CATCH YOUR DEATH

To my family, for all your support

First published in the UK in 2023 by Usborne Publishing Limited, Usborne House, 83-85 Saffron Hill, London EC1N 8RT, England, usborne.com.

Usborne Verlag, Usborne Publishing Limited, Prüfeninger Str. 20, 93049 Regensburg, Deutschland, VK Nr. 17560

A CIP catalogue record for this book is available from the British Library.

ISBN 9781803705422   JFMAMJJAS ND/23   8000/01

Printed and bound using 100% renewable energy at CPI Group (UK) Ltd, Croydon, CR0 4YY.

MIX
Paper | Supporting
responsible forestry
FSC® C171272

CATCH YOUR DEATH

USBORNE

CATCH YOUR DEATH is a work of fiction but it
deals with many real issues, including descriptions
of violence and domestic abuse.

THE DEADLIEST DINNER: SUDDEN DEATH OF PHILANTHROPIST EMILY VANFORTE BEING TREATED AS "SUSPICIOUS"

By Janice Evernight

A police spokesperson has confirmed the sudden death of Emily Vanforte is being treated as "suspicious", though no new details are being given at this time.

Initially reported as a heart attack, the police spokesperson has confirmed something more sinister may have happened to Emily Vanforte on Saturday night when she died suddenly at her multi-million-pound estate, aged fifty-eight.

According to an insider, Emily Vanforte was hosting a family dinner for her husband, celebrated politician Charles Vanforte (57), her nephew, Tate Astur (17), her daughter, Lottie Vanforte (17), and Douglas Treefair (17), son of controversial car tycoon Nicholas Treefair and reportedly Lottie Vanforte's boyfriend.

The Bramble Estate had been snowed in, having lost power earlier in the day. The combination of the snowstorm and the estate's isolated location meant it was cut off from the outside world for over fifteen hours. The police were only informed of Emily Vanforte's death late on Sunday morning, when Lottie Vanforte and Douglas Treefair braved the extreme conditions in order to hike to the nearest village.

"It was very odd," said Shelly Jones, a local resident. "I thought I was seeing things when they showed up on my doorstep – the Vanfortes have always kept themselves to themselves, no interest in the community at all. Douglas Treefair asked to use my phone. Lottie Vanforte never said a word – just started sobbing. Next thing you know, police are swarming the village and driving up to the estate."

"It's bizarre," added Peter Harkin, owner of the village pub. "There's something off about the Bramble Estate. Us in the village have always said so. We all steer clear of it, if we can. And I think— [cont. on page 5].

PART ONE

THE HOUSE

Extract of Transcript of Interview 7
Re: Death of Emily Vanforte
In Attendance – Inspector Adams (IA),
Devi Mistry (DM)

IA: So, just so we have it on record, you'd never met the deceased before the night of her death?

DM: Nope. [Pauses] We weren't exactly in the same circles. Her being a super-rich old woman and me... er, not being super rich. Or old. And living like a million miles away from the Bramble Estate – although she had a London home, didn't she? All those rich people have London homes. I'm from London, but the crap part—

IA: Great, thank you. A simple yes or no would suffice for these basic sorts of question.

DM: I'm just trying to paint a picture.

IA: Thank you, Devi. We do want to find out exactly what happened.

DM: And you're the best person to solve this, right? We need the *best* people on this case to solve it ASAP, before someone tries to kill me for seeing something I didn't know I saw. In fact, I still don't get why I'm not in witness protection, or why you're not giving me twenty-four-hour security—

IA: I'll keep those suggestions in mind. Now, what would be very helpful is if you could set the scene of your arrival at the Bramble Estate: who you spoke to and what you did when you got there...and just your general impressions of the others at the estate.

DM: But this is what I'm trying to tell you – the murderer has to be one of those four rich prats. What if they come after me for telling you what I saw? I've got *more* than a theory about who did it. I've got those four suspects all sussed out; I know which one of them did it.

IA: Oh – well, good, I would love to hear your suspicions. But to begin with, it would be most helpful to get a straightforward account of what happened.

DM: There's nothing straightforward about it – you know this whole thing is weird, right? It's like a murder-mystery scenario you see in films. The death happened in a locked room with only five people, including the victim, inside. No one else entered or left. The poison must have been in Mrs Vanforte's *glass*. Not the wine bottle, because everyone else drank from that. And she'd been using that same glass all evening, which means someone in the room put the poison in her drink at some point during dinner. Which *means* there's only four suspects. So, let's go back to the whole thing about how *I'm in danger.* The killer thought they could get away with murder in front of three witnesses in that room – but they knew those people, so maybe they knew how to fool them. And there should have only been one other possible witness to everything going on in the house: old Ms Bromley, the housekeeper – but her hearing's going and her eyesight is *bad*. The trouble is, the killer was unlucky, because the snow meant we were stuck there too – three strangers who *weren't supposed to be there.* Three strangers who might have noticed something the family didn't. We're the flaw in the plan, Inspector... You know, poisoning someone when there's three other people in the room? That's the action of someone who isn't afraid to take risks. And...

IA: Yes?

DM: I'm scared.

Devi
Before the Murder

I've had some bad luck in my time, but I kid you not, the day I ended up at the Vanforte mansion was probably the worst string of bad luck *ever*.

I'd made plans to visit Nani (my grandmother on Mum's side) up north a few days after New Year's Eve, but then the weather forecast started giving ominous warnings about Snowstorm Sara and I was like *hell, no*, I'm not driving in a blizzard. I'd only just passed my test a few months before and I was mainly used to London roads, where you can never go above twenty miles an hour because there's so much traffic. Plus, I barely drove anyway, since Mum's car is a beat-up piece of junk she'd got for cheap, because she was like its one-hundredth owner, and I simply *couldn't* be seen driving around in it. Dad wouldn't let me drive his car because he was worried I'd crash it (and there is *no* foundation to that worry at all. I passed my test first time, thank you very much. So what if I accidentally skidded right afterwards and hit a postbox? Cars are made to be dented).

But Nani was one of those old people who always said stuff like, *When I was your age, I used to hike fifteen miles in the heat just to go to the toilet,* and, *What if I die tomorrow and you never came to see me? You're going to miss me when I'm dead.* Rain or shine or snow, she expected me to make the trip.

Mum and Dad were busy working at the restaurant, so they couldn't come with me. I set off from London early, making great progress down the motorway. *Zoom, zoom, zoom* – I got into the fast lane and started racing people. The miles roared away. It was great to see how fast Mum's car could go – fast enough that no one would have a chance to see who was driving.

My phone was blasting rock music, the singers screaming at the tops of their lungs, and I had never felt more peaceful.

But the motorway got progressively quieter as the snow started to fall, and it all went to crap when I had to turn off onto one of those smaller roads – and then onto horrible country lanes. Nani lives in the middle of nowhere, because she married some man she met at a bingo night after Nana (my mum's dad) died. Step-grandfather (or as he insists I call him, Gerry) lives in a village with an access road so narrow only one car can drive down it at a time. It's *incredibly* inconvenient.

The snow was falling thick and fast, and the world was blanketed in a sharp white that made my eyes sting. I could barely tell where the road was. There weren't any tyre tracks, so clearly I was the only one stupid enough to be out. The car heater gave one last little puff of warm air before dying out. At once the temperature seemed to drop a thousand degrees.

I sucked in my cheeks, bringing the car to a stop so I could put my hat and scarf on. It didn't make a lick of difference because I was already starting to freeze. My coat was big and puffy and I hated driving in it, so I'd put it in the boot with the rest of my stuff – but I was regretting my choice. My old faded jeans and worn-out hoodie weren't doing anything to keep me warm.

I briefly considered getting out to fetch my coat, but I was worried that if I stepped outside I would turn into an icicle. The snow was falling so thickly that the world had become a continuous stream of white falling from an endless grey sky.

I turned my music off. It felt out of place on the quiet country road, and I wanted to focus on figuring out how much further I had to go. I zoomed in on the satnav I'd set up on my phone – and that was when I realized the bloody screen had frozen miles earlier and it had no clue where I was.

"Well, great," I said, tapping my phone a few more times. I had no signal – I truly was in the middle of nowhere. All country roads look the same to me at the best of times, and the snow made it impossible to recognize anything.

I thought about trying to turn the car round and heading back to the motorway, but I didn't know how far away from it I was – and whether the lack of heating would mean I'd freeze before I got there. Plus, I had a feeling I was pretty close to Nani's village, and Mum didn't raise a quitter.

There was only one thing for it; I still had almost three-quarters of a tank of petrol, and the road I was on had to be going somewhere.

My windscreen wipers were going at a hundred miles an

hour to keep the snow off, and I squinted, trying to make sure I stayed on the road and didn't veer into a bush. Without my music, all I could hear were the choking noises coming from the engine. I wasn't alarmed; the engine always sounds like an old man hacking up phlegm.

To my right, something loomed up out of the white. My window was frosted with snow, so I had to roll it down to see, letting in a blast of freezing air. It was a sign reading *The Bramble Estate*.

It said something else in smaller letters beneath that, but the words were hidden by snow.

The name rang a bell. I think Nani had mentioned the Bramble Estate before, and I had a vague idea it was the name of a fancy hotel about a half-hour drive from her house. I sighed with relief. I could park up at the hotel, maybe go inside and order a hot chocolate, and wait for the storm to blow over. The snow was slowing down anyway, and once I was in the hotel I could get directions to Nani's.

The snow crackled under my tyres as I turned off onto the estate's road, and the hacking noises from the engine changed to a few tired spurts, like it was dying.

"Crap," I muttered. The wheezing didn't sound good at all. I put the tired noises out of my mind as I drove up to two enormous black gates, with pointed tops that looked like little knife blades.

I waited impatiently for them to open, assuming they would be automatic and work via sensors – what kind of hotel had ominous gates like a fortress to keep their guests *out*?

If I'd been more sensible, I would have turned round and

driven on my merry way, risking freezing to death in the snow. But I was too obsessed with the thought of a nice hot chocolate. And at that point I had no idea that I was driving straight into a horror story – you know the ones I'm talking about, where people like me die first because we're too busy looking the other way to run from the danger—

Extract of Transcript of Interview 7
Re: Death of Emily Vanforte
In Attendance – Inspector Adams (IA),
Devi Mistry (DM)

IA: Ahem.

DM: What? I was on a roll there – really painting the scene.

IA: I think it would be best if you told your story without...any retrospective elements. Don't tell me what you know *now* about things – tell me your thoughts and impressions as they were at the time.

DM: With all due respect, *Inspector*, you said to tell my story in my own words—

IA: And, of course, you must do so! But I highly doubt at the time you were thinking to yourself, *I don't know it, but right now I am driving into a horror story.*

DM: [Pauses] You don't get it – everything that's happened... It affects *everything* I do. I'm seeing enemies everywhere. Right now I'm looking at you and I'm wondering how easy it would be for the Vanfortes to pay a policeman off. Or else get someone to infiltrate the police and pretend to be one of you.

IA: I can show you my badge. Here, look. I'm exactly who I say I am.

DM: That could be a fake. And you could still have been paid off. But fine, I will do my best not to be too *retrospective*.

IA: Great. Let's get back to it. And please can you note the rough timings of when things happened? It's helpful for us to build a timeline of events.

DM: Okay. Well, I arrived at like 4 p.m. – ish. Can I crack on with my story now?

IA: Please, go ahead.

Devi

Before the Murder
(Without Retrospective Elements)

I got annoyed just sitting and waiting for the gates to open – I wanted my hot chocolate and was starting to become genuinely concerned I might freeze to death. It only occurred to me then that the gates might not be automatic – there could be an intercom system, or maybe they were on a latch. Either way I would need to get out of the car.

"Stupid," I huffed, leaving my car dying slowly as I got out to take a closer look at the gates. My trainers sank into several inches of snow, the wetness leaking to my socks.

I gave one of the gates a gentle push and it swung open.

Great, I'd spent ten minutes freezing outside an unlocked gate for no good reason.

I hurried back to my car and drove into the grounds. The road sloped downwards to an enormous gothic mansion, made of a dark grey stone that looked bleak against the backdrop of the sky. Ivy crept up the walls, and there were only a few cars parked in the driveway, half buried by the snow. It was probably off-season at the hotel.

"Wow," I muttered as I slowly edged my car along the icy road. I'd never stayed anywhere half as fancy as this place – we normally picked cheap self-catering places when we went on holiday, because Mum always said we were hardly going to be in the room anyway, or else three-star hotels with decent enough online reviews. I had told Mum many times I would take well to the five-star lifestyle, but for some reason she ignored me.

But looking up at the hotel…I didn't think I would *want* to stay in a place like this. The grounds were too big and empty, and there was nothing for miles around. A holiday here would probably be incredibly boring. I liked places with a bit more of a buzz to them. Apartments near the seaside where the roads were full of tourists, caravan holidays that made it super easy to befriend kids from other families, or even a cheap resort in Spain where I could dance to the cheesy music at the shows in the evening.

My musings were rudely interrupted by my car giving a little sputter and the engine cutting out. I coasted to a stop in the middle of the driveway and groaned.

I knew what that sputter meant, but tested my theory by turning the key anyway. The engine gave a few sad chokes, but the car didn't roar to life like it should have done. It was dead.

"You stupid piece of *crap*," I said, banging my hand against the steering wheel. Obviously, the car did not respond. All I managed to do was send a slice of pain through my hand.

I checked my phone, but it still had no signal. Well, the hotel would have a landline, and then I could call Nani and tell her to make Gerry come and pick me up. My socks were damp and freezing as they clung to my feet, and I was fed up.

I got out of the car, flutters of snowflakes landing in my hair and eyes as I stomped up to the front door and tried to push it open. Nothing happened. I pulled at the door handle, but it still didn't budge.

The door was locked.

It occurred to me then that this might *not* be a hotel after all. There wasn't any signage. And hotels don't generally lock their guests out. But I still had the niggling feeling I had heard of the Bramble Estate before.

In the centre of the door was a metal lion, its mouth open like it was roaring. Dangling from its lower lip was a golden ring, which I guess served as a knocker.

To the left of the lion was a circular, rusted gold doorbell with the word *Press* engraved into the metal above.

I obeyed without thinking, and immediately a peal of noise clanged away inside. The reality of the situation began to dawn on me as I stood for an age waiting for the door to open. I was in the middle of nowhere at a private residence that looked about the size of Buckingham Palace with no phone signal and a dead car. The people inside could have been axe murderers or English cousins of Dracula. As I eyed the stone lion, its face morphed so it looked less like it was roaring and more like it was screaming.

I had half a mind to turn round and take my chances in the wild, snow-covered countryside, when the door slowly creaked open.

I waited, expecting someone from the Addams family to peek out. Instead, a willowy blonde girl about my age stared down at me. She was dressed in clothes no normal person wears at home – flowing white trousers paired with high-heeled boots and an expensive-looking top. Probably cashmere, it was a massive contrast to the food-stained old tracksuits and grey, elephant-skin-like T-shirts *I* wear at home. Everything I own always looks slightly lumpy on me, so I go for comfort above all else.

The girl's lips were painted blood red and she was wearing golden eyeshadow and pink blusher that stood out against her pale skin. Her fake lashes looked like spider legs. I've never got the hang of make-up – my best friend Priya used to slather it on for me, insisting she knew what she was doing. I trusted her every time, walking around like a clown until I caught sight of myself in a mirror and shrieked with horror.

The girl's head tilted as she looked at me, her diamond earrings dangling. I quickly summed her up – a spoilt and loud rich girl who probably thought the world revolved around her.

"Er…" she said, her voice softer than I was expecting. "Can I help you? Are you erm…selling something?" Her eyes flicked to my empty hands, and she flinched. "Sorry, that was a silly question."

The silence stretched between us, and it was getting weird that I hadn't spoken. But she was so awkward, which contrasted too much with how well put together she looked. It was unsettling.

"I lost my way in the snow and my car's broken down," I said. "I was hoping I could use your landline to call my grandma?"

22

Call me stupid, but the fact this girl looked to be my age made me trust her more. What harm could a seventeen-year-old do, right? In another world, where I'd been born rich, we might have gone to school together.

"Oh, you're lost?" The girl's eyes widened. Was I imagining it, or had her accent become less posh – more like mine? "I'm really sorry, but I don't think we can help you. The phones and Wi-Fi are down, because of the storm... We're cut off."

I blinked at her a few times. Crap. Crap, crap, crap. Crap on a stick. Crap in a river. Crap everywhere. What the hell was I supposed to do now? The temperature had dropped about a thousand degrees in the time I'd been talking to the girl, and my coat was still in the bloody car because I hadn't thought to grab it. I was going to die of frostbite, I could feel it.

"Who's that, Charlotte?" a woman's voice called from somewhere in the murky depths of the house.

The friendliness slipped off the girl's face. It was replaced by a pinched expression as a woman appeared next to her. The woman was well built, with hair such a bright white it had to be dyed. Her skin was almost flawless, apart from a few wrinkles round her mouth that were half hidden by her face powder, and she had large brown eyes. She had the same thin lips as the girl, though hers were painted a soft pink, and wore a plain beige top and trousers, paired with a dark-brown blazer. I was immediately struck by the *life* pouring from her. This was a woman who knew what she wanted. This was a woman who Got Stuff Done.

Emily Vanforte.

I *recognized* her from gossip accounts I followed online. *This* was why the Bramble Estate was familiar to me – Nani had once

23

mentioned it was the country home of the Vanforte family, nestled in the hills in the middle of nowhere, well away from the intrusive flashing cameras of the London paparazzi. Charles Vanforte was a politician and former businessman, and his daughter Lottie Vanforte was one of those teens blessed with good looks and money – the sort of person the paparazzi love to photograph. She had been snapped a few times at dinner with her dad and other rich families, or attending speeches her dad was making, always looking so poised. She never looked happy with the attention, but I assumed that was probably part of her act – to seem as aloof as possible, like she was above the cameras.

But for some reason I couldn't put together the ethereal girl I'd seen on gossip websites and the girl before me – Lottie seemed to have shrunk in the few seconds her mum had been standing beside her.

Her mum, who was one of the richest women in the country.

"Well, what do we have here?" Mrs Vanforte said, her voice sharp. At least *she* fitted the impression I had of her – that she was fierce; someone to be feared.

"I'm… I'm…" The words stuck in my throat. I'm not a shy person, but something about Mrs Vanforte intimidated me. The way she loomed over me, the way I knew from all the press about her that she was nearing sixty but only had the faintest wrinkles, like ageing wasn't something that happened to her (or, maybe only to her hair). That might be why Lottie seemed to be slightly afraid of her. I couldn't imagine someone like Emily Vanforte to be very…*mumsy*. There would be something like a ten-year gap between her and my mum, but it wasn't the age difference that made me think Emily Vanforte and my mum

24

would never get along. I couldn't imagine Mrs Vanforte helping me get past hard levels on my PlayStation, for one thing.

"She says her car has broken down," said Lottie. Her voice was stilted now. She seemed uneasy, keeping her eyes fixed on me rather than her mother. Weird dynamics there – maybe Mrs Vanforte had refused to pay for a new pony for Lottie and she was sulking (I knew I was being judgemental and I didn't know Lottie at all and she might be absolutely lovely, blah, blah, blah, but despite her awkwardness she was wearing enormous diamond earrings at *home*, for goodness' sake. Was she not worried about losing them? I would have been). "And that she's lost."

"Well, you must come in," said Mrs Vanforte at once, her voice firm, like she was settling the matter. "Out of the cold. I'll get someone to take a look at your car, to see if we can get it running again. Have you got much of your journey left?"

"No," I began. "I was on my way to visit my grandma—"

"But of course you can't drive in the *snow*," continued Mrs Vanforte, speaking right over me like I hadn't said anything. "Perhaps you had better stay for a while—"

"Oh, but Dad might not like that." Lottie pushed her hair out of her face, her back slightly straighter, like mentioning her dad gave her strength. "He told me about a scam where criminals send in a child who's pretending to be hurt, and while the homeowners are distracted the criminals rush in—"

"That's ridiculous." Mrs Vanforte cut across her daughter, her tone disparaging. I raised my eyebrows at Lottie, expecting her to snap back at her mother. But Lottie pressed her lips together, her eyes drawn to the ground. She almost seemed to wilt, like a flower without enough sunlight. I couldn't even be annoyed with her for suggesting I was a criminal. "Those scams involve five-year-olds, little cherubic angels."

"That's definitely not me," I said helpfully, looking from Lottie to Mrs Vanforte. I was now really shivering, the cold biting at my face, the wind finding its way through tiny holes in my cheap hoodie and nipping at my skin. I had never wanted to be warm so badly in my life, and now the possibility of getting indoors had been mentioned I was eager to nudge that idea along. "I thought this place was a hotel – the gates weren't locked…"

"They're electric," said Mrs Vanforte. "They probably broke down because of the snow." Her eyes scanned me, like she was trying to read my mind. I felt a strong need to apologize for something, even though I hadn't done anything wrong. She reminded me of one of the strict teachers at my school, who could shut an entire class up with a single death stare. "You're not going to steal anything, are you?"

"I'll try not to," I quipped, and Mrs Vanforte's mouth twitched as she stepped aside to let me in. I gave Lottie a victorious smile as I entered the house, finding myself in a grand foyer. Black and white squares tiled the floor, and in the centre of the room was a wide set of stairs. About halfway up they reached a landing, at which point they split into two narrower stairs that led off in opposite directions to the first floor. High above us was a chandelier. Two curved chaise longues were set up against the walls, and hanging above them were several abstract art pieces featuring weird-looking circles that, if you squinted hard enough, *could* look like faces.

It was barely warmer inside than out, the air as chilly as the inside of a fridge – or a mausoleum.

"Well, there you go," said Mrs Vanforte, as she closed the door behind me, the sound echoing around the vast space. "She said she's not going to steal, so she won't."

"I just know Dad wouldn't really like it…" Lottie trailed off.

I gritted my teeth. I didn't like being discussed as though I wasn't standing right beside them – especially since Lottie still hadn't given up on the whole "she might be a criminal" thing. Absolute insult: if I was a criminal I'd be way smarter – not knock on the front door, for one thing.

Lottie must have seen my expression, because she immediately backtracked. "Not that you're not welcome, of course," she said to me quickly. She tried to smile, but nervously shot her mother a look as she did so. Mrs Vanforte rolled her eyes.

"This random stranger off the street is more welcome than the *other* person who decided to show up on my doorstep," she said. "I didn't realize your boyfriend was Douglas *Treefair*. Left that bit of information out when you told me he'd be coming."

Lottie went red. "I didn't leave out his last name on purpose. You weren't home the other times we visited. And he's been wanting to meet you and Dad for ages…"

"From what I've heard of Douglas's parents, he's not the sort of person you should be mixing with," said Mrs Vanforte.

Obviously, this discussion didn't involve me, and they both had *way* bigger problems to worry about than letting me in so I didn't freeze. I'd never argued with Mum in front of anyone else – Priya used to come round all the time, and her visits sometimes coincided with me having pissed Mum off (me pissing Mum off happened a lot, because…well, sometimes I'm annoying. At least I'm self aware, I guess). But even when she was furious, Mum *always* waited until Priya was gone before sniping at me.

For all Mrs Vanforte and Lottie knew, I could have been an undercover reporter, planning to sell the story to the press. Headline being: VANFORTES HATE EACH OTHER, subheading being: ANONYMOUS SOURCE PAID £10,000 FOR THE DETAILS.

"Douglas is nice, Mum," said Lottie, her voice almost a whisper.

"He's nice because he wants a taste of your money," snorted Mrs Vanforte. "Didn't his father just go bankrupt?"

Lottie didn't reply, crossing her arms over herself like they would protect her from her mother's jabs.

Mrs Vanforte drew herself up to her full height. "Never mind. It all worked out for the best. You'll soon see why." She had clearly forgotten about me standing close by; her eyes were fixed on Lottie as she said, "Because one of the people coming to dinner tonight is a crook and a liar. And I'm going to expose them."

5

Extract of Transcript of Interview 8
Re: Death of Emily Vanforte

In Attendance – Inspector Adams (IA),
Elizabeth ("Lizzie") Newton-Hill (LNH)

LNH: I'm so sorry, Inspector. I really don't know what I can tell you. After...*it*...happened I was so scared I couldn't tell my left from my right.

IA: You'll be very helpful, I'm sure.

LNH: I hope so. [Hiccups] Sorry – I've been crying so much after the past few days. To think...Emily Vanforte is...is *dead*, you know? And that I was *there*. [Loud sniffle]

IA: You were a stranger to the deceased?

LNH: That's right. Mrs Vanforte's assistant contacted Mum, saying she *really* wanted to buy one of Mum's necklaces – Mum owns an independent jewellery store. The assistant really wanted to know about this diamond necklace Mum had – it was *so* lovely... Just beautiful – eight carat leaves of white gold filled with flawless diamonds – the highest possible quality—

IA: Yes, yes, great. So this necklace was very important to Emily?

LNH: Yes. The assistant said that Mrs Vanforte was *really* interested in buying the necklace; except she wanted it the next day...

IA: Why did she want it so urgently?

LNH: For an event she was holding, I think. She said she wanted to look her best and the necklace was stunning and would make her sparkle. Mrs Vanforte was offering a lot of money for it – more than it was worth, actually... Obviously we told her that. Mum isn't a swindler or anything. But Mrs Vanforte insisted on paying almost double for it – kept saying it was a fair amount considering how lovely it looked.

IA: So why was fast delivery an issue? Surely you could have booked a courier to deliver it?

LNH: Well, Mrs Vanforte said it would tie her whole outfit together and she didn't want it getting lost, and since it was so valuable to her she didn't want to trust a courier with it. So she said Mum should drive up and deliver it in person, then stay in a hotel and go back the next day. She said she would pay for everything, but she *had* to have the necklace, and it *had* to be that weekend... It was all settled. Mum was going to deliver it – you don't say no to someone like Mrs Vanforte. But then Mum got one of her migraines, and I wanted to be helpful because it was such a huge sale, so I said I could go to the Bramble Estate instead.

IA: So you arrived when?

LNH: At half past three in the afternoon. But then I was stranded because of the snow – it got so bad that I couldn't leave.

IA: And did you speak to any of the family that afternoon, prior to the dinner at 8 p.m.?

LNH: Yes. Mrs Vanforte obviously. And Mr Vanforte. I also spoke to Douglas Treefair – though he didn't speak *to* me, more...near me. And Tate Astur, I suppose, but only very briefly... That's the point I should have tried to leave – when I met Tate. I should have *known* something was wrong then – in fact, I *did* know something was wrong, deep down, but I told myself I was being silly. I wish I'd never stayed. I wish I'd risked the snow. It would have been safer.

IA: So, do you have any idea as to who could have poisoned Emily Vanforte?

LNH: Oh – well, no – I really don't think *any* of them could have done it. It's too horrible to think about. *I* thought some awful outsider had broken into the house... It was such a large place, you see. So many places someone could hide...

IA: There were no footprints in the snow leading to or from the house. Emily Vanforte was alone with her family – that is, with her husband, daughter, nephew and Douglas – in the dining room when she died. All four persons of interest have confirmed no one else entered or exited the room between the time when dinner was served and her death.

31

LNH: Well, I did have one theory. But the others thought I was being ridiculous. I'm really not sure if I should say.

IA: Please do.

LNH: I heard a ghost story about the Bramble Estate. Maybe the killer is a ghost?

IA: [Indistinct laughter which turns into a cough] I see. [Coughing] Well, let's put that to one side for now and get started with your full account of the events that night.

6

Lizzie

The Day of My Arrival

In an ideal world, I would have been able to do a dry run of the journey to the Bramble Estate in person the day before, checking the route to make sure I didn't get lost. Then, I could have gone back home and done it again for real. But the estate was much too far away from home, so I settled for using the little yellow person on Google Maps to visualize the way. But Google maps only went as far as the big sign saying *Bramble Estate – Private Property – KEEP OUT*, so I had no idea what the estate looked like. In the camera image online, the sign had been clear to read, but now half of it was hidden under ice and snow.

The black gate juddered open as I nudged my car forward slowly, because the snow was thick and my visibility was poor. I was very relieved to finally arrive – when Natasha and Hannah, my closest friends, had found out I was going so far on my own, they had laughed, because I'm not exactly a confident driver. I hate motorways, with all the cars racing past me while I remain in the left lane. My knuckles were white as I gripped the steering wheel and prayed that no one would come on from one of the slip roads. I hate driving through towns even more. Being surrounded by unpredictable drivers who might risk their lives to shave a few seconds off their commute.

And now I've learned that I hate countryside driving – the narrow roads twisting and bending. The probability of a sheep suddenly popping up in the lane might be low, but it's never zero.

I inched down a wide driveway that led to an enormous house made of soft grey brick, with huge windows and a columned front porch. I like visiting stately homes with Mum, wandering through old-timey rooms and pretending I'm the owner. Those homes are usually buzzing with visitors, and there's always a sort of hushed appreciation. I cut my car engine; here, everything was simply hushed.

There were a few flurries of snow just beginning to fall. I was later than I had planned, because of an accident on one of the motorways. I'd been forced to take an unexpected detour through back roads that I hadn't seen on Google Maps. I don't like it when things don't go according to plan, but I was trying to be optimistic: if I could be on the road again as quickly as possible and get to my hotel, I might make up for lost time… And avoid the blizzard that was surely coming.

I clutched the velvet-green box that housed the necklace Mrs Vanforte had been so desperate to buy, and crunched through the snow. I was wearing thick boots, which were old but comfortable. Mum had splashed out on them a few years ago, and I'd done my best to look after them – they were my most expensive shoes, and they did a great job of keeping out water.

The sweeping front steps were icy, so I made my way up slowly, images of myself falling and breaking my neck flashing through my mind. But thankfully I reached the top without anything bad happening, and pressed the doorbell. My breath came out in frozen puffs. Cold nipped at my face, but other than that I was nicely wrapped up in layers, finishing with my thick winter coat that went down to my ankles and my big hat that covered my ears.

The door was opened by Emily Vanforte herself. She was tall, much taller than she appeared to be in the newspapers and in online photos – of course, I'd done my research on her the moment I volunteered to hand-deliver the necklace for my mum. It was hard to determine if she would be scary in person from a few blurred paparazzi shots, and carefully posed pictures of her at charity galas, but I had done my best. I concluded she *would* be scary.

I was absolutely right. Mrs Vanforte stared down at me, her face oddly expressionless, as if it belonged to someone much younger. She was wearing what looked like a Chanel outfit – I thought I recognized it from their new line. I can't afford clothes like that, but I like to pore over the pictures, imagining myself as someone more glamorous, more confident…

"Ah, *Elizabeth*," Mrs Vanforte said, clasping her hands together. Her mouth twitched, like she was trying to smile but couldn't quite manage it – I wondered if she'd had Botox, or something else to freeze the icy expression on her face. "You've made it!" Her eyes flicked down to the necklace box. "Is that…?"

I nodded, holding it out for her.

"Excellent," she said, opening up the box at once and nodding at the necklace. "*Excellent.* I've got a surprise planned at dinner that I wanted to look my absolute best for, and this necklace is simply *stunning*. It will tie my whole look together." She snapped the box shut, and looked at me. "You must come in for a cup of tea now – I know you stepped in for your mother last minute, and had such a long drive, all to satisfy my little whim. But when you get to my age, you see that your whims *must* be satisfied, because there's very little else to do to pass the time."

I knew she was fifty-seven, which isn't *that* old, but she was talking like she was almost a hundred.

"Oh, thank you for the offer," I said. "But I should get going – my hotel is still quite far…"

"Nonsense," said Mrs Vanforte, her voice firm. "There's always time for tea." Her tone had changed, from being happy to see me…to cold. I wondered if she was used to hearing the word *no*. From the sound of it, probably not – and I didn't want to be rude. Even though I *really* wanted to get going – the flurries of snow were getting thicker and I was starting to feel slightly panicked at the thought I still had another thirty-minute journey to get to the hotel. Except, with the speed I drive in normal conditions and the snow, it would probably take me something closer to an hour.

"Okay," I mumbled, stepping inside. My heart was starting to pound, but I tried not to let my nervousness show on my face. I barely paid attention to my surroundings, catching a glimpse of a large space before Mrs Vanforte led me into a side room.

It looked like a tea room, with flower-patterned couches grouped around a golden coffee table and cashmere throws scattered over the cushions. The wide window looked out on the blanket of snow. Mrs Vanforte left the room without a word, which was deeply unsettling.

I felt like I'd stepped into the past, like I'd been let in behind the scenes of a period drama. I was small in the big room; insignificant. My home is large, with four bedrooms and a garden, and it's by the sea so has lovely views. But it's nothing compared to this.

I wanted to be as polite as I could, so I sat down on one of the couches and laced my fingers together in my lap, trying to keep my back as straight as possible. I anxiously waited for Mrs Vanforte's return. She came back a few minutes later, followed by an old lady bent over with age and clutching a silver tray. The old lady was wearing a plain red apron over a bobbly knitted jumper that looked home-made; she half reminded me of a grandma from a storybook.

With a gentle smile at me, the old lady set the silver tray down on the table. It held a teapot patterned with red roses, two cups and saucers made of fine china, and an entire Victoria sponge cake lightly dusted with sugar.

"Thank you," said Mrs Vanforte, obviously dismissing the woman, who had to be some sort of housekeeper.

Mrs Vanforte sat down opposite me, cutting a generous slice of cake and pushing it across the table. I didn't want to eat, but I also didn't want to risk her displeasure, so I took a big mouthful. I was too on edge to taste it.

Meanwhile, Mrs Vanforte stroked the necklace box. "You

know, my husband has always been slightly stingy when it comes to jewellery. He doesn't like spending money on things like that."

"That's not true," said a soft voice. I jumped, and a shudder passed through me, though I didn't know why.

Charles Vanforte had entered the room so silently he might have been floating. I recognized him straight away. Mum loves keeping up to date on politics, and my friends Natasha and Hannah don't ever really want to meet up with me on evenings and weekends. It means I spend a lot of time with Mum curled up on the sofa watching the news and listening to her takes on current affairs. Mum had told me all about Mr Vanforte's meteoric rise to power after his previous life as a businessman. He'd owned some clothes shops, then moved across into the construction industry – and then pivoted into politics.

The Mr Vanforte in front of me was shorter than he looked in the papers. He was wearing a double-breasted two-piece suit – made, I guessed, by an Italian designer, to match his loafers. He had thick, bushy grey eyebrows and green eyes, with a wide smile. I smiled nervously back, wishing he would leave quickly. Mrs Vanforte alone was intimidating enough – I didn't need him here as well.

Plus, there was suddenly an odd tension in the room.

"What stories has my wife been telling you about me?" Mr Vanforte asked. "They're all lies of course!" He laughed heartily, placing a hand on Mrs Vanforte's shoulder. She shrugged away from him at once, snapping the necklace box closed.

"It wasn't a story, it was the truth," said Mrs Vanforte as she stared at him, her eyes hard. "You never have liked spending money on me – and I know I've never wanted pretty necklaces, but some flowers on occasion might have been nice. At least I know there's a good reason for your stinginess *now*."

I didn't know where to look, so I took another bite of cake to pretend to be casual and act like this wasn't the beginning of a row. One of the crumbs went down the wrong way and I coughed, then tried to force myself to stop coughing, which only made it worse.

Mr Vanforte's eyes flicked down to me, then back to Mrs Vanforte. "If flowers are what you want, my dear, then flowers you will get." His voice was smooth, sincere, like an old-fashioned hero in one of the black-and-white films Mum forces me to watch, but I actually secretly enjoy.

My eyes were streaming, so I took a gulp of tea. It scalded my tongue but I managed to get it down without embarrassing myself again.

"Oh, don't act like you don't hate me." Mrs Vanforte's voice was frosty as she poured herself a cup of tea and added three spoons of sugar, stirring it in slowly, like she had all the time in the world. "And let's be honest, I don't *actually* want you to buy me flowers – since it would be *my* money you would be using, I assume."

"What's that supposed to mean?" snapped Mr Vanforte. "Why would I use *your* money?" It was like a mask had slipped. Gone was the film hero, replaced by a hostile man who had had one argument too many.

"Isn't it obvious?" said Mrs Vanforte softly. Whatever she was talking about *was* apparently obvious, because Mr Vanforte took a step back, shock on his face.

My cheeks were heating up – I don't cope well with conflict. Mrs Vanforte finally seemed to pick up on my discomfort, because she raised an eyebrow at me. "Now, we must not argue in front of poor Elizabeth," she said drily, like I was a delicate flower for feeling uncomfortable.

And at once the mask was back on Mr Vanforte's face, only now I knew there was cold steel behind the genial expression. I supposed you couldn't get to where he was, a politician with real influence over the entire country, without needing to wear different masks; amiable, to gain votes, but tough to make change. I wondered which mask was real.

"Forgive us," said Mr Vanforte with a laugh. "We argue like…well, like an old married couple." He gave a little shake of his head, then looked at his watch. "Oh no, is that the time? I've got a lot of work to be getting on with – well, it was lovely to meet you…"

"Lizzie," I said, realizing with a start that I'd forgotten to introduce myself. Mum would have told me off for being rude.

"Lizzie," he repeated, like he was tucking it away in his mind. "Well, have a good rest of your day, Lizzie." And with that he left, striding out with his hands folded behind his back.

"Oh, *dear*," said Mrs Vanforte, looking out of the window. "Look at that snow – it's falling so thickly."

The blizzard had started earlier than I thought it would. Panic shot through me as I put my teacup down and got to my feet. "I wanted to be at my hotel long before the storm started," I said, wringing my hands together as I squinted out of the window. The snowflakes were enormous. "Do you think if I set off now, I'll be okay?"

But Mrs Vanforte was shaking her head. "It'd be silly to set off in that – there isn't anyone for miles around and no phone signal, should you run into trouble. No, you must stay here tonight."

"I couldn't," I protested. She had her dinner party planned out – she'd gone to the effort of asking me to drive the necklace all the way up. I didn't want to get in the way of it – especially with the tension brewing between her and her husband. Nothing would be more mortifying than being anywhere near them if they started arguing properly. "I don't want to be a bother…"

"It's no bother at all," said Mrs Vanforte. I couldn't tell if she meant it or not – her voice seemed to be naturally sardonic. "It's my fault, really, insisting you bring the necklace today. But you see, it *had* to be today…" She trailed off, shaking her head.

"Well, if you're sure…" I said, biting my bottom lip. Mum always tells me it's rude to impose on someone's hospitality, but at the same time the thought of attempting to drive through the snow sent shivers through me. I'd hated the solo journey to the estate, but I'd also really wanted to help Mum make the sale – and if Mrs Vanforte's offer meant I could cut off an hour of driving, I would take the opportunity. Then I would set off first thing in the morning. "Well…would it be okay if I use your telephone to call my mum – just to let her know I've arrived?"

Mrs Vanforte frowned. "I'm afraid you can't do that, my dear. The landline is dead."

7

Extract of Transcript of Interview 9
Re: Death of Emily Vanforte
In Attendance – Inspector Adams (IA),
Jayne Faraway (JF)

IA: Er... So, Jayne. Please tell me in your own words how you came to be working as the housekeeper's assistant at the Bramble Estate.

JF: [Long pause] Who else's words would I use?

IA: Let's try again. You had only been employed at the Bramble Estate...a few months earlier?

JF: Yes. I'd been employed for four months. I worked Saturdays and a few evenings during the week, after school. I've just started college and I wanted to start saving a bit of money. I helped cook and clean. It's a big house.

IA: Yes. And, er, as to my first question...

JF: They advertised. I applied. I got the job.

IA: Ms Bromley said she didn't get many applications – only you and one other girl applied? [Silence] A nod isn't enough, Jayne – you need to say yes

42

or no for the transcript.

JF: Yes.

IA: But the job is well paid, for what it is. I'm surprised more people didn't apply.

JF: People say the estate is haunted.

IA: And that didn't stop you from wanting the job?

JF: I'm not scared of ghosts.

IA: Lizzie Newton-Hill became convinced the Bramble Estate was haunted.

JF: That's not a question.

IA: Okay. Right. Well, please can you tell me about your time at the estate then...

JF: In my own words?

IA: Yes, exactly. And, also, can you tell me if you have any personal thoughts on which one of the four might have been responsible for Emily Vanforte's death?

JF: [Pause] Yes.

IA: What?

JF: Yes, I have thoughts on which of them killed her.

IA: Well? Which one do you think did it?

JF: All of them.

Jayne

I did odd jobs at the estate in the evenings, some weekends. Whatever Ms Bromley, the old housekeeper, wanted me to do. Mainly dusting rooms that hadn't been used in years and helping her prep meals. It was a good job, since it still gave me time after college to do schoolwork.

Ms Bromley is seventy-one, but seems even older. Her face is lined with wrinkles and her hands tremble as she lifts things. It looks like it's painful for her to walk – her back is hunched and she needs a stick if she goes any further than a few metres. She told me why she hasn't retired. She works three days a week because otherwise she would be bored. It didn't make sense to me, but I didn't press for more details.

The Saturday of Mrs Vanforte's murder, I arrived at my usual time in the morning. Ms Bromley told me to get started on prepping a large dinner Mrs Vanforte had requested. I thought the ratio of food requested to the number of guests was off by about three and a half times, but I didn't question it. That wasn't my job. My job was to do as I was told, and get paid £5 an hour more than the minimum wage for my efforts.

People do say the estate is haunted – the Vanfortes of old were apparently violent and their ghosts supposedly still roam the hallways looking for fresh victims. Guests have reported locked doors being opened from the inside and hearing scratching sounds behind the walls.

But, like I said, ghosts aren't what scares me.

I was supposed to clock off early that day, so was Ms Bromley, because Mrs Vanforte wanted to serve the meal herself. Ms Bromley lives in a small cottage in the estate's grounds. I was meant to go home too, but Mrs Vanforte said I should spend the night in the main house, because there were some other girls staying and she wanted me to look after them – make sure they had food, bedding and all that. Ms Bromley and I continued to make dinner…

Extract of Transcript of Interview 9
Re: Death of Emily Vanforte
In Attendance – Inspector Adams (IA),
Jayne Faraway (JF)

IA: Jayne. I'm going to need a bit more from you. Between you, Lizzie and Devi, I believe you spoke to all four members of the family that day. You, in particular, have a unique insight because the family weren't strangers to you...

JF: Yes, they were. I just spoke to Ms Bromley. Only Mr and Mrs Vanforte were normally at the estate and I never ran into them. Lottie lived at boarding school – she'd been home before for holidays, but I hadn't seen her about. It's a big house, and Ms Bromley says it's our job to stay out of the Vanfortes' way. If Douglas or Tate were ever around, it was on a day I wasn't working. The job was part-time, after school, occasional weekends – it's not like I was there all the time.

IA: Okay. Right. Well... Tell me everything you

remember... [Pause] I wonder...if ghosts don't scare you, what does?

JF: [Crackling silence]

IA: Er...did you hear the question?

JF: I did, Inspector. I was just thinking. People.

IA: What?

JF: That's what scares me. People. They're the scariest things in the world.

Jayne

I was peeling carrots when Douglas Treefair came down to the kitchen. It must have been…3.24 p.m. at that point. I was timing myself to see how fast I could peel the carrots.

I suppose you want to know what Douglas looks like. He is seventeen, tall and wiry, with blond hair that falls in curtains around his face. He was wearing jeans and a bright orange shirt with a pattern of green birds.

Ms Bromley had told me all about him. She likes to gossip. That's how I knew Lottie and Douglas had been dating for around a year. Lottie went to an all girls' boarding school, and Douglas was at the neighbouring boys' one. Apparently, they'd got into loads of trouble for sneaking out to see each other, and that's why Emily Vanforte thought he wasn't good enough for Lottie. She thought he was leading Lottie down the wrong path. There was also something to do with Douglas's dad needing money that Mrs Vanforte didn't like. Which didn't make sense to me, because his dad was supposed to be a big car salesman with lots of cash.

From what I could tell though, Mrs Vanforte didn't like Lottie very much either. Or Mr Vanforte. Or anyone. She could put people down with a single glance.

I stayed out of her way.

Ms Bromley also didn't like Douglas. Unlike me, *she* had been around when Douglas visited the Bramble Estate previously. Apparently he treated her like she wasn't even a person.

Ms Bromley likes to talk a lot, and I don't, so that's why we get on – as well as I get on with anyone, which doesn't say much.

So, Ms Bromley talked, I listened, and we both prepped dinner. Sometimes there were other people around the house. Mrs Vanforte's assistant, her masseuse, the gardener. But on that Saturday it was only me and Ms Bromley working. Ms Bromley struggled to stand for long periods of time, so she was sitting at the kitchen table as she prepared the vegetables.

"How are things going in here?" asked Douglas as he came into the kitchen. He gave one of the pots a stir, splashing some of the sauce onto Ms Bromley's stone floor. "Oh, sorry," he said, with a smirk. He didn't sound sorry at all.

"That is quite all right," said Ms Bromley. But I knew it *wasn't* all right because I once spilled orange juice in the spot Douglas was standing and Ms Bromley had yelled at me for five minutes and thirty-two seconds. I timed it. "Jayne – get the mop and clean up the floor," Ms Bromley continued. "Douglas, why are you down here? We've got work to do."

"It's Mr Treefair to you," said Douglas, taking the lid off another pot and sticking his finger into the sauce. He took his finger out and licked it, frowning slightly. Then he stuck it in again and had another swirl. "This is disgusting," he said. "Maybe you should learn how to do your job."

Ms Bromley's nostrils flared as I balled my hands into fists. She'd spent all morning on that sauce, and now he'd double-dipped his spit in it and called it disgusting.

"Maybe you should *get out of my kitchen*," she said through gritted teeth.

"You can't talk to me like that," said Douglas, his lip curling. Ms Bromley glanced at me, raising a single eyebrow. Wondering why I hadn't followed her instructions.

I went over to the cupboard, got out the mop, wet it, and started cleaning.

"I can talk to you however I want," said Ms Bromley, folding her arms. "You know why? Because I've worked at this place since before you were born, and I'll probably die here too. You're just a mistake Lottie is making."

Douglas smirked.

The bell rang, probably Mrs Vanforte wanting tea.

"I'll get that," said Ms Bromley, rising slowly to her feet and grabbing her walking stick. I would have offered to go instead but I knew Ms Bromley would snap my head off if I even suggested she might need help. She hobbled from the room.

I wrung out the mop, and then put it away to get back to my vegetables, doing my best to ignore Douglas, who was now staring at me.

"What's your name?" he asked, tilting his head.

I looked at him, and then started chopping.

"Hello," he said, slightly louder. "Do – you – understand me—?"

I moved onto the potatoes, my knife slicing through them with ease. I didn't want to talk to him. And even though I got the sense he *knew* I didn't want to, he stayed, watching me with a small smile on his face.

I hadn't washed my hair in a few days, and it hung in lank black sheets around my face. Just the way I like it, keeping me hidden.

"What are you making?" he said, speaking slowly and clearly.

Go speak to your girlfriend, I wanted to tell him. But I didn't. I'd always keep my thoughts to myself, and I wasn't about to change that now.

I glanced up to see his mouth twitching. Making me uncomfortable was a game. I was entertainment. I turned back to my potatoes. They were all finely diced into squares, but I kept chopping, making the squares smaller and smaller. I wouldn't look up again, wouldn't meet his eyes.

"Fine," he said at last.

He turned on his heel and *finally* left.

I threw the potatoes in a pot as Ms Bromley hobbled back into the kitchen, her cane tapping on the floor as she looked around. "Good – at least Douglas is gone." She sat down with a sigh. "Mrs Vanforte would like some tea and cake – could you please prepare a tray and I'll take it up?" Her lips were pursed as she spoke and I got the feeling she wasn't happy about something. I waited, because she usually explains what's wrong without prompting. "I overheard Mr Vanforte speaking to

Lottie about buying her a new car – as if she needs *that*. What she needs are parents who *care*." She shook her head. "Let's just get through tonight and hope no one else decides to come and visit us."

11

Extract of Transcript of Interview 7
Re: Death of Emily Vanforte
In Attendance – Inspector Adams (IA),
Devi Mistry (DM)

DM: Sorry about that. I drank a bucket of tea before I came here, which was stupid of me because I've got a bladder the size of a pea. I'll probably need a lot more loo breaks, just so you know. In fact, I think I already might need to go again...

IA: Before your, er...bathroom break, you were telling me how you'd just arrived at the estate, and you'd overheard Emily telling Lottie that she wanted to expose one of the people who was having dinner with them that night for being – let me find the quote – *a crook and a liar*. But Emily didn't say which guest she was referring to...

DM: Yeah, that's right. I think that's why she wanted to have this fabled family dinner in the first place. She wanted to reveal this big secret about one of them. Must have been a great motivation for murder.

IA: Hmm. What did Lottie do after Emily's declaration?

DM: What any normal person would do. Walked off.

IA: And was that the point when you decided you would be staying at the Bramble Estate for the night?

DM: Hell, no. I'm not stupid – Mrs Vanforte's threat was *weird* – besides, that house... I know you said don't mention my *retrospective* thoughts or whatever, but even before Mrs Vanforte's murder it had an odd vibe to it.

IA: How so?

DM: Well, it was enormous for one thing – why the hell would anyone need to live in a place that large? Anyone could have been lurking. And the atmosphere... [Pause] I've never liked old houses. There's a high chance at least one person has already died inside.

IA: Ah, you believe in the supernatural, do you?

DM: No. [Snort] But I was raised superstitious, right? If you sneeze before you leave the house you need to eat something sweet, and never buy steel on a Saturday – that sort of thing. And there was...well, something *evil* about that house.

Devi

Before the Murder

"Douglas will look at your car..." Mrs Vanforte paused. "What was your name?"

"Devi," I said quickly. "Devi Mistry."

Instead of replying, she turned on her heel and marched off, her shoes clacking on the tiles. I didn't know who Douglas was, but she seemead to be very sure he would help me.

My shoulders slumped in relief, because I would rather have faced the snow than stay with her while she turned her family dinner into a massive family row. Although...it would make a good story. And I *love* a good story. That's how I got into watching reality shows – everyday life taken and distorted into plot lines for entertainment. I've always said I'd make an excellent reality star. I've got a great personality – that's what the teachers at school say (though it's usually followed with a "but": *but Devi needs to stop talking so much in class and save her great personality for home time*).

Mrs Vanforte left me standing alone in the grand foyer, looking at the abstract art and thinking about how ugly it was. There were a few bowls filled with flower petals on the side tables, along with golden candlestick holders with no candles. I took a photo on my phone, and wished I could send it to Priya – but I couldn't send messages to *anyone*, obviously.

I wondered what Priya would say if I told her about the Bramble Estate. Probably that I needed to leave as soon as possible. She was always the more sensible one out of us two. Sometimes I wonder if Mum would have preferred her for a daughter, but I that was just me being slightly bitter at the fact Priya *was* a lot better than me. She was nicer to everyone and used to be able to make friends with anyone, she got better grades, all the boys had crushes on her. I didn't mind though – if everyone thought she was awesome, and she thought *I* was awesome, then by definition everyone thought I was awesome too. Basic science.

"Who are you?" asked a posh voice from behind me.

I turned round, and recognized the owner of the voice at once: Charles Vanforte. I obviously don't, like…watch political stuff, and he doesn't really feature on the gossip sites, but the news is sometimes on right before the new soap Mum and I have just got in to, so I've caught glimpses of him. He looked exactly like he does on the telly, with salt-and-pepper hair, and light green eyes – though he's definitely shorter than I expected. He was wearing suit trousers and a shirt and a grey waistcoat, the whole outfit held together with a blood-red tie.

I told him who I was. He raised his bushy eyebrows. For some reason he reminded me strongly of the Grinch.

"Oh, so you just *happened* to get lost and arrive here?" he said, shaking his head. "Sending a child out in a snowstorm. This is low, even for the tabloids. Who sent you? The *Daily Express*? The *Daily Mail*?"

Good lord he was paranoid about the press. Did he *often* get teenagers acting as undercover journalists coming up to the house? "The *Financial Times*," I said drily. "They want to run an exposé. Or the alternative is that I actually did get lost. You can decide."

He looked slightly taken aback – I bet he wasn't used to snarky comments. "I do apologize," he said, with a rueful smile. "Forgive me – it's just the sort of thing the papers would do. The price of being a public figure, I suppose. I'm a politician, you see," he said, like he thought I wasn't smart enough to keep up with current affairs. I don't, but that wasn't the point. "I'm Charles. Mr Vanforte to you."

He held out his hand for me to shake. I took it and gripped it tight, shaking once while I looked him in the eye, trying to show I wouldn't be intimidated by him or his huge house.

"And where exactly were you driving *to*, Devi?" His eyes flicked over my face, and there was a slight curl to his lip – I bet there weren't a lot of Indian-looking folk in these here parts, so he must have thought it was a bit odd for me to have been passing by.

"My grandma's house," I said. "She married a man called Gerry." That explained everything he needed to know. Something about him raised my hackles – I wanted to be confrontational. I think it was the way he was talking to me, all condescending, like he thought I was a kid.

"Of course she did," said Mr Vanforte. He crossed to a window next to the front door, peering out with his hands behind his back. "Your car is the small one? I'm sure it's fine – it's probably just cold. And then you can be on your way as soon as possible."

"Nonsense," said Mrs Vanforte, bustling back in with a tall, sandy-haired boy with freckles. He was wearing the ugliest effing shirt I had ever seen, an orange so bright I wondered if it would glow in the dark. I thought it was patterned with flies until I looked properly and saw they were birds. His trainers were so white they looked like they were straight out of the box.

"Seems my expertise is needed," the boy said, folding his arms as he smirked at Mrs Vanforte.

"Maybe you can *finally* be useful," said Mrs Vanforte with a sniff. "Devi, this is Douglas – Charlotte's…friend." She grimaced as she said *friend*.

"Boyfriend," said Douglas. "You can't stop us being together, you know – I love her. And I *am* useful – hence why I'm the only one you could ask for help." His smirk widened into a grin, like he had just told the punchline to a joke.

"Of course you love Lottie," said Mr Vanforte proudly. "My daughter is wonderful."

"Douglas will check over your car," said Mrs Vanforte to me, like her husband hadn't spoken. "Though really, the day is getting on and the snow is still falling. I think perhaps the best thing for you to do would be to stay the night and then set off in the morning when the storm is over."

"No," I said, at the same time as Mr Vanforte. We were startled, looking at each other – it was weird to be on the same page as someone who seemed so different from me.

Because even though these people did not look like the Addams family, I still wanted to be on my way. I had a prickly feeling down the back of my neck – they were so blunt and hostile, like they all *hated* each other. And yet they were stuck in this mansion in the middle of nowhere, with no one else to speak to, and no internet to keep them entertained. I was getting seriously bad vibes.

"Devi should be getting on her way," said Mr Vanforte smoothly. "She is off to visit her grandmother and *Gerry*, who I'm sure will both be very worried about her. Please could you go and help Devi?" he added to Douglas.

I didn't like the way Mr Vanforte kept repeating my name, like he thought I should be impressed that he had remembered it. Mum once said that repeating someone's name in a conversation makes them feel more relaxed around you, which sounds like a load of crap – and even if it isn't, I'm too smart to be taken in by psychological tricks.

"I'll just turn the key a few times and Dev will be on her way," said Douglas.

Gee, guess I'm stupid because I didn't think to turn my key a few times myself. I bit my lip to stop myself from saying that out loud. "My name's Devi," I said instead, loud enough for him to hear. He looked at me properly for the first time. The smile slipped off his face.

"Dev-ey," he repeated, the pronunciation wrong.

"Day-ve," I corrected. It was only two syllables and not hard to pronounce at all, but I've run into loads of people who act like it's the most complicated thing in the world. I always tell people when they get it wrong – it's my name, which means it's important to me.

Douglas shrugged, like it didn't matter. "Whatever, Dev. Let's go fix your car."

I didn't bother to correct him again. With any luck, I would be on my way soon and he'd no longer exist to me. Out of sight, out of mind and all that jazz.

We went outside into the freezing air. The snow was already about two inches deeper than it had been when I arrived, still falling thickly.

We traipsed across to my car, and it quickly became apparent that Douglas didn't have the first clue about how to fix a car. I had no idea why Mrs Vanforte thought he might, apart from the fact he has a general air of smugness about him that suggests he's the type of person to blag his way through life.

After doing a full circuit around the car – and starting to shiver in his stupid shirt – he took my key off me, grimacing as he opened the door, and peered at the ripped seats. He flinched as he climbed inside, like he expected the roof to collapse, stuck the key in the ignition and turned.

Nothing happened.

"It just needs a few revs," he said, but although the engine spluttered, it didn't roar to life. He got out, then popped the hood open and peered at all the mechanics inside. "Er, right, well there's the engine. And that's the battery."

"And *that's* the car," I muttered.

He slammed the hood down. "Well, in my opinion this thing is dead – why don't you get a new one? My dad actually owns a dealership for luxury sports cars…" He trailed off, his eyebrows rising as he looked at me. "Though, er…they might be a bit pricey for you. Just a *tad*. But still, I can suggest a few good cars – although I don't think I'll have heard of anything you can afford."

"Yes, yes, *that's* what I'll do," I said, folding my arms. "I'll just pop out to the local car dealership down the road right now and buy a new car with my *parents'* money."

"Get the chip off your shoulder," said Douglas, rolling his eyes. "It's not a good look."

I narrowed my eyes, biting down on my bottom lip to stop myself from swearing at him. "How far is it to walk to the nearest village?" I said through gritted teeth. Once there I could get to a phone box and ring Nani and then in a few hours I'd be nice and toasty, eating her roti and daal and gossiping about all the old people who live nearby. All this just because I'd let her guilt-trip me into visiting her. Although, it wasn't like I had any other plans before school started and I had been looking forward to staying somewhere other than our little house in London. I'd spent New Year's Eve sitting at home with Mum and Dad watching the fireworks on the telly – well, with Dad. Mum fell asleep at 10 p.m. At midnight, I'd messaged Priya to wish her a Happy New Year. She hadn't replied. I knew she wouldn't, but I sent the message anyway. It's tradition.

"About fifty minutes on a good day," Douglas replied as he stood back and examined the car, pushing his blond hair back and leaning on his back leg. It looked like he was posing for a photo – ruined by the fact that he was still shivering, except he hadn't acknowledged that part, like he thought he was too cool to be cold. "But I don't fancy your chances of not getting lost on the way. More likely to die in a snowdrift somewhere." He paused, a slow, sly grin spreading across his face. "But, by all means, feel free to attempt it."

Since we'd only known each other twenty seconds, the fact he'd told me to go ahead and die seemed just a *tad* aggressive.

I was on Mrs Vanforte's side – I didn't like him at all. Considering Mr Vanforte also seemed to be a bit of a twat, maybe she was right to be hostile to everyone in her house. I certainly wouldn't have been able to put up with them.

Douglas's eyes slid past me and the grin vanished from his face.

"What are you doing out here?" he called.

I spun round to see another boy of about our age walking round the outside of the house, heading to the front door. He was Douglas's height, with curly black hair, thick black eyebrows, and dark brown eyes. His hands were stuffed into the pockets of his black leather jacket, and his face was deathly white – apart from his nose, which was red, probably from the cold.

Damn. He was fit. Which also meant he was bad news. I'd been known to have inappropriate crushes in the past – I always pick people I can't have, to prevent me ever actually having to have a proper relationship.

I haven't delved into *why* I don't want a proper relationship, because that would open a whole can of worms. I had my first crush when I was thirteen – on Dylan, Priya's older brother, who had gone off the rails slightly when he fell in with the wrong crowd at school…which somehow made him more attractive. I never said anything, because there was like a four-year age gap (inappropriate I know, blah blah) but I had all these stupid daydreams. It'd be just like a film, me dating my best-friend's brother. We'd fall in love, and get married one day, and Priya would be my sister properly, and we'd all be happy.

Things never work out the way you want them to, though.

"Emily invited me, remember?" the boy said to Douglas, his voice lightly sarcastic.

"You know that's not what I meant," said Douglas with a growl.

"I was going for a walk," said the boy with a shrug. He seemed laid-back, unbothered by Douglas's rudeness. "That's not illegal, is it?"

"In the freezing snow?" Douglas replied, tilting his head. He was right to question the boy – he looked like he was seconds away from turning into an icicle.

"Yup." The boy's mouth twitched slightly as he looked at me, his expression curious. "Who are you?"

"Devi," I said, folding my arms. "My car broke down." I nodded at the pile of junk behind me.

"This is Tate Astur," said Douglas. "He's Lottie's cousin." His lip curled, and I could sense tension between them. I took back what I'd thought about how seventeen-year-olds couldn't possibly be dangerous – Douglas seemed like the type of person I'd want to steer clear of. "Well, like I said, there's no way your car can be fixed, Dev. See you around." He trotted back up to the house, sticking his hands in his pockets and whistling as he went.

Tate clicked his tongue against his teeth as he watched Douglas's retreating back.

"You want my advice?" he said, then pressed on before I had

a chance to answer. "I'd risk freezing to death by spending the night in your car rather than going back into that house."

"What are you talking about?" I asked.

"Aunt Emily hates us all," he said. "She can't stand Uncle Charles or Lottie. Thinks Uncle Charles is a waste of space and hates Lottie for actually *liking* her dad – shock horror that Lottie would get on with the parent who is actually nice to her. I don't think many people like Douglas to be fair – he's, er…an acquired taste. Of course, Aunt Emily hates me just as much. I'm from Uncle Charles's side of the family, after all. I'm a waste of space, just like he is – according to her, anyway. Honestly, no idea why she's invited me tonight." Puffs of white clouds blew away from his mouth, but he didn't seem to notice the cold.

"Maybe she likes the drama," I suggested. He looked so miserable and moody I just couldn't take him seriously. "If I was a rich old lady, I'd definitely pick arguments just for the fun of it."

"I don't think Aunt Emily knows what fun is," muttered Tate, kicking at the snow.

"You know, you could have just turned down the invite to dinner?" I pointed out. "Stayed at your own giant house, eating caviar and polishing your gold? You don't *have* to stay."

Tate's mouth twitched – was that almost a *smile*? "I'd be stupid to say no to Aunt Emily."

"Well *I* have my own mind," I said. "No one tells *me* what to do." That wasn't entirely true – I had, after all, been guilt-tripped into making the journey to visit Nani – but Tate didn't know that. "And no one scares me either."

Tate's dark eyes flicked over me, and there was a new light

in them – something in his expression had shifted. "Well then, you won't mind me telling you that the house is a *dangerous* place to be." He glanced around, like he was afraid of being overheard – stupid, because we were in the middle of bloody nowhere with no one else around, which was why I was stuck talking to him. "There's a murderer inside."

I blinked at him, not sure if I'd heard correctly – especially since he'd said it so matter-of-factly. "What?"

His eyes slid to my car. "Maybe it isn't any safer out here, though," he said, as he went past me and tapped the bonnet, like he thought that might get the engine to start working. I carried on staring at him. "There could be a murderer outside too." He lowered his voice. "It might even be me."

Lizzie
The Day of My Arrival

Mrs Vanforte showed me to the kitchen, where she said I might "make friends" with "Jayne". I sucked a breath in as I took in the room. It was a large space with wood-panelled walls, red tiles on the floor and a large fire crackling cheerfully. I was still slightly on edge – Mum wouldn't like me intruding, but she'd also want me to be careful and not risk my life by attempting to drive in the snow. There were pots bubbling on the stove, and a pile of dishes in the sink.

The old lady who had delivered the tea tray earlier came bustling forward, and I felt more at ease as she twinkled at me. "Do come and make yourself comfortable. I'm Ms Bromley – and now, my dear, let's get some food in you!"

I hadn't properly eaten the sponge cake Mrs Vanforte had given me, and my last meal had been a horrible burger at a service station hours earlier. I normally have dinner later – it was still only 4 p.m. – but my stomach grumbled at the word *food.* I smiled to show my appreciation as Ms Bromley spooned me some soup out of a pot, serving it alongside home-made bread dripping in golden butter. It was delicious – warm and thick and just what I needed. I found myself digging in, inhaling a few spoons of soup before I realized Ms Bromley was watching me. She gave a satisfied nod as I looked up and met her eyes.

"Do you want anything, Jayne?" she asked.

With a start, I realized we weren't alone in the room. I'd thought *Jayne* was Ms Bromley's first name, but it turned out she was a tall girl about my age, skulking in the corner of the kitchen. She had pale white skin, thick black hair that fell in a sheet around her face, and sharp cheekbones. She could have been a model if she'd been wearing nicer clothes – she was dressed in an oversized black hoodie and baggy black jeans. Although, I suppose the grunge look is actually in again now.

Jayne grunted in response to Ms Bromley's question, then turned back to wiping down the countertops. Ms Bromley didn't seem to expect a reply, because she sat down and turned to me to continue chatting. "We're getting ready for a dinner Mrs Vanforte is serving tonight, aren't we, Jayne? It's being made into something of an occasion." Ms Bromley lowered her voice slightly. I think she wanted a good gossip with me, but Mum always says it's rude to gossip. I shifted in my seat uncomfortably – but Ms Bromley didn't seem to notice my discomfort, continuing to speak. "Mrs Vanforte is eating with her husband for one thing – they *never* eat together. She simply *loathes* him, and the feeling is very much mutual. I don't understand why they haven't separated – although I suppose it'd be hard dividing all their money up in a divorce…"

"Yes," I mumbled, not sure what to say. I reached for another piece of bread, to make myself look busy, and Ms Bromley poured more soup into my bowl without me even needing to ask.

This was the wrong decision. The thought blasted through my mind unbidden. I had never stayed away from home alone before. I went on a school trip to an adventure site when I was ten, but other than that I've only ever gone away with Mum – and Dad, when he was around. I'd been mentally prepared to stay in the hotel, and I had done all my research on it, read all the reviews. I knew what television channels the room got and exactly what time breakfast was served in the morning. I knew nothing about this house, or who these people really were.

Was it too late to leave? Chance the snow? I'm not usually a risk-taker – but staying here, with strangers, was a risk as well. There was no right choice.

The mental image of Dad's face surged into my mind. I always associate him with bad decisions, though it wasn't *his* fault he had a heart attack and died in front of me.

"Mr Vanforte prefers going to dinner with his friends rather than eating with Mrs Vanforte." Ms Bromley shook her head. "Horrors, those men. There's James Marton and – a Smith of some kind… What was the first name? It was such a common one… Oh, it's right there on the tip of my tongue. Oh, well, it will come to me. Now, Mr Vanforte *really* doesn't like people talking about Smith… I heard Mrs Vanforte yelling about him once, this Mr Smith, saying she didn't want Mr Vanforte using Smith any more – *Edward*. That's his name – Edward Smith…"

She shook her head, looking at me expectantly, like she wanted more input from me.

I had no idea what to say, so I ate more soup – and tried to swallow my anxiety down with it.

There was a movement to my right – Jayne was now staring at Ms Bromley.

Devi
Before the Murder

Of course, I didn't let Tate bother me with his whole *there's a murderer inside the house* thing. He obviously just wanted to wind me up – I could see the little glint in his eyes. He was testing me. He's probably one of those bad boys at school, who sit away from everyone else and look all mysterious, and everyone thinks they're super cool when they were actually a giant knob. Just my type, but obviously I wasn't here to form inappropriate crushes on rich boys.

"I could be a murderer too," I said, making sure I didn't blink. "But let's go back inside before we're both killed by the weather." He didn't want me in the house for some reason – so into the house I would go. It's a slight sickness, my need to do the opposite of whatever other people want.

Tate's eyebrows went up, and his mouth twitched again – he tilted his head, likely to admit defeat. One point to Devi.

I smiled at him as I headed back in. In the hall, Mrs Vanforte was standing by the window. She'd clearly been watching us. Mr Vanforte was sitting on one of the chaise longues, tapping his fingers on the material, and Douglas was standing by the stairs with his hands in his pockets.

"I just went for a walk, Aunt Emily," Tate said to Mrs Vanforte as he shut the front door behind him. She looked at him in silence, failing to hide her disdain as she turned away without acknowledging he had spoken. "And, as ever, my superpower of invisibility remains in check," he muttered.

I felt a twinge of sympathy – it's not nice, being ignored and having to pretend like you don't care. I find I often have to be the loudest person in the room to get people to listen to me, but even then they don't really want to hear what I have to say. It's why I like to come up with outrageous stuff, just to test whether people are paying attention.

"Devi, Douglas said your car won't start – you must stay the night," said Mrs Vanforte to me, her face still carved of stone even though she was making a really nice offer.

My heart gave a small flutter of panic. *Stay?* My initial impression had been that this place would make one hell of a creepy hotel, and it made an even creepier home. Plus hanging around this lot was already incredibly awkward. I immediately tried to come up with another solution – maybe one of them would let me borrow their car, just to get to the nearest village. Although the darkness was creeping in, and the snow was still falling…

"It's settled then," Mrs Vanforte said briskly. "Devi, do you have a bag?"

I nodded. "Yeah, it's in my car boot."

"Right. *Tate* will go and get it for you." She waved her hand towards the front door without looking at him, saying his name like it was a swear word.

The moment of vulnerability I'd briefly seen on Tate's face was gone. "Why can't she get it herself?" he said, folding his arms.

"You were delighted to be outside just a second ago," said Mrs Vanforte, still not looking at him. It was like she thought he was Medusa and would turn her to stone if she made eye contact. I gave Tate my car key, and he rolled his eyes and stomped back outside.

"Emily dear, she really should be setting off," said Mr Vanforte, standing up and striding over to his wife. "Her grandmother will be worried about her."

He was keen to get rid of me. Too keen. It kind of made me want to stay – even if I *did* have a choice about leaving – just to see what he wanted to keep hidden from me.

Mrs Vanforte simply stared at him, with her arms folded.

Tate returned, clutching my tattered bag away from his body like he thought it might make him ill. The seams were coming apart and it was very close to ripping; something so cheap had probably never entered the house before.

"*Why* is this so heavy?" he said, dropping it by my feet, along with my key. "What do you have in here – bricks?"

"Yes," I said. "I'm actually a famous brick smuggler."

Douglas started, his eyes widening as he gaped at me. "Is that street talk for drugs?" he said, and I almost smiled at him, because for a moment I could see someone who loved a bit of gossip just as much as me.

"Douglas," cut in Mrs Vanforte. "Why don't you take this bag up to the West Wing – the Blue Room, if you please." Douglas stared at her. "*What?*" he asked. "Surely you're not going to put her in there…"

Mrs Vanforte blinked at him. "Excuse me? Who are you to question what I do or don't do in my own home? Where's Lottie – isn't the whole point of this visit that you're here for her?"

Douglas cleared his throat. "I, er…like giving my opinions on things. And it's just…I've seen that room, and it's horribly cold, and she looks like someone who'd prefer somewhere warmer. Wouldn't you, Dev?"

I looked around. "Where's this Dev person?" I asked pointedly, the brief moment of connection between us gone. "You keep talking to someone called Dev, and I don't know who they are."

"Devi," he said through gritted teeth. "Don't you want a nice, toasty bedroom to stay in?"

"I prefer feeling like I'm going to freeze," I said in the most pleasant voice I could manage. No way on earth would I have agreed with him.

"She's going in the Blue Room," said Mrs Vanforte, in a voice that made it clear the argument was over.

Douglas looked from her to me – and then to Tate, who shrugged. Tate was keeping back, away from the conversation, but I could tell he was listening intently to every word from the way his dark eyes flicked around from person to person.

Douglas's nostrils flared, and his face went red. I wondered if he'd ever not got his way before. "Fine," he said, and turned on his heel and walked off.

"You'll forgive me if I ask you to eat dinner later, in the kitchen, rather than with me and my family…and Douglas…" said Mrs Vanforte, turning to me like the tense exchange hadn't happened. "I've been planning this *special* dinner for so long."

"Oh, she's still here?" Lottie appeared at the top of the stairs, looking from me to Mrs Vanforte. "Weren't we able to fix the car?" Her voice was timid as she spoke to her mum.

"She's staying the night," said Mrs Vanforte. "Isn't that utterly delightful." Her words didn't match her tone, which stayed caustic.

Mr Vanforte cleared his throat, and I looked over to see him raising his eyebrows at Lottie. "She's a stranger," said Lottie, though she didn't sound convincing. She glanced at Mr Vanforte, like she was searching for his approval. He gave a small nod and the tension in her shoulders loosened slightly. Interesting – she was willing to say whatever her dad wanted. I bet she didn't actually have any sort of problem with me staying, but I also lost any respect for her.

Tate snorted. He had slipped into the shadows, his eyes briefly meeting mine – and my stomach flipped. I found him *very* attractive, which meant he was *definitely* a bad guy.

"Pish, there's nothing to be worried about, Charlotte," said Mrs Vanforte airily. "I'm putting Devi in the Blue Room, in the West Wing. It'll be nice and private for you," she added to me. "The West Wing can be turned into its own little annexe once it's locked off."

"And if it helps, I'm not a thief or anything," I butted in, ready to wrap up the conversation. "Really, I was just driving up from London to visit my grandmother. She lives in Fickleburry

– a really small village. More sheep than people around."

Surprise flashed across Lottie's face as she walked slowly down the stairs towards me, grasping the handrail for support. "Fickleburry?" she said. "But that's miles back. You've gone past it."

And that was when I learned my satnav had really screwed me over.

I swore, then grimaced as I looked at Mr and Mrs Vanforte in case they found that rude. "I mean – oh no." My *oh no* sounded insincere even to me, but luckily neither of them commented on it.

"I, erm…still don't think you should stay here?" said Lottie again, once more sounding completely unconvinced. She was looking at Mr Vanforte, who was nodding at her like he was proud of her.

"I am *not* going to throw this poor girl out into the snow," said Mrs Vanforte, with a glint of steel in her eyes. This argument was about something way more than just me staying the night. "*I* have morals, and what I want is all that matters. I have the final say here – this is *my* house after all. And besides…" She looked at Mr Vanforte. "The alternative would make a terrible story for the papers – if it happened to get leaked. *Politician and family kill child by leaving her to freeze in the snow.*"

Mr Vanforte jerked to attention, like he'd been shocked. For the first time I saw what appeared to be genuine hatred in his eyes. "You're absolutely right, Emily, as ever. Of course she should stay. Lottie was wrong to suggest otherwise – right, Lottie?"

Hurt flashed across Lottie's face – but she still nodded, like she really was the only one who had been opposing me staying. "Right."

Mr Vanforte tilted his head as he looked at me. "Now, Devi," he said. "There's going to be a few costs in letting you stay the night. You know, for food – and heating up your room –"

"I will not be charging a single penny –" cut in Mrs Vanforte.

"– though *of course* we will let that slide tonight. Really, Emily, how could you even *suggest* that I would ever consider the thought of charging this unfortunate child for a room." Mr Vanforte's eyes zipped over me with new interest, and his tongue darted out to lick his lips. I half expected it to be forked, and was a bit disappointed to see it was completely ordinary. "But perhaps there are…other ways you could pay us back. Perhaps if you just…shared your story with others." He seemed to be warming to me now he thought I could help him tell a positive story to the press. Mrs Vanforte pursed her lips at him, looking unimpressed with his suggestion.

"You want me to tell everyone you're a hero?" I said, folding my arms. "Beacon of light in the community, blah, blah? Sure, I can do that."

"What a way to put it!" he chuckled. His laugh was always the same – three *heh, heh, hehs*, a small snort, and then silence. It was really disconcerting, because it felt like fake amusement, as if he was putting on a performance. "But you *can* say it if you want to."

"Sure," I said, putting on a fake enthusiastic voice. "You clearly *do* have a heart of pure *gold*."

If he caught my sarcasm, he didn't say anything. In the shadows, however, a smirk played on Tate's lips.

"We'll lock off the West Wing at about half past seven," said Mrs Vanforte. "You'll still be able to go outside if you want to – all I'll be doing is cutting the West Wing off from the rest of the house for the sake of everyone's privacy."

"Sounds good," I said, and I meant it. I'm not stupid – them locking off the West Wing was for their safety, not mine, because I was obviously a weird stranger to them. But it meant I would be safer too.

Tate was still watching silently and the rest of them were acting like they'd already forgotten he existed.

"I'll show you to your bedroom," said Mrs Vanforte, apparently unaware of the frosty atmosphere – but I had the feeling she wasn't oblivious at all, and generally enjoyed pissing off her husband… And everyone else. It was almost like they were entertainment for her. "I'll point out how you get down to the kitchen as well."

She set off without waiting to see if I would follow. I hurried after her, up the grand staircase and along a dim corridor leading off the first floor. The floorboards creaked underneath us, and there was a musty smell in the air. Definitely an old house.

There were loads of portraits on the walls, of grumpy men and women wearing dark outfits. They were all frowning, their eyes almost following me as I went.

"The Vanfortes," said Emily, seeing where I was looking. "My ancestors – Charles took my name when we married, of course."

"Very, er, modern of him," I said, trying to think back to what I knew about Mr Vanforte. As far as I knew, he also came from a rich family – because unlike the crap you read in fairytales, I know rich people like to marry other rich people. Princes don't pluck randos off the street and decide to shower them with wealth – not unless they're beautiful. So I had no chance, because according to the boys at school, I'm ugly. My face isn't symmetrical, and my eyes are too close together and blah, blah.

Someone at school actually once called me ugly to my face. He said I was the last person in the world he'd ever date. I replied that me going out with him was never a possibility because, as a general rule, I would never date anyone who obviously had no taste. The rest of his friends had high-fived me and from then on they treated me like one of the lads – and no one called me ugly again. But also no one ever asked me out.

Anyway – the point is, from what I knew, Charles Vanforte had started off with a loan from his parents, but his family's level of richness was nowhere near Mrs Vanforte's – that had to be why he'd changed his name. People like him always want more power.

"This is actually my ancestral home," continued Mrs Vanforte. She took huge strides, like she had several other places to be and no time to waste. I had to half jog to keep up with her. "Although I've added a few things to modernize it – like a swimming pool and such. Do feel free to use the pool – though of course you won't have your bathing things. I'm sure Lottie will have a spare if you want to ask her?"

I imagined myself sidling up to Lottie and asking for a swimming costume. She was a giant and it would probably look like I was five trying to dress up in my older sister's clothes. "That's okay, thanks," I said.

Mrs Vanforte led me down dark corridors, then down another set of stairs. She pointed out the kitchen on our way, then seemed to get into the tour and started telling me what the other rooms were – almost like she was showing off to me.

"Charles's and Lottie's bedrooms are down that way, along with mine," she said, nodding at a hallway we were going past. "I've put Douglas and Tate in guest rooms down this corridor." One of the doors was just shutting – I guessed it was Douglas returning from dropping off my bag.

I got a feel for the scale of the house as we walked through – so big I bet someone else could hide inside and live their life in secret, like that horror film about the serial killer who lived in the attic of a house and only came out to steal food and murder people.

We passed through an enormous wooden door.

"This is the West Wing," Mrs Vanforte said briskly. "Like I said, it'll be locked off at seven thirty, but as the kitchen is in the main part of the house I'll keep it open until then. Feel free to wander around if you want to before, though – and do try not to steal anything. I wouldn't want today to be the first time ever that my daughter's judgement has been right." Her tone was as dry as ever, but she seemed to enjoy getting in a dig at Lottie. *Super* weird – I almost felt sorry for Lottie. It probably sucked to have parents like hers.

Mrs Vanforte paused at the beginning of a dead-end corridor, getting a few towels out of an airing cupboard and passing them to me. "And through there is your room – I'll put the other two girls who are staying over tonight down this corridor as well, in the other spare bedrooms."

"Huh?" I asked. "Other girls?" What other girls? She'd only mentioned the people going to her family dinner.

"I employ a local girl to help around the house – she comes after college sometimes, and on the odd weekend. She's staying over to look after you," said Mrs Vanforte. "Just in case you need anything. And, er…well, I accidentally got a delivery driver stranded here. Long story – she's about your age, though. Maybe a little younger."

For a wild moment, the story of Hansel and Gretel flashed up in my mind – Mrs Vanforte was the witch luring people inside her (relatively) warm home before stuffing them in her oven to roast them. What if *we* were going to be main course at the dinner she kept banging on about?

I snorted, letting the thought pass.

Devi
Before the Murder

My room was incredible. Against the far wall was a *huge* four-poster bed – I'd seen them in films and stuff and always thought they were so cool. I waited for Mrs Vanforte to leave before dropping the towels she had given me and taking a running leap, bouncing onto the bed and sinking into the pillows. My clothes were a bit grubby from my car ride and traipsing back and forth in the snow, so I got a small amount of grime on the fresh white sheets.

I sat up, taking in my surroundings properly. The walls were panelled with wood painted a dark blue, and instead of a main light there were loads of dim lamps with blue lampshades. There was a thick, dark blue rug in front of an empty fireplace. Clearly, the room's name was literal.

Beside the fireplace there was a rickety old heater, which wasn't doing much to give warmth to the room. I swear I could see my breath coming out in white fog. So, Douglas hadn't been lying about it being freezing – but it was still weird that he had cared at all.

My room was on the ground floor. I peered out of the window, to find I had a view over the front of the house. The driveway was buried by the snow and there was a mess of blurred footprints around all the cars. It had stopped snowing, but the clouds looked like they were deciding whether to burst open again.

Beside my window was a red sports car. I don't know anything about cars, but I'd be willing to bet it had cost a few hundred thousand, and that it belonged to Douglas. I thought about chucking a snowball at it, but as it was already buried in inches of the white stuff, I didn't think my effort would make much of a difference.

I checked my watch – quarter past five. Well past the time Nani had been expecting me to arrive. I wished I could find some way to get hold of her and let her know I was safe. But she's a smart lady. When I didn't show up, she'd probably figure out I had holed up somewhere for the night. According to her, she'd survived hundreds of battles in the rural village in India where she had grown up. She was a tough old cookie and expected the same from me and Mum.

I continued to explore the room, discovering an en-suite that was probably about the size of my living room at home. I'd never had a bathroom just for me before.

Figuring I *was* pretty gross, I swam around in the bath for a bit and changed into fresh clothes. Then I stood in the middle of the room, my hands on my hips, wondering what I should do. It wasn't like I could just play around on my phone – there was no internet and no signal, so my usual go-to for entertainment was a bust. I wished I could message Priya and let her know what I was doing, though. I'd love to have seen her thoughts on the mansion – she would probably have been bouncing off the walls in excitement, nosing through everything, trying to find out all the historical background of literally everything, because she was a *massive* history nerd.

On the one hand, this whole situation was super weird, and the most sensible thing to do would be to stay in my room, and be as polite a guest as I could be.

But on the other…the Vanfortes were so *strange*. So different from how they appeared in the papers. There was a good story here, I could feel it. It was like a film come to life, where I was the protagonist, about to find out some shady detail from their past… Though even if I did, I wouldn't even sell it to the press, because they *had* taken me in after all. But it would be a juicy scoop to share with Priya.

Deep down, I knew I was just manufacturing drama in my head to stop myself getting bored and being alone with my thoughts in this creepy old house.

But, Emily Vanforte *had* said it was fine for me to *go for a wander* and I figured in the worst-case scenario, I would say I'd got lost on the way to the kitchen.

I left the West Wing and made a few random turns. It became clear pretty quickly that I *was* lost, so at least I'd have a real excuse if I ran into anyone. I was just looking into a dusty lounge when I heard a door closing and clacking heels coming down the corridor. I dived inside the room and peered through the crack I'd left between the door and door frame.

Lottie Vanforte was striding past, clutching a few sheets of paper. The way she was walking, all furtively, looking back over her shoulder, seemed weirdly suspicious and I guessed she had taken papers she wasn't supposed to. One fell to the ground as she disappeared around a corner and I darted out to scoop it up. It looked to be a newspaper article from a few years ago about a construction company that had gone bust – but there was something weird about it. The formatting looked off, and there were lines of red pen blocking out sentences – it seemed to be a draft. I frowned, scanning through until I caught sight of a familiar name: *Charles Vanforte.* He'd been the owner of the company. The red pen was thick, so I could only see odd words that hadn't been crossed out – the most interesting were *corruption* and *close to bankruptcy.*

I bet Lottie had been taking this clipping to her father. She'd only wanted to kick me out earlier because that was what Mr Vanforte wanted, so she'd probably do anything he told her to. But also…I was suddenly filled with a burning curiosity to find out what Lottie was up to, and why. I'd started exploring the house because I was bored and didn't want to be alone with my thoughts, but what if there actually was a story worth investigating here?

While I love trashy soaps and reality TV, another favourite of mine is mysteries – Mum and I often watch reruns of the old detective shows on TV, curled up on the sofa all Sunday afternoon. There is something comforting about mysteries, how you always know they're going to end with the brilliant detective figuring everything out. A question with an *answer* – how many times had I wished for that? For years it felt like all

I ever had was questions – how could someone who meant so much to me die? How could I ever move on?

This was definitely a mystery, and with my thoughts spiralling I needed to keep myself busy. Even if the solution was unimportant, it would likely be one I could figure out. And how else was I going to pass the time?

I couldn't hear the clacking of Lottie's heels any more, so I peeked down the corridor she'd walked along. There were only two rooms coming off the corridor, so it had to be pretty easy to figure out which one she'd been rifling through. I tiptoed into the first: a small library Priya would have loved. Then the other: a room that looked like Emily Vanforte's private office – jackpot.

There were papers everywhere, but stacked really high in neat piles. I bet Mrs Vanforte had a proper system in place so she could find everything easily. She struck me as someone who liked to be in control.

This had to be where the papers Lottie had taken came from.

Above the fireplace, exactly where someone else might hang a group family portrait, there was an oil painting of a frowning man I took to be one of the Vanforte ancestors. Mrs Vanforte didn't have any pictures of Lottie or Mr Vanforte, but there were several framed certificates hanging on the walls, thanking her for donating money to various places. She even had a few newspaper clippings in frames of her shaking hands with important-looking people, while the headings said things like VANFORTE SAVES THE WHALES AND THE CHILDREN.

A shiver of intrigue went down my spine. Had Lottie's father asked her to steal those clippings for him? And why did Mrs Vanforte have them in the first place? Mrs Vanforte obviously loved *good* press – but the bit of the newspaper clipping I had seen seemed to be negative, something that might have embarrassed Mrs Vanforte if it ever got out.

It felt as if I was just scratching the surface of something – but I didn't know what. Logically, though, it felt like the best place to start was by looking further into Mrs Vanforte's office. Perhaps I could see where Lottie had got the clippings from and dig a little more into whatever else was around.

I started skimming through the papers on her desk, but got bored pretty quickly – they were just lists of random numbers: sixty million (and three pounds) to this foreign account, fifty million to that foreign account, twenty million to this charity and ten million to that… Just staring at her money all day every day looked to be a full-time job. But from the little glimpses I saw, it seemed Mrs Vanforte had a very generous heart… Although maybe not towards her own family. There were a lot of charities listed – and all the donations were from her alone. I thought that was weird, because Mr Vanforte seemed like the kind of person who would *love* to take credit for donations.

But from the papers I had scanned, it was also pretty clear that this was all *Emily* Vanforte's money – the accounts were all in her name. I remembered what she had said about the house – how it was *her* ancestral home.

I've always thought in a marriage everything is supposed to be fifty/fifty and all that, but then I remembered Nani telling me about how a woman should always hide money for herself, in case she ever needed it to escape from a man. Nani meant *literally* hide money – like in a waterproof bag in her toilet cistern – and it was smart that she did that because Nana, from what I had gleaned from the rare times he had been brought up, was not a *nice* man. More of the old school beat-with-a-belt type. And he liked to *glug, glug* if you catch my drift.

That was why it was so good when Nani met Gerry. Good old dependable Gerry, who does the *Times* crossword every Sunday and won't touch a drop of the devil's sauce because he needs to watch his health. It was a scandal in our community in London – no one ever discussed the fact that Nani and Nana had separated, so when he died, people expected Nani to mourn him for ever. Three weeks later she announced she was getting married to Gerry.

But anyway, I know there are legal ways of protecting your money, and I bet the Vanfortes of old set up trusts only a Vanforte by blood could touch. I thought back to the arguments I had seen between them already. If they disagreed like that in front of strangers like me, what must they be like in private…? And why they were even still together? Although I guessed Mr Vanforte could be staying for the money anyway, even if he didn't control it. Maybe, like Nani, he was worried Mrs Vanforte might get vindictive – but for someone like Mr Vanforte, I guessed everything probably came down to money.

I gave up on the desk and started looking around the room. In the far corner, what looked to be a cupboard door was swinging open slightly, like someone had been trying to shut it in a hurry but hadn't latched it properly. I headed over – it seemed to be a safe, like the sort of thing you might find in a hotel.

"Excellent," I muttered. But I was disappointed when I peered inside to find yet more folders – I'd been hoping for a few bars of gold or something.

There were several files under a paper tab marked *Employees*. I flicked past two thin folders marked *Doris Bromley* and *Jayne Faraway*. The Bromley folder was empty – weird… What was the point of even having it? Jayne's had an application form for a job. Under *Why are you applying for this position?* she'd written "I need the money". My type of girl.

There were separate folders marked *Family*, *Friends*, and *Acquaintances*.

It looked like Mrs Vanforte had folders on *everyone* she knew. Tate's and Douglas's folders were together, and I pulled out Douglas's first. It had notes detailing fights he'd been in at school and report cards from teachers saying he was an average student, but was in danger of failing most of his classes because he kept skipping them. Tate's folder was thinner with just a few report cards, all saying he was a quiet student who kept apart from the other pupils, but had excellent grades.

"Creepy," I muttered to myself. Why the hell was Mrs Vanforte gathering information like this on her nephew and her daughter's boyfriend?

I glanced at the door, wondering how much time I had. If I was caught, there was no way I could talk my way out of this. From where I stood, the eyes of the man in the oil painting seemed to be fixed directly on me, his frown showing his displeasure over what I was doing.

But, oh well – in for a penny, in for a pound. Nani always tells me and Mum that we needed to finish what we start. I had started looking through the safe, so I absolutely needed to finish.

I skipped past other folders with names I didn't recognize

before I came to Mr Vanforte's. It was filled with stuff I didn't understand, papers covered in numbers and figures about some old business that looked like it had been shut down – probably the construction company in the newspaper article.

At the back of the folder were a few bank statements for a current account. Mr Vanforte had a grand total of £74 waiting to be spent. He couldn't be broke, surely – a big politician with the salary to match. There had to be other accounts scattered about with loads of money in them. But if there were, Mrs Vanforte wasn't keeping evidence of them.

There was no folder for Lottie, so using my powerful skills of deduction I worked out that was probably what she had been in the office to nick, alongside the newspaper clipping. Or else, Mrs Vanforte hadn't made a creepy folder on her own daughter. I bet it was the first option, though.

I thought I heard muffled voices floating down the corridor, so quickly stuffed the newspaper article about Mr Vanforte that Lottie had dropped into my pocket and left the office, ambling along like I hadn't been doing something dodgy.

Douglas and Mrs Vanforte were walking towards me.

"What are you doing?" said Douglas, as they both came to a stop.

"Looking for the kitchen," I said. Why the hell wasn't Douglas hanging around with Lottie – I don't think I'd even seen them in the same room together at that point… And on that note, why was he with Mrs Vanforte? The woman obviously hated him.

Mrs Vanforte nodded at me. "I realized I forgot to lock my office, and ran into Douglas heading the same way…" She frowned at him. "Where were you going again, Douglas? You know it's just the West Wing this way – why do you want to go there?"

"Er...I just wanted to check to see if Dev had settled in okay," said Douglas, nodding at me.

I bit down the urge to scream *My name is Devi!* at him – I didn't want to be rude in front of Mrs Vanforte, seeing as she was the one hosting me. "Which way's the kitchen?" I choked out instead.

Mrs Vanforte smiled, like she knew the great pains I'd gone to not to spew a bunch of insults at Douglas. He was definitely lying about wanting to check up on me – he didn't give a rat's arse about me, or his own girlfriend either, apparently.

I quickly forgot the directions Mrs Vanforte gave me, but tried not to show my confusion. I was sure I'd figure it out, and I wouldn't mind getting lost and having to wander around a bit more, maybe figure out what Lottie was up to. Her boyfriend seemed to be so uninterested in her – why would she put up with that?

"Actually, Douglas, I wanted to get your opinion on a new painting I bought," Mrs Vanforte said, glancing at him. "Come with me."

He looked baffled as she led him away, but I couldn't help noticing that he glanced back as he went, his eyes looking slightly desperate. I thought about how he'd been really alarmed to hear I was going to be staying in the Blue Room – and if it was just the West Wing this way, maybe that was where he had been heading. He'd definitely not wanted me in that particular room...

If there was something odd about the Blue Room, I wanted to know what it was. I was supposed to be *sleeping* in there, for one thing. Plus, rich people always have skeletons in their closets, and now my mind had gone down the avenue of there being something super horrifying in there – like a literal skeleton.

I was on the case now. So instead of going to the kitchen, I turned on my heel and headed back to the Blue Room.

16

Jayne

I got tired of listening to Ms Bromley gossiping at the new girl. She'd been at it for nearly an hour and showed no signs of stopping.

Lizzie was painfully awkward, her face red. I took in everything they were saying, but my mind was elsewhere. Chopping vegetables, sautéing fish, preparing pastry. Wiping down the counters to keep the workspace tidy. Doing the dishes as I went. I like cooking and cleaning. I like using my hands.

Ms Bromley got the last few things in the oven. Then she put Lizzie to work, sending her across to the dining room with all the cold food that could be set out early on the table.

Lizzie seemed to be happier once she had something to do. It was clear she's someone who doesn't like to sit still.

Even though she told me she was seventeen, she seemed younger than me for some reason, with her blonde hair that bounced around her face and big blue eyes. She half reminded me of a porcelain doll my mum tried to give me when I was little.

Ms Bromley looked at the clock hanging on the wall – 5.02 p.m.

"All the food's done, so we just need to make sure it's warm when we plate it up for dinner. Emily says she'll take it through herself." She looked at me. "Jayne…you'll be staying in the big house tonight, down the West Wing corridor?"

I nodded, as Lottie came into the kitchen. She was wearing a dark blue jumpsuit, her hair curled up in a bun.

"Er…hello," she said, hovering by a saucepan of soup that was simmering on the stove. "I'm so sorry to bother you, I don't want to waste your time or anything, but I was just wondering –" she knocked against the pan, and flinched – "I'm so sorry, I'll get out of your way. I just wanted to ask… Have any of you seen Douglas?" Her eyes flicked over Ms Bromley, then she gave me a small smile. I stared back at her.

"Good evening to you too, my dear," said Ms Bromley. "We saw Douglas a little while ago. He wanted to…check up on the food."

He wanted to lord it over us. But Ms Bromley obviously didn't want to upset Lottie. Or else she thought it would be rude to say Douglas had walked in and spilled sauce on the floor. He was a guest, after all.

I wouldn't put her straight, of course. Even though I wanted to. Better to stay in the shadows – and keep my job.

Lottie sucked her cheeks in, biting her bottom lip. "If you see him, can you tell him I'm looking for him, please?" she said. "He was supposed to spend time with me – he said that was the whole point of this visit…"

17

Extract of Transcript of Interview 9
Re: Death of Emily Vanforte
In Attendance – Inspector Adams (IA),
Jayne Faraway (JF)

IA: Just one second please, Jayne. What was Lottie wearing?

JF: What?

IA: You said she was wearing a dark blue jumpsuit. [Sound of shuffling paper] Devi mentioned, however, she was wearing a cream top and white trousers earlier, when she let Devi into the house.

JF: [Silence]

IA: A shrug isn't an answer, Jayne. You need to say something, for the transcript.

JF: You didn't ask a question.

IA: Why did she change her clothes? She would change again later, for dinner...

JF: I don't know. Why don't you ask her?

IA: I will. I will...

Jayne

"We don't know where Douglas is now," said Ms Bromley. "Where did you last see him?"

Lottie let out a puff of air through her nostrils as she thought. "About an hour ago? I missed him in the entrance hall twenty minutes or so ago – he was just done fixing that girl's car."

Lizzie's back snapped straight. "Er…" she said timidly, like she thought Lottie would turn and bite her. "What's wrong with my car?"

Lottie's eyes widened. "Oh, no, I didn't mean you. This other girl got lost and her car broke down. I'm not surprised, it, er… looked like it was on its last legs, to be honest."

"Jayne should take a look at the car," said Ms Bromley, turning to me. "She's good with technology."

I wanted to point out that helping her when her phone froze by turning it off and putting it back on again did not make me *good with technology*, but I bit my tongue. Ms Bromley was looking at me expectantly, and I didn't want to let her down.

"Is the battery dead? Did Douglas try jump-starting it?" I asked Lottie.

Lottie shook her head. "I don't know." She hesitated, then tentatively smiled at me. "You're Jayne, aren't you? I've been wanting to meet you…"

I looked at Ms Bromley, then back at her. "Why?"

"Why have I been wanting to meet you?" Lottie's smile faltered. "Well…you know. We're, erm…both the same age, and…you work here and…" She bit the inside of her cheek, looking flustered. "I should go. It was nice speaking to you all. Thank you for your help."

She turned and scurried out.

Ms Bromley wheeled round to face me. "Why don't you go and see if you can sort that car out, Jayne?"

I nodded, glad of an excuse to leave the kitchen and spend some time alone. I knew Mrs Vanforte kept jump leads and tools more generally in the cellar.

I headed down a narrow, windowless corridor behind the kitchen, in the same direction Lottie had gone. The dim light from a line of naked bulbs hanging from the ceiling barely made a difference. They were further apart than made any logical sense. It felt like I was walking through twilight. I guessed Mrs Vanforte had never bothered redecorating here; the corridor was hardly used, and guests never saw it at all.

A plain wooden door that marked the entrance to the cellar was set into the stone wall about halfway down the corridor. I pushed the door open, and the weak light from the bulbs in the corridor only revealed the beginning of a set of wooden stairs leading down into the darkness. I flicked the switch for the cellar, but nothing happened.

The beam of white light from my phone torch revealed the stairs were steep, stretching away into yawning darkness. They creaked as I went down, and when I tried to hold the handrail it shifted slightly. The temperature dropped. I bet Mrs Vanforte didn't bother to put on the heating in the cellar, if there even was any heating down there. I might as well have been walking into a freezer.

I'd taken trips to the cellar before, to root around for very specific cooking equipment for Ms Bromley, so I knew it was an enormous space divided into sections by freestanding metal shelves. Cardboard boxes were stacked on the shelves, but there was no logic as to what was stored where.

I decided to start rooting through the boxes nearest the door. I thought jump leads would be pretty easy to find. But as I searched boxes of old crockery, it occurred to me that Mr and Mrs Vanforte probably *didn't* ever need to jump-start their cars, not when they had a small fleet in their garage. It's almost like a showroom – a flashy white space with a row of super expensive cars. The jump leads were probably buried somewhere deep in the cellar, out of sight – if they even had any.

I flashed my torch over the rows of boxes and realized it would take ages for me to look through them all. There was nothing else for it. I'd limit myself to fifteen minutes of searching. If I didn't find the leads by then, I'd give up. It was too cold and dark to be thorough.

Somewhere in the cellar there was a leak; I could hear a *drip, drip*, loud in the silence.

I moved along, crouching to examine the boxes stacked against one of the walls. The cardboard was damp to my touch, and I flashed my beam of light over it – and fell backwards, onto the dusty floor, my heart thudding.

Inside the box was a severed head.

I scrambled backwards, breathing heavily as I stared at the box. It took a few seconds for my brain to start working again. Obviously, Mr and Mrs Vanforte didn't keep severed heads in their cellar. But I still had to force myself to slide forward and lift my phone up to the edge of the box, to take a proper look.

My light revealed waxy skin, staring blue eyes – it was a mannequin's head. Just a mannequin's head. I shook myself for being stupid and getting scared so easily. Of course there was a rational explanation.

I examined some nearby boxes and found a whole stack of the heads – eighteen in total, stored across four boxes – the plastic eyes staring up at me. Counting them, focusing on the numbers, helped calm me down.

Ms Bromley had told me that, years ago, Mr Vanforte owned a bunch of clothes shops, which had gone bust. Obviously, he had decided to keep the heads as a souvenir, or maybe he'd thought they might come in useful one day.

Drip, drip.

I'd found the source of the dripping at least. Above me was a damp patch that spots of moisture were seeping through, occasional drops splashing down.

I got to my feet, deciding that the jump leads probably weren't going to be stored near the mannequin heads. As I turned round, a blast of ice-cold air hit the back of my neck.

I spun round – there wasn't a window near me.

Once more my heart started to hammer and the thought of a ghost briefly crossed my mind. There are loads of stories about the Bramble Estate, including a tale of one of Emily's ancestors, who apparently loved the house so much that she didn't want to leave it when she died. She insisted on her corpse being buried in the walls, and her ghost has haunted the house ever since.

But then I spotted a grate, high up, through which cold air could blow. The moment of stupidity passed.

I moved along. One of the boxes on the shelf in front of me had hammers and screwdrivers. This felt more promising – there might be jump leads somewhere nearby.

My heart continued to thud. The mannequins had put me on edge. All I could think of now was severed heads. The idea of long-dead ancestors floating through the walls didn't scare me for long, but *real* horror, caused by real people – *that* sent shivers through me. All of a sudden the cellar felt a thousand miles away from the rest of the house, down in the bowels of the earth.

I started rooting through the boxes in front of me, pushing aside the Vanfortes' Christmas decorations.

Crash.

I jumped as the noise thundered in my ears. I held up my phone's beam, to find a box had toppled into the middle of the room, the candles it stored spilling out. There were several boxes stacked precariously, and I supposed the one that had fallen could have been sliding for a while before deciding to crash.

Or else someone had accidentally knocked it over.

I flashed my torch over the dark space, but the beam of light was small and there were loads of boxes to duck behind. I didn't bother saying *hello* or anything like that. If someone else was in the basement with me, they would see my torch. If they wanted to, they could easily make themselves known.

I waited, but no one called out. Whoever was there with me didn't want to say.

I switched off my torch and stood in the dark, glancing over at the exit door at the top of the staircase, with the weak beam of light from the corridor shining towards me. I strained my ears and thought I heard footsteps – quiet ones – on the other side of the room.

There are a lot of exits from the cellar – and lots of hidden passages across the Bramble Estate as well. I'm not supposed to know about them, but Ms Bromley had told me, because she's worked at the place for years and knows all its secrets.

I decided it was time to leave.

But as I was heading back to the stairs, the light in the corridor went out, plunging me into complete blackness – and someone started screaming.

Jayne

I put my torch back on, and hurried up the stairs, down the dark corridor and into the kitchen. It was now lit only by the crackling fire, which cast shadows onto the walls. Darkness was falling outside, the last of the winter light quickly gone.

It was Lizzie who had screamed.

"Sorry," she said, standing so close to the fire she looked like she might jump into it. Her cheeks were flushed and she was shaking. "The dark – I don't like it. I wasn't expecting… What happened?"

"Power cut," said Ms Bromley grimly. "Not completely out of the blue, given how bad this storm has been. But not ideal. We used to have an Aga which would have just needed a match to get it going, but Mr Vanforte wanted to switch everything to electric, even though he's never cooked a thing in his life. His insistence on modernizing means the family will have to eat the food cold, since Mrs Vanforte wants the meal to start at 8 p.m.

I've worked for her long enough to know she won't change her plans." She shrugged, then looked at me. "You couldn't find the jump leads?"

"No," I said. I didn't mention that I'd thought someone else had been down in the cellar. Ms Bromley and Lizzie wouldn't be able to shed any light on that.

"Nothing's going right today," said Ms Bromley with a sigh. "What's the time? I can't read the clock in the dark."

I squinted at my watch. Its face was just about visible in the dim light. "5.24 p.m."

"Well, I guess you can just plate up the food then, Jayne," she said. "I'm off for the night – no point hanging around now." She ran her eyes over us both. "Maybe you should put on a few extra layers of clothing – coats perhaps. I've seen power cuts like this before – they usually take a long time to get sorted and, in the meantime, you don't want to freeze."

"You're going to walk *home*?" said Lizzie, her eyes wide. "In the snow? Are you sure you can make it? What if you get lost? Or freeze?"

"My cottage is in the grounds – it's only across the fields," said Ms Bromley, as she put on her coat and hat and scarf, her hands trembling with age as she wrapped the clothing around herself. She went to one of the cupboards, rooting around before pulling out a huge torch. "The electricity will be gone there as well, but don't you worry – I've been here for many a power cut. And I've done the walk across the fields thousands of times." She clutched her torch in one hand, and her walking stick in the other, and her eyes were steely even as she stood hunched over.

"You can't go out there – in the dark on your own," protested Lizzie, hugging herself. "Perhaps...perhaps we should walk you to your cottage..." She was trembling as she spoke.

I snorted. Lizzie looked terrified at her bravery in even *suggesting* the idea.

Ms Bromley paused by the door. "It's perfectly safe," she said with a smile. "What exactly are you worried is going to happen to me?"

"I don't know," said Lizzie, as she glanced at the window, then back at us, her eyes wide. "You could fall, you could be blown away – a bear could try to kill you." I held back a snort as she shuddered. "And in the countryside...there's no one around. Anything could come out – anyone could be lurking. I watched a film, the other day, about home invasions..."

"Calm yourself," said Ms Bromley, as she did up the buttons on her coat, and flicked her torch on. The beam was so powerful half the kitchen was doused in honey-yellow light. "I've been working at this place for over fifty years – I know the way to my cottage like the back of my hand. Bears have been extinct in England for who knows how many years. And as for a home invasion –" she shook her head – "dear me, girl, there's no one around for miles. It's just us here, I promise you."

With that, she opened the kitchen door, letting in freezing air that slapped my face and a roaring wind that rattled my teeth.

The door closed, cutting off the wind – and Ms Bromley.

Lizzie and I stood in silence for a moment.

"What do we do now?" said Lizzie, her eyes wide as she stared at me.

You leave me alone, I thought. But I could tell that wouldn't happen – Lizzie was clearly already making up her mind to follow me around everywhere.

"Let's get our coats before we freeze," I said.

Lizzie

The Day of My Arrival

Ms Bromley had taken the most powerful torch from the kitchen. Jayne and I were left with small ones with yellow beams that flickered, and I immediately began to worry that they might need new batteries, and that there might not *be* any new batteries around, and the end result would be us being plunged into the dark.

I was going to ask Jayne about it, but she traipsed on ahead of me. She didn't seem to want to chat, which made me worry, because I take silence as a sign that someone doesn't like me and I didn't know what I could possibly have done to offend or annoy her. I knew I wouldn't ever see her again after tonight but I still had a desperate need to be liked.

Her coat was in a closet by the kitchen – if I could even call it a coat. It looked thin and woolly, more like a fleece. Did she not feel the cold?

I'd left mine in the tea room, and we had to go through dark corridors to get it. I was glad to be with Jayne – I couldn't think of anything worse than getting lost in the twisting passages, maybe even accidentally running into someone from the family. How intrusive – this entire situation was already awkward enough.

I flashed my torch around the tea room. Everything looked different in the dark. The paintings of Vanfortes now felt like people silently watching in the shadows. The first time it happened I flinched back, before realizing it was just a portrait. I chuckled nervously to myself, then stopped in case Jayne thought I was weird.

My beam landed on my coat, and I picked it up and slipped it on thankfully, comforted when it wrapped round me like a hug.

As I turned to leave once more, my beam caught on a pair of eyes.

There was someone standing in the corner of the room.

This time I did scream, loudly. I flashed my torch back over to find myself staring at a boy with dark hair and thick black eyebrows, one arched as he looked at me. He was wearing a black jacket, blending into the shadows.

"Hello," he said, like it was the most natural thing in the world to be standing alone in a room in complete blackness. "Who are you?"

Jayne had sidled up next to me. "I'm staff. Lizzie's staying the night. You're Tate."

The boy unpeeled himself from the wall. "That's right," he said. "How long's the power going to be out for?"

Jayne shrugged.

"Why were you in here in the dark?" I asked, still feeling shaky. Tate's hands were behind his back as he rested against the wall.

"Well, *everywhere* in this house is in the dark," he said. "I thought I would set up camp in here. Maybe even get a fire going. I was just thinking about it when you two walked in." His voice was light, and a small smile played on his lips. I couldn't read him at all – was he amused because he'd frightened us? Or because he'd been caught doing something odd and was embarrassed? That was unlikely – he didn't seem like someone who cared what other people thought.

Jayne's face was in shadow, so I couldn't tell what she was thinking. I just wanted to leave, but for some reason she hadn't made a move to go. That was odd, because she didn't strike me as the kind of person who would want to hang around and chat.

"We'll be in the kitchen," she said after a moment of silence. Then she turned round and left without another word.

"She doesn't say much, does she?" Tate said to me, his teeth flashing in the beam of light from my torch. My mind froze, but then I came to my senses and followed Jayne out, risking one more glance over my shoulder as I left.

For a moment, my heart stopped beating at what I saw. Then I sped up to catch Jayne, who was marching onwards. I shook my head – my eyes had to be playing tricks on me. The room was dark, I was already jumpy...

It was only when we were in the kitchen with the door firmly closed that Jayne turned to face me.

"Did you see that?" she asked.

"I...I don't know," I said, my heart sinking. Because if she had seen it too, it *couldn't* be a trick of the light, or my overactive imagination.

She stared at me. "You did see it."

Slowly, I nodded.

Her eyes slid past me, to the closed door. "Why does Tate Astur have a gun?"

21

Extract of Transcript of Interview 8
Re: Death of Emily Vanforte
In Attendance – Inspector Adams (IA),
Lizzie Newton-Hill (LNH)

IA: Of course, Emily Vanforte was *not* killed with a gun. And Tate is insisting it was just a toy gun.

LNH: I'm sorry, Mr Inspector, but...that doesn't make sense. Why would Tate be playing with a toy gun in the middle of a blackout?

IA: It's certainly a question to be asked.

LNH: So...where's the gun now?

IA: That's not really relevant to you.

LNH: Please?

IA: [Sigh] We don't know. Apparently, Tate left it in his bedroom before dinner. And when he went back after dinner, it had vanished – and it's still missing.

Devi
Before the Murder

It was clear pretty quickly that there weren't any skeletons hanging around in the room Mrs Vanforte had put me in. I half wanted there to be – a mystery I could solve, a drama to distract me.

The thought had lodged in my mind now and even though everything seemed fine, I still did a thorough sweep of the room. It only took about fifteen minutes, because while the room was large there weren't really many places to look. I started to get irritated by the stupid floorboards that creaked every time I went over them. One floorboard in particular, hidden by the rug, squeaked way louder than the others.

Mrs Vanforte had all the money in the world and she still hadn't had the creaking fixed. I shifted my weight back and forth, so that the floorboard played a nice tune. Maybe there wasn't anything else to find – maybe Douglas hadn't wanted me to stay in the room because he simply hadn't wanted me to stay.

The floorboard squeaked again, and I frowned. It felt like it was almost…shifting beneath me.

I tugged at the blue rug covering most of the floor, but it was too heavy and large to lift. Instead I rolled it up, revealing an expanse of dusty floorboard beneath. One of the boards was darker than the rest, and I kneeled down to examine it.

The lights flickered as I found a small groove in the corner. I experimented by placing my finger underneath; when I lifted, it came up easily.

It was a hiding place for…

I swore, just as the lights went out.

Underneath the floorboard was a huge stash of gold knives.

Extract of Transcript of Interview 7
Re: Death of Emily Vanforte
In Attendance – Inspector Adams (IA),
Devi Mistry (DM)

IA: You found...knives.

DM: Yup. Big ol' knives, all sharp and pointy and stabby. Would you be able to get me another bag of crisps? [Background crackling noises] I've just finished these ones and I'm still really hungry.

IA: I will in a moment. Just carry on, please – what did you do with the knives? And don't make a mess – it's not really *done* to be eating in this interview room—

DM: This is just between us. Well, the crisps are. I guess you can edit this bit out of the transcript? [Silence] Okay, yes, fine, I'll carry on. The lights went out just as I found the knives. I didn't panic or anything – I'm calm under pressure, I want to make that clear. But you know, strange house, lights go out and I have no idea why – I wanted to find some other people. I thought I'd finally go down to the kitchen and ask what the hell was going on – in a calm way.

IA: You *left* the knives?

DM: Well, what did you expect me to do with them? I wasn't exactly about to go up to Douglas and ask him about them. The electricity was gone, everything was pitch black – and I figured – you know what? – the knives could be some weird rich-person game. Like hide the antique or something – I hardly suspected they might belong to a murderer. And anyway, they'd only need one, right? Not a whole collection. And when I went back to the room later—

IA: Let me guess. They were gone?

DM: Yeah. But it's obvious who took them, right? Douglas clearly wanted them—

IA: So we have knives that went missing. And meanwhile, Emily Vanforte was *poisoned*.

DM: I don't know what to tell you, Inspector. You're the one who's supposed to be figuring this out.

Lizzie
The Day of My Arrival

I tried to discuss Tate's gun with Jayne, but since it was clear neither of us knew why he might have a gun, there wasn't much to say. I questioned whether we should find Mrs Vanforte and tell her, but then I thought it was her house, what if she knew about his gun? And we were being rude by asking about it?

Jayne looked troubled. "I don't normally speak to Mrs Vanforte. I'll tell Ms Bromley about it in the morning, and she can decide what to do."

We lapsed into an awkward silence, which stretched on and on – until another girl came into the kitchen. She had light brown skin and thick black hair that curled wildly around her head. She was wearing jeans with rips in them that didn't look intentional and a faded hoodie with a few coffee stains on the cuffs. I assumed she was the girl Lottie had mentioned earlier, whose car had broken down.

"I'm Devi," the girl said, not bothering with niceties. She

seemed to be breathing quite quickly, like she had been walking fast. "What happened to the lights? None of them are working – I had to use my phone torch to get down here, got massively lost on the way as well, everything looks the same in the dark… I'm guessing you two are the other girls Mrs Vanforte said are staying here? Any idea what's happened?"

"It's common in a snowstorm for there to be a blackout," said Jayne gruffly. "The whole area probably lost power."

"Great," said Devi, huffing as she sat down. "Just great." Her shoulders sank for a second, but then she seemed to shake herself, and launched into telling us how she had ended up at the house, asking us who we were, how we'd got here, where we were from – so incredibly chatty it made my head spin. She probably could have had a conversation with a brick wall if she wanted to, and I realized I was glad she was there; the silence with Jayne had started to become oppressive.

We started on a dinner of sandwiches and crisps, much earlier than the special meal Emily Vanforte had planned for her guests.

"So, Jayne, you work for the Vanfortes?" asked Devi. Her tone was casual, but her back had straightened and there was a slight tension in her shoulders. "How long for?"

"Not long," replied Jayne. "Why?"

"Erm… The thing is, right, is that you know…the Vanfortes seem like a normal enough group of people. Bit ratty with each other, but what's a family gathering without a few arguments…?" Devi set down her half-eaten sandwich. "But I found something weird in the room I'm staying in. A bunch of knives stashed under the floorboards… Any idea what that's about?"

"Knives?" I said. The word came out as a squeak, and I cleared my throat. I looked at Jayne in alarm, but her face was carefully blank, like she was trying not to show a reaction. I decided to tell Devi about the deadly weapon Jayne and I had just seen. "We met Tate Astur about twenty minutes ago and he had a gun…"

"A gun?" Devi gaped at me. "What the *hell*…" Her expression turned thoughtful as she titled her head. "Er – you know how it's dark because of the power cut…?" She cleared her throat. "Maybe it wasn't a gun. Maybe it was a…a boomerang and you just couldn't see it properly."

I blinked at her. "Why on earth would he have a boomerang? No, it was a gun – Jayne and I both saw it." I looked to Jayne for support, and she nodded.

"I don't know – I think both of you are a bit on edge, you know, with it being a touch spooky in this house without the power – maybe you saw something that wasn't there." Devi picked up the sandwich again, her voice getting more certain; I could almost feel her convincing herself that she was right.

"Well, maybe *you* didn't see the knives," I pointed out. "It was dark, wasn't it? Maybe they were…rubber ones or something."

"Maybe," shrugged Devi, but I could tell she didn't believe it. I must have still looked worried, because her expression softened. "Chill out – nothing's going to happen to us here, in *Emily Vanforte's* home." She started on the bowl of crisps, shovelling handfuls into her mouth and spraying crumbs as she spoke. "You know what *is* weird though – that they've left us alone. If I was putting a stranger up for the night, I wouldn't just bugger off. I'd want to keep an eye on them."

"I guess…we're not alone," I said, nibbling my bottom lip as I nodded at Jayne. "We're being…hosted. By a member of staff."

The host in question was now tucking into a fourth sandwich; she didn't even seem like she was listening any more.

"I wonder what *they're* doing right now," said Devi. "Or what they're going to be talking about at dinner. I guess they're worried about it getting heated…" We lapsed into silence. I didn't know what to say; I wanted to talk more about how odd the situation was, with the gun and the knives – but I also wanted to block out my fears. Devi was right; there probably was a reasonable explanation for it all.

The clock ticked closer to ten past seven and the time we were supposed to head to the bedrooms we'd been given. The only noise came from the crackle of the fire. We really could have been the only people in the world.

No, that wasn't true, because muffled yells floated into the room.

"What's going on?" said Devi, hopping to her feet. "Sounds like an argument…" A grin stretched across her face, and she licked her lips in anticipation. "Maybe we should go and listen in."

"It's not really our business," I said uncomfortably. There was a small part of me that was curious, but eavesdropping felt a bit too much, especially as we were just unexpected guests – and strangers to boot…

"Of course it is," said Devi, wrinkling her nose at me. "If they didn't want us to hear, they wouldn't yell!" She grabbed one of the rubbish torches and switched on the tiny beam. "*I'm* going to see what's going on."

"Use your phone torch," I said, shuddering at the thought of her walking through the darkened corridors with nothing but the weak, flickering light.

"No way," said Devi, already by the door. "I'm saving what's left of my battery for when I need a *real* bright light."

"You could charge it in your car," I said, trying to be helpful.

"Her battery's flat," grunted Jayne.

I jumped at her low voice; she *had* been listening. Her eyes flicked over me, then back to the plate sitting on her lap.

"Even if the battery *wasn't* flat, I can't believe you'd think there'd be a way to charge a phone in my car," snorted Devi. "It's still got a cassette tape player – you know what tapes are, Lizzie?" She wheeled round to face me. "It's what they used to play music with in the Stone Age." She didn't wait for my reply, that I *did* know what a cassette tape was, thank you very much (thanks to Mum's love of 80s films) and in any case I believed *Jayne* was the youngest of the three of us. But Devi had already charged out of the room, clutching her little torch.

I turned to Jayne. Surely, she would agree with me that Devi shouldn't eavesdrop. This was her employer's home, after all. But before I could say anything, Jayne shrugged again, and got to her feet. She grabbed a torch too and silently followed Devi out into the dark corridor.

I was left alone in the kitchen, with only the snapping fire for company. I looked out of the window nearest me, which revealed nothing but pitch blackness. My reflection stared back, my eyes wide in my round face.

If someone – or some*thing* – was standing outside in the snow, they would be able to see me – but I might not be able to see them. The thought blossomed unbidden in my mind, the roots tightening to the inside of my skull.

I shivered, trying to force it away – but the thought had lodged inside me. My hands were shaking as I picked up a torch. I followed the other two down the corridor, whispering, "Wait for me."

I caught Jayne up quickly, and together we found Devi, standing at the end of the passageway leading to the kitchen. She had turned off her torch, and Jayne and I did the same. Beyond the passageway was the grand foyer, where the commotion was taking place.

Devi pressed a finger to her lips, but that was unnecessary because all of us knew to be quiet.

Emily Vanforte was standing at the top of the stairs, at the point where it split into two smaller staircases going in opposite directions. She was holding a candle in front of her, looking down at four people standing at the bottom of the stairs. Each of the four were clutching candles of their own, their faces eerily lit from the bottom.

I recognized Charles Vanforte, Tate and Lottie. There was one other boy I hadn't seen before, so I guessed he was Douglas.

Lottie was wearing a sleek black dress, which pinched in at her waist and fanned out beneath. It was paired with sheer black tights and black high heels, which she tapped against the floor. Douglas was next to her, wearing a blue shirt so bright it nearly glowed in the dark. They looked good together – Lottie in her dark clothes, Douglas in his bright ones – like they had planned their outfits to complement each other.

I felt slightly in awe of them standing there together, with Douglas's hand resting on the small of Lottie's back. They seemed much older than me, their lives so much more glamorous than mine.

Douglas looked to be breathing quite heavily, his face splotchy with anger; he had to have been the one who'd yelled. Mr Vanforte was standing next to the two of them, but Tate was further back, alone. In the flickering light of the candles his face was half-lit, just enough for me to see the smirk playing on his lips. It seemed like he was enjoying the scene.

"I *do* have a special surprise for one of you tonight," said Mrs Vanforte, her amused voice echoing around the large space. "Thank you for mentioning that, Douglas – I did want to wait until dinner to bring up the topic, but...I suppose you were too eager to discuss it. Yes, the surprise is a secret I discovered, that I want to share. With you first – and then the world." She had changed into her dinner clothes, a long, deep purple dress, and was dripping with diamonds – the necklace I had brought hanging in pride of place. She reminded me of pictures of old royalty. She seemed powerful, to be holding all the cards, as she looked down on her subjects, the queen of the house.

Douglas took a step forward, like he wanted to physically stop Mrs Vanforte from saying anything else, but Lottie quickly gripped the back of his shirt – the action appeared to be automatic, like this was something she was used to doing. Their eyes remained fixed on Mrs Vanforte – and I couldn't blame them, because my eyes kept being drawn back to her as well, the way her dress fanned out behind her, over the stairs, like she had purposefully draped it that way.

"*All* of you have disappointed me in some way," Mrs Vanforte continued. Her voice was soft, calm, at odds with what she was saying. "You know, Douglas, I've never respected anyone with a temper – apart from the rudeness, it suggests you would act rashly... And I've always been a fan of biding your time, waiting for the right moment..."

Mr Vanforte folded his arms, staring up at her. The poor lighting meant I couldn't read the expression on his face, but his entire body was rigid and unmoving, like he'd become a statue.

Douglas let out a low growl. "Stop taunting us," he snapped, and I shivered at the venom lacing his voice. How could he *dare* speak to Emily Vanforte, his girlfriend's *mother*, in such a way? He looked like a wolf backed into a corner and ready to pounce, his hackles raised, the light from his candle bouncing off his clenched jaw. The sort of person you'd run from if you came across them in the dark. "You keep dropping these ominous hints about us – what do you think you know? I don't even have anything to *do* with you – I'm just dating Lottie..." He stepped back next to her, and his arm circled her waist, pulling her closer to him – like a prop. Lottie stumbled, but didn't say anything.

"The tables are turned now, Douglas, and I don't think you like it very much," said Mrs Vanforte. She held her candle a little higher, the tiny light revealing that she was smiling down on them all.

"What's *wrong* with you, Mum?" asked Lottie, her voice shaking. "Why do you hate us so much?" She sounded like she was crying, but in the dim lighting I couldn't be sure. My heart went out to her – first because she was upset…and secondly because of what she was asking. I couldn't imagine ever saying something similar to my mum – I would never think for a second that she hated me. In fact, sometimes I think she loves me just a little bit *too* much. After Dad died, she said I was all she had left. I haven't wanted to let her down, because I know how she only wants what's best for me. Because of that, sometimes I'm overly cautious.

Douglas seemed to have noticed Lottie was crying, because he removed his arm from her waist and instead started gently rubbing her back, like he was trying to reassure her.

"I don't hate you," whispered Mrs Vanforte. "But the rumours turned out to be true – and now I must punish."

"What *rumours*?" said Douglas, dropping his hand from Lottie, the brief moment of genuine comfort over. His voice was sharp – I wondered what he could possibly be worried about Emily exposing. There had to be something, or else he wouldn't sound so angry. But then his eyes widened. "The rumours about your family? But they're *all* obviously rubbish – like the ones about how the Bramble Estate is haunted, or that Mr Vanforte had an affair years ago and now has a son out in the world somewhere, or that you do rituals on strangers to keep yourselves young, or that the Vanfortes are up to their eyeballs in debt—"

"Hush, Douglas," said Mr Vanforte softly, as I forced back a gasp, shocked that Douglas would say those things in front of the Vanfortes, even if they *were* untrue. Devi sucked in a breath – I wasn't the only one surprised.

Tate snorted. He was the only one who hadn't changed into

an expensive-looking dinner outfit, but I supposed he still had plenty of time – there was just under an hour until the grand event. Although, I wondered if he simply wasn't going to bother. I would have, if I was him – I imagined Mrs Vanforte wouldn't appreciate him turning up to her special meal in his leather jacket, not when she had gone to so much effort to look so nice herself.

"Emily, as ever, you have caused a scene," continued Mr Vanforte, his voice mild, as if they were all discussing something mundane, like what time the bins were supposed to go out in the morning. He didn't sound bothered about the affair rumour Douglas had just brought up, or the debt rumour – but then again he was a politician, and Mum always says they're the best at hiding how they're really feeling. "You've forgotten we have guests."

A spike of panic went through me as he nodded towards our passageway. I wanted to sink into the ground and disappear – what we had witnessed was a private scene, nothing to do with us, and yet we were standing essentially in the open, jaws scraping on the floor. We might as well have had popcorn – Mum would have been so embarrassed by me. She's always told me to be polite and have manners, that my behaviour reflects on her, and I don't want to ever disappoint her, not when she went through so much after Dad died.

But Devi had no shame. She marched out, holding her torch up. "We've just finished dinner," she said cheerfully, acting like she'd just arrived at the scene. She was so convincing I half believed it. "I'm going to go to bed, if that's okay with all of you? Thanks so much again for letting me stay, I really do appreciate it."

She walked past the four of them like it was the most natural thing in the world, and mounted the stairs. "Left or right for the West Wing?" she called over her shoulder. "I can't remember."

For a moment, no one responded, all four staring up at her. I shuddered, because alone on the stairs, trapped between Emily Vanforte and the four at the bottom, she looked so small and vulnerable. Like a mouse tricked into a trap by some cheese, moments before the metal jaws swung closed.

"Right," said Lottie at last. Douglas looked at her like she had uttered a disgusting swear word – he obviously didn't want her to be helpful. Tate grinned.

"Thanks," said Devi, disappearing off.

Five sets of eyes turned to look at Jayne and me. I tried to hide behind Jayne, but that wasn't easy to do, even though she was so much taller than me.

Jayne stared back at all of them, and I could tell the silence that bothered me so much made no difference to her. It wouldn't press down; it would fall lightly, like a blanket, caressing her.

"Dinner is on the trolley," she said at last. "You'll have to eat it cold though."

"Off to bed with you, my dear," commanded Mrs Vanforte. "And you as well, Elizabeth. I can't believe I've caused a *scene*, for goodness' sake. Can't do anything to ruin the reputation of this family, Charles's career is *so* important—"

"That is *enough*, Emily," cut in Mr Vanforte, his voice suddenly so venomous I flinched.

"It is enough when *I* say it is enough," said Mrs Vanforte, her voice hard. "That goes for all of you. And when this weekend is over, I'm going to expose *you,* so the world knows exactly what you are."

From her vantage point, it was impossible to tell which of the four she was talking to – but I got the sense it was just one of them. The *you* didn't sound collective.

"I don't think I want to come to dinner any more," said Douglas, his eyes flicking over to Lottie. "Not when you're standing up there thinking you can talk to me like that. I've had enough."

Lottie looked at him. I thought I heard her quietly mutter *please* but I wasn't entirely sure.

Mrs Vanforte smirked. "You'll come to dinner, I know you will – you won't be able to help yourself, because you'll want to know exactly what it is that I have to say."

Douglas's nostrils flared, but then his face suddenly switched into a pleasant smile. "Whatever, Emily." He walked away then paused, looking back at Lottie, who was staring after him like she didn't know whether to follow. He jerked his head and she hurried along, nearly tripping over herself. I recognized that behaviour in her – it's the same sort of gratefulness I feel at school, whenever Natasha and Hannah wait for me to join them at break-times. It's born out of times when they *don't* wait for me, going off on walks and leaving me to sit by myself and act like I'm not bothered. I never know what mood they'll be in – whether they'll want to exclude me, or let me in. It feels like I'm always walking a precarious path, unsure if it will be smooth or crumble beneath my feet. I've learned to balance on my toes, just in case – always treading carefully, always prepared for the worst.

Tate had disappeared, I wasn't sure when – that left only Mr and Mrs Vanforte. And us.

We scuttled across the foyer – well, I did. Jayne sort of sloped. The atmosphere was tense as I went past first Mr Vanforte, then Mrs Vanforte standing at the top of the stairs.

I reached the next level, and went to continue on, before I realized I had no idea where to go. Jayne came up behind me silently, and clicked off my torch, then her own.

"What—" I began.

"Shush," came the hushed response. I could see her outline beside me, facing towards Mr and Mrs Vanforte, still standing and looking at each other. They were each clutching a candle, their tiny flames flickering in the vast, empty blackness surrounding them, locked in some sort of silent battle of wills.

But then Mr Vanforte suddenly blew out his candle. Outside was pitch black, with not even the weak silver light of the moon shining through the windows. It meant Mr Vanforte disappeared into the darkness, and it occurred to me that we might not have been the only ones lurking in the black spaces. That the others might have run off but remained within hearing distance of the foyer. Watching for what Emily Vanforte did next.

Which was to say, "You don't frighten me – I'm a Vanforte. *Nothing* scares me."

But out of the darkness came a soft chuckle, echoing around the vast space so it was impossible to tell where it originated from.

Devi
Before the Murder

When I got back to my bedroom, it was to find the rug had been put back into place, covering the floorboards. I didn't really need to check underneath it, but I thought I might as well. I wasn't surprised to find the knives were gone – Douglas must have found a moment to sneak into the West Wing while I was having dinner with the others.

I didn't know why he wanted the knives or why he'd hidden them there, but I didn't like the thought of him carrying them around. This was going beyond creepy – this was starting to feel dangerous.

Like that scene with Mrs Vanforte and the others – I appreciate drama when I'm not involved. I'd been entertained by their sniping at each other earlier – but what I'd just witnessed was something else.

Now I must punish.

What did that mean? Which one of them was she going

to punish? *And why did Douglas need all those knives?* Jayne and Lizzie had said Tate also had a gun – what for?

I shook my head. I was being stupid, making things up in my head. I was taking the whole mystery thing too far. It was time to be sensible, so I lit a few candles with matches I had found in one of the drawers when I'd searched the room earlier, and placed them in candleholders. It would have been easier to keep my torch on, but the battery was flaky and I didn't know how much juice it had left. I didn't exactly relish the idea of traipsing around the house looking for a spare one.

The bedroom was freezing, and I wished I could light a fire. Or scroll on my phone. Or do *something*. Instead, I could only pace, and think about what we'd overheard. Mrs Vanforte had said there was a rumour that had turned out to be true, and that she needed to punish someone. With the little I knew about them, I considered whether Mr Vanforte, Lottie, Douglas or Tate was most likely to be the one she was wanting to expose at dinner.

Lottie was her own daughter, so surely Mrs Vanforte wouldn't want to ruin her life. But I remembered the way she had spoken to her when I first arrived – with contempt, like Lottie had disappointed her and that was the end of it.

Tate was Mrs Vanforte's nephew, through her husband. I didn't have too much of an opinion on him, because I'd only briefly met him. Though it was enough time for me to decide he was fit…and had something of a dangerous edge to him. Mrs Vanforte didn't like him – I had no idea why.

It was obvious why Mrs Vanforte didn't like Douglas, however. He was a massive bellend, incredibly rude. If there was a nasty rumour about any of them, I could believe it would be him… He didn't seem to care about Lottie at all.

And then there was Charles Vanforte. I tugged my coat tighter round me, but the cold in the air seemed to seep into my bones. Out of all of them, he was the one Mrs Vanforte was the most likely to hate…surely. He was her husband – on the soaps I watch, adults fall out all the time because of lying, or affairs, or drugs or money problems. Plus, he was a politician. There were *bound* to be loads of skeletons in his closet.

My teeth chattered. Pacing was making no difference in keeping me warm. The sheets on the bed were slippery and cold, but it looked like burrowing under might be my only option, if I didn't want to become an ice cube. My little home in London would have been way nicer to be in right now – cosy and toasty – even though Mum and Dad have both started to worry about the heating bills and are considering limiting the time the radiators are on.

Maybe Jayne or Lizzie would know how to light the fire. Well, I didn't think Lizzie would, but Jayne seemed like the type to go camping in the deep wilderness, and she probably had to light fires for the Vanfortes all the time anyway. I figured I would ask her. Plus, all I could think about was this messed-up family. Speaking to someone else would help me get my mind off things.

I went out into the corridor and knocked on the door opposite, where Jayne had told me she was staying. Jayne peered out, frowning at me in the light of my candle.

"Can you light my fire?" I asked. "Please?"

"Sure," she said. "That's why I'm here tonight – Mrs Vanforte wanted me to look after you two."

She'd done a bloody awful job of it so far, because I'd been about two seconds away from turning into an ice cube. I didn't say that out loud, though – I still needed her help.

Somewhere nearby, someone coughed. It didn't sound like Lizzie. I looked at Jayne.

"They were supposed to lock off the West Wing at seven thirty," she whispered, her eyebrows twitching together in confusion. "There shouldn't be any of them down this way."

I glanced at my watch: 7.36 p.m.

"Maybe they're just having a wander around," I replied. There was a prickling feeling down the back of my neck. I was beginning to wish more and more that I didn't have to stay in this house. "It's not that weird to walk around your own pitch-black mansion at night…"

Something was wrong.

Jayne looked at me, her eyes unreadable.

"You work here, don't you? Do you feel like something's… off?" I spoke as carefully as I could, keeping my voice low to avoid anyone listening in. I didn't want to insult anyone and be drawn into their arguments. It went against my usual instincts, which are to speak loudly and freely – but I'm not stupid. I was on edge, never forgetting that I was in a house full of strangers in the middle of nowhere. "Is it normal for them to be as argumentative as they've all been in front of other people?"

"No," she said. "It's not."

I felt a small rush of relief that I wasn't being overly dramatic. "Maybe we should go and check they're actually locking off the West Wing," I said. "I mean, I know it doesn't make much of a difference because…well, they'll have the key, but you know…

I'd feel better if I saw it was actually locked."

Jayne nodded, and we headed towards the entrance of the West Wing. The big door was still wide open, and there was someone walking away, down the corridor past Mrs Vanforte's office. In the dim moonlight that was filtering in from outside I could make out the shape of them – bulky, tall.

They went round a corner and disappeared.

"Who was that?" I said to Jayne. It couldn't have been Lottie or Mrs Vanforte – both were too short.

"Charles, Douglas or Tate," she whispered back, staring at the spot where they had vanished.

I bit my bottom lip. "Douglas wanted to come to the West Wing earlier," I said. "I think to get the knives he put in my room… But when I came back just now they were gone, which means he's already *been* down this way. Why would he come back?"

Jayne was silent for a second. "I don't know."

"Maybe that was Mr Vanforte we saw just then," I said half joking, half serious, trying to keep the tremor out of my voice. I don't usually scare easily; if I'd been the lead in a horror film, I'd be the last girl standing, and if I was in a detective story, I'd be the one calling all the shots. There was some sort of logical explanation for what was going on. "Douglas had the knives; Tate had a gun – maybe Charles Vanforte was trying to find a weapon as well."

The explanation felt wrong – *silly*. But what if I was right? And if I was, what the hell was going to happen at Mrs Vanforte's dinner?

Extract of Transcript of Interview 7
Re: Death of Emily Vanforte
In Attendance – Inspector Adams (IA),
Devi Mistry (DM)

IA: Lottie Vanforte has also said in her interview that she saw a man emerging from the West Wing – she was put in charge of locking it off, but was slightly delayed. I asked Charles, Tate and Douglas if the person you saw was one of them – and they all denied it.

DM: Well, one of them is lying.

IA: Tate and Douglas were together at that time in the tea room. They'd got a fire going in there. Charles was apparently with Emily in the dining room...

DM: Mr Vanforte could easily be lying about being with Mrs Vanforte – it's not like she can say otherwise now. Tate and Douglas could be lying about being together... Unless...unless it was someone *else*?

IA: No one else entered or exited the house – there were no other footprints...

DM: Maybe it was that old cook woman—

IA: Ms Bromley went to her cottage and didn't return – there were no footprints leading from her cottage, because she was there all night. And you, Jayne and Lottie are all very sure it was a *man* – why's that?

DM: I don't know. It was dark – he was...tall. Very tall. Looked big, bulky...

IA: Emily and Lottie Vanforte are both tall, but neither of them could be described as bulky...

DM: Well, you say no one else entered or left the house because there were no footprints in the snow. So...what happens if there was someone else in the house *before* it started snowing? Like...they hid? A random stranger in the house with us the entire time – and they might have killed Mrs Vanforte?

IA: Emily was with Tate, Douglas, Charles and Lottie when she died. The poison given to her was in her wine glass. Therefore it must have been administered *at dinner*. And the four of them are quite certain no one entered or left the room during dinner...

DM: What if they're *all* lying? And the random stranger walked in during dinner, killed Emily and then pissed off? And they all collectively decided to protect the stranger because they all hated her? [Pause] Yeah, yeah, I know the theory's flawed. Anyway, I'm telling you, random man in the house aside, I know who killed her. Honestly, I could do your job for you.

IA: Well, please do enlighten me.

Jayne

"It was Douglas," I said. He'd been creeping around a lot since he'd arrived the night before. And I didn't like him. I'd hated how rude he was in the kitchen earlier.

If it *was* Douglas that we'd seen, I didn't want to run into him. But I also wanted to know why someone would have been walking through the West Wing. This was *my* place of work and I felt protective over it. If Douglas was up to no good, it would be nice to have the details. Maybe if we caught him out Mrs Vanforte would ban him from the house. That way I'd never have to see him again.

"Are you two okay?" Lottie appeared at the doors, clutching a bunch of keys dangling from a string. She was obviously in charge of locking up.

"Her voice sounds weird…" muttered Devi. "Shaky – like she's been crying. Go and speak to her. Find out what's going on."

"I don't think…" I began.

"I'm a stranger!" said Devi. "She knows you!"

That was untrue. I was basically just as much a stranger as Devi… And I didn't *want* to speak to her. As I got closer, I saw her face was pale and there were tear-stains on her cheeks. I didn't want her to start crying in front of me. I turned to tell Devi I couldn't do it, but Devi had already gone – back to her bedroom, probably.

"Erm… How's it going?" I asked.

"Good," said Lottie. I was used to people eyeing me like they thought I might attack them or something – I guess there's something *unnerving* about me. But Lottie didn't look at me like that at all. She straightened up, pinching her lips together as her eyes scanned over me. Her expression was…almost curious. She gave a small smile. Maybe she was trying to find a friend.

Well, it wasn't going to be me.

"You won't be able to get into the rest of the house now," she said.

I eyed the bunch of keys in her hand. There was only one key for the West-Wing door – Ms Bromley had grumbled about Mrs Vanforte losing it once, and said they needed to get a locksmith out. But the key had shown up, so they never bothered.

Out of Mr and Mrs Vanforte, Douglas, Lottie and Tate, I trusted Lottie the most. She didn't have a knife or a gun, and she was our age. But that trust meant very little. She would give her father the key if he asked. Or Douglas.

If he came back to the West Wing again, though, I would be listening. Ready to catch him out.

"Goodnight," I said, turning on my heel.

"Wait." Lottie's voice was small and shaky, and that made me stop. I looked back at her. "What do you think of my outfit?"

"What?" I stared at her.

"Do you like it?" She smiled uncertainly at me. "You like dark clothes, don't you?"

I only wear dark clothes because there was a sale on at the local supermarket a while ago and most of the stuff in my size was black and grey. Gran stocked up on new tops and trousers for me. I don't care about clothes at all.

She was wearing a black dress that seemed fine. "Er...yes, looks good," I said. I walked away quickly, and when I glanced back it was to find her staring after me.

Devi

Before the Murder

Jayne didn't come back with any good gossip – just that Lottie had locked off the West Wing, and Douglas was on the other side with everyone else. Unlike Jayne, I wasn't convinced it *had* been him walking through earlier, but I didn't have any credible alternative theories. Either way, I decided to put him out of my mind for the moment, because I had a bigger problem: I was really, *really* starting to freeze.

It turned out Jayne did know how to light a fire. She crouched down in front of the fireplace, fiddling around with the wood and a lighter and some papers. I couldn't see exactly what she was doing, but a few minutes later flames sprang to life. All at once, a light was dancing cheerfully on the walls and the room went from gloomy to slightly cosier – but only just. The light didn't reach the corners, which still remained in shadows.

She straightened up as I went to the flames and toasted my fingers, wishing the heat could cover me completely. The cold from the rest of the room continued to stab at my back.

"Thanks," I said. I'd been impressed by the size of the room before, but now I was noticing the downsides. It would take ages to heat up and the bed was nowhere near the fire, so basically I would be spending much longer with my coat on.

Jayne didn't acknowledge my thanks, heading to the door in silence. But before she got to it, it opened and Lizzie peeked inside.

"Oh, why are we all in here?" Lizzie said. I tried not to roll my eyes. I didn't think much of her: she's the type who gets scared by bugs and the dark, stuff that isn't scary at all. I was too impatient to get along with her, and I was also blunt enough to accidentally say it to her face as well.

"We're not," grunted Jayne, stepping away from the doorway as she glanced back at me. "You'll need to put more wood on to keep the fire going, but let me know if it goes out." She left my room, taking her torch and disappearing into the room opposite.

"Jayne got my fire working too," said Lizzie, leaning against the doorway. "Isn't this fun? It's like we've been transported back to the olden days." She didn't sound convinced by her own words – more like she was asking for reassurance.

I could have made a rude comment, like how the olden days probably would have sucked for someone like me. But I didn't, because I could tell she meant well and it would have been like kicking a puppy. Plus, I often say things for the shock value, rather than actually meaning it. It gives me a sense of power. I like feeling powerful, even though I'm scrawny, with slightly crooked teeth and grades no one believes I should be getting –

because I talk too much in class (even though no one ever listens). In reality I have no power, none at all.

So, I kept my mouth shut for once and nodded.

"Should we, er…play a game or something?" asked Lizzie. "There's a pack of cards in my bedroom…"

"No thanks. I'm very tired." I said it pointedly, hoping she would take the hint that I didn't want her to hang around for a cosy chat and an attempt to make friends. Tomorrow we'd part ways, and I would never see her or anyone else from the house again. I just wanted to be with Nani, accidentally mixing up salt and sugar as we attempted to make cakes that didn't rise.

I felt a pang of worry – Nani would have had to let Mum know I hadn't arrived at hers. Hopefully, Nani would stop Mum from being too concerned, and would float the *she's holed up somewhere safe for the night* explanation.

Lizzie looked disappointed. "Goodnight," she said, and closed the door, leaving me alone.

It was 7.49 p.m. Almost time for the Vanfortes' dinner. I sat on the edge of my bed and was wondering what I should do – whether it was too soon to get into my pyjamas and go to sleep – when I heard footsteps going past my bedroom. There was someone moving around – Jayne or Lizzie, probably.

But then I frowned. Something niggled in my mind. It took me a few seconds to work out why the footsteps were odd: the corridor was a dead end, and Jayne's room was opposite mine, and Lizzie's to the right. Neither of them had a reason to go past my bedroom.

I waited, but the footsteps didn't come back. Which meant someone was simply standing at the end of a dead-end corridor.

I tried to remember what was at the end of the corridor – just a window that looked out onto darkness. And the Vanfortes had made such a big point about locking off the West Wing – why would they go back on that?

I curled my fingers, digging my nails into my palms. The knives, the gun, the argument, the tall person walking silently through the West Wing. Someone else waiting outside our rooms. A third of me wanted to barricade myself into the room, a third wanted to flee into the night – and a third wanted to know what the hell was going on.

It was the curious third that won – I wanted answers. I would confront whoever it was and ask them what they were doing.

Pushing down the spiking feeling of nervousness that was suddenly shooting through me, I grabbed my torch and peered out into the corridor, holding the beam up to try and illuminate the dead end.

There was no one there.

The door opposite me opened a crack. Jayne's eyes glinted in the light of her candle as she looked out. "Was that you?" she said. "Going past just now?"

She'd heard the footsteps too. "No," I said. "Was it Lizzie?"

We both looked at Lizzie's closed door. I went over to it, turning the knob and entering. Lizzie was sitting cross-legged in front of the fire, warming her hands.

"What's up?" she said, looking confused.

"We heard footsteps," I replied. "We thought it was you."

Lizzie frowned. "I heard footsteps, but I assumed it was one of you two."

"The rest of the house is definitely locked off, isn't it?" I said to Jayne.

She nodded. "Yeah, but that was for their benefit. A few of the doors leading outside have old locks – they could be broken quite easily. Someone could walk in from the grounds."

A shiver ran down my back, though I tried to hide it from the others.

Lizzie didn't bother attempting to appear brave. "Home invasion," she said breathlessly, her eyes wide and panicked. "A stranger has just walked in..."

I rolled my eyes, the shiver gone – when Lizzie said it aloud, it sounded stupid. The house was isolated, cut off by the snow – surely that meant it was *less* likely a stranger might be lurking about in an attempt to do a home invasion. But on the other hand, it *was* better to be on the cautious side, seeing as we were *staying* in this house...

Jayne was frowning. "The house has secret passageways – Ms Bromley mentioned it once. She and Mrs Vanforte know all the ones on the estate." Her voice was low, and it was almost like she was speaking to herself more than us. She didn't explain anything further, just left the room in silence.

"That was helpful of her," I muttered, following Jayne out. "So, you think someone walked past and disappeared down a secret passageway?" I checked my watch: 7.54 p.m. They'd be cutting it fine if they wanted to make it to dinner on time.

In the corridor, Jayne was holding her candle up to the wall panels with one hand and tapping them with her other.

"Er, are you going to set the house on fire?" I said, wincing as the tiny flame got close to licking the wood panelling – it was

141

so old it would probably easily go up in flames. "Because I don't think burning down the house with us in it is a good way to figure out where this so-called secret passageway is."

Jayne continued to ignore me, tapping away. Then she must have hit a hidden switch, because part of the wall silently slid back.

She stood back, nodding once. "I was right."

"This is so cool," I muttered. "Where does it go?"

"No idea. But I'm guessing that's why whoever it was came down this way. This secret passageway leads somewhere they wanted to get to."

"What if it's got something to do with the knives?" I said. "And the gun Tate had." My heart was hammering with a mixture of fear and excitement as I held up my torch and shone the light into the dark space. It was a thin passageway, and barely high enough for me to go down. Anyone taller would have to crouch. I didn't want to go back to my bedroom, not when someone was wandering the corridors, and there were knives and guns floating around. The mystery surrounding the Vanfortes wasn't in my head. There was *something* going on. Something – *potentially* – dangerous. That we needed to solve, in case we were put in *more* danger.

I was getting the beginnings of a bad feeling, an instinct I had learned the hard way never to ignore.

"Well, what are we waiting for?" I said. "Let's explore."

Jayne

My candle was barely giving out light. I went back to my bedroom to grab my torch, coming back to find Lizzie with her feet firmly planted on the ground. "I'm not going down that passage, no way," she said. "What if whoever went down there is *still* in there? If they had to sneak past our bedrooms to get into it, this must be the only entrance. Which means we might run into them."

"Unless it's a ghost," said Devi with a straight face. "In which case they'll just walk through the walls."

Lizzie looked at Devi, horrified. I forced back a smile at the mischievous sparkle in Devi's eyes.

"Look, either way I'm finding out what's going on," said Devi. "I'm not going to bed until I'm sure we're completely safe from this weird family. Hey, maybe it's Ms Bromley – she only pretended to leave and now she's running around the house she has access to all day. Or, maybe she *died* on the walk home and that was her ghost – really ties the two theories together, doesn't it? A ghost with footsteps."

"That's not something to joke about," said Lizzie. Her eyes were shiny.

Devi peered at her. "Hey – are you crying? It was a *joke*. Toughen up a bit, yeah? We'll be fine as long as we stick together."

She set off down the passageway, holding her torch aloft. I made to follow her, but Lizzie grabbed my sleeve.

"You can't be serious – there could be anything down there," she said.

"It's just a passage," I said with a shrug, then entered it. I had a strong feeling the person sneaking around the West Wing was Douglas. This was *my* place of work. *I* was in charge of the West Wing tonight, looking after Devi and Lizzie. He couldn't just do as he pleased.

The passageway was narrow and I had to bend slightly because the ceiling was low.

Devi was ahead. Every so often I heard her swearing to herself, and that gave me a warning that the passage was going to dip sharply, or the floor was going to get slightly uneven. Lizzie groaned and entered behind me, quietly whimpering. I wondered why she hadn't just waited in the corridor if she was that scared. Probably thought there was safety in sticking together, as Devi had said.

My watch said it was 8.06 p.m. and I knew Mrs Vanforte wouldn't take kindly to anyone arriving late. I didn't think we would run into the person coming back through; they were probably now at dinner.

Devi came to a sudden stop. "It's a dead end!" she said.

"Where has the person gone then?" Lizzie squeaked from behind me.

"Through the wall?" Devi suggested. "Obviously there must be some sort of hidden panel, like the one we came in by." She squeezed back past me, accidentally elbowing me as she did so. Then she shoved me forward towards the dead end. "Right, tech whizz – you found the entrance. You find the exit."

My neck was starting to ache from all the crouching. I just wanted to get out of the corridor. So I held my torch up, squinting at the stretch of brick in front of me. All I had done before was feel for a bump in the wall, for the slightest indication that I wasn't touching a panel at all, but a hidden switch. I started running my fingers along the wall.

"Do you hear anything on the other side?" said Devi. That made me pause, because I'd been so fixated on finding the exit, I hadn't even thought about the mysterious person we had followed down the passage.

I strained my ears, but I didn't hear anything except Lizzie's loud, jagged breathing. She sounded like she was on the verge of tears, and I remembered she was afraid of the dark.

I shrugged, even though I knew Devi wouldn't be able to see. It's my usual response when I don't want to say anything. I went back to my task.

Lizzie shrieked, the sudden noise making me wince. "Something touched my neck!" she said. And then—

"Ow! You punched me!"

"Well then, don't yell!" Devi said. "We've no idea where we are – for all we know, on the other side of that wall is the dining

145

room. We could be walking straight into Mrs Vanforte's weird supper."

But I didn't think accidentally walking in on the meal was a concern for us. From my knowledge of the house, we'd walked in the opposite direction to the dining room. Emily and the others were far away from us. All the same, I could see why Devi didn't want to be too loud.

"But something *touched my neck*," whined Lizzie. "It wasn't you, was it? Playing a trick on me."

"Obviously not," said Devi. "I'm a cow but even I have my limits."

"Well then – is there someone behind me, who touched my neck?" said Lizzie. Silence followed her question. I stopped, straining my ears and trying to work out if I could hear anything other than Devi's and Lizzie's breathing.

There *might* have been a noise coming from the blackness beyond Lizzie – extra breathing from someone standing in silence with us in the dark passageway. Or it could have been my mind playing tricks on me.

It appeared Lizzie couldn't take the silence any longer. "There's someone behind me, isn't there? Shine your torch."

"Why don't you shine yours?" came Devi's immediate response.

"I don't want to turn round," said Lizzie. "If there is someone behind me, I am going to cry." It sounded like she was already sniffling.

"You've probably scared them off anyway," said Devi. "But *fine*, I'll look."

I tuned them out, trying to figure out where the button to

leave was – although, maybe this *was* just a dead end. It'd be a fairly pointless passageway, though. And the person who'd walked down it couldn't have simply disappeared.

There was shuffling behind me. "See, there's nothing there," said Devi to Lizzie.

"They could have moved down slightly – I swear I heard footsteps – can you stand behind me and protect me?"

"So they can stab me first? I'm not a human shield, *no* way—"

"So you agree there's someone in here with us?" Lizzie said to Devi.

I crouched down, and my finger finally ran over a bump on the wall. I pressed, and the wall slid back to reveal a darkened room. For a moment I stood in shock, that I had found the switch – it was hidden further down than I expected.

Then I held up my torch, took a deep breath, and stepped inside.

Lizzie

The Day of My Arrival
(although at this point it is night. So to be accurate, it is the night of my arrival)

It turned out there was nothing behind me, but I did find Devi laughing off my fear rude. If there *had* been an axe-murderer or a ghost behind me, my alertness might have saved us all. I didn't know *why* I had axe-murderers or ghosts on my mind – there was just something about the house that set me on edge. The darkness. The emptiness. The loneliness, out in the middle of nowhere. The fact the snow had us all trapped, and we were cut off from the outside world. It all added up to something out of a nightmare.

I wished Mum was with me – or my friends. Mind you, Natasha and Hannah would have stayed in their bedrooms…or if they had decided to walk around, they would have probably left me behind to watch the entrance to the secret passageway, in case someone else came along. I would have hated that a lot more – being alone, waiting for everyone else to come back. At least Jayne and Devi had let me stay with them.

We entered what looked to be some sort of study.

"This is Mr Vanforte's," said Jayne. "He normally keeps the room locked – only lets Ms Bromley clean it while he's there."

"He could just clean it himself if he's that paranoid," said Devi. "Though…I can't imagine him cleaning *anything* himself." She paused. "So if this is Charles Vanforte's study, that must mean he was the one going through the passageway earlier! Then again, why the hell would he sneak through to his own study?" She didn't wait for an answer – she started digging through some papers stacked on the windowsill.

The study was a mess, with papers everywhere, and a collection of used coffee mugs on the bookshelf. Despite my own worries about being in there, I wavered – a quick look around couldn't hurt, just to see what sorts of things he owned.

There was a large black folder sitting open on the desk. It was packed with newspaper clippings carefully cut out and stored inside plastic pockets. I held up my torch to squint at the pages. The articles were all about an old construction company Mr Vanforte seemed to have owned. According to the articles, it had been doing really well, making lots of money – but the articles stopped abruptly after one newspaper reported that he'd made a multi-million-pound profit. I wondered what had happened to the company; why he had decided to move across into politics.

He had underlined positive quotes about himself in neat, straight lines.

"Look at this watch collection," said Devi, peering into a drawer. "I bet these are worth *thousands*." I abandoned the newspapers, because the watch collection seemed much more interesting, though I couldn't help but tut at the way he had dumped the watches in a pile.

"He's treating them so poorly," I muttered, the beam from my torch reflecting the gold. I wished I could pick all the watches up and carefully place them in a box. Mum has always taught me to look after jewellery properly – as well as how much it's worth, it often has sentimental value... Though I supposed that didn't matter so much to Mr Vanforte.

"He'll just buy more," said Devi with a shake of her head.

Jayne, meanwhile, had done a loop round the room, tapping at the walls. I guessed she was looking for more secret passageways. Finally she arrived at the far door and tried the handle – it was unlocked, leading out into a dark corridor.

"I thought Mr Vanforte kept this room locked?" I said nervously.

"He might have forgotten to lock it," said Devi. "Anyway, I really don't think he would have snuck into his own study – but that still doesn't explain why someone's wandering around when they should have been going to dinner, and what the hell happened to those knives."

Jayne and Devi hadn't taken my theory about the stranger wandering about the house seriously, and maybe it *was* a slightly ridiculous idea. But while the Vanfortes had every right to be walking around in their own home, Jayne knew as well as I did that one of them had a gun. We didn't need to get on their bad side.

"Can we go now?" I asked, my voice coming out low and pitiful. I gestured at the passageway, even though I couldn't stand the thought of heading back in there, trapped within the walls, the air so musty, I was worried we would all die from dust getting caught in our lungs.

The entire time we were walking I had been expecting to come across skeletons entombed for ever, with scratches on the wall above them, where they'd clawed at the passage roof in an attempt to get out. Plus, even now we were in Mr Vanforte's study I still couldn't get rid of the idea that *someone*, or *something*, was watching us.

Mum and I read stories about the Bramble Estate and its long history when we were googling directions for how I could get here. One tale was about a woman called Victoria Vanforte, whose father was going to force her into marrying one of his friends in order to make more money. She refused, so the father, along with all her brothers, killed her for disrespecting his wishes. They laid her to rest in one of the bedrooms while they dug a grave – but when they returned her corpse had disappeared, never to be found.

Over the years, everyone involved in Victoria Vanforte's murder met a grisly death of their own – and Victoria's ghost is said to continue walking through the house, vowing revenge on all Vanfortes and their friends for evermore.

To distract myself from the thought of long-dead eyes watching me, I peered at the paintings on Mr Vanforte's walls. There was one of the Bramble Estate, and the rest were of people I didn't recognize, but I assumed they were past generations of Vanfortes. I went back to the painting of the Bramble Estate, examining it as best I could with the dim light of my flickering torch. I hadn't really got a good look at the house in all the snow, so here was my chance. It seemed just as large as it had when I saw it from the outside, with all the windows and rooms stretching onwards.

"You know art is one of the easiest ways to launder drug money," came Devi's helpful voice from behind me. "It's true, I read it online."

She got bored and wandered off as I continued to peer at the painting. The artist had drawn in the shadow of a person in a room at the end of the ground floor – a room with…bars over the window.

"What are you looking at?" asked Jayne.

"Are there any windows in the house with…those over them?" A shiver went up my back as I pointed at the bars.

"No, of course not," said Jayne, as she squinted at the painting. "Actually…that room with the bars…is *this* room. We're in the corner of the house, near the West Wing, and there's two big windows."

"The painting isn't that good," called Devi from behind me. "Good paintings should have people in them, I think. What's so great about drawing a building?"

"Why would someone draw bars over *this* window?" muttered Jayne.

"Maybe for fun," said Devi, and before I could stop her she had slid next to me, reached up and poked the bars in the painting.

"Art is not interactive!" I shrieked – but it seemed this piece was, because the painting, and the panel of wall it was attached to, swung forward to reveal a hidden room.

"What the hell," said Devi, holding her torch up. "Another secret room – Jayne, did you know about this one?"

Jayne shook her head.

"Awesome," said Devi with a grin. I clutched her arm, suddenly overcome with the fear that *something* was going to come lurching out of the space. Corpses flashed across my mind and I stumbled backwards.

Nothing attacked. Instead, we found ourselves looking into a stone chamber, big enough only for a bench against the far wall. The weak light from our torches revealed a single naked light bulb hanging from the ceiling.

"You would never be able to tell this room was here unless you were actually measuring proportions," said Jayne, coming up silently to stand next to us. "But then again – the walls are so thick they probably disguise the space – look, it's cut *into* the stone."

Devi stepped inside to take a closer look – and the door swung shut behind her, the room vanishing once more.

Devi
Before the Murder

I was trapped in the stone tomb. I couldn't see any sort of switch to open the room from the inside and I couldn't hear Jayne and Lizzie, even though I yelled for them to let me out. I swore at them. For all I knew, they could have been the type of people who'd just leave me to die while they trotted along on their merry ways. Especially since I had enjoyed taking the piss out of Lizzie so much, and Jayne was probably cold enough to calculate how long it would take me to die from inhaling my own recycled carbon dioxide after my oxygen ran out.

But then the wall swung open, wedging to a standstill. Lizzie's nervous face peered around.

"Sorry – I wasn't pressing the painting hard enough," she said. "Are you okay?"

I glared at her, both for her slowness and for suggesting I had been at all worried during my time in the tomb. I am not a coward. I am a Mistry – I am tough. It takes more than the thought of being entombed alive to faze the likes of me. "Do you reckon Mr Vanforte has kept prisoners in here?" I said, trying to keep my voice smooth.

"No," said Jayne shortly, shutting down my suggestion instantly.

"Charles Vanforte is a respectable man," said Lizzie. "There's rumours going around that he's going to be *knighted*."

I rolled my eyes, because in my view being knighted doesn't mean you're respectable. But I managed to rein myself in from making a snarky comment (an effort which I think was truly deserving of national recognition) and turned to have another look around the space.

There wasn't much to see; if I stood in the centre I could stretch my arms out and brush both walls. A bench was bolted to the wall, and clearly wasn't used often because there was dust all over it – except for a small section in the corner.

I used my fail-safe method of pressing and was rewarded when the top of the bench slid backwards into the wall. Whoever had built all these secret passageways and hidden spaces *really* didn't have much of an imagination.

The bench was hollow inside and also empty. I frowned, feeling disappointed – but then I saw a small bit of white peeking out of the far-left corner.

It was a false bottom. I grinned, sliding my fingers round the edges and pulling. The thin wooden board came up easily, to reveal a trove of papers hidden underneath.

"Jackpot," I said. Hidden room, hidden papers – something dodgy was going on, and I was getting closer to finding out what.

I bundled the papers up in my arms and went back into the main room, crouching down and spreading them across the floor.

"What are we looking at?" I asked. Like the papers I had found in Mrs Vanforte's office, they all seemed like gibberish to me, rows of random numbers and names. What's with rich people and their secret papers? Why can't they just stash bars of gold away somewhere?

"No idea," said Jayne, running her fingers over the ink.

"Okay, we've looked through these papers," said Lizzie, who had only taken one quick look before getting to her feet. "Can we *go* now? This is really terrible of us – the Vanfortes have let us into their home and trusted us and we've repaid them by going through their private things… Someone could come in at any minute!"

I'd half forgotten about what the Vanfortes might be doing. Mrs Vanforte had said she was going to *punish* someone at dinner. Were they having another screaming match right now? Or else, eating cold chicken in tense silence? Although…what if dinner finished early because they couldn't stand to be in the same room any more? It *was* half eight, and I'd been going on the assumption we'd have more time.

I figured I'd see what the papers said, and then we would go. They were all addressed to different people – David Allen, Richard Gower, Edward Smith, Joseph Ship. Each one looked to be a receipt for a small amount of something that sounded like a drug – I'd never heard of it. The drug had been bought from a company called Noviroam. I guessed they were the manufacturers, or else a pharmacy or something.

I paused flicking through the papers, to look at a printout of an email chain between Edward Smith and James Marton at Noviroam. "Who's Edward Smith and why's Mr Vanforte got his emails?"

Jayne shook her head, though she frowned. "The name rings a bell…"

"It's a generic name, of course it rings a bell," I said impatiently.

"He's a friend of Mr Vanforte's," whispered Lizzie from behind me. I glanced back at her – she was hovering by the door to the study, rocking back and forth on her heels like she was preparing to take off at any moment. "Ms Bromley told me, in the kitchen – she said Mr and Mrs Vanforte would have arguments about Edward Smith… That Mrs Vanforte didn't want Mr Vanforte using him any more, whatever that means…"

"Interesting," I said, as I read through the email chain:

From jamesmarton@Noviroam
Edward –
Can I just confirm this is the correct amount? In this
quantity, it would be lethal.

From edwardsmith@mail
Yes. Just want a stock, don't intend to take it all at once!

From jamesmarton@Noviroam
Edward –
This will cost significantly more.

From edwardsmith@mail
You'll get the money.

"It's *drugs*," I said. "A *lethal* amount that this guy Edward Smith was stocking up on." As I spoke there was a noise outside the room, a sort of scratching. It could have been a mouse (or the ghost Lizzie kept insisting was haunting the estate). Either way, it spooked Lizzie (not me, obviously).

"We need to *go*," she said, crossing over next to me and starting to gather up all the papers. "Let's put these where we found them and go back to our rooms."

"Wait," I said. I got my phone out and switched it on. I had drained most of the battery using its satnav during my car journey. It was now at ten per cent, and *still* showed no signal, but at least the camera worked fine. I put the flash on, snapped pictures of all the papers, then turned it off again. Mr Vanforte had hidden them in a secret compartment in a secret bench in his study. If that didn't say "illegal", I didn't know what would. Whatever or whoever Noviroam were, they were selling a type of drug, directly to Mr Vanforte's friend, Edward Smith. I felt as if I was getting somewhere. That my instincts about there being something deeper going on were right. I could actually solve a case. No more armchair detecting for me. All those Sundays watching old men in tweed coats had finally paid off.

Edward Smith couldn't be a fake name for Mr Vanforte: I knew Mr Vanforte had £74 to his name and apparently money wasn't an issue to Edward Smith… Although I only knew about Mr Vanforte's money status from the bank statements Mrs Vanforte had – maybe he had secret accounts hanging around.

Or he'd spent all his money buying drugs.

Mr Vanforte had basically only let me stay the night because he wanted to make himself look good in the papers – if he was doing something *really* wrong, why should I help him keep his image clean? Exposing him was the morally correct thing to do.

"Come *on*," said Lizzie. By now all the papers were tucked under her arm. I rolled my eyes, but then I helped, taking them from her and putting them back into the bench with the hidden bottom and closing the lid once more. Mr Vanforte would never know.

Lizzie headed towards the doorway.

"No," said Jayne, nodding back towards the secret passageway. "We need to go this way – they've locked off the West Wing, remember?"

Lizzie let out a little whimper and a small chuckle escaped me before I managed to change it into a cough, patting my chest a few times for good measure.

I entered the passageway first, only this time I held my torch higher, to reveal thick cobwebs hanging from the ceiling. I'd found the hand that had stroked Lizzie's neck. Behind me, I heard the wall slide back into place, sealing off Mr Vanforte's study.

I started walking, and we were a little way down the passageway when Lizzie called out for me to stop. I glanced over my shoulder, to find Lizzie was looking behind her, at Jayne.

Jayne was staring at the wall with a frown on her face.

"Yes, that's a wall," I said impatiently. The passageway was freezing and the air was musty, and even though we hadn't found the person who had entered the passageway in the first place, we'd at least found those papers, hidden away. I was itching to go back to my room and have a proper look at the pictures I'd taken.

"This little wood panel slides back," said Jayne. "It's not an entrance to another room… It's too small."

I frowned, squeezing past Lizzie to take a look.

"I just want to get out of here," Lizzie said, making no move to either carry on going, or to look at the panel. I'd been just as eager to get out of the passageway, but now here was a new puzzle to solve.

Jayne slid back the wood to reveal a small hole, at stomach-level, which looked out into a dark room. I crouched, but with only the light from the torches I had no idea what was inside.

"Whereabouts do you think we are?" I said to Jayne.

"I think…maybe one of the sitting rooms?" she said. "Hang on."

She went past me, and Lizzie heaved a sigh of relief. Maybe she thought we were going to keep walking. But then Jayne stopped a little way ahead of us.

"Devi – come here," she said. I went, once more squeezing by Lizzie.

"Please can we just go?" Lizzie said. "I really don't like it in here – what happens if the walls don't open again to let us out? No one would be able to hear us screaming…"

"Oh, I think they would," I said with a grin, because what I was seeing was wildly twisted. Jayne had found yet another hole, looking out into another dark room. "This passageway doesn't just link Mr Vanforte's study with the West Wing –

it has secret peepholes into each room. You could listen in on conversations in any of the rooms it runs past."

Lizzie let out a low moan. "I don't like this – I don't like this at all."

I looked at Jayne; the torches made her face look orange. Her expression gave away nothing of what she was thinking.

"You reckon Charles Vanforte walks along these passages and listens in on everyone in the house?" I said. "This is *so* twisted…" I thought about the folders Emily Vanforte kept on basically everyone she knew. She was definitely a messed-up lady – maybe she was the one who used the passages. After all, she'd made it very clear this was *her* family home.

"Let's go back," said Lizzie, and she gave me a little shove. "I want to go back."

"You reckon they all spy on each other?" I said, ignoring her. "Or worse – you reckon people from *outside* the estate come in and use these passageways?" I didn't really believe anything I was saying, I was just winding Lizzie up.

But then I thought back to the horror film about the person in the attic living their life in secret, only coming out at night.

The Bramble Estate was *so* large – what if there *was* someone else in the house with us?

"The passages are secret," grunted Jayne. "The family would have had to *tell* an outsider about them."

Her common sense burst my horror bubble, and I couldn't help but feel secretly relieved. "Okay, let's get out of here," I said.

Lizzie
That Night

I had never been as happy as I was when we left that horrible secret passageway and returned to the corridor with our bedrooms. Jayne closed the passageway off, and it looked like an ordinary stretch of wall again.

Devi waved her hands over the panelling. "You wouldn't even know there was a passage running past…"

Jayne had gone into her bedroom and there was the sound of something being dragged across the room.

"What's she doing?" asked Devi, as we went into her bedroom. Jayne was pulling one of the armchairs over to the far wall near the door. "Er – why are you rearranging the furniture?"

"There's a peephole looking into this room," said Jayne, straightening up. "And one looking into Lizzie's. Not sure about yours, Devi, as it's on the other side of the corridor." "Oh *no*," I said, running into my bedroom and staring at the wall. I didn't know what I was looking for, but Jayne followed me in and pointed at a patch of wood which was slightly darker than the rest.

"That's the passageway we were just in. I saw these peepholes as we went past."

I shook my head, horror flooding through me. "Block it off."

Jayne yanked an armchair in front of it, like she had done for the hole in her bedroom. Now, even if someone opened it on the other side, all you'd be able to see was the back of an armchair.

"They'll still be able to listen in, though," said Devi, standing in the doorway and holding up her torch.

Fear squeezed my heart. "Do you think one of them might eavesdrop in the middle of the night?" I knew I would simply be asleep, but the thought of someone standing behind a wall and listening to me at my most vulnerable did not appeal.

"Don't need ghosts, do you, Liz?" said Devi with a grin. "Not when these people can all walk through the walls."

"Easy for you to say," I snapped, starting to get irritated with her. "*You* might not even have a passageway going past your room."

"I'm happy to swap, if that makes you feel any better," said Devi unexpectedly. I looked at her in shock, because it was a genuinely nice offer. But then I saw she was smirking. "Of course, this way at least you *know* you've blocked off the peephole by sticking something in front of it – no one can watch you. In my room – who knows? Maybe there's a secret entrance in there to a passage filled with bodies. Imagine waking up in the middle of the night to a nice, waxy corpse staring at you with its maggot-filled eyes—"

"Oh *stop*," I whimpered, putting my hands over my ears.

Devi's smile widened. "You know, I'm being a cow because... Well, I am a cow and it's fun. But I'm sure the Vanfortes have better things to do than creep along in the middle of the night and listen to us sleeping." She paused, her smile flickering. "Except we still don't know what Douglas was doing with those knives..." She swallowed, and a moment of fear flashed across her face, gone the next second. She was scared, but trying not to show it. That didn't make me feel better – I preferred it when she was acting like everything was fine. "Jayne, let's just see if we can spot any sign of a secret passageway or a peephole in my bedroom," she said.

Jayne followed her out, and a few minutes later they returned to my bedroom, shaking their heads.

"Nothing there," said Devi, settling down on the armchair like she never planned to leave. Gone was her eagerness to be alone in her bedroom. "So, what do we think's happening at dinner? It's been about forty-five minutes since it started. Reckon they've all kicked off yet? Or else they've all eaten as quickly as they could and then headed off to sleep?"

I didn't want to speculate. I wanted to leave and never come back. I was deeply regretting ever bringing the necklace in the first place.

"I'm going to bed," grunted Jayne as she left the room. Devi looked disappointed – I guess I wasn't much reassurance safety-wise.

"Maybe I should go as well," she said uncertainly, rising from the armchair. "The quicker we're all asleep, the quicker tomorrow will come and we'll all be on our way." She hesitated, looking like she wanted to say something else. Maybe she wanted to stick together, but didn't want to say the words aloud. That was how I felt – if I asked her to stay then it would be admitting I thought there might be something wrong. The secret passageways had deeply unsettled me in a way I couldn't properly explain – the thought of the empty space behind my bedroom, of the room not being secure…

"Goodnight, Devi," I said, hoping she would hear the plea in my voice, that maybe we should stick together, and that she would take charge and suggest it. But instead she nodded, and left.

I closed my door, and was about to slide a bolt across and lock myself in – but then I remembered that wasn't enough; Mr Vanforte's study was usually locked and we still managed to get in by bypassing the main door.

I got ready for bed, and climbed between the freezing sheets. The fire was just dying out and for a while I lay staring at the glowing embers.

I must have fallen asleep because the next thing I knew I was being shaken awake. Someone was looming over me clutching a torch. A shriek burst out of my throat before my senses caught up with me, and I realized I was staring at the white face of Lottie Vanforte.

My instinct was to apologize for yelling. "I'm so sorry." I clutched my sheets to my chest. "I didn't mean to shout – you just took me by surprise, that's all." *And why are you in here?* But even though someone coming into my room while I was asleep had been my fear, it would have been too rude to ask.

"The power is still out," muttered Lottie, clutching her torch.

She looked like she was in shock – I half wondered if she had come into the wrong room, or if she was sleepwalking or something.

"What's the time?" I asked. The room was pitch black – it had to be the middle of the night.

"Midnight," said Lottie. She sat down on the end of the bed, taking deep breaths. It took me a second to realize she was crying, her shoulders rising and falling. "Can we borrow your car, please?"

"What?" I said, sitting up and rubbing my eyes. "What's going on?"

Lottie turned the torch towards me, right at my face. I shielded my eyes and she lowered it, her face in shadow. "Sorry," she said. "But none of our cars are working and I can't figure out why." She took a deep, shuddering breath, sounding like she was on the verge of tears. "I know Devi's car is dead and I wanted to test yours – I just don't know what to *do*. What are we supposed to *do*?" Her voice turned to panic, and she swung the torch about, rubbing at her eyes.

A shiver ran through me. "Why do you need a car?" I asked. "What's happened?" I had an awful feeling in the pit of my stomach.

"We're still cut off," said Lottie, her voice shaking. "No phones, no Wi-Fi, no way to call anyone. We need help."

"But *why*?"

"Mum's dead."

PART TWO

THE MURDER

Lizzie
That Night

I woke up Devi and Jayne, my entire body numb. I couldn't believe this was actually happening and it felt wrong to let them stay oblivious to it all. I couldn't think of anything worse than having a good sleep only to wake up and discover hours later that Mrs Vanforte was dead.

Lottie followed me in silence, like she didn't know what else to do with herself.

Devi showed a complete lack of delicacy. "Was it a heart attack?" she said. "If she's already dead, what help do we get? A doctor can't do anything now."

I flinched at the suggestion it was a heart attack, remembering my dad. But I didn't want to show any fear, or nervousness – not in front of Lottie. She had just lost her mother.

Jayne didn't react – at least, she didn't show a reaction. But her eyes flicked towards Lottie, who was staring at her. I think Lottie wanted a hug, but I wasn't entirely sure so I didn't try to give her one in case I'd misread the situation.

"Let's go look at your car," said Lottie to me. "See if it's working." Her chest was still rising and falling rapidly, her eyes blinking back tears that shone in the dim light of our torches. I nodded, about to follow her.

"Wait," said Devi. "I don't know about you lot, but I don't want to freeze to death." She looked pointedly at our pyjamas – Lottie was still in the black dress she'd worn to dinner. It would have blended in well at a funeral.

It's like she knew.

I pushed the unbidden thought away, because of course Lottie hadn't known Mrs Vanforte was going to die. In silence, I went back to my bedroom and fumbled for my bag, putting on two jumpers over my pyjamas, and boots, tucking in my trousers. I buttoned up my coat, my hands shaking – although the house was still freezing, the shakes weren't from the cold.

"Hey," came a soft voice from behind me. It was Devi, shining a torch at me – she had put her hoodie back on, and a puffy off-white coat that made her look like a snowman. "Are you okay?"

I nodded my head, but it might have come out uncertainly because Devi pressed her lips together. "It's going to be fine," she said. I knew she had no clue whether things were going to be okay or not, but her back was straight, her eyes were narrowed, and she looked like nothing would faze her. It reassured me, gave me a little courage – enough to stop my hands shaking so much, so I could do up the last of my coat buttons.

We went out into the hallway, where Lottie and Jayne were waiting. Jayne was also in warmer clothes now, but Lottie was still wearing the black dress. She didn't look cold – her face was flushed red now, from tears.

"Come on," she mumbled, leading the way through the silent, dark house. From what I could tell through glimpses out of the windows, there was a thick cloud blocking any stars or the moon, so the world outside was pitch black. It almost felt like I was in a dream, and any second I would wake up at home nice and safe.

Lottie stopped by the front door to retrieve a thick trench coat from a closet and slip it on. It looked too big for her, like it didn't belong to her – but at least it covered her up. I had thought she might be considering walking outside in just her dress, which would surely lead to her catching her death from cold.

Outside, our feet crunched over the snow. The house had been freezing but this was another level; even with my thick coat on I was shivering, the cold biting at my ears and my fingers. I wished I had thought to put on a hat and gloves.

My ankle twisted painfully to one side as we followed Lottie.

"Where are the others?" asked Devi sharply. I stumbled again, because that thought hadn't even occurred to me. Mr Vanforte, Tate and Douglas felt like distant memories now – we could have been the only people left in the world. "Are they with…with the b-body?" Devi stumbled over the last word. Perhaps she wasn't as unfazed as she appeared.

I couldn't believe that Emily Vanforte had actually keeled over and died. Not the hurricane-force woman I had seen, not the woman who had stood at the top of the stairs and looked down at the rest of her family like she owned the entire world.

I remembered the last image I had of her, standing with a single candle in the darkness, bold, unafraid. I couldn't understand how a few hours later she was dead.

"I don't know where Tate is," said Lottie after a pause. "Douglas and Dad are with…with Mum." She cleared her throat on the last word. The beam from her torch revealed a mess of footprints over the snow, leading up to my car.

"Who's been out here?" asked Devi. She swung her torch and picked up loads of footprints around all the cars.

"Well, you have – earlier, when you were checking your car," said Lottie. "And I've been out with Douglas to have a look at the cars just now. We've checked the other cars in the garage – Lizzie, yours is the only we haven't looked at."

I slipped into my car, while Lottie and the others waited outside. I turned the key. Nothing happened.

Lottie shook her head. "I knew it," she whispered, staring at my car like she could make it work with the power of her mind.

"What?" said Devi, a touch of panic creeping into her voice. "What's wrong?"

"None of the cars are starting," said Lottie. "Not mine, or Douglas's or Tate's – none of Mum's and Dad's."

"What – *all* of them?" said Devi. "They've all collectively died? The thing that happened to my car isn't contagious, is it? No – what am I saying, that's stupid."

The implication hung in the air. For one car to die was bad luck. For *all* the cars to die had to mean someone had *tampered* with them. But why?

I let out a low moan of fear. Someone had clearly been watching the house, and had sabotaged all the cars. Maybe they had killed Mrs Vanforte, and they were going to murder us all one by one.

The Vanfortes and Douglas and Tate were powerful people who must have enemies... Of course, my theory didn't square up with the fact that Mrs Vanforte had been threatening to spill a big secret belonging to Mr Vanforte, or Douglas, or Tate or Lottie all day – then she'd conveniently died. But I simply didn't want to think of the alternative theory – that one of the four people at dinner had killed her. Because that would mean one of the people I had met, who was still in the house with me now, was a murderer.

"Crap," said Devi, her teeth chattering. I didn't know if it was from the cold or from fear. "Jayne, can you hot-wire one of them? Like they do in the films?"

"Why would she know how to hot-wire a car?" I asked.

"You can't hot-wire new cars," said Jayne.

"Well, *I* don't know," said Devi. "I'm only trying to offer up realistic solutions here. How the hell could this have happened? Plus, if you look at the whole picture – the phones being off, and the power being gone..."

"Yes," said Lottie, pausing for a second. "We should check, shouldn't we?" She waited, like she wanted Devi to take charge and tell her what to do. Devi nodded.

"Yeah," said Devi. "We should."

I had no idea what they were talking about, but followed Lottie and her big beam back into the house. I closed the front door behind me, but it made little difference; the temperature was still icy, the corridors draughty and my breath was coming out in puffs. Pain was cutting through my toes and I wondered whether it was possible for frostbite to be setting in.

We walked past the kitchen, where the fire grate still had a few dying embers, to a door set in the wall.

Lottie pushed it opened and disappeared down into the bowels of the earth. I flinched at the idea of going into the dark, damp cellar, where spiders and rats had probably made themselves at home. But the others were already pressing on and the thought of being left alone in the corridor where anything could get me was even worse.

I tried to keep as close to Devi as I could, clutching at her sleeve, reassured by the fact I wasn't alone.

A cold breeze blew across the back of my neck as we made our way across the room. I barely paid attention to anything around me, aware that there was a lot of space where anything could have been lurking. We stopped in front of a rusty old box attached to the wall, which Lottie opened.

She shone her torch over it and gasped. I knew nothing about this sort of thing, but even I could see the wires had been slashed, and were now a tangled mess.

"Well, there you go," said Lottie in a small voice. "That's the reason for the power being down."

"I heard someone," said Jayne suddenly. "When I came down here earlier for some jump leads to see if I could get Devi's car working…"

"Well, there's no way you could jump-start it now," said Devi, her voice bitter. "We need to connect the leads to another *working* car to be able to get it to start. What about the phone and internet lines? Should we check those?"

"I guess…" said Lottie. We went to the far side of the room, where Lottie held up a wire that had been neatly snipped into two.

"Mice?" I suggested half-heartedly.

"Yes, *mice* got into the power box and *mice* cut the phone lines and *mice* destroyed everyone's cars," said Devi. She turned to Lottie, holding up her torch. "What the *hell* is going on?"

Devi
After the Murder

Lottie didn't answer my question and helpfully explain everything. Instead she suggested we go up to the drawing room to talk. It was a huge, grand room that served no use as far as I could tell. It could have been a living room, but there wasn't a TV and the antique-style couches with white fabric and golden edges were centred around a fireplace. The room was *too* big, the fire only lighting half of it, leaving the rest in shadow – though I could make out a few chairs dotted around, pushed up against the walls.

Jayne silently got the fire going, and Lottie sat down heavily on a couch in front it, staring blankly at the flames. It was like she'd forgotten the rest of us were in the room with her. Jayne slunk back, folding her arms, and Lizzie sat awkwardly on another couch, shooting Lottie anxious looks, like she wanted to comfort her but didn't know what to say.

It seemed neither Jayne nor Lizzie were going to be asking

for answers. It was down to me. "So, are you going to tell us what happened to your mum?" I asked as I sat next to Lizzie. I knew I should be gentler… Her mum had just died after all and she was obviously upset. But we'd also just been woken up in the middle of the night to find out the cars had all been tampered with, the power and phone lines were cut – and somewhere in the house with us was her mum's dead body.

I needed to know what exactly had happened at dinner, because if Mrs Vanforte had died of a heart attack, I'd eat my shoe.

Lottie raised her head and stared at me in silence. "Mum's *dead*," she whispered.

"Yeah, but *how*," I pressed. I felt Lizzie shift on the sofa beside me, and wondered if she was going to tell me off for being insensitive.

Lottie shook her head, and I thought she might start crying again. It was odd that she was hanging around with us, actually – three strangers – over her dad and boyfriend and cousin, any of whom could have comforted her properly. She pulled the trench coat tighter around her.

"This was Mum's," she said suddenly. "This coat. I disappointed her, you know. I didn't mean to, but I did."

I wanted to ask her another question, but Lizzie placed a hand on mine and shook her head really subtly. I bit my tongue, because it was the sort of thing Priya would do – stop me from putting my foot in my mouth. Lizzie was right to get me to shut up, because Lottie kept speaking.

"There isn't much to tell," said Lottie, her eyes fixed on the fire. "We had dinner – we talked for a while. Then Mum gave

177

a little gasp and slid forward. I thought she'd had a heart attack – I checked her pulse. There was nothing…"

"A heart attack," whispered Lizzie. "Oh, poor thing."

I rolled my eyes. The death combined with the cars being damaged and the power being cut – was Lizzie really that naïve? Surely the reality of what had happened at dinner should be dawning on Jayne and Lizzie as well. Mrs Vanforte had been dropping hints from the moment we walked in that one of her family was going to be exposed at dinner, that someone was going to be punished – that family member had obviously taken her seriously, and offed her. I'd literally *seen* knives in my bedroom earlier – Jayne had said Tate had a gun. Mrs Vanforte had folders on everyone she knew, and peepholes all over the house to watch and listen in on everything that was happening.

She'd been murdered, and there were only four suspects – one of whom had cut us off from the outside world.

Well, there was still the secret psycho option – that someone had been hiding in the walls. I snorted to myself at the ridiculousness of the idea, and Lottie looked at me confused – that brought me back to the present, and the facts as I knew them.

We had purposefully been cut off from the outside world. We were in danger.

If it was a family grudge behind Mrs Vanforte's death, me, Lizzie and Jayne were now witnesses, who might be on the hit list. And all I knew was that I wanted to survive until morning.

And hell, yes, my instincts to snoop about had been dead on. My gut had led me to the knives in the house, the weird folders Mrs Vanforte kept on her family, and the secret passageways and peepholes. Considering the fact that any hiding places I found might have *also* had a hidden entrance inside them, which meant nowhere might be safe inside this murder house, I figured my best bet to keep myself alive was to gather information on who was most likely to be the killer. That way, at least, I could be extra on my guard around them.

"Was there anyone near her when she died?" I asked cautiously. Now that I'd decided Mrs Vanforte had been murdered, I couldn't wrap my head around *how*. She hadn't been stabbed, because someone would have seen – and she hadn't been shot at, because someone would have heard…

Lottie shook her head. "No, that's why it's so strange. She was sitting at the head of the table, eating…"

"She, er…didn't choke, did she?" I said. It was probably a stupid question – but better to ask it than wonder.

"No," said Lottie. "Well, she made a few choking noises, like she couldn't breathe…" She closed her eyes for a second. "Sorry, I can't talk about this…"

A bolt of electricity went through me. Mrs Vanforte had been eating her food, she'd made a few choking noises, and then she'd died. What if she had been poisoned? We had literally *found* emails from a guy at Noviroam to the mysterious "Edward Smith" talking about lethal amounts of drugs. Which meant someone in the house could have pretended to be called Edward Smith, bought the drugs, and used them to kill Mrs Vanforte – although… The Noviroam guy hadn't *named* the drug. For all I knew it could have been something like paracetamol – a drug that could be lethal in high dosages, but in such a huge quantity Mrs Vanforte would definitely have tasted it. And she wouldn't have died instantly either…

If the detective films I've watched were accurate, the killer would have slipped something sufficiently deadly into their victim's food without it being visible.

"What is the dining room like?" I decided to try a different course of questioning, rather than asking Lottie to continue describing her mother's death. "Is it quite large? I guess it wasn't lit well because of the power outage? Did you see anything…odd?" *Like…someone poisoning Mrs Vanforte*. I didn't say that aloud – even I'm not that blunt. "Or else hear anything odd – maybe your mum said something strange?"

"Mum was always criticizing me," muttered Lottie.

I stared at her, confused. "So your mum didn't say anything strange? She just…criticized you?"

"No," said Lottie, annoyingly vaguely. I exchanged confused looks with Lizzie, who pressed her lips together. I knew she was telling me to be quiet. It was weird, how quickly I could read her, even though I barely knew her at all. Maybe it was because this was such a weird situation that we were forming the beginnings of a bond.

"The dining room is large," said Lottie. She balled her hands into fists, shaking her head. "We were eating by the light of the fire, by the light of candles. We were serving ourselves from the sideboards. Everyone was moving around… Except Mum. She'd filled up her plate at the beginning, and she sat at the head of the table, alone. She talked to Dad for a bit. Then to me. And then she died."

She looked at me, and though her face was half in shadow there was a pleading tone to her voice. Maybe she was hoping

I would say *don't be silly, it* couldn't *have been anything other than a heart attack that killed your mum.*

Except I couldn't give her that comfort. "Did you all eat everything?" I asked. I wouldn't say the words aloud – *your mum might have been poisoned.* But we were on the same page – she knew why I was asking these questions.

"Yes," said Lottie. "We all had some of everything. We opened a new bottle of wine. Dad let me, Douglas and Tate have a glass."

So the food and wine hadn't been tampered with... Unless something had been slipped directly into Mrs Vanforte's drink. The room had been dark, after all, because of the power cut. The fully intentional power cut.

"Did you see or hear...*anything*? Could anyone have put something in your mum's drink? Or did your mum say the wine tasted weird?" I felt slightly desperate, but I wanted to at least run through the theory.

Lottie's eyebrows knitted together. Her tongue darted out, to wet her lips. "No," she said after a pause.

I had a strong sense that she was lying, but I couldn't put a finger on why – maybe because she wouldn't meet my eyes.

"Devi," said Lizzie warningly, and I rolled my eyes, changing tack. Lizzie's comments while we were sneaking through the passageway came back to me.

"Is there any way someone *else* could have got into the dining room without you seeing? This is a huge house..." I trailed off, because the psycho hiding in the walls angle had been a joke. But what if it wasn't?

Lottie shook her head. "No one entered or left the room the

entire time. And…I don't know if any of you know, but there are secret passageways all over this house. The first Vanforte was a paranoid person and wanted lots of escape routes, lots of secrets just for him. I don't know where most of them are… Mum would never say. But I *do* know the dining room is one of the only rooms in the house where there *isn't* a passageway – no way in or out of the room other than the main door. There's no way for anyone to listen in…" She buried her head in her hands. "There were only the five of us in that room," she whispered, more to herself than to us.

It was wrong, but my mind was whirring – if Lottie had seen or knew something – and I thought she must have, based on the way she was acting – who would she be more willing to protect? Not Tate, they didn't seem close. So, either Douglas or Mr Vanforte… And from what I could tell, it had been her and her father against Mrs Vanforte.

"What do we do now?" I said, more to break the silence than anything else. I couldn't help but look at Lottie differently – had she been involved in killing her own mum? "There's no phone lines or anything – do you have neighbours anywhere near?"

"It's about an hour's to walk to the nearest village on a good day," said Lottie, her voice muffled because her head was still in her hands. She looked up, leaning backwards as she rubbed her chin. "But it would be worse in the current conditions, especially if we got lost on the way – which we might do, considering how deep the snow is."

"We can't do anything until morning," said Jayne. I jumped, because I'd half forgotten she was with us. "We need daylight. Half seven or so should be okay."

I checked my watch – seven hours away.

"Let's all stay in here tonight," said Lizzie, hugging herself and shivering. "We can sleep on the couches, keep together."

"There is no need for that," said a soft voice from the doorway.

We all jumped, turning round to find Charles Vanforte standing in the shadows. He was holding a candle and still in the outfit he'd been wearing for dinner. Unlike Lottie, he didn't look upset. He seemed completely calm.

Like he's putting on a show.

The words nestled in my mind. I hadn't liked him when I first arrived – he'd been eager to get rid of me, send me on my way. Why?

"You're all perfectly safe," he continued, and there was a smile on his face. It could have been comforting, in another scenario – but under these circumstances it was creepy. He'd read the room wrong – we were all tense. I bet the knowledge we were trapped with a murderer was circling everyone else's mind as well as my own. "I suggest you all go to sleep now – really, Lottie, I don't know what you were thinking waking them all up. They've got nothing to do with this."

"I wanted to check Lizzie's car…" said Lottie, getting to her feet. "Sorry," she added, the word a mumble.

Mr Vanforte sighed. "It's most unfortunate – my wife has died of a heart attack. I never realized she had such a weak heart – *most* unfortunate."

He repeated it was unfortunate, but he didn't seem sad about it at all. It occurred to me, suddenly, that a rich lady like Mrs Vanforte would have had a will. She'd said again and again that the money was *hers* and not Mr Vanforte's. Well, she was dead now, so I wondered what would happen to it all, and whether Mr Vanforte would get anything. Whether it would finally become his. Even if he *did* have more than £74 to his name, he wouldn't say to a couple of extra millions, would he?

"If it wasn't a heart attack, a coroner would know," I said suddenly, staring at Mr Vanforte and trying to see if his facial expression changed. It was too hard – in the light of the fire and the candle – to see.

"What does that mean?" said Mr Vanforte sharply. "What *exactly* are you trying to suggest? She died *of a heart attack*." He strode forward, his pale green eyes fixed on me, anger radiating off him with enough heat to melt the snow outside. "If you repeat anything else, it will be a slanderous *lie* – and I do not care if it is the middle of the night and what my wife would have wanted, and what the papers would say, I will throw you out into the snow and you can disappear for ever."

I took a step back, my heart hammering. His hands were balled into fists. I didn't think he would deck me, but the switch in his personality was terrifying. One moment he was all smooth and calm – the next he was basically threatening to kill me.

"Hey, calm down, Uncle Charles." Tate was leaning in the doorway, one hand holding a torch, which he was aiming directly at the ground, so it didn't do much in terms of lighting the room. I couldn't see his facial expression in the dim light, but his head was tilted. "I don't know *how* you're going to deal with this bad press without killing off three *more* people." Like Mr Vanforte, he didn't sound upset about Mrs Vanforte's death... And from what I could tell he'd just accused his uncle of killing his aunt. He'd made wild comments earlier to wind people up – he'd tried telling me there was a murderer in the house after I said I didn't scare easily – but I hadn't taken him seriously then. Now was different, though – there was an edge to his voice. And it definitely wasn't the time for jokes.

Mr Vanforte looked at him. I thought he was about to start screaming at him, but instead he just shook his head. He glanced at me, and I stared back as defiantly as I could. Then, without another word, he left the room, pushing past Tate to get by.

"Glad you got the fire going in here," said Tate smoothly, entering the room properly and clicking off his torch. "Nice and toasty."

"I'm going to bed," said Lottie, her voice shaky. She followed Mr Vanforte out. That was interesting. Was she leaving because Tate had arrived, meaning she couldn't stand the thought of being in the same room as him? Or because she wanted to speak to her father about Tate suggesting he was a murderer?

Tate perched in front of the fire on a footstool, warming his hands in front of the flames.

"What the hell did you mean about Mr Vanforte?" I asked. I didn't need to worry about upsetting Tate – he didn't seem at all affected by what had happened.

"Careful," whispered Lizzie to me. "He's got a gun." Her whisper was too loud because Tate picked up on it.

"I don't have a gun," he said, glancing back. His face was in shadow. "I, er…had a toy gun. It was a good replica – it shot water. Someone took it from my bedroom."

A *toy* gun? I didn't believe him. He wouldn't have been trotting around in a power cut with a *toy* gun.

185

By now, I was completely convinced someone had killed Mrs Vanforte, and that there was no way her death was natural. The coincidences were too much otherwise. I'd ruled out shooting because…well someone would have noticed if a murderer whipped out a gun and shot Mrs Vanforte. "Maybe the murderer took it as a backup in case they didn't have the opportunity to give Mrs Vanforte the poison." I was speculating more to myself than to Tate, but he seemed to think he was part of the conversation.

"It was a *toy*," said Tate, turning back to the fire. "But I do think one of the others killed her. We were all moving around, getting our food and stuff. Douglas kept trying to go to the door, like he wanted to leave. I'm fairly sure Uncle Charles was the only one to actually *speak* to Aunt Emily – I think they were having an argument, they kept whispering in the corner and it looked pretty heated. Actually no…Lottie spoke to Aunt Emily just after that. And then boom, Aunt Emily sat down, and suddenly slumped forward." He glanced at me. "My best guess is poison too." Like Lottie, I couldn't figure out his angle – why was he sitting in here with us? But it was like he could read my mind, because a second later he said, "I've just lit a fire in my bedroom, but it's absolutely freezing up there. Got to wait for it to warm up a bit, I think."

I was completely focused on him now. "And what happened after that?" I asked. I didn't trust him to tell me the truth – he seemed too smooth, too casual despite what had happened to Mrs Vanforte. A woman had literally died in front of him, and he didn't seem at all affected. And the comment he had made when I first met him was still ringing in my mind: *there might be a murderer in the house – it might even be me.* I'd thought it was just a flippant comment at the time – but maybe he knew something.

"Lottie sort of froze," he said. "Douglas immediately started saying he hadn't been anywhere near her – and Uncle Charles smiled."

There was a moment of ringing silence.

"He *what*?" gasped Lizzie.

My heart started hammering, but I wanted to finish questioning him. "And what did *you* do?"

He glanced back at me, and I couldn't read the expression on his face. After a pause he finally said, "I watched."

Extract of Transcript of Interview 7
Re: Death of Emily Vanforte
In Attendance – Inspector Adams (IA),
Devi Mistry (DM)

DM: Mr Vanforte reacted so weirdly to his wife's death. Why was he so insistent that it was a heart attack when it was so obvious there was something else going on? And according to that leak in the paper this morning, she had all the classic symptoms of poisoning by an overdose of that sleeping tablet with the super long name...chlorobenzo...flurodie... benate... You know what I mean. You should keep an eye on the people working on the case – make sure they don't let anything else slip.

IA: So...What do you think of Charles Vanforte?

DM: He's a prat. Implying he wanted to chuck me out into the snow if I didn't keep my mouth shut – and I was right, wasn't I? Mrs Vanforte *didn't* have a heart attack. But he wanted to punish me for telling the truth. I am a *child* – well, technically

I am, according to the law. Imagine saying you want to chuck a *child* out to freeze to death.

IA: It was his home, after all. And you had offended him.

DM: It's *not* his home, it was Mrs Vanforte's. Importantly, it's all bad press for him. He only ever cared about his image and now look at him and all the headlines. *Politician's Poison* and all sorts. And yeah, I get that it suggests he isn't the murderer – if he was so worried about his image, why would he get himself wrapped up in a situation where there were only four suspects, blah, blah, blah. But he can get them to close ranks, can't he? They're all connected to him somehow – though I guess Douglas is the weakest link. I reckon he's making them all stay silent. That's why the papers keep saying the police know nothing, even though it's been like a week since her death and, as you said, there's only four suspects.

IA: Has it ever occurred to you that the papers might not be correct?

DM: Nope. I'm pretty sure you haven't got a clue. How could *none* of the four of them have noticed Mrs Vanforte being poisoned? At least one of them is lying, to protect the killer. [Brief silence] You know, if the police can't figure out who did it, the murderer will go on their merry way quite happily and this whole thing will be forgotten, leaving them free to kill again. And if it *was* Mr Vanforte, even if there

189

is a nasty rumour about him having murdered his own wife, he'll be fine. People like him *always* get away with it, in the end.

IA: Then why are you so concerned for your own safety? Surely the murderer wouldn't want to harm you – that would point to them being the killer.

DM: They'll want revenge. Even if they have to wait years – and there's ways of making murder look like an accident. I've seen it in detective shows. I'm *telling* you, I *know* who did it – and they won't like that.

Jayne

We had seen Mr Vanforte, Lottie and Tate. But no Douglas. Which was odd – surely he'd want to be with his girlfriend?

We went back to our corridor in silence.

Devi hovered outside her bedroom. "I'm going to barricade myself inside," she said. "And if you hear me screaming, know that the murderer has come for me – so try your best to help, okay?"

"Mrs Vanforte died of a heart attack," said Lizzie, balling her hands into fists. "There's no… There's no…"

"There's a murderer," said Devi decisively. "And I reckon none of us should sleep until morning. We're not the targets – we weren't even supposed to *be* here." She sounded frustrated that we were tangled up in this. I knew how she felt. "But we should still be alert."

I nodded. Even though I headed back to my bedroom, sleep was the last thing on my mind. Ms Bromley might have a heart attack when she found out what had happened to Mrs Vanforte. She had been working for her for so many years. Longer than Mr and Mrs Vanforte had been married.

I wondered about going across to her cottage and telling her, but she would be asleep and it was news that could wait until morning. Plus, I was uneasy about going outside in the dark on my own. Devi was right. We needed to be alert.

It took a few tries, but I got my fire going again, warming my hands near the flames. As the heat licked over my fingers, I thought I heard faint…voices. I frowned, looking behind me. I was alone in my bedroom, obviously. I wondered if it was Lizzie and Devi talking. Except they had both gone to their own rooms.

I took a step closer to the fire, wishing it would warm me up faster. But as I turned towards the bed, someone started knocking on my door.

Devi

After the Murder

I placed a candle in the candleholder on the bedside table. I still didn't want to waste the battery in my phone or torch, and I figured that the risk of the candle toppling over in the middle of the night and burning me to a crisp was worth taking if it meant I didn't have to lie in the dark. I'm not a coward like Lizzie, I'm not afraid of the dark – but all the same…

I wouldn't be going to sleep, but I figured the warmest I would be was in the bed. The wind was howling, rattling at the windowpanes, and I burrowed down, pulling the sheets over my head and curling into a ball. I tried to be positive: at least the snow had stopped, and hopefully it wouldn't restart again – surely there couldn't be any flakes left in the clouds to fall?

But even as I lay there trying to keep my ears pricked, on alert for anything weird, I thought I heard scuffling. Maybe a mouse, I thought to myself.

"*Ow*," someone said.

Adrenaline shot through me, because unless the Bramble Estate was built on a radioactive waste site that made mice talk, that was definitely a human.

There was someone in my room with me.

I lay still in bed, my heart pounding, wondering if I should let the person know I was awake – maybe leap up and attack. Or else pretend to be asleep and hope they would just leave.

But I felt way too vulnerable in bed, with my sheets on top of me, weighing me down. Anyone could come along with a pillow to smother me, or a knife to stab me, and that'd be the end of one Devi Mistry.

My candle was still alight, flickering away. I tried to tilt my head up, to see the room, without making it too obvious that was what I was doing.

There was a light coming through the cracks of wood in the wall.

Someone was watching me from a secret passage we hadn't found.

I made my breathing regular, so they would think I was sleeping, but I was pretty sure they'd be able to hear my heart pounding, because it was basically the only thing I could hear. Why the hell was I being watched? *Who* was watching me? What could they possibly want?

I squinted again to see the light was still there. The person hadn't moved – they must still be staring, which made it even creepier. At least try to get into the room – do *something*. It seemed like they just wanted to watch me sleep.

I dug my nails into my palms as I tried to push past the fear roaring inside me. From a logical point of view, I knew it had to be Mr Vanforte, Lottie, Douglas or Tate watching me. Maybe they knew I was awake and this was part of some sick game to mess with me.

Screw that.

I acted quickly, sitting up and grabbing my torch before leaping from my bed, shrieking, "Get away from me, you pervert!"

The light disappeared at once and there came the sound of someone running heavily along the inside of the wall.

I started banging on the wall with my free hand so hard my palm started to sting. "Come back and fight me, you little coward." I was too wired to think sensibly, that *obviously* I couldn't fight anyone, but the words spewed out of me all the same. Either way it didn't matter: the noises had disappeared – whoever it was had gone, scurrying away like a rat in the wall.

I took a few deep breaths to calm myself. Jayne and I had looked around my room for hints there might be one of the peepholes somewhere. I'd searched this wall, but clearly I hadn't done a good enough job. Now, however, I had a frame of reference – the light had been near to the edge of the wall, halfway up.

I peered at the dark panelling, but it didn't look any different to the rest of the wall. Except – there was a darker patch. A black hole just big enough for me to look through – whoever had been looking through the peephole hadn't thought to close it before they ran off. I shone my torch over the space, but all I could see was a dusty, empty passageway.

There had to be a way inside. Jayne had described the entrances as discoverable by a bump or a ridge set into the wood. It took about fifteen minutes of careful searching for me to find the world's smallest indentation set into the wall, near the floorboards. I hooked my fingernail in and pressed. The wall gave a shudder and a narrow section slid back to reveal the passageway.

I stepped inside cautiously, ready to leap back if the wall decided it was going to slide shut and trap me inside. But the passageway remained open. I was at the end of it, the darkness stretching onwards.

I went in a little way, just to find the grate where the person had been looking through. I could see the outline of my four-poster bed. The peeping tom would have been able to see more, because my candle had been lit, shining on me.

As I examined the grate, something caught my eye: a sharp, rusty nail protruded from the wall and on the end was a piece of torn fabric – bright blue, the colour Douglas had been wearing for dinner, with a few splotches of blood staining the material. No wonder he had said *Ow*. He must have been stabbed by the nail.

At least I knew who'd been watching me. Pervert. I thought about charging down the passageway after him, to see where he'd gone – but he'd had a huge head start, because it had taken me so long to find the damned entrance.

Plus, there was a possibility he was not a pervert, but a murderer. Or a pervert *and* a murderer. People can be more than just one thing.

I stepped out of the passageway, staring at the enormous gap in the wall. No bloody way would I ever be able to go to sleep now. Hell, I didn't even want to stay in my bedroom on my own. Why hadn't I suggested holing up with Jayne and Lizzie in a cupboard?

Jayne and Lizzie. I should have asked them for backup before I explored the passage! But why hadn't they come running? They must have heard me yelling.

I slipped out of my room and hurried across the corridor, knocking on Jayne's door.

"Jayne," I whispered. I waited a second but there was no reply. "*Jayne*," I said, louder this time, knocking harder. The door creaked forward a fraction; it hadn't been fully closed.

I pushed it open, cautiously stepping inside.

The room was empty.

Devi
After the Murder

"What the hell?" I muttered. "Jayne?" I said at normal volume, half hoping she would suddenly pop up. But the silence remained, the only noise the howling wind. There was a tree outside of Jayne's window; the branches scraped against the glass, like something knocking to get inside.

I lost my head slightly, looking under the bedsheets even though there was no lump, and checking the bathroom and the wardrobe just in case Jayne had been one step ahead of me and already decided on the barricade-yourself-in-a-cupboard option.

But my search made it clear that Jayne was gone.

Had she decided to go for a walk through the house? I wouldn't put it past her – she seemed like the kind of person who decided they wanted to go traipsing around in the middle of the night.

I sighed – I would have to speak to Lizzie then, even though she was a total wimp and would be absolutely no help.

I went next door, holding up my torch to shine the thin beam of yellow around the room.

It was also empty.

"What the *hell*?" I said again, louder this time, my voice taking up the empty space.

I was alone.

Had they done a runner and left me? Had something horrible happened to them? There was no sign of a struggle – and I hadn't heard anything, and Lizzie wasn't the type to go quietly – she'd have screamed her little blonde head off.

Which meant they had disappeared willingly. Why had they left me? Where had they gone?

More importantly, what the hell was I supposed to do now? I went back to my room – and the passageway that lead off to the unknown.

A shiver went through me, because I was now properly alone. I couldn't just go wandering around – what if I came across someone in cahoots with Douglas? I was at a disadvantage because I hardly knew anything about the house. A cupboard I picked to hide in could have a false floor that would send me shooting down to a dungeon with spikes sticking out to impale me.

I bit the insides of my cheeks as I continued to stare at the passageway. I needed to make a decision. Instinct told me it would be stupid to stand around gormlessly, waiting for someone to decide I was going to be the next murder victim.

A small part of me still wanted to hide, but a bigger part thought it would be smarter to be proactive. The passageway led *somewhere* and curiosity was biting at me. Besides, I knew who my enemies were: I bet I could outrun Mr Vanforte and Lottie seemed the sort to simply roll over in a fight. Tate was more of a problem – especially if he still had that "toy" gun.

Right now, though, my biggest issue was Douglas. If he knew about this secret passageway, he could know about others. Plus, he had those gold knives. From the brief look I got before the lights went out, the edges had seemed dull with age – but I'm not a knife expert and they could probably still do serious damage.

On the other hand, if this was going to turn into a game of cat and mouse, I wanted to be the hunter.

My mind was made up. I would be going down the passageway to see where it went. But first things first: Jayne and Lizzie needed to know Douglas might be dangerous – and if he did manage to get me, I didn't want my death to go unexplained. Of course, I didn't *seriously* think he'd manage to off me – I'm too smart for that. But it was better to be prepared, just in case.

I tore a few sheets of paper from the notebook on the desk, grabbed a pen from one of the drawers, and wrote a note – IF I AM KILLED, DOUGLAS DID IT. DEVI XOXO.

I copied the note a few times, and left one on Jayne's bed, one in Lizzie's room, one tucked up in my bed, one in Lizzie's bathroom and one in a lampshade in the corridor. Then I left one final note out on the desk in my room, in plain view. There – if Douglas circled back, he would see and destroy the most obvious note, not realizing I'd hidden several more about the three bedrooms.

Genius, if you ask me.

Now I'd sorted that out, I clutched my torch, looking around the bedroom for anything I might be able to use as a weapon, if it came down to it, half wishing Douglas had played fair and thought to helpfully leave behind one of his knives. There was a small lamp by the bed. I took off the shade and unscrewed the light bulb, gripping the base. I could batter someone over the head with it if I needed to.

Feeling much more confident, I set off down the passageway.

Lizzie

The Night of the Murder

I paced my bedroom, still wearing my coat and wondering if I would ever be warm again. The wind outside howled and I listened to it rage, rattling against the windowpanes like it was desperate to get inside.

And just underneath the wind was a second noise…voices, whispering. I shook my head. I was just imagining things. Ghosts on the brain. The voices I was hearing were just a by-product of the wind, somehow. Because I was alone in my bedroom – and we were alone in the West Wing.

I stopped pacing though, straining my ears. The wind started to die down slightly – and the voices continued.

Coming from the walls.

"Oh *no*, no, no, no," I said, listening harder. I hoped I was imagining the voices, but they echoed around me, making goosebumps rise on my arms. I couldn't make out the words, but the noises were hissed – angry.

It was Emily Vanforte's ghost – she had died an unexpected death and she was still in the house. Furious, looking for revenge, having an argument with…someone.

I looked up slowly, half expecting a ghostly apparition to appear above me.

But I was alone. For a moment I was frozen, too scared to move. My entire body tensed as I tried to figure out what I should do. If I moved, would that alert the ghost to my presence? Would it turn its attentions to me? But if I stayed – then what?

The voices went silent for a second and I let out a sigh of relief. Perhaps it was over – but then they returned, the noise distorted. They seemed to be everywhere, echoing all around the room.

I couldn't stand it any more, so I grabbed my torch and edged towards the door, my heart thumping painfully as I pushed it open.

The corridor was pitch black, and I tiptoed to Jayne's room next door to mine. There was a thin beam of orange light filtering out from the gap between the door and the wooden floorboards. I knocked gently, praying she was awake.

It only took a moment for Jayne to open the door, looking confused. Her room was half lit by a crackling fire and was a lot warmer than mine, though she was still wearing her jacket.

I put my finger to my lips, warning her to not make a noise. Not that that was much of a concern; Jayne isn't the sort of person to chat. I gestured at her to follow me, leading her back to my bedroom.

"Listen," I breathed to Jayne. She stood in front of me with her eyebrows raised, waiting for me to explain what was going on. "Can you hear them? The voices?"

Jayne still looked confused, and I could immediately tell why. The room was quiet: the voices had finally stopped. Her confusion turned into a frown and I knew she was considering leaving. Even though I was glad that the voices had stopped, I still willed them to return – I wanted proof that someone else could hear them, that the ghost wasn't targeting me alone.

But then came a horrible muttering, droning on and on—

I strained my ears, only hearing snatches.

"It's what needed to be done…"

I couldn't tell if it was a man's voice or a woman's. It was too quiet.

Jayne's eyes went wide, her mouth falling into an O of surprise – probably because she hadn't believed I was telling the truth. But that didn't matter – all I cared about was that she could hear the voices too. Relief swept through me.

Her head moved left and right, like she was trying to pinpoint the location of the ghost. But then her eyes narrowed and a look of intense focus appeared on her face.

She crossed to the far wall, running her hands along it.

"It's coming from the passageway we went down earlier," she said.

Embarrassment made heat rise in my cheeks – in my panic I'd forgotten about the passageway. That made a lot more sense – but it didn't make me feel any better. Somehow, the idea that the noise was coming from the hidden passageway was even worse than if it was originating from somewhere in my bedroom. It was the idea of the unknown, the black space on the other side of the wall.

"The passageway runs past your bedroom as well," I pointed out. "Why couldn't you hear it?"

Jayne shook her head. "Your room is further along than mine," she said, which didn't give me an answer. Surely, she had heard *something*. "At least we know that the passageway leads to Charles Vanforte's study... Maybe we should go and take a look."

"No," I said at once. "We should just leave whatever it is alone... I mean, whoever it is."

"I'll go by myself, then," she said, taking her torch and stomping out into the corridor.

Surely she couldn't be serious. There might be anything lurking in the walls – we knew there was a murderer in the house. "The best thing to do is to leave them," I said in a small voice. I wanted to stay inside the bedroom, curled up in a corner, but I couldn't just let her go off on her own. I followed her out into the corridor, ready to run back as quickly as possible.

Jayne ignored me, opening the passageway and going inside before I had a chance to suggest we get Devi and decide what to do. I followed her, meaning to call out and tell her I was going to wake Devi, but then the passageway door slid back silently into place, blocking me off in the darkness. I briefly scrabbled against the wall, my heart pounding. I couldn't figure out how to open it again, and Jayne's light was already disappearing further down the passageway.

Leaving me in the dark.

I made a decision, stumbling after Jayne, hurrying so I could catch up with the rapidly disappearing light. The darkness was so thick it felt like someone had blindfolded me. The voices had stopped, the silence pressing at me on all sides.

"Wait," I whispered. "Jayne, wait for me!"

The light stopped moving.

I couldn't see Jayne properly in the darkness, but she huffed impatiently.

"Look," she whispered, pointing ahead. The darkness was broken up by a tiny light filtering through a peephole. "That hole wasn't open when we came down the passageway earlier – someone's been down here. Someone's been listening."

And my fears of ghosts returned, irrational though it might have been.

Jayne crouched low and looked through the hole. She was silent for a second, and I couldn't see her facial expression.

"What?" I breathed, not daring to speak too loudly, not now I knew how easily sound travelled down the passageway.

Jayne stood aside and gestured for me to take a look as well. I shook my head – I didn't want to see, I didn't want to know.

But she just stared at me, and I had no choice but to look through the hole and see what was inside the room.

Devi

After the Murder

The passageway was narrower than the one I'd walked through earlier with Jayne and Lizzie – and mustier as well, like it was poorly ventilated or rarely used. There were splotches of blood on the dusty floorboards. Douglas must have cut himself quite deeply on that rusty nail. Despite everything, I couldn't help but feel slightly pleased. Good. He deserved it, for spying on me.

I made my way carefully down the passageway, having to go sideways like a crab at one point before the walls widened slightly and I could walk normally again. Ahead of me there was a faint glow and I paused, worried it was Douglas's light.

But the glow stayed in the same place, though it shifted slightly. Like firelight.

I edged forward. My torch was flickering badly now, barely giving out any light at all. I wished I'd been smart enough to bring a spare candle and matches as a backup. I hadn't even thought about what might happen if I was left in the dark, having to find my way out through feel alone. I had my phone, of course, in my coat pocket, but it was probably on a few percentages of battery, about to die. I couldn't rely on it.

The firelight was coming through one of the weird peepholes dotted along the passageway. I peered through, switching off my torch so that I wouldn't be seen. On the other side, there was a room with a fire crackling – and someone sitting in front of it.

Their head was tilted upwards, to look at a portrait...of Emily Vanforte.

A shudder went through me as I stared at the half-lit painting. It was scarily accurate, right down to the formidable eyes boring into me. It must have been painted recently, because it captured the wrinkles at the corners of her eyes, and her greying hair.

As I crouched, I saw a few more splotches of blood on the passageway floor, glistening in the light of my torch. Douglas had been here recently. Listening. Watching.

The person was sitting in front of the portrait, and I couldn't tell who it was. They were wearing a thick coat, their form bulky, and the hood was up. They were holding what looked to be a few pieces of paper in their right hand, but they placed them down on a side table as they got to their feet to move closer to the portrait.

It couldn't be Lottie – she might be tall, but she isn't bulky. Douglas had been somewhere in the passageway wearing his bright blue shirt. Could he have got out, found a black coat to change into and positioned himself in front of Emily Vanforte's portrait...?

No, the person in front of me was either Tate or Mr Vanforte…

Something creaked in the corridor outside the room and the person exited through another door – they obviously didn't want to be seen.

I waited, but no one came into the room – and the person had left the papers on the side table. Curiosity burned through me as I searched the wall for an exit, running my hand over the smooth wood until I found a little ridge that I pressed. A panel slid back, leaving a gap just wide enough for me to squeeze through. I darted forward to grab the papers, hurrying back into the hidden passageway and quickly pulling the panel back into place.

My torch was barely giving out any light now, and I had to squint to read the squiggles on the pages, catching snatches.

I loathe her, with everything in my heart—

Things would be so much easier if she was dead—

I stopped, my heart pounding as I forced myself to start at the beginning of the page. I was reading a diary extract, that was basically a tirade against "her". The writer loathed "her", whoever she was.

I did everything she ever wanted me to, I stayed with her for the show. But she uses me. She needs to p̲a̲y̲.

The word pay was heavily underlined. The next page was filled with similar stuff, a tirade of epic proportions about how much the writer did for "her", spewing hatred until the last sentence, which was on a new line – maybe written a different day.

I gave my daughter £1000 for her university fund. I don't have the money, of course, but what can I do? She deserves—

"What the hell are you doing?" said a voice beside me. My heart stopped beating as I looked up from the extracts to find Douglas looming over me, holding up a torch. He had a bandage around his arm – and in his other hand he was holding a knife.

Devi
After the Murder

I jerked backwards, my eyes fixed on the knife. I'd been so fixated on reading what I'd found that I'd forgotten where I was.

"I've been planning this for *months*," he hissed, his hands tightening round the knife. "And you've already screwed things up for me—"

"Just…just calm down okay," I said. I felt weak and stupid and clueless and I had no idea what to do.

"I don't deserve Lottie, but I *needed* her, okay? And after this I was going to end it between us – I'm not a bad guy." His fingers played over the knife. I had no idea why he was telling me this – maybe he mistook my fear for judgement, as if I cared at all about his relationship with his girlfriend. "I'm *not* – I just have no choice. And now, you're going to come with me and we're going to have a little talk about the fact you're creeping through the walls. And keep quiet too, or else…" He held the knife up, his hand shaking – and it was either being told to keep quiet, or the fact that he was trembling just like me, that made something in me snap.

"Like hell I will," I said and I threw my head back and screamed. "HELP, DOUGLAS IS TRYING TO KILL ME, HE'S A MURDERER, HE'S A MURDERER."

Douglas's eyes went wide. "What the—?"

I swung my lamp stick like a bat, right at his nuts. He bent over, dropping his torch. I chucked my crap torch, grabbed his, and legged it past him, shoving the papers into my hoodie pocket as I ran.

I could hear Douglas groaning behind me as I ran along the passageway, almost tripping over myself. I had no idea where I was running to – and I didn't know whether there was anyone else around who might hear me. And if there was, would they help me, or silently listen to me get murdered?

I was panting, a stitch forming in my side, the light from the torch bobbing up and down to reveal the passageway stretching on, on, on.

I should have stayed in the room with the portrait of Emily Vanforte and risked running into the mysterious person. Now there was no way out – I was trapped in the walls with Douglas.

Extract of Transcript of Interview 7
Re: Death of Emily Vanforte
In Attendance – Inspector Adams (IA),
Devi Mistry (DM)

IA: Just to reassure you, Douglas has said he's not going to press charges. For, erm, assaulting him with a lamp.

DM: *Reassure* me? Did you not listen to what I just said? In *what world* would Douglas ever be able to press charges against *me* – he's the one who had the bloody *knife*! You know how ridiculous that would be—?

IA: Yes, sorry, completely agree. Let's change the subject. Those extracts you found, left by the person who was looking at the picture of Emily Vanforte. They are what appear to be diary entries – written by Charles.

DM: [Muttering] Douglas is a bloody twat, isn't he? [Normal volume] Yeah, I kind of figured the extracts were Charles's, though I didn't get a chance to really think about that bit until later. So the whole *I loathe her with everything I have...* Damn. He *really* didn't like her. I mean, it was obvious they didn't get *on...*

IA: And you don't know who left them there? Or *why* they were looking at the portrait of Emily?

DM: Nope. I mean...it had to be Tate, right? It couldn't have been Mr Vanforte, because why would he leave something like that about himself lying around? And it couldn't have been Douglas, because he was in the passageway. Tate's the only one left – the person was too bulky to be Lottie... And Jayne and Lizzie were together. But I guess Tate didn't mention diary extracts when you interviewed him? Otherwise you'd know about them. Except...why would he leave out diary extracts – where would he have got them from? Who did he want to find them? You know what I think?

IA: If it's okay, I'd like to go back to asking you more questions—

DM: —I think it's some sort of weird game they were playing. This *whole* thing is *weird*. But if you're looking for motivation, that diary extract gives you a seriously good clue.

IA: This is an odd case, I must say.

DM: You know what? I'd say it's pretty straightforward... Why are you smiling? I'm not making a joke.

IA: Devi...

DM: Yeah, yeah, I'll carry on with my bloody story.

Lizzie

The Night of the Murder

The peephole in the passageway running to Mr Vanforte's office was just large enough for me to peer through with one eye. Jayne remained tensed beside me as I looked through into a large sitting room with a lit fire. Charles Vanforte was pacing, while Lottie stood by the flames.

I couldn't be sure, but from the tension in the air they seemed to have been arguing. Which was odd, considering Mr Vanforte's wife and Lottie's mother had just died, and from what I could tell the pair of them had got on better with each other than with Mrs Vanforte.

"That front page of the draft article was the main bit," said Mr Vanforte. "I can't *believe* you were so careless."

"I can still go back," Lottie was saying, her voice shaking. "We can search for it – I think I only dropped it right outside her office—"

"It's too late now," Mr Vanforte snapped.

I held my breath, looking back at Jayne. She edged forward and slid the wood panel partially shut.

"So they don't see our light," she whispered. "We can still hear them." She pressed a finger to her lips.

"But surely this information is available online anyway – it might have come out no matter what—" Lottie sounded like she was on the verge of tears.

"The article that came out was nowhere near as damning. I used my connections to make sure of it," said Mr Vanforte. "But, of course, even the draft doesn't have the whole story… And you're *sure* there was nothing else in that folder that might…might suggest I don't have as much money as I want people to think?"

"Yes," replied Lottie. "I mean…I only looked quickly. I was so worried about being caught… But, Dad…why does it matter if Mum knew you were struggling with money?"

"It's the sort of thing she'd lord over me," said Mr Vanforte, his voice wary. "She kept the draft article as insurance, just in case she could hang that over my head. But she thought all my money issues were sorted – and the fact they're not is the secret she was hinting about all day, it *had* to be. The one she was going to reveal at dinner, then tell the world about – the press would have loved it, especially with my whole policy on getting responsible with money."

"But…" Lottie's voice got softer, more hesitant. "But that doesn't matter now, right?"

"What do you mean?" snapped Mr Vanforte.

"Well… Her will. Everyone knows she's leaving you ten million pounds…"

"And you the rest," said Mr Vanforte, his voice thoughtful. "To make sure we're taken care of. She did love us, in her own way."

A shiver went through me, that they were so callously talking about wills and money when Mrs Vanforte had only just gone cold.

"So you'll be okay," said Lottie, sounding like she was trying to reassure herself. "The issue of your debts will go away. The secret doesn't matter. None of the secrets matter... Not even the one about..."

She trailed off. I guessed Mr Vanforte must have given her a look that made her shut up. My breathing was coming out in sharp gasps as I worked through what we had just heard – the secret Mrs Vanforte had been hinting at was about Mr Vanforte's money problems. Mr Vanforte had thought she was going to expose him.

Then she died – and Mr Vanforte was set to inherit millions of pounds.

"Did you hear that?" asked Mr Vanforte suddenly. "That... scuffling noise?"

I looked at Jayne, feeling confused as I leaned back from the peephole and strained my ears for a scuffling sound. There was silence from the sitting room, and all I could hear was my own breathing as I waited to find out what they had heard.

Then suddenly Charles Vanforte was staring through the partially open peephole, straight at me.

I screamed, as Jayne grabbed my arm and yanked me forward. In our panic, we didn't go back towards the bedrooms – we went the opposite way, towards Mr Vanforte's study.

Behind us, there was a scrabbling noise, like Mr Vanforte was trying to find a way into the wall. I hoped there wasn't an entrance into the passageway from that room, because if there was and Mr Vanforte got in with us...

I didn't know what would happen, but I didn't think it would be good.

"Hurry *up*," Jayne said to me, pulling at my arm. I didn't point out that she was the one slowing us down, not me – I might have been a slow runner, but adrenaline was pumping through me and I wanted to *sprint* to safety. But I couldn't because Jayne was in the way – she was too tall for the low passageway, and because she was having to bend over to move along she was slowing us down.

Ahead was the end of the passageway, leading to Mr Vanforte's study. As Jayne attempted to open up the room I looked behind me and then immediately wished I hadn't. The darkness was so thick I was worried it would swallow me whole.

"Hurry up!" I moaned, but instead of saying, *Yes, Lizzie, I'm working as fast as I can,* Jayne swore.

"The door's stuck or something," she said, and it was the first time I'd ever heard panic in her voice, which made *me* want to panic even more.

I glanced behind us again, half expecting a monster to lurch out of the darkness – or worse still, for Charles Vanforte to appear.

But then Jayne got the hidden door open and we went through, the wall sliding shut behind us.

Mr Vanforte's study was lit by a ghostly moon and I took a deep breath. Bending over, relief flooded through me at the fact we were free, we'd made it out of the passageway. Mr Vanforte and Lottie hadn't followed us – maybe they couldn't figure out a way in.

"What happened in here?" said Jayne. The study had been a mess before – now it looked like it had been ransacked. Drawers had been taken out of the desk and flung everywhere, the chair had been knocked over, the windows were open, and freezing air was blasting into the room.

"I don't know – let's just *go*," I said, making my way towards the door. Mr Vanforte might not have followed us through the passageway, but maybe he knew where it led. He could be heading to us as we were speaking.

"These weren't here before," said Jayne, picking up yellowing papers from a stack on Mr Vanforte's desk.

"Just take them and let's *go*," I said, heading towards the door – Jayne seemed to have forgotten that we weren't safe yet, but my words jerked her back to reality. She went past me, folding the papers up and sticking them into the pocket of her jacket. Her pace quickened into a light jog, and then a run – but even as we went, I wondered where we were running *to*. This was the Vanfortes' house, after all. Our only option was to flee into the snow.

Yet still, we ran, turning down corridors left and right and left and—

I smashed into Jayne, who had slammed into someone sprinting the other way.

Devi

After the Murder

I found an exit from the walls that had been left open – probably the one Douglas had used to enter the passages – and was happily barrelling through along the corridors and internally screaming at the fact that Douglas had *pulled a knife on me* when I literally ran into Jayne and Lizzie.

"Where the *hell* were you?" I said, once I had got past the pain of colliding into them.

"No time to talk," said Lizzie. "We were running from Mr Vanforte and Lottie—"

I wasn't going to be outdone. "Yeah, well I was running from Douglas and he had a *knife*—"

"I don't know what you're talking about," said a voice from behind me. I whirled around to find Douglas standing before me. He had silently come up in the darkness. "I found you in a passageway and you shrieked like you thought I was a ghost and ran."

"I smacked you in the nuts with a lamp first," I reminded him. He had lost the knife and was clutching my old torch.

"What is going on?" said another voice. Mr Vanforte and Lottie appeared from a different corridor. Mr Vanforte's eyes flicked from Jayne to Lizzie to me.

"*Why* are the three of you running around screaming on the night of my wife's death?" asked Mr Vanforte. "Have some compassion, for goodness' sake." But instead of sounding upset he was snappy.

"He was peeping in my bedroom," I said, pointing at Douglas. "From one of those secret passages that are all over this house."

"She's lying," said Douglas quickly. "I knew the second I saw her that she was a liar." But his eye twitched slightly, his nostrils flaring – *he* was lying, and he…didn't like having to do it. Did the guy with a knife have a conscience? Who cared – he had a *knife*.

"Oh, Dougie, you're hurt," said Lottie, squeezing past me and Jayne to get to Douglas. She looked at the bandage on his arm. Douglas jerked away from her, wincing as he did so, as if he didn't want her to touch him. She stood for a second looking up at him, confusion on her face like she didn't understand what had just happened.

"It's interesting, isn't it, that there are so many secret passages about this house," said Mr Vanforte, ignoring Douglas. "I don't know about many of them, but it appears others do. For example, I didn't realize there was a passage leading past the room Lottie and I were in just now. I'd be very interested to hear what you think you heard, Jayne and Lizzie."

Jayne and Lizzie weren't stupid enough to reply, but I looked at them with wide eyes to let them know they absolutely had to tell me later.

Mr Vanforte must have caught my expression, because he tilted his head at me. "What were you saying, Devi? About Douglas?"

"I followed Douglas into the passageway after he spied on me," I said. "And he showed up and attacked me with a knife."

Douglas chortled, though the laugh didn't reach his eyes. He swallowed hard. "I have no idea *where* this knife you're talking about can have come from."

"What's going on?" Tate appeared from behind Douglas, looking at us all.

"Of *course* you're here," said Douglas. "Of course you are – have you literally spent your entire life lurking?"

"Why did you have a knife?" I said to Douglas, because people seemed to be trying to get me off track, and I wouldn't be distracted. "In fact, why were you *hiding* knives in the room I'm supposed to be staying in?"

Douglas looked at me, and I thought I saw something like an apology in his eyes as he said, "I have no idea what you're talking about."

I looked at Jayne and Lizzie helplessly, because it was just my word against Douglas's.

"Tate had a gun earlier," said Lizzie suddenly, her face going red like she couldn't believe she'd had the nerve to speak up.

"For the last time, it was a *toy*—" began Tate, but there was a flush to his cheeks. He was flustered, his eyes darting towards Douglas.

Lottie's eyebrows were furrowed as she looked at Douglas, then me. "Knives?" she said quietly to him, like it had some sort of special significance.

"She's *lying*," said Douglas again, his voice turning pleading. "Please, Lottie, who are you going to believe – your boyfriend, or some random stranger?"

"He's right," said Mr Vanforte calmly. "We know Douglas. We do not know Devi – which means it's clear who to believe here."

"What did the knives look like?" Lottie said to me. She looked confused, uncertain. I realized this was my moment to convince her, to get her on my side.

"They had gold hilts…" I said, trailing off because I didn't remember that much about them. I had only caught a glimpse and besides – they were *knives*. Surely she knew what a knife looked like. "They were being stored in the Blue Room, where your mum told me to stay – under the loose floorboards."

"It's true," said Douglas suddenly, his eyes wide.

I gaped at him, not understanding where the sudden change of heart had come from. I couldn't believe he was actually confessing.

But he wasn't looking at me. He was looking at Tate, whose eyebrows were furrowed together as he stared back.

"Someone sent me a note saying they were going to kill me if I came tonight," Douglas said, his voice earnest. "And, if I needed proof, I should look under the floorboards in the Blue Room that Dev's in. I thought it was a joke…someone obsessed with the Vanfortes or something… But when I went to the Blue Room, I found *knives*."

"It is *Devi*," I started, before I actually processed what he was saying. I knew it was stupid, but sometimes my mouth has a hard time listening to my brain. "Hang on," I said. "Someone threatened to *kill you* for coming tonight and you *showed up*? You didn't like, hide in a bunker somewhere?"

Douglas turned to look at me. "I thought it was a joke," he repeated. "I don't know how the knives got there, or who put them there or why they threatened *me*."

"But this doesn't change the fact that *you had a knife and you tried to use it on me*," I said, because Mr Vanforte looked grim, and Lottie was clutching at Douglas's arm and trying to hug him, even though he kept pushing her away, and Tate had his arms folded as he frowned. They all seemed to have forgotten the key bit of information I'd told them, focusing instead on Douglas's proclamation.

"Why would someone want to kill you?" said Jayne, her voice quiet.

Everyone jumped, turning to look at her. Her dark eyes were fixed on Douglas.

"What?" he said.

"Why would someone want to kill you?" Jayne repeated calmly, her face and voice devoid of emotion.

"I don't know," spluttered Douglas. "That's what *I* want to find out—"

"But you're not dead," I pointed out, once more speaking without thinking. "*Emily Vanforte* is dead."

"I didn't kill her," said Douglas at once, his voice vicious. Any hint of apology or that he was torn in two about accusing me of something I hadn't done was gone.

I took a step back, holding my hands up – I had struck a nerve.

"You will not accuse Douglas of anything," said Mr Vanforte. His face was half lit, his voice soft. "You will go back to the bedroom we've so kindly offered to you for the night, and you will *stop* with all your lies—"

"I'm *not lying*—" I started.

"I'll walk them back," said Tate suddenly.

"I don't need to be *walked back*," I said, but Tate shook his head at me, a tiny movement that I was sure only I was supposed to see. He strolled away, his hands in his pockets, and I looked at Jayne and Lizzie, not knowing what to do.

I trusted him as much as I trusted any of this messed-up family, and that was not at all. But I was sure he was trying to tell me something.

Jayne followed him without hesitation, and Lizzie scuttled after her – clearly she'd decided to appoint Jayne as her protector at some point. So I went as well, because no way was I going to stay back to hang around with the boy who had threatened to stab me, his girlfriend, who didn't care that he had threatened to stab me, and his girlfriend's dad, who *also didn't care that his daughter's boyfriend had threatened to stab me.*

Tate took us back to the West Wing. Jayne went into her bedroom and Lizzie silently followed, looking back at me and jerking her head, her meaning clear: the three of us would be staying together from now on. An excellent idea if we were going to survive the night. Maybe she had a bit more street smarts than I'd initially thought.

Tate lingered, though, so I didn't immediately follow them

225

in. "You should have stayed out in the snow," he said, folding his arms as he looked down at me, his dark eyes searching my face.

"What is *wrong* with you all?" I asked.

"Look, Devi, I don't know you, you don't know me. And I think maybe if we'd met somewhere else we would have got on quite well." He lowered his voice. "But you're giving the impression you won't, er…keep quiet about stuff you've seen tonight."

"Good," I said. "That's exactly the impression I want to give off."

Tate grimaced. "Uncle Charles is a very private guy. He won't like that."

I stared at him. "Are you trying to warn me about him?"

He looked like he was on the verge of saying something else, but then he shook his head. "It doesn't matter." And, after being so incredibly helpful, he turned on his heel and walked away. "Goodnight," he said over his shoulder.

I shook my head as I went into Jayne's room. Jayne was sitting on the bed, watching as Lizzie paced back and forth, her hands balled into fists. She looked like she was on the verge of tears.

"The police will be here in the morning, won't they?" she asked as she came to a stop. She looked from me to Jayne. "And we can tell them… Everything, right? About how Mrs Vanforte was acting and what the family was saying to each other and… Why are you looking like that?" she said to me.

It's one of my few weaknesses: I can't hide what I'm thinking. My face was probably showing the mixture of deep irritation and impatience that I was feeling. "Who gives a crap about what we're going to say to the police in the morning?" I said, the words coming out snappier than I meant. But I was on edge and hyper alert and that meant I'd lost what little tact I'd normally have. "The four of them – they've all got links to each other. They all know each other – they'll want to protect each other. So even if they all weren't involved in murdering Mrs Vanforte, they might want to protect whoever did. And we're three loose ends. So, right now, all I care about is staying *alive* until morning."

Lizzie
That Night

Silence followed Devi's speech. My entire body was trembling and I looked at Jayne, but she just shrugged.

"And how do you suggest we stay alive?" I asked as I sank to the floor. "Apart from keeping together for safety."

"New tactic," said Devi. "From now on, we have each other's backs – we stick with each other. We don't go wandering off. And we can take it in turns to sleep. One of us is always awake and keeping watch. And, when morning comes, we are getting the hell out of here."

Jayne frowned as she shifted on her bed and felt something. She reached behind her and pulled out a note. "What's this?" she asked, holding it up. I squinted at it – it said something about murder and Douglas.

Devi shrugged. "My contingency plan in case Douglas got me. We need to be smart here, if we're going to stay alive.

Speaking of which –" she turned to me – "have you got your phone?" she asked.

I frowned and nodded. It still had a fair bit of charge left, though of course with the power gone and no signal there wasn't much point to it beyond its strong torch beam that would probably drain all the remaining battery.

"Hand it over," commanded Devi.

I did as she said, feeling confused – was she planning to somehow turn it into a weapon? But instead, she immediately started blasting music.

"Er – is now really the time for that?" I said, having to bellow over the noise.

Devi placed my phone directly below the place we knew the peephole was hidden.

"Try listening in now, you twats," she said victoriously to the wall. I raised my eyebrows, feeling rather impressed. "Now, tell me why you two abandoned me in the middle of the night."

We filled Devi in on what had happened, explaining the voice we heard in the passageway, the conversation we'd overheard between Mr Vanforte and Lottie, about how he thought the secret Mrs Vanforte had been planning to reveal was that he was bankrupt, and that they thought they were included in the will.

Jayne pulled out the new papers she'd shoved in her pocket. "I also grabbed these from Mr Vanforte's study – they weren't there before... Or else we missed them because they were buried under other papers." She spoke as her eyes scanned over the pages. "They're...emails. From Mr Vanforte to...a friend, I guess. This one's asking for a loan – he says he's basically bankrupt and needs money fast. And the friend has replied saying he knows Mr Vanforte won't be able to repay a penny, and why doesn't he try a loan shark instead. Or else, erm…steal more money from his wife."

Devi whistled. "Okay, so Mr Vanforte's definitely broke. But more importantly…I think I might have found the article Mr Vanforte and Lottie were talking about – she dropped it and I picked it up. It was a longer draft of an article that I think was later printed – with the more damning details deleted – about a construction company Mr Vanforte owned going bust. It talked about corruption and bankruptcy – maybe in relation to him." She hesitated. "And earlier I found a bank statement in Mrs Vanforte's office, which showed Mr Vanforte has £74 in his current account. If he's broke and he's in Mrs Vanforte's will… that's a real motive for murder."

The words hung in the air.

"And the emails between Edward Smith and Noviroam…" I began, speaking slowly as I tried to order my thoughts. I had only been half listening when Devi was monologuing about the emails when we originally found them, because I'd been so eager to leave Mr Vanforte's study and stop snooping. But it was coming back to me now. "Talking about a lethal amount of… presumably drugs. If Edward Smith is actually Mr Vanforte then he'd have a way to murder Mrs Vanforte…"

"But how would he have paid for the drugs?" asked Devi, sounding slightly frustrated. "If he's broke…"

"He could have stolen from Mrs Vanforte," said Jayne quietly. "That's what his friend suggested he do in his email to him."

I took a deep breath. "Okay," I said. "But what about the

death threat Douglas received? *Mrs Vanforte* died, not him."

Devi shrugged. "Douglas's whole story doesn't make sense – I can't work out how it connects with everything else, but he's definitely hiding something." She bit her bottom lip, shaking her head. "You know what…? Let's just get through the night, okay? And worry about all this when we're tucked up and safe – anywhere but here."

I nodded, as Devi started dragging the desk chair across the room, propping it under the door handle then standing back to admire her handiwork. "Even if it doesn't work as a barricade, if anyone tries to get into this room, we'll know," she said. She turned off the music playing from my phone, and silence fell. "And we keep each other alive, okay? Until we're safe with the police, we stick together. Deal?"

I swallowed, then nodded. Even though I'd only met these girls a few hours ago, I trusted them both deeply. We *were* in this together.

"Deal," said Jayne.

"Good," said Devi. "Right, which one of you wants to take the first shift?" Before either of us had a chance to respond, she continued, "You know what, I'll do it. Get some rest, Jayne, I'll wake you in two hours. Then Lizzie can take the shortest shift. It'll be morning before we know it."

"Why am I taking the shortest shift?" I mumbled, as I crawled onto the bed, beside Jayne. It was big enough to fit the three of us comfortably, but Devi had sat cross-legged in the armchair beside the fire, warming her hands.

Devi didn't bother to reply to my question, but I didn't need her to. I obviously didn't know Devi and Jayne that well, but out of the three of us I was clearly the one who needed the most looking after, something I loathe about myself. I want to be fiercely independent, someone who can survive anything without getting scared, or continue on boldly despite the fear… But that's not me.

"Night," said Jayne after a pause. She curled up under the blankets, and a few seconds later her breath was steady.

"That's a gift, that is," said Devi, nodding at Jayne. "I'd never be able to fall asleep that quick – in fact I don't even think I'll need to come off watch. I don't think I'll be sleeping tonight at all."

"Me neither," I muttered, sitting up in the bed. I was too wired to go to sleep.

"I just keep thinking about Mrs Vanforte," said Devi, staring at the fire. "How she's in a room in this house somewhere… dead. It's morbid to say so, but right now all I can think about is how I…I can't imagine it. I've never been able to wrap my head around death. Around the fact a person is just gone for ever and you'll never speak to them again." She snorted. "I've never even seen a dead body."

"I have," I said without thinking, then immediately wished I'd kept my mouth shut.

But it was too late, the words were hanging around in the open. I had to explain. "My dad. You know, he died a few years ago, of a heart attack. Right in front of me."

Devi was silent for a second. "I know it doesn't help, but… I'm sorry." She gave a hollow laugh. "I used to hate when people told me they were sorry. Sorry doesn't change anything. It doesn't bring them back. My best friend…" She stopped speaking, her voice getting thicker. "This is stupid. Why are we even talking about it?"

"Because it helps," came Jayne's soft voice, making me jump. Okay, maybe she *hadn't* gone to sleep.

Devi gave a sniff – was she crying? In the half-light, I couldn't tell.

I wondered what Natasha and Hannah would say if I could tell them what was going on and how scared I was. Texting them was always something of a game of chance. Would they reply? Maybe a message now would sound interesting enough to grab their attention. The thing about Natasha and Hannah is that they really are good friends. They're *best* friends – to each other. They went to primary school together, and so when I met them in high school they were already an inseparable pair. They let me join their group, but whenever we had to pair up for class projects, they always chose each other, and I always ended up alone. If we went on school trips and the coach only had rows of two, I ended up sitting across the aisle, acting like I didn't care.

I've always been the third wheel, the hanger-on. But Devi and Jayne didn't even know me at all, and yet I felt a deep kind of connection with them I hadn't felt with anyone else before. *We were in this together.* We were a team, and we were going to survive.

The next thing I knew, Jayne was shaking me awake for my shift to keep watch, so I must have fallen asleep at some point. I felt disorientated – it was still dark outside. I checked my watch – half past six.

I was only about ten minutes into my shift, though, when someone started knocking on the door.

46

Devi
The Morning After

Jayne was on her feet at once, crossing the room to remove the chair I'd used as a barricade in front of the door.

"Wait," I said, unplugging and picking up a lamp, its weight reassuring in my hands. It had worked well as a weapon against Douglas, and even though I highly doubted the murderer would politely knock before entering the room, I wanted to be on the safe side. "Okay, go," I said, as Jayne pulled the chair back and opened the door. I tensed, waiting for someone to come bursting in with their knife/gun.

"Hello," said Mr Vanforte. He was holding up a torch, shining it at each of us in turn. "It'll be daylight soon. There's still a few flurries of snow but we're gathering in the kitchen to make a plan to get help."

"Great," I muttered, because honestly at that point I didn't care if the sky opened up and dumped all the snow ever to fall in one giant pile – I was going to be getting out of that house no matter what. We'd made it to morning – we were on the home stretch. I'd ski to safety if I had to.

"I'd like to speak to you about what happened last night," said Mr Vanforte, turning to look at me. Not Jayne and Lizzie, even though they were the ones who had actually overheard him talking to Lottie about stealing from Mrs Vanforte's office and how they were both included in her will. Did he know that I had *seen* Lottie stealing from the office? And picked up the draft construction article?

"Go on then," I said, folding my arms. I was still clutching the lamp – his eyes flicked down to it and then back to me.

"No, not here," he said, his voice silky smooth. "Alone. But of course, just across the corridor. I know how…jumpy you get." One more eye flicker to the lamp, as if that proved his point.

"If you try to attack me, I will fight back," I said, swinging the lamp to show I meant business.

"And, er…you'd have to get past me and Jayne too," said Lizzie with squeak. I rolled my eyes, because she sounded so terrified it was clear she was not a threat. But still, the sentiment was nice, I had to give her credit for that.

"Don't be silly," said Mr Vanforte, his voice disparaging. He led the way across the hall, to the Blue Room, closing the door behind us. "I don't know what Jayne and Lizzie think they heard last night," he said, examining his fingernails as he dived right in to the conversation. "And I don't know what they told you – but they're wrong."

I thought about keeping my mouth shut. I thought about faking ignorance, that Jayne and Lizzie hadn't told me anything.

I thought about reassuring him that even though I *did* know that Lottie had snuck into Mrs Vanforte's office and tried to take the article, I wouldn't ever say anything.

They were all the sensible options.

But he was still focused on his fingernails, like even though he viewed me as a threat I still wasn't important enough to look at.

I was so sick of people in this house treating me like I didn't matter. So I decided to show him exactly how much respect he should give me, if he wanted his secrets kept quiet.

"I really don't know much," I said sweetly. "I just wonder *why* Lottie was rooting around Mrs Vanforte's office a few hours before her death? Who put her up to it?" I stopped myself from going further, from twisting the knife in that his net worth was likely lower than mine, which was *really* saying something. I had already said enough to get him to stop looking at his fingernails. There was a flash of anger in his snake-green eyes as he stared at me, gone the next second like it was hidden behind a mask. He went back to smiling pleasantly and somehow that was worse – his wife had just died. He shouldn't have been able to smile so easily.

Although, there was a very good chance his wife was dead because he had killed her less than twelve hours ago.

"I have no *idea* what you're trying to imply," said Mr Vanforte. His nostrils flared, and any pretence that he was being nice was dropped. "If you leave this house and spread anything about me or my family…" His voice was low. "Well, it won't end well for you."

"Are you threatening me?" I asked.

He went back to smiling. "Glad we're on the same page."

"And what happens if I *tell* everyone you threatened me?" I said, folding my arms.

"Well, it's like Douglas and that knife of his," said Mr Vanforte pleasantly. "Who are people going to believe? You or me?"

Extract of Transcript of Interview 7
Re: Death of Emily Vanforte
In Attendance – Inspector Adams (IA),
Devi Mistry (DM)

IA: [Papers shuffling] According to my notes from
my interview with Charles, during that conversation
with you he simply wanted to make sure you were
okay. He said he was worried the stress of the night
had taken a toll on you.

DM: He's lying. Funny, isn't it, that he picked on me
out of the three of us – even though Jayne and Lizzie
were the ones who actually heard the conversation
between him and Lottie.

IA: Why do you think that was?

DM: He thought I was the biggest threat to him in
terms of actually going out and running my mouth
about what they'd heard.

IA: The issue I'm having here, Devi, is *both* Douglas
and Charles have called *you* a liar. Douglas has said
again he did not chase you down the corridor with
a knife—

DM: I told you about the knives in my bedroom, under the floorboards.

IA: Yes, but I have no proof they were actually there. And if they were, there's no proof they belonged to Douglas.

DM: Look, you wanted to know what happened the night I went to the Bramble Estate – I'm *telling* you.

IA: This is a bit of a he said, she said situation.

DM: That's *utter* crap. It's a he said, *we* said situation.

Lizzie
The Morning After

Devi and I gathered in the kitchen with Mr Vanforte, Lottie and Douglas. Jayne went off to tell Ms Bromley what had happened – I didn't know where Tate was. He didn't strike me as the kind of person who liked hanging around with other people, but I couldn't imagine wanting to be alone after last night. I'd be terrified I was going to be the next victim.

The snow was falling thick and fast again. Devi was muttering something about how rich people always kept skis, and I couldn't help but look at her oddly, because was now really the time to find a hill and go skiing?

"It looks like we're going to have to wait until the snow stops properly before we go for help," said Lottie. She was wearing dull grey trousers and a matching grey top, and was sitting next to Douglas. She looked at him as she spoke, possibly hoping he would agree with her. Instead, however, Douglas was focused on chowing down on a sandwich he'd insisted she make him.

"There was a bit more this morning, and there's still a few flurries now. We don't want to be walking only for a blizzard to start up," she continued.

Douglas reminded me of Mr Vanforte. Both of them seemed to either ignore Lottie, or talk down to her. And yet she appeared almost desperate for their approval – which was weird, because before yesterday I would have assumed she had everything she could possibly want. She was rich, and beautiful and *should* have been full of confidence – but she wasn't.

Mr Vanforte was sitting in the corner of the kitchen, his eyes flicking from Lottie to Douglas – to Devi and me. This morning he was wearing a long coat over another suit.

"Nope," said Devi, shaking her head in response to Lottie's suggestion that we needed to wait to be sure of the weather. "I am not having it – there is a road underneath all that snow, and I'm going to be following it to freedom."

"Well then you'll get lost and die," snapped Douglas, looking up from his sandwich. "Which would be a *big* shame." He sounded sarcastic, but surely that couldn't be right, because it would be an awful comment to make. "We should wait," he continued, his voice final. "It's slowing down now – let's just hold on a few more hours and then we can all go."

"Where's your *urgency*?" asked Devi. "We need an…an ambulance or something. I mean, I know Mrs Vanforte's dead or whatever and she's past being saved, but her body's still in the house somewhere just…"

Rotting. The word came into my mind unbidden. I was being ridiculous of course – a body in a cold room would basically be preserved – it wouldn't have started decomposing or anything, I knew that. And yet the word was still lodged into my mind.

"Not *all* of us are going," said Mr Vanforte. "I'm staying right here – I'm not leaving Emily alone in this house."

"You won't be," said a crabby voice from the doorway. "I'll be here too."

Ms Bromley hobbled into the room, with Jayne by her side. She looked much more withered than she had yesterday, hunched over her walking stick. Jayne helped her to a seat, and as she sat down she placed a shaking hand on Jayne's arm, giving it a squeeze.

Relief went through me at the sight of Jayne. I hadn't realized how dependent I'd become on her steady, practical presence until she had gone, leaving me with the drama and chaos of the Vanforte family and Devi, who seemed to enjoy fuelling it as much as possible.

"You can't stay alone in the house," said Devi, and she looked over at Mr Vanforte. There was an awkward silence, Devi's meaning clear. Ms Bromley wouldn't be safe alone with Charles Vanforte and the dead body.

"I hope you're not suggesting what I think you are," said Mr Vanforte, tilting his head.

"I'm not going to be alone," said Ms Bromley quietly. "Jayne's staying with me, aren't you, Jayne?"

Jayne looked startled, but nodded.

"What about Ms Bromley's car?" asked Lottie suddenly. "Is that still working?"

Ms Bromley shook her head. "The engine's been scrambled," she said. "Jayne already checked for me."

"Were there footprints by the car?" said Devi urgently. "Did you notice what size they were?"

"No footprints except mine," said Jayne. "It's snowed – that might have covered them."

Ms Bromley shook her head slowly as she looked at Mr Vanforte. "I spent hours cooking that dinner," she said. "Mrs Vanforte insisted… She *insisted* that everything had to be perfect." Her voice caught. "She did not die of a heart attack, Charles Vanforte. I know it – you know it. I just can't understand…" A tear rolled down her cheek. "Tate has always stayed out of my way, I've only had terrible encounters with Douglas, Lottie will just do whatever you tell her to and… and *you*…"

The room was deathly silent. Mr Vanforte's eyes were locked on Ms Bromley, his lips pressed together.

"It was a heart attack," said Mr Vanforte, his voice cold and final; that would be the end of the conversation. But Ms Bromley was still staring at him like she had never seen him before.

"My landline was cut," said Ms Bromley suddenly. "I don't know when – I only noticed it yesterday evening when I got home. I last used my home phone two days ago."

A shiver went through me, as Devi's head snapped up. "Everything's so well thought out – to cut this house off from the outside world. It's obviously proof someone *planned* for all this to happen – to kill Mrs Vanforte – and they might have more plans—"

"Let's just focus on getting help," said Mr Vanforte through gritted teeth.

"I for one suggest Devi," said Douglas. "She's got an impeccable sense of direction – would *never* get lost in the snow."

Devi rolled her eyes at the dig. I could tell she was trying to work it out – one of the Vanforte lot would need to go, because they would know the way to the village. Maybe Devi and I should go as well – but I couldn't think of anything worse than traipsing through the snow and hoping against hope we didn't get lost. I could tell Devi was really itching to be out of the house, doing something, but then I'd be worried about her being with a potential murderer. Plus, we'd said we'd stick with Jayne until the police came, and she was staying in the house with Ms Bromley.

Devi's face squeezed up. "Lottie and Douglas should go," she said finally.

"Hang on, you're not telling us what to do—" began Douglas, but then Lottie spoke up.

"Devi's right," she said quietly. "I know the way to the village. And you'll come with me, because you're my boyfriend. Mum's *dead*, Douglas, I just…" She shook her head, looking exhausted. "I need to do *something*."

Douglas stared at her, his face unreadable. His mouth opened and closed, like he was considering arguing with her – but even he must have decided it would be cruel to fight with Lottie when she was so vulnerable.

"Fine," he said shortly. He didn't look pleased at all.

"Great," said Devi. "And if you're not back in four hours, we'll assume you're dead."

Jayne

After Lottie and Douglas left, we sat around in the kitchen in silence for a bit longer. Mr Vanforte kept looking at me, Devi and Lizzie.

"You'll be on your way soon," he said to Devi and Lizzie. I obviously lived nearby, so wasn't really trapped the way they were. But we'd made our pact to stick together. And I wanted to protect Ms Bromley.

Even I could feel the hostility coming from Devi as she glared at Mr Vanforte. "That's the hope," she said, folding her arms.

Mr Vanforte rolled his eyes. "I'm going to my office. Let me know when Lottie and Douglas return." He left without another word.

"I've worked for the Vanfortes all my life, you know," Ms Bromley said, her eyes watery as she sipped her tea. "I watched Mrs Vanforte grow up. More than just my employer, she was.

She was my friend." Her voice wavered on the last word. "I always thought, when I started getting older, that the worst thing that could happen to me would be dying. But it's not – it's outliving the people you love... People you never thought you would outlive. If...if Mrs Vanforte was murdered, like Jayne said she was..." Her hand trembled as she put the cup of tea down. "I suspect Lottie and Mr Vanforte. Surely, it had to be them. It *had* to be..." She looked troubled as she shook her head. "I don't understand how they could do it though... How *could* they?"

Devi looked from Lizzie to me, then back to Ms Bromley. "It's the worst, isn't it? When you lose someone you love and then you have that unanswered question hanging over you... That *why*... My friend, Priya, she..." Devi swallowed hard, her throat bobbing. "We could find out who did it," she said quickly. "While we're waiting for Lottie and Douglas to come back. What if we have a look through their stuff? They might not have had a chance to throw away the evidence..."

I had been watching the scene in silence. I'm not used to other people. I prefer machines, mechanics, maths and figures. Things that have a solution you can always solve. People don't suddenly make sense if you're smart enough to figure them out. They're messy, they do things you don't expect. They let you down.

But last night, I had been comforted by both Devi's and Lizzie's presence. For the first time I found myself starting to think that maybe, even if I didn't always understand them, some people *didn't* let you down. Sometimes they'd stay with you – even after your employer was murdered by one of her own family.

So I decided to engage in the conversation. "What exactly would we be looking for?" I said to Devi.

"A giant bottle of rat poison, I don't know," said Devi. "A huge stash of drugs to overdose someone on. A journal saying *I killed Emily Vanforte last night.* My point is, there *could* be more evidence, right? Beyond the stuff we've found so far. For all we know, Mr Vanforte wanted to stay behind to *hide* said evidence. And where's Tate, huh? No one's seen him this morning."

"What do you think, Jayne?" said Lizzie, suddenly looking at me. "Do you think Devi's right and we should go looking for more clues? *I* personally think we should stay here where it's safe."

"It's not safer in here," argued Devi, getting to her feet and drawing herself up to her full height (which wasn't much). "We're *only* fifty per cent safer than we were an hour ago, because two of them have just left the house to get help... Although..." Her eyes grew wide. "Wait here. I'll be right back."

She ran from the kitchen, and I frowned after her. What she had said *wasn't* true, because that would mean all four of them were *equally* likely to have killed Emily Vanforte. I didn't know if we could believe that. Of course, if *all* of them had been in on it, then the probability of us being in the house with a killer hadn't changed at all.

Ms Bromley poured more tea. "I think you should search," she said. "I think you should find out who did it and... Mrs Vanforte won't be able to rest in peace until her killer is found." The teapot slipped out of her hand and crashed to the floor. It cracked down the side, but didn't completely break. Ms Bromley stared at it, motionless, like she didn't understand what had just happened. Then she let out a sob and quickly clamped her hand over her mouth, steeling herself. "When Devi comes back, you go look and you find out what happened."

"Yes," I said. Then I picked up the teapot. The crack was surface level – none of the hot liquid inside had sloshed out. But I still emptied the remnants of the tea, and then threw the pot away.

We waited in silence for eight more minutes, before Devi returned, panting.

"I just wanted to check that Lottie and Douglas *did* actually leave the house and set off," Devi said. "And they did – there's two sets of new footprints in the snow, leading right out of the house and onto the road."

That was smart thinking. I nodded in appreciation.

"So, Douglas and Lottie are gone now, right? Well, let's have a nose around their bedrooms, see if we can find anything," said Devi, her voice eager. Having something to do seemed to give her purpose.

She was looking at me and Lizzie.

"Ooh, I *really* don't want to…" said Lizzie, nibbling her lip as she glanced at Ms Bromley.

Ms Bromley smiled at her kindly. "That's okay, my dearie. You can stay down here with me and protect me in case anyone comes to get me."

Devi looked at me.

"Let's go," I said.

Devi

After the Murder

Jayne and I left the kitchen and went up the grand staircase. Since I couldn't ski to freedom, searching for clues felt like the next best thing – to burn off my nervous energy. I couldn't stand the thought of sitting still, watching the clock tick.

I let Jayne lead the way, obviously, because otherwise I would have got lost. The corridors still didn't look familiar to me, and even though it was daylight, everything was stuck in a state of dim.

"All their bedrooms are this way," said Jayne. "The guest ones too."

I was thinking about Tate, how it *was* weird that he hadn't come down to the kitchen. For a moment my mind went flying to the idea that he'd been murdered and we were all going to be picked off one by one… In which case maybe we should try to find him, and make sure he wasn't lying dead somewhere.

Or maybe *he* was the murderer, and had done a runner in the middle of the night.

This area of the house had lots of windows overlooking the fresh paper of snow that blanketed the world. My eyes stung at the view; the white was too bright after the darkness we'd just walked through.

"That's Mrs Vanforte's bedroom," said Jayne, nodding at a large door. My hand was on the knob at once, to search – surely there would be loads of information inside there. But then a shiver washed over me – I looked back at Jayne.

"I'm not being dramatic here or anything but… Is this where they've put her body?" I asked. Jayne shook her head – of course, she didn't know. I held the handle, taking a deep breath as I closed my eyes. If Mrs Vanforte's body wasn't in this room, we'd be missing a prime opportunity to have a look around. But if it was…

I know I can be heartless sometimes, but searching the room while Mrs Vanforte's body was there drew the line for me.

"I'll just quickly…" I didn't give myself enough time to get scared. I opened the door and peered inside. It was an enormous room, with a four-poster bed – and that was the only thing I saw. Because underneath the sheets was a lump – they'd tucked her up, like she was asleep—

"Bloody hell," I said as I pulled the door shut, my heart hammering. I almost wanted to throw up – I had never seen a dead body before and on the other side of this thin piece of wood was the woman who had let me into her house and out of the snow just a day earlier.

Jayne's dark eyes were fixed on the door, her face pale.

"Let's go," she said, turning on her heel and continuing down the corridor. I trailed behind. The silence between us was heavier now and I kept thinking back to that lump underneath the covers...

"That's Tate's room," said Jayne, nodding at a door from behind which classical music was playing.

Oh – so there went my theory that he'd done a runner. It was good to know he wasn't dead. "I'd have taken him to be into weird indie music," I said. "The type he could shove down everyone's throats so it's clear how much of a loner he is." I was making comments, but my mind was now back on Mrs Vanforte – if they'd been able to get an ambulance to her last night, would she have lived?

Did she regret anything about her last few hours alive?

"Here's Douglas's room," said Jayne. "We can search this one."

I gasped as I followed her inside. It was about double the size of the room I had been given (and my room was *huge*), with a gigantic red rug covering the floorboards and enormous windows that looked out over the back of the house. There was nothing to see but snow stretching away in all directions.

Douglas was messy, with his clothes flung about everywhere and designer shirts that probably cost more than my parents made in a month lying crumpled on the floor. His suitcase was shoved under his bed; he hadn't bothered to unpack anything into the chest of drawers which stood underneath the window.

I went straight to his suitcase and began rifling through it, but it just contained more clothes, nothing of interest there.

Jayne looked through the desk drawers, and wandered into the bathroom.

We searched the space quickly, but didn't find anything beyond loads of designer stuff.

"How long was Douglas planning on staying?" I said, frowning as I picked up a tropical T-shirt that looked like it should be worn on a beach somewhere, not in an English house in the middle of winter.

"It was supposed to be a few days," said Jayne, grimacing at a particularly hideous pair of bright orange trousers.

Despite all the stuff I'd said in the kitchen, I wasn't really expecting to find anything, but it would have been nice. Once more that lump under the sheets flashed in my mind. It would have been really nice – to get justice for Mrs Vanforte... And to make sure we knew who to be wary of, so we didn't end up like her.

"At least we tried," I said to Jayne as cheerfully as I could as we left Douglas's room and headed towards Lottie's. Tate was still blasting Mozart like he thought it was a banger.

Lottie's bedroom was weirdly empty. There weren't any clothes in her drawers, or her wardrobe, the dressing table was bare and there was a single suitcase for all her belongings. She looked like more of guest than Douglas did, even though this was actually her home.

Except, there were two photos pinned to the wall. One of Lottie and Mr Vanforte, and one of Lottie and Douglas. In both of the photos, Lottie was looking at the other person and they were smiling directly at the camera.

"There's nothing to search," muttered Jayne, as she peered

into the bathroom. I got down on my hands and knees and looked under the bed. It was an obvious hiding place, so I wasn't expecting to find anything, but there was a dark shape in the middle of the space underneath the bed frame.

"Jayne, do you have your torch?" I asked.

"No," she replied.

I shimmied forward and poked at the shape, praying it wasn't something disgusting. Instead, I found myself tapping at a box. I moved my hand along and felt a handle, which I pulled, tugging the box out.

I sat cross-legged as I stared at it. It looked like a make-up box, with a silver clasp at the front.

"Weird place for her to store her make-up," I said. "Especially when she's got that enormous dressing table." Jayne came and crouched beside me. I twisted the clasp, the box snapping open to reveal—

Pictures. A huge stack of them, of older guys with dark hair. They looked like they had been collected from different social media accounts, and were all personal photos, of the men at the beach or in nice fields or in restaurants posing for the camera.

"Ew, gross," I said, thinking for a second that this was a box of Lottie's crushes or something. But then I picked up a photo and turned it over, to see she had annotated the back.

Simon Burgious, twenty-six, adopted by one of Mum's acquaintances.

I pawed through the rest of the photos, and they all had the same weird annotation.

"What is this?" whispered Jayne.

"It's a bunch of men – all in their mid-twenties. All linked to

253

Mr and Mrs Vanforte in some way…" I paused at one photo. On the back, it said, *Hope he's not my brother, his haircuts are awful.* On another it said, *James could be older brother? Lots of people said Dad had an affair nine months before James was born?* I looked up at Jayne as my mind whirred. "Remember that rumour Douglas brought up, about Mr Vanforte having a son from an affair? What if it wasn't just a rumour? What if he actually does have a child out there somewhere? And Lottie's been looking for him. A man in his mid-twenties…bulky, dark-haired…"

"Lottie knew the rumour was true," muttered Jayne, sifting through a few of the photos.

"What exactly are you two doing?" came a voice from the doorway.

Devi

After the Murder

I scrambled to shut the make-up box and got to my feet, quickly kicking the box towards the bed. It slid a few inches and came to a stop – still in plain view. I cursed under my breath – my sleuthing skills needed work.

Tate was leaning against the door frame with his eyebrows raised. He was wearing his leather jacket again and somehow looked even paler than yesterday, with dark rings under his eyes, his hair sticking up like he'd spent the whole night running his fingers through it.

"I thought this was one of the historic rooms of the house," I said, trying to sound as casual as I could. "I wanted to, er…see all the lovely details. Like, you know, the fireplaces and stuff." I'm normally a better liar, but my brain had jammed at the sight of him looking all moody and on the edge of death – I really have to get over my attraction to boys who look like they're going to be trouble, but I don't think it'll be happening any time soon.

"You're snooping," said Tate coolly. "To try and figure out who killed Aunt Emily?" His mouth twitched, like he was amused, but a second later his face was sulky again. I had a ridiculous moment of feeling pleased with myself, that I could make him smile, before I remembered what we were discussing. I scrambled to come up with a proper excuse for what we had been doing, but Jayne spoke first.

"Yes," she said, tilting her head as she looked at him. "And we found loads of pictures of people Lottie thinks might potentially be her older brother. From an affair that Mr Vanforte had."

A flicker of surprise darted across Tate's face. "So Lottie wants to find herself a sibling? I wonder why. Maybe that's the secret Aunt Emily was going to reveal at dinner – who Uncle Charles's love child was."

"So you think the secret was about Mr Vanforte then?" I said, back on track – I wasn't going to let him distract me again. Mr Vanforte had thought the secret was about his finances – but he could have been wrong. Either way, he still had the strongest motive.

Tate shrugged. "I mean…I don't know who else it could be about. Aunt Emily didn't have any dirt on me and, well – Douglas has done a whole bunch of stupid stuff. The question isn't what he *has* done – it's what he hasn't. But how would Aunt Emily know about it?"

I scowled at him. He looked so calm, coolly discussing things with us even though he'd caught us rifling through Lottie's room.

"I'm guessing you've also searched Douglas's room?" Tate's

eyes glittered. "Do you want to have a look through my stuff? See if you can find any clues?"

A prickle of irritation ran through me and suddenly he didn't seem so attractive. Clearly, Tate thought he could call my bluff and intimidate me. But as far as I was concerned, he'd just openly invited me to search his room. I charged forward and down the corridor into his bedroom.

It was empty, like Lottie's. Except, of course, Tate was *actually* a guest. There was a single backpack lying in the centre of his room. I yanked it open, to find a few changes of clothes.

"Is this all you brought?" I asked Tate, who had followed me into his bedroom, looking startled – likely at how fast I had moved. I felt a flash of satisfaction to see I'd managed to dig past the calm attitude to get him to reveal some emotion. Jayne was peering round the door with interest.

Tate nodded.

"I wasn't planning on staying long," he said, his voice taking on a dry tone.

"Well, do you *often* stay?" I asked. He'd made it clear he disliked his uncle – but how well had he known his aunt?

Tate shrugged. "My dad sends me here a few times a year when it's school holidays and he doesn't want me alone at home. But he normally just calls Uncle Charles up and tells him that's what's happening – I've never been *invited* before. The dinner thing came super out of the blue."

Another thought occurred to me. "How long are you going to be staying now?"

"It'll be a while," said Tate, as he ran his fingers along the dusty desk, like he didn't want to meet my eyes. "To speak to the police and whatever. About what happened in the dining room."

"When you killed Mrs Vanforte?" I asked. It was for the shock value – I wasn't expecting him to confess to murdering his aunt. His eyebrows furrowed.

"Why would *I* kill her?" he said. "Aunt Emily doesn't – *didn't* – like Uncle Charles's side of the family, she made that clear enough – we hardly ever spoke, even when I stayed over. I barely knew her – and nowhere near enough to want to *murder* her. Plus, like I said before, I think it was Uncle Charles – he *hated* her…" His voice became more thoughtful. "He spoke to her just before she died – was the only person *near* her, which means he had the best opportunity to poison her… Apart from Lottie, of course. But Uncle Charles and Aunt Emily had a whole conversation. Aunt Emily just said something to Lottie really quickly – something that made Lottie roll her eyes. So it *had* to be Uncle Charles."

52

Extract of Transcript of Interview 10
Re: Death of Emily Vanforte
(second interview with Devi Mistry)
In Attendance – Inspector Adams (IA),
Devi Mistry (DM)

IA: Thanks for coming back to see me. It's been a
long few days interviewing the three of you. You
were my last interviews though.

DM: Thanks for all these snacks. [Rustling] I'm a big
fan of these crisps. [Munching] So, Inspector, do you
know who did it? Who killed her?

IA: We have a theory, yes. But there are a few
things which are...odd.

DM: Oh? But you know who killed Mrs Vanforte.
Charles Vanforte – obviously. He had the motive –
he had no money, he was in debt, he knew he was in
the will, he hated his wife – just look at that diary
extract you said was written by him. He had the
means – he could have bought poison, he's got
connections, that could definitely have been him in
touch with "Noviroam". I googled it afterwards,

when we got out and I could get onto the internet again. That's a drug company, that's where he could get the poison from surely. And Tate said he saw Mr and Mrs Vanforte having a conversation at dinner – no one else got close to her apart from Lottie. Which means he had a good chance to put the poison into her drink. So he had the means, the motive and opportunity. I've seen enough detective films to know what you're supposed to be looking for, and it all points to Mr Vanforte.

IA: The sleeping tablets that killed Emily were bought by one Edward Smith a few months ago – illegally, of course, lots of bribes were given. But the company confessed to selling them at a high dosage, without a prescription. They're under investigation too.

DM: Edward Smith is clearly a fake name for Mr Vanforte. He was obviously planning this for months, waiting for the exact right time. But then Mrs Vanforte screwed that up by deciding to have this dinner where she was going to reveal a big secret. So, he had to act fast, right? But it was fine, he could get things back on track – he had the drugs, he could slip them into Mrs Vanforte's drink at dinner. He would cut off the phone lines to make sure people couldn't get help, same with the cars. Everyone else in the house had ties to him – he could bank on them to be silent. But he wasn't expecting me, Lizzie and Jayne to be there. That's why he was so eager to kick me out in the snow. It's always the husband.

IA: Hmm...

DM: What do you mean, "Hmm?" Have you not been listening to anything I've been saying? He had the motive, the means – everything!

IA: Oh, I don't dispute that.

DM: So why are you looking at me like that?

IA: Like what, Devi?

[Long pause]

DM: Like you think I'm lying.

INTERLUDE

Devi

One Year Before
Emily Vanforte's Death

The driver didn't speak to me. Not once. Even when I asked him really basic stuff that was super easy to answer like *What's your name?* and *How long have you been a driver for?* I sat at the back of the car twiddling my thumbs and biting down all the comments I wanted to make about the countryside flashing past – *Look how many cows there are! What happens if you get lost in these woods? Why would people want to live in the middle of nowhere like this?* I don't often get to travel outside London and I felt ten years younger, bursting with excitement like I was off on a holiday. Except this wasn't a holiday, obviously. This wasn't supposed to be fun.

"This is the road that leads up to the building," the driver said at last. I jumped, because his voice was deeper than I had been expecting it to be. So he *could* talk – I'd been bored since about an hour into the journey and he'd missed out on loads of my wittiest thoughts. Apparently, rich people's drivers are taught to stay silent.

He glanced back at me, but since he was wearing dark glasses I couldn't properly read his expression. He was bald, wearing a black suit – I'd wanted to make a joke about him working for MI5 or something with the way he was dressed, but I knew it wouldn't be appreciated.

We inched down a narrow road, and the hedges on either side were too close – the leaves scratched the side of the car.

"Just drop me off here," I said, slightly concerned we might end up wedged in between the hedges, and have to smash our way to freedom through the back window in awkward silence.

"My instructions are to go right up to the door," he said.

"Stop talking my ear off," I muttered, as the car continued to inch forward.

The car turned a corner to reveal a single-storey building before us, the weak winter sun reflecting off the windows, which were tinted black. It reminded me of the sort of building people might put at the bottom of their garden – like an outdoor office.

The road widened out – plenty of room for the driver to turn round and leave. It'd be easy for me to stay in the car as well, go back home. It'd be the *much* easier option.

But I've never done things the easy way. I like a challenge.

I repeated that to myself as I undid my seat belt and got out, grabbing my backpack and steeling myself to march up to the building. There was something sinister about the black windows revealing nothing but my own reflection, staring back at me and asking me what the hell I was doing.

The car door slammed shut behind me – the driver had reached back to close it. Before I could change my mind, the car was turning away to leave me, and within seconds it had disappeared back into the hedge tunnel. Hours and hours together and the driver didn't even say goodbye.

The front door of the building was flung open, and a woman wearing a grey suit stepped out.

"Welcome," she said, smiling at me. "I am Emily Vanforte. And you must be Priya Patel?"

I grinned. "Nope. I'm Devi Mistry. It's a pleasure to meet you."

Devi

One Year Before Emily Vanforte's Death

Emily wanted me to leave. I wasn't part of the plan.

"Well, sucks for you, because I'm muscling my way into this show," I said. I'd come too far to give up now, and she wasn't going to get rid of me that easily. I mean, I'd *literally* come too far – London was bloody hours away and this journey had better be worth it.

There were two other girls already waiting in the building Emily had called her "bolthole", which she said was about ten minutes' drive away from her home. She introduced the girls as Jayne Faraway and Elizabeth Newton-Hill, who squeaked as she said she preferred to be called Lizzie.

Jayne looked as though she'd been cast as a lead in an emo vampire film; Lizzie had the air of someone who would much prefer to be at home with her teddy bear. They sat around a circular table in what looked to be the main room of the building, though there was a door in the corner I guessed led to a bathroom. There was a desk against the far wall, and a sofa placed in front of a television, with a kitchenette behind it.

The black glass distorted the world outside, making it look like it was the middle of the night.

Emily pursed her lips at me as I sat down at the table, where she had laid out tea and cake. I didn't touch the food or drink, sliding in opposite her and sitting back with my arms crossed to try and seem all calm and collected, like I crashed plans all the time.

"So, erm…Mrs Vanforte," said Lizzie. "Why are we here?"

"Call me Emily, dear," said Emily, and even though the words were sweet, the steel in her eyes didn't vanish. She seemed like the kind of person who didn't take crap – the kind of person I normally liked and admired… But not today, because today I had pulled the biggest load of crap, and I needed her to be forgiving.

"Okay," squeaked Lizzie. "Okay…Emily. Please could you tell us why we're here?"

Emily tilted her head. "Well, as you know, I am a philanthropist and mother and have the misfortune of being married to Charles Vanforte. A while ago, I had an idea. A bold idea – of course, I've always considered myself as someone bold. Someone who isn't afraid to take risks. But this is a cut above the rest – I have finally outdone myself. And to put my bold plan into action, I wanted to invite three teenage girls to this estate, three teenage girls with one unpleasant thing in common – Charles Vanforte ruined your lives…and got away with it."

Lizzie almost fell off her chair as she scrambled to get up. "Is this some sort of joke?" she asked. "Some sort of game?"

Jayne hadn't reacted, but I'd noticed her hands were curled into fists.

Emily continued on as if nothing had happened. Her eyes fixed on me. "Of course, that's not true for you, is it, Devi? Charles Vanforte didn't ruin *your* life. Why are *you* here?"

I tilted my head at her, while I considered my response. I didn't owe her an explanation. I didn't owe any of these people a damn thing. But I had the feeling she wouldn't let me get away with that if I said it aloud, that she'd toss me out if I didn't say *something*.

"Priya couldn't come," I said. I wanted to add *obviously*, but I didn't. "So I came instead. In her place. Trust me, it's better this way. Charles destroyed her life – but mine too."

Emily's eyebrows bunched together, like she couldn't work out what to make of me. But she didn't tell me to get out, so I figured I was safe for the moment, while she decided what to do. Instead, she turned away from me, like I was invisible, focusing on the two girls she'd actually invited. "All my life, I have wanted to be a good person. I have given to charity, I have helped the poor and needy. I have been blessed with wealth, and I have helped where I could. But my husband… He has not been so good. He has failed and failed and failed – and destroyed countless lives in the process. And yet – he has climbed the ladder. Failed *upwards*. His motto has always been *Seek forgiveness, not permission* – but he has never actually sought forgiveness. I rather think he doesn't believe he *needs* forgiveness. If a few lives are ruined here and there – if a few people *die*… Well, what does that matter to him? *He* has never stabbed anyone – he has never picked up a knife or a gun and looked a person in the eye as he ended their life. Therefore he is innocent."

"He's a murderer," said Lizzie, still on her feet. "I don't care what the law says. He's got away with murder." The words were venomous. It was surprising. I'd have taken her for a quiet girl who let people walk all over her. She was blinking rapidly, like she was surprised by her own ability to speak up.

"I would like your help," continued Emily, with a small nod at Lizzie. "I have come to the realization – even though I have *wanted* to be good…I am not. Charles and I have led separate lives for many years now, but it has remained convenient for me to stay married, so I did. I ignored his actions – they weren't *my* actions after all. But I've had some news recently, which made me reconsider. You see, I've been diagnosed with a tumour – dreadful little thing. I have a few years left to live. And with my own mortality staring me in the eyes, I have begun to question myself, my actions. I have given away lots to charity, I have helped lots of people. But I have been selfish. I have done what is convenient, what is easy for me – instead of what is right. So, when I got my diagnosis, I realized I must stop doing the convenient thing. I have decided that Charles is finally going to get the justice he deserves."

"I don't understand," said Lizzie. "What does this have to do with us?"

"You're right, dear, Charles has murdered people over the years – though not with the knife or the poison or the gun – nothing the law can touch. And he has destroyed countless lives through his greed, his desire to rise to power. So, I have decided that, if I am to die, Charles is going to be the one who kills me – and you are going to help."

55

Devi

One Year Before Emily Vanforte's Death

There was a long silence following Emily's little speech. I tried to process what she'd said, but it still didn't make sense to me. Maybe Emily was so used to getting her way, with all her money and connections, she thought she could ask for the most ridiculous things and snap her fingers, and she would have everything she wanted.

I hadn't been expecting *this* when I'd decided to take Priya's place.

Priya was my best friend, we'd grown up together, her house is a few doors down from mine. We were even born just a few days apart – I was the older one of us two, the protector. When another kid stole Priya's teddy at nursery, a mangy old thing she carted around everywhere, I was the one who pushed the thief over in the sandbox and got it back.

Our lives had been intertwined from the very beginning – we'd gone to primary school together, then high school. She was more than my best friend. She was my sister – her family was *my* family too.

The invitation to visit Emily Vanforte had come in the post, addressed to her. She would have ripped it up and never spoken of it again if I hadn't been there to ease it from her trembling fingers. She wanted to put the whole thing with Charles Vanforte behind her – she wanted to put *everything* behind her, pretend like she wasn't haunted by the past, like the life hadn't been sucked out of her. But there were glimmers of the old Priya still buried deep inside her, the Priya who was curious about everything, who was *adventurous* – who would have dug for gold in the middle of the night in a snowstorm if someone gave her a map. And those tiny sparks of Priya from Before wanted to find out why Emily had sent her a letter.

So, I said I would go along in her place. I'd have done anything for her – for any of her family. And they would have done the same for me, if they were able to.

The silence continued to stretch on, so I decided to speak up. "What the hell?" I said.

Lizzie and Jayne were nodding along with me; it looked like we did all have something in common after all. They were looking between Emily and the door, as if trying to calculate how long it would take them to run out and not look back.

"I am going to take some poison," said Emily, ignoring me. "I am going to set it up so that Charles appears to be the one who kills me – but there is a problem with this plan, you see. Charles has got away with a lot before and I'm afraid he'll get away with it again after I'm gone. I can manipulate things to a certain extent up to the point of my death – but I cannot do

273

this alone, especially not once I am gone and the matter is in the hands of the police, and Charles's lawyers. I need help to get him sent to prison, where he belongs."

She stopped, looked at Lizzie and Jayne.

"So, will you help me?" she asked. "I would have loved Priya to be here too, but that's not to be, unfortunately…" She glanced at me, irritation creeping into her voice.

Lizzie shook her head. "This is ridiculous," she said, making her way to the door. "I'm really sorry about your diagnosis, and I know Charles Vanforte is a horrible man – but what you're suggesting is…illegal. It is *perjury*. It would be sending an innocent man to prison—"

"The man's not innocent," I said sharply, a hot flash of anger spiking through me. "Just because he wouldn't have committed *Emily's* murder, doesn't mean he's not a murderer. You said it yourself."

Emily looked at me, and the irritation was gone. Instead, there was a gleam in her eyes. Admiration.

"You know where the law got my friend Priya? Nowhere," I continued. "And I bet it's the same for you as well, else you wouldn't be here."

Lizzie had paused by the door. She looked back at me, her eyes sad. "You don't know anything about me."

"I know you're desperate," I said. "Only a desperate person would have come here, to speak to the wife of the person they think ruined their lives. You know as well as I do if the law was good for something, Charles Vanforte would already be in prison. But people like him…" I paused, a lump in my throat. "No one wants to believe they're the bad guys. Or if they do think they're bad guys…they don't care. They get away with things anyway."

"Exactly," said Emily, nodding at me. She seemed to have warmed up to me, had forgiven me for barging into the scene she'd constructed so perfectly in her head. "Summed up beautifully, I must say. Someone like Charles – they look very favourable in court, come across well. They say all the right things. They can hire the most expensive lawyers, be coached to come across just so in front of a jury – you'll be surprised what the law lets you get away with, if you look the right way, if you talk the right way, if you have enough money. So, please," she said to Lizzie. "Sit back down. At the very least you can share your link to Charles with the group. Share your story. I have a feeling no one has listened to you properly before, and I'm sure you want to get it off your chest."

Lizzie sat back down, but her lips were pressed together. She didn't look like she was going to be speaking any time soon.

Once more the silence lingered long enough to become awkward.

I cleared my throat. "Why don't I go first?"

56

Devi

How Charles Vanforte Killed My Best Friend's Brother

Dylan was Priya's older brother. There were five years between them.

But he wasn't just Priya's older brother. He was also my friend. I grew up with *both* of them and one of my earliest memories was him sitting for hours and playing Barbies with me when Priya had a cold and couldn't come over. He helped me chop off their hair and give them tattoos with felt-tip pen, and then took all the blame when Mum told me off for ruining my toys.

But as we got older, he got in with the wrong crowd. Started bunking school, failing classes…becoming someone else. His parents were working constantly, just trying to keep a roof over their heads, so they weren't around as much as they would have liked. He left school with no plans for the future, and drifted apart from Priya and me. But that didn't change anything – I'd love him no matter what.

When we were thirteen, he got a job working on a construction site, owned by Charles Vanforte's company. Things were looking up – instead of going out with his horrible friends every Friday night, he would stay in and watch films with me and Priya, telling us both how he was planning on turning everything around. And he wasn't just saying it – Priya told me he'd offered to help his parents with the bills, that he'd deleted his social media to get away from his dodgy friends and start a clean slate.

Then one day, there was an accident.

Health and Safety at the site was lax, we all know that now, we all saw the investigation – though it concluded Charles and his company had done *everything reasonably expected of them*, like Charles couldn't have known that a crane which had dropped heavy concrete blocks three times before *might, just might*, do it again – and right when Dylan was standing under it too.

People said Dylan had been mucking about on the site, that it was his fault. Showing up late to work, not wearing the proper clothing, fiddling around with the equipment – all sorts of crap. They said he had caused his own death by not following basic safety procedures. A stupid teenager, who messed up at school and messed up everything else.

Priya and I didn't believe it. Dylan had been taking the job so seriously – he'd come home and tell us all about his day, and everything he was learning, and how he was going to save up and buy his own place. And I did my research on Charles Vanforte, digging into stories about him and his family. I knew how rich his wife was – he had access to the sort of money that could make sure any investigation found in his favour, with his fancy lawyers billing eight hundred pounds an hour to pull all-nighters putting together the "evidence" in a way that made sure he came out on top.

We decided we were going to figure out what really happened.

And we did. We spoke to a member of staff who had been on site – an accountant – who said the accident had happened after work, when most people had gone home. Dylan had volunteered to take a late delivery, and the accountant was the only other person around. Charles happened to be there to pick up some documents – and when the screams of agony started, Charles went to investigate, and came back and told the accountant not to call the ambulance.

The accountant did eventually, but not before Dylan had fallen unconscious. Charles had to have gone out there, seen Dylan and known that, if he lived, he could have testified against him and the corners he had cut. And he was in the right place at the right time to make sure that didn't happen – because things always work out for Charles Vanforte, don't they?

It's not illegal to watch someone die, did you know that? To stand back and do nothing. There was a window of time where if Dylan had got to the hospital, he might have been saved – but that window was missed, because Charles wanted to save his own skin.

And that accountant who told us all that didn't say it at the inquest – his story changed: Charles apparently called the ambulance the moment he knew the accident happened. I guarantee you, Charles threatened that accountant, or paid him off, or did whatever he needed to do to shut him up.

But no one would listen to Priya and me. We tried telling the police but they said the investigation was closed – and, anyway, Charles walking away from Dylan while he was dying, *if that even happened*, wasn't a criminal act, and he had done all that he was reasonably required to do. We tried to tell the press, but they didn't care either.

Who would believe us – two teenage girls – over successful businessman and politician Charles Vanforte?

57

Devi

One Year Before Emily Vanforte's Death

"We never got justice." I half spat out the words. Emily, Jayne and Lizzie were all staring at me – and I stared fiercely back. As I'd been telling my story, something had cemented in my mind: I wanted to be involved in this, in putting Charles in prison where he belonged. The helplessness, the *powerlessness*, I'd felt as the investigation was closed, had come rushing back to me. And the anger as well, burning inside me.

A few years ago, Priya would have wanted to as well. But after Dylan's death, and the police not listening to us, and Charles walking away like nothing had ever happened, she'd retreated into a shell. Gone was my sweet best friend who believed she could be anything, who believed she could change the world. She was replaced by someone uneasy in her own skin, unsure of everything, someone who barely took interest in the outside world. It was almost like a big part of her had died too.

And I got louder and louder, hungry for attention. To prove I had something to say, to show the police and the press that they had been wrong to ignore me. To prove we *all* had something to say.

Dylan could no longer speak for himself, so other people painted him any way they liked – *delinquent boy, poor boy*. Charles Vanforte, the *hero*, had given him a chance to turn his life around. Charles Vanforte, who was born into everything, didn't need to display humility or tell everyone how grateful he was – whereas Dylan was the brown kid who messed up his big opportunity.

There was that final layer. *Brown boy*. Somehow, that element always came up when the press were discussing the accident at the construction site.

I wanted to scream until my lungs were raw at the injustice of it all, but I'd started to learn that being too loud meant no one would listen to me. People are okay around me if they think I'm a good little Indian girl – if they think I serve chai and samosas to guests who come round, and help my mum cook the roti on Saturdays, and study quietly every evening. They don't like it if I argue back, if I am spiky and overconfident – if I don't fit into the role they want me to play.

But I didn't say any of that aloud to Emily, Lizzie and Jayne. I didn't want them to think I was a loose wire, and I *really* wanted in on this, because this could be the ending that made Priya see there was some fairness in the world. That healed some of the extra damage that had formed around the scar caused by her brother's death. This might be the way I could do something for Dylan, after everything he had done for me –

being there, while I was growing up. My best friend's brother, my friend.

"I know you wanted Priya, but I'm willing to help do this," I said to Emily. "I get it's risky – but all we're doing is nudging the police towards something we already *know* is true, right?"

Emily considered me, her eyes scanning my face. At last, she turned to Lizzie, her expression unreadable. "Why don't you explain your connection with my husband?" she asked. "I believe your story picks up right where Devi's left off."

Lizzie stared back at her – then she looked over at me. "I can't," she whispered, and I wanted to roll my eyes. She had wanted to hurry away, and now couldn't even tell us how Charles ruined her life? "You might... You might hate me." And she looked at me, not Emily.

"*I* might hate you? I don't even know you. And unless you killed Dylan and not Charles..." I shrugged. "I think we'll be okay."

Lizzie shook her head. "No, I didn't. But I..."

"There's no judgement here," said Emily gently. "And truly...keeping things to yourself...it's no good, Elizabeth. It only makes things worse, trust me."

"And also," I added, because my curiosity had been roused, since Lizzie was being so cagey about things, "why the hell should you care what I think anyway?"

Lizzie blinked a few times. "Fine," she said. "But you need to promise me you won't...pass judgement."

"Yeah, yeah," I said. "No judgement, got it. Now what did Charles do to you?"

Lizzie

My Connection with Charles Vanforte

Mum and Dad and I were happy. We had a nice house in a nice part of the world.

Dad worked hard and often late, but he always said to me that hard work would pay off in the end, that it would all be worth it one day. It was gruelling, I know it was, and he had bags under his eyes and sometimes he seemed to sink into himself a little when he thought I wasn't looking – but he always had a smile for me, and he always repeated that his hard work would be rewarded.

He believed in the good in people, always.

He worked for Charles Vanforte's construction company, in the office. I knew something had gone wrong at one of the sites, but Dad didn't talk about it, not with me. I remember one day, when I was thirteen, he came home and had an argument with Mum. I didn't want to listen. I tried to stay in my bedroom and turn up my music. But above the singer wailing about heartbreak

I could still hear snatches of their conversation.

"I'm going to say something – Charles lied in that inquest… He stopped me calling the ambulance. That boy's blood is on my hands…"

Mum said, "You *know* Charles is a bad man and could ruin your life. Don't say anything—"

"We're out of debt now, but I've sold my soul to the devil, Melissa—" That was my dad again.

I turned my music up even more, and buried my head under my pillow. I didn't like it when they argued.

Dad went away to a conference with Charles a few weeks later. He came back, cheery as ever, and he told Mum he was going to do what needed to be done. That he wouldn't let Charles get away with the injustice.

A few days later, he had a heart attack.

It happened in our living room. He was watching the news while I did my maths homework on the coffee table. He would help me out whenever I got stuck, talk through problems with me – and not just about maths. I have always been something of a worrier – I tend to see issues and then make them bigger in my head, turning small problems into insurmountable mountains – but chatting things through with Dad always made them better. It helped me see the whole picture, rather than just one tiny part of it. I don't even remember what we were talking about that last time – a problem of mine I had probably thought was life-ending, but obviously didn't really mean anything.

I was in the middle of saying something, I remember that much. And he gasped, this horrible noise coming from him, this choking – and I turned round and watched him fall to the floor – and then my memory becomes flashes.

I remember screaming and crying and not being able to stop, even when I phoned 999, and I remember waiting for the ambulance to come and I remember knowing that I would be too late.

Dad was a strong man – my rock, my shield. He'd been there for my first breath.

I was there for his last.

And the horrible thing is, while I remember random flashes of that evening, I don't recall the last thing he said to me – or what I said to him. I hope it was nice, something that made it clear how much I loved him. But I know it was probably something stupid because *I'm* stupid – how did I not know what was happening? If I'd reacted faster, got to the phone faster, known how to do CPR or…*anything*…maybe I could have saved him.

He had a heart condition his whole life, managed by little pills he used to tell me were his special protectors. The coroner did tests to try and understand why the medication had stopped working, and found none of it in his system.

He hadn't been taking it they told us, apologetically. But I knew better. I saw him gulp that round white pill down with his morning orange juice every single day at breakfast – he'd never missed a dose in his life, because he was someone who was responsible, who you could rely on.

I wanted them to test the pills, but they wouldn't. It was an open and shut case to them, and they had other stuff to deal with, and besides he'd apparently been really busy at work and that had probably made him stressed and forgetful.

But I knew the truth. Someone had killed my father.

The thoughts kept going round and round in my head, as I tried to replay the exact moment he died, wondering what I'd missed. But even though the memory of that moment is foggy, I have complete clarity about the fact that *he always took his pills*.

Which meant the pills he was taking weren't doing anything. Which meant someone had swapped them out.

And I knew who: there was only one person with any motive; one person who would have had access to my dad's heart medication when he went away for the conference. One person who wanted to stop my dad telling the world that Charles Vanforte let a teenage boy die.

But I had no proof, and the police closed the case – and Charles Vanforte got away with it.

Lizzie

One Year Before Emily Vanforte's Death

I finished my story. My face was red – I'd been expecting Devi to interrupt me the second I got to the part where I'd overheard Dad admitting he'd let Charles stop him from calling the ambulance. I'd always wondered whose blood Dad had thought was on his hands. And now I knew – eighteen-year-old Dylan Patel, who had just been trying to do better.

Mum and Dad had been in debt – they'd got behind on the mortgage payments, and the lovely house that I'd lived in all my life was close to getting repossessed. We were going to be homeless, and Dad had done whatever it took to make sure that didn't happen, even at the expense of what was right, by delaying calling the ambulance and withholding information that could have made a difference at the inquest – by taking a bribe from Charles. Because Charles had preyed on his desperation, his need to protect his own family.

And that was one of the things that tied me up in knots.

I had always been so worried about everything, seeing all the things that could go wrong, deliberating over decisions in case I made the wrong one. Dad had been a constant, a rock. I had thought he was a good man, someone I could rely on. But he had taken a bribe to save the house from being repossessed over the life of someone else – a *teenager*.

Devi had narrowed her eyes at me. "Your dad made mistakes," she said. "He made…big mistakes. He called the ambulance – but too late. He was going to tell the truth – but too late."

Tears were pricking in my eyes. "I can't listen to this – you said no judgement, I—"

I didn't want to hear that Dad was a bad man, because I had already felt a lifetime's worth of guilt over the poor decisions he had made. Would I have been brave enough to do anything differently?

But Devi reached out and gripped my hand. I startled at the touch, as she looked intensely at me. "Your dad made mistakes, but he wanted to do the right thing. He *would* have done the right thing – but Charles Vanforte stopped him. I don't blame the people Charles has exploited. I blame *Charles*. There's shades of grey with what your dad did – but I don't see any shades of grey when it comes to Charles." Her voice was angry, fierce. She pulled back from my hand, staring at her own like she couldn't believe she had reached out to hold mine.

"It would have been a disaster for Charles if your father had blown the whistle on what happened at the construction site – the *real* reason that Dylan Patel died," said Emily, who had leaned back in her chair and coolly watched me as I spoke, her expression never wavering from one of detached satisfaction that I was doing what I was told and sharing my story. "The crane was unsafe – Charles had got other staff to falsify safety records. He stopped your father from calling the ambulance at the time when it might actually have made a difference… He tried to make sure your father wouldn't tell the truth afterwards. Your father was one of the only people in the *world* who wanted to stand up to Charles. He was a brave man."

I didn't know how long I'd been waiting to hear those words. *He was a brave man. He would have done the right thing eventually – if he'd had the chance.* "So I *was* correct?" I asked Emily. "Charles Vanforte killed my dad?"

Slowly, Emily nodded. "Of course, he never said as much. Not to me. But I knew enough of the circumstances to know an employee had been making noise at work, noise that would spell disaster for Charles. And I overheard him discussing heart medication on the phone with someone, even though he doesn't have a heart problem, and then the next thing I knew the problem was gone, because his employee had conveniently died…of a heart attack."

It was a weird moment, being told I was right. No one had believed me, not even Mum. She'd thought me wanting to blame Charles was my way of grieving for something senseless that had happened and I could see it was hurting her every time I brought it up. I didn't tell anyone else what I thought, not even Natasha and Hannah. Even freshly after Dad's death, I could tell they were getting tired of my sadness. I'd noticed they were slightly off with me, their messages short and snappy, until one day Hannah came out and told me I was turning into a black void and sucking up all their energy. She said both of them felt all I ever wanted to do was vent and I hadn't even been happy for Natasha when she'd got into a big music programme for the next summer – like I *cared* about that at all, since my dad was *dead* and that was all I could think about.

So I stopped talking about Dad. And the knowledge of what Charles had done stayed lodged in me, buried like a stone trapped behind my heart. Every time my heart beat, I had a shudder of pain going through me to remind me of what had happened to him.

And a second shudder of pain followed, because I then kept wondering if dad *deserved* it, if he really had someone else's blood on his hands. A horrible, terrible, cruel thought, because I was a horrible daughter. But that second bit of pain was gone now – I could, finally, see the whole picture. And at the centre of it all was Charles.

"So will you help your father get the justice he deserves?" said Emily to me, softly. And I wanted to, so badly. But I couldn't say yes. Dad's death had left me…afraid. Scared – even worse than before he died, because he used to be able to talk me through my worries, and now I didn't have him any more. Second-guessing myself and everything I believed in. I'd seen how easy it was for the powerful people in the world to get what they wanted, how easy it was to lose my voice when I should have been shouting the loudest to get him justice.

"Well, *I'm* in," said Devi, breaking the silence. "Let's send Charles straight to his grave."

Emily raised her eyebrows. "I have made it clear I'm not suggesting we all band together and murder my husband, haven't I?"

Devi shrugged. I wondered how she could be so sure of herself. Turning up when she wasn't invited, acting like what Emily was asking for wasn't something…ridiculous. We couldn't get away with what she wanted us to do. We couldn't outsmart Charles and the police and the *law*.

Charles did it, said a niggling voice in my head. *Why can't we?*

Charles was the centre of the picture. Charles was the problem.

Emily continued: "It was difficult to track you down, but not impossible, with my connections. For this ruse to work, your connection to Charles and to each other must be almost impossible to pick up on."

Devi nodded. "Which is why it makes so much more sense for *me* to be involved in this, not Priya. I'm not directly connected to Charles."

"It's really that easy for you to make this decision?" I asked Devi. "What Charles did is awful. But we're not master criminals, we're just…three girls. And we'd be taking on *Charles Vanforte* and all his wealth and his connections – and, morally, what we'd be doing…" I trailed off. Was it hypocritical, to talk about morals, after I'd just told them what my father had done?

"I've thought this plan through," said Emily, her voice calm as she poured herself some tea from the pot no one else had touched, stirring in some sugar and tapping the teaspoon on the side of the cup to remove excess liquid. "You'd show up at my home, the Bramble Estate, apparently coincidentally, and do your best to speak to everyone, listen in – find clues that have been planted – either by yourselves or by me, we'll figure out exact details later. And then you will report your findings to the police when the time comes, so that all fingers point at Charles. Things might go off track, of course, and you would need to improvise, but you're all clever girls. Jayne and Lizzie, I've thought about a way to get you to the estate – Jayne, I would hire you to work here a few months or so before. Lizzie – your mum has a jewellery shop?"

I nodded.

"Good. What I would do is have you come up to the house and deliver a necklace, and then figure out a reason for you to stay afterwards. You could even pretend you didn't *want* to stay, to really sell it. If you were to join in, of course. There is no pressure – you can walk away at any time."

"But what about me," whined Devi. "As far as I can tell, I'm the only one out of the three of us who has actually agreed to this – how do I get here? I mean, my grandma lives about half an hour from here. I could say I got lost on the way to visit her..." Her mouth twisted into something like a smile. "She'd be proud of me, if she knew I was doing this. You want to know why I find it so easy to agree to this, Lizzie? I suppose I can tell you three, because we're coolly sitting here discussing framing a murderer for murder. My grandad was a drunk. One of those old-school men, thought women were only good for doing the cooking and the cleaning and waiting on him like he was some kind of lord, while he sat there and drank and drank and drank. He hit me, once, when we were visiting and that was the final straw for Nani. She took the money she had been stashing in her toilet—"

"Where?" I interrupted, forgetting about my own problems for a second. I wasn't the only one listening to Devi completely transfixed. Jayne and Emily were too.

"In her toilet cistern," said Devi impatiently. "See, Nana never wanted Nani to have her own money, right? Mum moved out to live with Dad, but Nana still kept a grip over her, even when we were happy and living in our own home. And, obviously, he still controlled Nani. We didn't have enough money for ourselves, let alone to help Nani get out – and anyway, she wouldn't go. You don't divorce where Nani is from, you just accept your lot in life. Except, when Nana hit me for the first time, one time when we went round – I can still feel the belt buckle now, slashing against my cheek – Nani decided she deserved more, we all did. So, she took the toilet money and left. And she did what everyone told her she couldn't do – she divorced Nana, and met Gerry a few years later—"

"And he just...*agreed* to divorce her?" asked Emily, her mouth hanging open. It made me smile slightly, because ever since we'd arrived she'd been the one in control, knowing everything that was going on. Now it was Devi's time to shine, and I could tell she was enjoying every second.

"Yeah," said Devi. "Well, no, not exactly. I know it wasn't easy. Nani has made that much clear. And she won't give me the details surrounding the divorce. But she did it. And she got him to leave her alone – and us too. She lived with us for a while – that was a massive pain, let me tell you – Nani has an opinion on *everything* and she never shuts up. But then she met Gerry, boring as hell Gerry, who is also reliable as anything and would never *dream* of hitting anyone, and she went off with him. And that's why I'm okay with this – I want to do what no one thinks I can do. Because Nani did it – and she did it for her family. And I want to do the same for mine – because Priya and Dylan and their parents...they're my family too." She looked at Emily. "So if these two won't help, you've got me."

Emily chuckled, and I could see her feelings for Devi shift. Gone was the irritation that she'd arrived uninvited – it was replaced with admiration. "Well, hold your horses there. Let's see what Jayne has to say first."

We all turned to Jayne. I'd half forgotten about her – she had been so quiet the entire time the rest of us were talking.

"Do you want to share your story?" said Emily in the same soft tone she had used to get me to speak. "Like I said to Lizzie, sometimes it helps to say things aloud."

"I'm not much of a storyteller," Jayne grunted. The soft tone clearly wouldn't work on her. "And I'm not much of a sharer. But it's similar to Lizzie's. My mum isn't here any more because of Charles. And I know he deserves to pay for what he did." She stared at Devi, then at me, for the longest time, like she was weighing us up. I couldn't tell what she was thinking; her dark eyes were unreadable. But at last, she spoke. "Okay, I'm in."

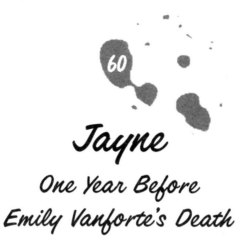

Jayne

One Year Before
Emily Vanforte's Death

No one pushed me on my story – which was good, because I didn't want to share it. I knew exactly how I felt about Charles Vanforte, and I didn't need to convince them that I hated him.

"Let me tell you more about my plan," said Emily. "I think we'd wait until we had a good forecast of snow – that would make it much easier for you all to have a legitimate reason to stay the night of my murder."

"Heavy snow's super rare though," pointed out Devi. "We might be waiting for ever for there to be enough to keep us indoors."

"Well, if there's no snow then I'll make sure the road leading to the village is blocked – tree fall, rock fall, I'll figure something out – and you and Lizzie would just need to arrive very late. No one would dream of suggesting you walk on the roads around here in the dark – no lighting, the speed limit is ridiculously high – and the nearest town back the way you came is much too far away." Emily smiled slightly, clearly happy with her suggestion. "As I said before, I'll figure out the finer details later, but the important thing is, you *would* be staying the night."

Devi nodded along, leaning forward with eagerness. Lizzie was still looking at the door, like she was deciding whether or not she should run.

"We can't make it too obvious what we're doing," said Emily. "So I will make sure there are one or two others in the house that night. Make it look like a nice, cosy family dinner. The police will get too suspicious if all the clues obviously point to Charles – he's not a stupid man and it needs to look like he's murdered me but, by a stroke of bad luck, slipped up enough to get caught. We need him to have a clear motive for killing me – and the means to do it." She was speaking faster now, excitement in her voice. She was looking *forward* to this. "The motive will be simple – money. I will post you a bank statement to plant that shows he's got no money. He's in debt – and has been trying to hide it from me." She snorted. "The man has been stealing from me, and thought I wouldn't notice because we're married and what's mine is technically his. But what's mine is *mine*." She half spat the last word. "And I'll make sure there are a few other bits you can pretend you found, and then take directly to the police."

"Wait, wait," said Devi, folding her arms. "Why the hell are *we* planting this stuff? You live there, surely you could do that yourself?"

"And risk Charles finding it and hiding it away or destroying it before you do?" Emily's voice was dry. "This evidence needs to be found in his study, for example. A place *I* never go. And I may not spy on him, but he has never had qualms about going through *my* things."

"Okay," said Devi, shifting in her seat. She seemed fine to take the lead for me and Lizzie. "But won't it seem weird to the police that we went snooping around?"

"Are you into detective stories?" asked Emily, fixing her gaze on Devi.

"Er…you mean the ones on TV on Sundays with the posh people wearing the weird hats? No," said Devi. "I'm more of a trashy soap kind of—"

"You're a detective story lover now, okay?" said Emily. "You *adore* them. You will get into the habit of watching them every Sunday. You want to live out your fantasies of being a detective. That's why you're going to be so interested in searching for this evidence, even before I'm actually dead…"

Devi snorted. "I feel like I could just start poking around because I'm nosy and bored…I feel like that's more in line with who I am…"

"Go with the lover of detective stories," commanded Emily. Obviously used to getting her way. "Now – the *means*. Charles must have the means to kill me. Poison is our best bet here – I could take it at dinner without anyone noticing. With anything else, physical evidence might show I did it to myself. Now, Charles sometimes has trouble sleeping, but his doctor won't prescribe him the sleep medication he wants. He's got connections with a foreign drug company – his friends from school now run it. He has a history of getting sleeping tablets on the side from them – under the name Edward Smith. I will pretend to be Edward, and procure a lethal amount of tablets from that company. It will look like *Charles* was the one to get them. He'll argue the truth, of course – he never bought them. But the history he has of doing this will work against him." For the first time since she'd begun running through her plan, she hesitated. "And the final thing Charles needs is...the opportunity to kill me..." She trailed off, her face going oddly slack. Like she was somewhere far away.

"Erm...Emily?" said Lizzie timidly.

"Mrs Vanforte," said Emily. "When you three are at the estate, I'll be Mrs Vanforte, Charles will be Mr Vanforte. We'll be your employers, Jayne. Your client, Lizzie, buying a necklace from me. And Devi, your saviours, helping you when your car breaks down. So, the *opportunity* to murder me. This will be key to the case. You three won't be able to help with this bit – you won't be in the room with me when I die. Otherwise you'd be under suspicion – and we don't want to introduce too many suspects, because that would make it more difficult for the police to come to the conclusion that Charles is guilty." She gave a small nod, like she was impressed with herself. "I will make sure I pull Charles aside before I take the poison – I'll make a point of it. The others in the room will see this. And then I'll tell my daughter, Lottie, that my wine has an odd taste to it. I hadn't noticed before, but it definitely tastes strange now. And then – I will pop the poison into my glass of wine, drink it, and then I will die. Lo and behold, only Charles could have put the poison into my glass."

"Is Lottie going to be in on it too?" frowned Devi. She seemed to have taken Emily's calm attitude to poisoning herself in her stride, but Lizzie had gone pale.

"No, of course not," said Emily with a wave of her hands. "My daughter couldn't be trusted with this." She paused, and let out a snort of laughter. "Sorry – just the thought of her trying to *cope* with something like this – she's always been a bit weak-minded, you know? She doesn't have the strength to do what needs to be done. No, what she'll do is parrot back what she heard to the police – she won't even figure out the importance of it, but it will help *us* immensely. Now, is everything clear to the three of you?" Her eyes swept over us. I glanced at Devi and Lizzie. They had to be reeling with the amount of information she'd just thrown at us. When no one spoke, she continued. "I can tell you where all the secret passageways are in the house – there will be one down the corridor where I'm going to put you up for the night. You can pretend to hear footsteps, and 'follow them' down the passageway that leads to Charles's study. Plant the clue regarding the drugs there for the police to find later – it's a big one, so take photos as well just in case something goes wrong and they can't find it. For dinner, I think two others, beyond Charles and Lottie, will make a good number of people… I'll have a think about who else should be in the house. I'll rile everyone by suggesting I'm going to reveal someone's secret, then start hinting at the motive."

"So you want us to tell a fake story to the police?" said Devi. She rubbed her chin. "But what happens if we contradict the stories of the other people who are there?"

Emily shook her head. "No, no, for the most part I want you to keep your stories to the police as true as you can – leave out things, of course, like the fact the evidence you find was planted there by yourselves. And the moment you come to the house and see each other – you must be strangers. You must keep up the act, even when you are alone together. That way your stories are less likely to be contradictory."

"But if you've got four other people in the house…" said Lizzie. She hesitated, like she was steeling herself to ask the question. "What happens if they do things you don't expect them to do?"

"I'm counting on it," said Emily. "I'm counting on them all being on edge – slipping up, discussing things… We won't be able to plan for every scenario, so you'll need to improvise – keep finding excuses to eavesdrop – and when you tell your story to the police, it'll help if you keep your stories as close to the truth as possible regarding what you heard and saw. Don't make up anything when you're one on one with anyone else. We want your accounts to match; we want them to trust your evidence."

"And what happens after you're dead?" said Devi bluntly, making Lizzie wince. I didn't want to draw attention to myself. I liked my role as observer. But I nodded along as Devi spoke, to show I thought it was a good question. "What happens if Charles Vanforte hires his best lawyers and makes it clear he wasn't involved?"

"He will," said Emily. "He'll hire the most expensive lawyers and they'll pour hours and hours of work into building a defence. But stick to drawing attention to the fact that he had the means and the motive – leave the opportunity part up to me. I believe you three are smart enough to make sure the police see the truth. Well…*our* truth."

Lizzie took deep breaths in and out. Her face was going red, her fingers were clenched. "It's too dangerous," she burst out. "This isn't just some game. This is real life – someone could get hurt!" Her eyes were wet. I wondered if she was thinking about her dad, and how easily Charles had disposed of him. "Or else... we could be found out – this is a *crime*. My mum wouldn't be able to cope if I was caught – I'm all she has left now. I just don't understand. Surely you know enough about Charles to expose him yourself? If not for the murders, then something else. I'm sure he's done loads of illegal stuff?"

"Well for one thing, he'll find a way to worm out of it," said Emily. "We need to actively work against him to bring him down. And for another – well, he deserves a punishment that fits the crime. In my mind, he is a murderer – and he deserves to be punished for murder. Don't you agree?"

Lizzie closed her eyes, tears flowing, but she nodded. "He haunts me," she said. "My dad...his ghost – it's everywhere. And I can't let go. And I can't move on – and I want to. I want to so badly." She opened her eyes, her bottom lip trembling. "I think...I'm going to try – to be brave – and...and if I try to quit, or walk away – don't let me. Help me be brave. Help me move on."

"So, you're in?" said Emily, beginning to smile, and I could see why. I'd only known Lizzie for five minutes and already I could tell she was the one who would have needed the most persuading. But Emily had done it. She had got us all on board.

"Yes," said Lizzie. "I'm in. Let's do this."

PART THREE

THE TRUTH

The Present
Devi

"Well, this is a nightmare," I say, slapping down a newspaper on the table so that the front page faces upwards. "I mean, I know we weren't expecting things to be easy, but this is beyond anything I could have imagined."

Lizzie looks up from her plain toast. It's been a week since Emily Vanforte died, and things have got weird. Lottie Vanforte is paying for us to stay in a hotel near the Bramble Estate while we're being asked questions by the police – I guess she wants to get to the bottom of what happened as quickly as possible. Theoretically I could just stay with Nani, but Lizzie didn't want to be in the hotel on her own and I really believe I deserve the chance to sample the five-star hotel lifestyle. I know Lottie absolutely could have put us somewhere cheaper, but she doesn't seem to have much concept of money. It probably didn't even occur to her – and, anyway, she seems like the type who'd want to host us properly, maybe even feels a bit guilty we've been dragged into her family's mess... No matter what the reason, I'm not complaining.

Nani has left Gerry in their village and is staying with me; Lizzie's mum is with her. They seem to be getting on well; they're both out, taking a walk.

Jayne doesn't need to stay in a hotel, because she lives nearby anyway and, unlike me, she doesn't seem massively interested in the chance to sample the rich people lifestyle. We haven't seen her in person since the night Emily died – we thought it might seem a bit odd for the three of us to be getting together. It's a shame though: I think she'd be a great person to talk things through with. When I first met her I thought she was an odd one, all sullen and silent, but she's *smart*. She cut all the power to the house without electrocuting herself and sabotaged all the cars, even Ms Bromley's when she went over to visit her in the morning. She even told me what to do to kill my own car when I first arrived, and she came up with the story of hearing someone in the cellar when she was down to "get jump leads" – all to make it seem like Charles was panicking trying to figure out how to kill Emily, before she revealed her big "secret".

She's definitely missing out on this fancy hotel; we have a suite of rooms and breakfast, lunch and dinner are provided – and even room service is included. I ordered loads of stuff off the breakfast menu up to our suite, and made my way through stacks of pancakes dripping in golden syrup, sausages, bacon, eggs – all kinds of eggs, in fact, poached, scrambled, fried – beans, toast, cereal, yoghurt and fruit. I figured it was easier staying in our private rooms, rather than going down for breakfast. We could talk freely in there without worrying about being overheard.

Lizzie keeps throwing everything up, from the stress she says. But it seems like she's just about managing to keep the toast down today.

The newspaper I was reading is reporting on the sensational murder of the famous Emily Vanforte, at the well-known Bramble Estate. The article uses most of its word count waxing lyrical about what a piece of crap Emily Vanforte apparently was, and how she used to bully staff and only gave stuff to charity because she wanted to be praised.

"Even if she was the biggest cow in the world – it doesn't mean Charles didn't kill her," I wail.

"He *didn't* kill her," says Lizzie, rubbing her stomach.

"Yeah, but *they* don't know that – the police have all the evidence that says he did do it," I say, sighing. We've pulled it off well so far – the only dicey moment we've had was when I had to ask the police guy interviewing me if he thought I was lying – he definitely looked at me oddly a few times while I was telling my story. Maybe because a few times I was a bit *too* unguarded with my thoughts – but I bet he'd lose all credibility with the rest of his team if he suggested anything even *halfway* near to the truth. Plus, as I left the station, I really hammered up how paranoid I was about someone coming after me. That way, I thought he could put down any behaviour of mine that didn't add up properly to a deep fear of Charles Vanforte's army of assassins.

We even caught a lucky break – Emily had dropped hints she knew about Charles's bankruptcy, which worried Charles so

307

much he made Lottie look through Emily's office. She found a few articles Emily had kept, including the draft one about the construction business – that showed the police he had secrets to hide. She didn't find Charles's bank statements showing he was broke, because I hadn't planted them at that point – or the hidden emails in the secret room saying that "Edward" wanted to buy drugs.

Plus, Lizzie and Jayne got to overhear them *talking* about the will – that was a really lucky moment, because it could cement the idea that Charles had killed Emily for her money. Emily put out that information herself, just so they could all get a nasty shock when they found out everything, apart from the Bramble Estate itself, would be going to charity. Lottie would be inheriting the estate, along with enough money to keep it running.

In fact, the only person who let us down…was Emily. I did as I was told and watched those detective shows like she said I should – Mum got really into them too, though I kept getting impatient and wanting a bit more drama. But I *did* sit through them all, which means I know our means and motive evidence is solid… It's the *opportunity* side of things is lacking. Even when I pushed Lottie, she wouldn't say that her mother told her the wine tasted funny. Emily was wrong – Lottie hasn't just parroted back what she heard. When I met her, I thought she'd be a rich airhead. But, while she's obviously lacking in confidence, she doesn't strike me as someone who wouldn't figure out the importance of what she heard. Which means she's deliberately protecting her father.

Emily underestimated how far Lottie would go for the one

parent who seemed to care about her – and it looks like things are hinging on that piece of evidence, because why else would the police not have made an arrest? They need a rock-solid case that will stand up against Charles's lawyers, and at the moment there's a small hole his lawyers will do their best to make bigger.

Of course, there's stuff I don't understand, and neither did Lizzie when I tried to talk it through with her. The biggest one is the diary extract, where Charles talked about how much he hated Emily. It was super helpful for proving his motive – but Emily couldn't have known about it, otherwise she would have given it to us to use, and she didn't. It wasn't part of her plan. Someone wearing a black hood had left it for me to find – I hadn't been lying about that part of the story when I told the police. And like I discussed with the police, the only person who could have left it out for me was Tate. But why the hell would he do that? He didn't know what we were trying to do. And maybe I want him to be on our side because I have a stupid, inappropriate crush that I'd probably said too much about while the detective was interviewing me, but also I don't like not being in control.

I guess it's not the biggest issue in the world – the diary had been helpful for us, after all. But I still don't like it.

There are a few other things I can't figure out. The gun, for one thing. Why did Tate even have it? And where had it gone? Tate said it went missing, and the police haven't been able to find it. No one had fired it – so why hide it? Was it really a toy gun, like he said? And what was up with Douglas and the knives he'd hidden in the Blue Room? Had he really received a death threat? From who? Why had he been creeping around in the walls? Lottie must have told him about a few of the secret passages she knew of – but what was *up* with their relationship? At first I'd thought he didn't care about her at all – he kept pushing her away, and she still clung to him. But I'd briefly seen flashes of what looked like guilt when he spoke to her.

Plus…we still didn't know who the person walking through the West Wing just before it was locked off had been.

"I'm going to be sick again," says Lizzie, hurrying to the bathroom.

Emily had predicted how Charles's lawyers might plan to discredit us, and he's clearly got contacts in the press, because the newspaper articles are theorizing Emily's death was a suicide, trying to suggest that my, Jayne's and Lizzie's evidence is worthless because we are worth *less* than the Vanforte family. They haven't named us, but "sources" have called us little girls who were traumatized and confused about the events of that night, and suggested we were seeing monsters where there weren't any.

The lawyers aren't going to poke holes in our stories – they are going to poke holes in *us*, diminishing us. We are the extras. We are the nobodies.

Plus, the fact that Emily was dying anyway has come out, backing up the theory she might have committed suicide.

Charles's lawyers say that Emily bought the poison using a fake name she linked to Charles. In fact, they've stumbled uncomfortably close to the truth.

Except for one thing.

No one suspects us.

The Present
Lizzie

I finish throwing up again, trying to be as neat as possible. My stomach keeps churning even though there's nothing left in there. I enter the living room of the suite again, wrinkling my nose as Devi starts to hoover up leftover croissants. She glances up at me and in the second our eyes meet I see steel – this isn't affecting her like it is me.

Why am I *not* more like her? We both experienced the same trauma, losing people we loved, knowing the man who caused their deaths walked free. I *saw* my father die, but there was nothing I could do. Devi has to walk around knowing her friend could have been saved.

And yet, Devi is tough and I am weak. The world tried to break Devi and she did not crumble; she wears armour, walks boldly through life. The world broke me, and it breaks me again and again. Even now, at seventeen, I'm still the thirteen-year-old who collapsed with her father and screamed at him that he needed to *wake up*.

My phone flashes up with a message from Natasha, who has never been more interested in me than now – when I am involved in a murder investigation. I ignore her – I may not know Devi and Jayne well, but we are a team. They are better friends than Natasha and Hannah ever were.

I wonder what Natasha and Hannah would think of Devi, who looks like she's worried there's going to be a national pastry shortage, the way she's digging into all the food.

I wonder what they would think of me, if they knew the truth about what we're really doing.

The Present
Devi

I spend the rest of the day with Nani, who is treating this whole thing like a free holiday. She knows that I won't be accused of murder or anything, because I have a rock-solid alibi, since I was with Jayne and Lizzie when Emily died, and she had to have been poisoned by someone physically in the room with her. That means Nani is going to enjoy herself. She makes me go to afternoon tea with her in a fancy café, and then immediately scoffs at the prices. Unsurprisingly, she's brought along some biscuits she got in a nearby shop and we share a pot of tea for £2 while sneaking bites of cookies when the waiters aren't looking.

"Have another cookie," Nani says in Punjabi. Nani emigrated to England years ago, and Mum was born here. Dad was born in India, and they had what Nani calls an arranged marriage, but wasn't really. Their families did introduce them, but that was basically it – they started dating all on their own. "You know, Priya would like this place."

The Priya of four years ago would think this place was great. But not Priya as she is now. She doesn't *enjoy* things any more – not since Dylan died. She studies a lot, and sits around at home, and ignores most of my messages. Occasionally she comes over to my house for dinner, but she doesn't really say much. All I want is for her to be happy again, to find some peace – and until then, and way after, I'll be there for her no matter what.

When we first decided to find out what had happened to Dylan at the construction site, she was eager, determined even. There was a fire burning in her, almost consuming her, but I didn't care because that same fire burned in me.

Then we found out the truth, and it was like the fire went out.

And I was left alone with all my anger.

I had been round at Priya's house when the letter from Emily arrived, and while she had been curious about it, she thought we should throw it away. I disagreed, and decided we should find out why Emily was contacting her. *Better to know than not*, I'd said to her. *It's worse wondering.*

I told her what Emily wanted to do, of course, the second I got home from the Bramble Estate. How she wanted to frame Charles for her murder and had initially wanted Priya's help instead.

Priya listened in silence as I told her I was going to take her place in the plan, that it would be better this way, because I have much less of a link to Charles – so it would be harder for anyone to figure out what we were doing.

She'd told me she didn't want me to do this. Because she didn't want to lose me as well.

"You won't ever lose me," I'd said. "But…I *need* to do this." Because my anger was still there – burning bright. I needed justice.

"You're the best friend I'm ever going to have," she'd said. "I can't risk you getting caught, Devi."

"What's life without a bit of risk," I'd said with a grin, only she hadn't smiled because she knew me too well. She knew when I was joking and when I was serious, and I think she knew I wasn't just doing this for her.

Anyone else would have told me I was selfish – that no matter how much I was grieving for Dylan, it didn't mean as much to me as it did to Priya. We might have played football together in the park when we were little (Priya and I would take turns in goal while he shot ball after ball past us and cheered and told us he was going to be on a national football team one day). We might have got in trouble together that time Dylan was babysitting us and we wanted to oven bake some chicken wrapped in foil for dinner. Only the oven at Dylan and Priya's house was bust, so we decided we would try to use the oven setting in the microwave and ended up microwaving the foil and setting fire to the kitchen. But in the end, she was his sister and I was not.

But Priya didn't call me out. She knew I wanted justice. I wanted it so badly that it kept me awake at night, staring furiously up at my ceiling in the dark as I let the rage bubble in my stomach.

I haven't risked texting or calling her, because I'm worried the police might randomly decide they want to see my phone. Besides, there's nothing I can share. Not when it feels like we're losing, because Charles still hasn't been arrested and anything less than that is a fail. She'd have read about Emily's death in the papers, I know. She'll be expecting news from me.

Maybe I am a coward.

Not like Charles though. Even at my worst, I am nothing like him.

Every so often the image comes, completely unbidden, of Dylan lying alone while Charles walked away, while he used his power to make sure Lizzie's dad didn't call for help or speak up. I wasn't there when it happened, of course – not like Lizzie when her dad died. I can't imagine how awful that must have been. The fake images in my head are enough to keep me up at night.

"You're too quiet today," says Nani as she passes me another cookie under the table, bringing me back to the present. I snort, because she normally tells me off for talking too much. Guess she doesn't *actually* hate it. "What's wrong?"

"Nothing," I say in English. I dunk my cookie in my tea, ignoring the glare from one of the two women at the next table, whose eyes widen as she takes in the carrier bag peeking out of Nani's purse. I want to stick a middle finger up at her, but I know Nani would smack me for that, so I settle on shooting a sarcastic smile instead as I turn back to Nani. "I'm just worried… about this whole investigation. It's not nice to be wrapped up in it." I speak carefully – Nani doesn't know the truth, of course – but she knows what happened to Dylan. She knows about the inquest into his death, and how Charles was involved – and she knows how much I hate him.

Lizzie's mum has made the connection with Charles as well, but seems to walk around in a bit of a haze, not really taking anything in – *a small world*, is all she said on the topic. Originally, she announced she would be delivering the necklace to the estate. I knew Lizzie had panicked about the plan going wrong, because obviously that was the excuse she was using to get herself to the scene. Lizzie had to persuade her it would be best if she went, because her mother was so much more anxious about it.

"Speak Punjabi," snaps Nani. I roll my eyes – if I do speak Punjabi, she'll tell me off for how crap I am at it. Although I can understand it, speaking in it has never felt natural to me. My tongue trips over the words, my thoughts don't move as quickly. "And if this doesn't go the way you want it to, you just move on, okay? No harm done." She adds in English, "Win some, lose some." She gives me a knowing look – I wonder how much she suspects; whether she has spoken to Lizzie's mum and worked out both Lizzie and I hold grudges against Charles. She won't say that aloud, of course.

She's wrong about there being no harm done if this doesn't end well. If Charles doesn't go to prison, he wins. He gets to stay out in the world, ruining lives and getting rich, and I just have to *deal* with it. I just have to go my whole life knowing I couldn't even do one thing for Dylan: get him and Priya and their parents the justice they deserve.

The conversation at the next table gets louder. "I just can't believe Charles Vanforte would kill his wife," says one of the two women, the one who glared at me for chomping my own biscuit even though none of the staff seem to care that much. Nani isn't even being discreet any more. She's just asked for a refill of our pot of tea, and a plate for the rest of the cookies.

"I heard nasty rumours about that Emily, you know," says the woman's friend. "Apparently she wouldn't let him divorce her." Emily said this would happen. That people might criticize Charles but she would take some of the heat as well, even though she was the victim. People might still find a way to try and blame her. White hot anger rages in me – *Charles* is the bad guy, and I'm more determined than ever to make sure he is found guilty.

Nani gulps down her tea. "Let's go."

I arrive back at the hotel to find Lizzie sitting on the floor outside my room, her face red. She leaps up when she sees us, her eyes flicking between me and Nani.

"Hello," she squeaks. "Devi, I was just wondering if you would help me pick out something to wear for dinner tonight." She's clutching a piece of paper and her eyes look wild.

Lizzie's lying is awful – she always sounds terrified. It worked fine at the Bramble Estate because we *were* supposed to be terrified, but it doesn't really fit now. Luckily, Nani isn't listening. She lets herself into her room, ready for her afternoon nap. Then she'll have a bath and get into bed and watch whatever's on TV. I've tried to tell her about streaming services, but she doesn't care. At six o'clock she'll order dinner and eat it in her room; she's done for the day and won't be leaving again.

"Sure," I say, as we go into Lizzie's hotel room. Her mum has a migraine and Lizzie says she'll be hanging out in her own room for a while.

I stop short when I see Jayne standing by the window,

holding a piece of paper and looking worried – well, it's hard to tell with her, but her lips are pursed and her free hand is clenched into a fist.

"What are you doing here?" I ask her. "We weren't planning on meeting up."

But Jayne looks very concerned – clearly now is not the time for me to get all cautious.

Lizzie is going redder and redder. "I am *stressed out*," she hisses at us. "What are we going to do. What are we going to *do*?"

"What are you on about?" I say, starting to get frustrated.

Lizzie thrusts the piece of paper at me.

TO ELIZABETH NEWTON-HILL,
CHARLES VANFORTE INVITES YOU TO DINNER AT
THE BRAMBLE ESTATE TOMORROW NIGHT. OTHER
INVITEES ARE CHARLOTTE VANFORTE, TATE ASTUR,
DOUGLAS TREEFAIR, DEVI MISTRY AND JAYNE
FARAWAY.

"What the hell?" I say. "He's inviting everyone who was there that night?"

"The concierge knocked on my door and gave me the message," says Lizzie. "But obviously you were out…"

"Someone put it through my letter box," chips in Jayne.

I go to my room and, sure enough, underneath the door there's an identical message. For a moment, I stare at the words. They are handwritten in capital letters – almost like the writer is trying to disguise their handwriting.

I go back to Lizzie's room, feeling lost for words – which is strange because usually I always have something to say. My heart is hammering, but I want to make it look like this doesn't faze me. If I *act* like I'm in control, then I will *be* in control.

"Do we think Charles is trying to figure out who killed Emily?" I ask, trying to keep my voice steady. "Bringing together all the suspects and witnesses?"

"Is he allowed to do this?" says Lizzie. "Contact us like this? Won't the police think this is really suspicious? And the Bramble Estate – isn't it a crime scene?"

"The dining room was, but probably isn't any more," I mutter, as I stare at the invitation. "The police have already searched the house – that's basically all they've been doing, besides interviewing us." There's something odd about the invite, random black markings in places. I realize there's something written on the back.

I turn over the page, where someone has scrawled:

I know what you three are doing

The Present
Jayne

"Charles knows about us," says Lizzie. "Charles *knows*." She is breathing rapidly, her face bright red. Tears drip down her cheeks. "Charles KNOWS." She has been repeating the same thing for the past three minutes, in between sobs.

My heart is jumping and I'm trying to take steady breaths. If I speak, it'll show them how worried I am. I need to stay calm, keep my emotions to myself. *In, out. In, out.* Just listen to them until I can think of something sensible to add.

"Okay, *someone* knows, but we need to think about this logically, right?" says Devi. She seems a lot calmer than Lizzie. At least she's not crying. "Maybe it's not Charles – if it was, we might all be dead by now. We know he's happy to commit murder to keep his secrets safe. So, it could be from Lottie, Douglas or Tate." She opens the hotel mini fridge and starts rooting around. "Ah, excellent," she says, as she emerges with a can of Coke. "Anyway, I reckon we've not got anything to worry about."

"How have you come to that conclusion?" says Lizzie.

"Well, they haven't turned us in, right?" says Devi. "So, either they're not planning to or they don't have enough evidence of what we're doing." She cracks open her Coke and gulps it down, her throat bobbing. She can't be that thirsty, but she keeps glugging. When she stops, her face is carefully blank.

"They can *get* evidence," hisses Lizzie.

A smile slowly spreads across Devi's face. "Can they?" she says. "I think we can use this dinner to our advantage…"

"You're not suggesting we *go back*?" says Lizzie, so alarmed she nearly falls off her bed, where she is perched. "We need to get out while we're ahead—"

"We're *not* ahead," points out Devi. "We've given that detective loads of evidence – Charles had the means and the motive, right? And yet he *still* hasn't been arrested – I guess because the opportunity part of the equation is still shaky. Plus it'll look odd if we don't go – and maybe we can…I don't know, see something suspicious while we're there or something."

"Emily didn't tell us to plant any more evidence—"

"Emily's dead!" snaps Devi. "So, it's down to us now, right? This was always the plan. For us to keep going."

We stand in silence as the three of us digest the words.

Devi swallows. "We *should* be in the clear, with all the evidence…" Her mouth hangs open. "The diary extracts…" She looks at me. "When I was at the estate, someone in a black hood left some of Charles's diary extracts for me to find. They were *bad* for Charles – he talked about how much he hated Emily a *lot*. I handed them over to the police, and in my interview I told them I thought it was Tate who left them. He could be the one

322

who wrote the message on the back of the dinner invite. Maybe it's not a threat – maybe he's offering help."

"We need to go to that dinner," I say slowly. My thoughts whirl as a concern starts to niggle at me.

"Great," says Devi with a grin. "Then it's all settled. We're going back to the Bramble Estate."

65

The Present
Jayne

I wake up early the next morning. Earlier than Gran. I consider trying to go back to sleep, but I know I won't be able to. So I head down to the living room, which is small and dark, crammed with furniture and knick-knacks Gran has collected from car boot sales. The sofas are covered in faded blankets.

My plan is to spend the day in front of the TV. I already know I won't be able to focus on anything but the thought of dinner at the Bramble Estate. Speculating why Charles Vanforte is inviting over everyone who was there on the night of Emily's death. Or else wondering if Devi is right and Tate is trying to help us.

Gran comes down for breakfast, and places a stack of buttered toast on the table in front of me. She doesn't try to speak to me. But I know the toast means, *I love you.*

At midday, Gran goes out to see her friend Shirley. It has crossed my mind several times that it's probably sad my gran has more of a social life than me. I don't *feel* sad about it, though.

I can't help but glance at the clock as I watch a show about people trying to fix their houses or their relationships or something. Five hours and thirty-two minutes to go. Nervous anticipation thrums through me.

I am curious to see what Charles, or possibly Tate, wants. I want to see the plan through.

But that's not the only reason I want to go back. Devi called late last night to point out that if the person who sent the message saying *I know what you three are doing* is working against us, it still doesn't matter: there's no proof. Plus, it's not like we actually did much – Emily was the one who got the drugs from the company. Charles *was* in debt. All we did was plant the evidence. Draw attention to it. Let the police draw their own conclusions.

Except—

I've been sloppy.

It's not like me at all, but I was bound to make a mistake eventually.

I just wish it wasn't such a big one.

The Present
Devi

I've told Nani that Lizzie and I are going round to Jayne's for dinner. If I said we were going back to the Bramble Estate she'd insist on coming with us, and I don't want her anywhere near that house.

Lizzie and I ride the lift down in silence and head into the car park, where Jayne is waiting in her car. I know Lizzie thinks this is an awful idea – she's said as much several times, and she keeps shooting me daggers, like I'm forcing her to come at knife point. But at least she's quiet now.

The three of us know the plan – keep our mouths shut, stick to our original stories, act like we don't know anything and that we're terrified. Obviously, Lizzie won't even need to worry about acting terrified, because she's been visibly shaking for about an hour.

Jayne drives slowly and carefully – though it hasn't snowed for a few days, rainfall last night has meant the snow is now frozen under a layer of ice, so the roads are treacherous. As we near the estate I start to feel flutters of nervousness in my stomach – I'm worried about what we are walking into, even though I won't admit it to Jayne and Lizzie.

The enormous gates silently slide open – at some point in the past week Charles took time out from mourning his wife to get them sorted. The driveway is clear of snow, but the surrounding grass is still buried. Jayne drives us right to the front door, which opens as she cuts off the engine.

Lottie Vanforte steps out. She's wearing a black jumpsuit and a black jacket that wraps round her – I wonder if these are supposed to be mourning clothes for Emily. Her hair is pulled up into a bun and her lips are painted a deep red.

"Ah," she says. "You came." Her voice shakes as she speaks.

"You sound surprised," I say. Her face has a pinched, nervous expression to it. I glance at Jayne and Lizzie – both of them seem as confused as I am.

"Follow me," Lottie says, her voice high-pitched. "Come *on*," she says, pausing when we hover in the doorway. I'm intrigued now – why's *she* meeting us at the door, and not Charles or Tate? But curiosity wins over any annoyance at being ordered about, so I follow, Jayne and Lizzie behind me.

Lottie leads us through to the dining room, closing the door behind us. I look around with interest. This is the first time I've ever seen it, even though I've heard about it so many times. It's a long room, with a huge table in the centre. Emily Vanforte probably sat at one end, Charles on the other, miles apart. The walls are dark red, and the chandelier hanging from the ceiling gives off dim lighting.

I imagine the scene that night with Emily, how easy it would have been for her to slip the poison into her drink while no one else was looking. Would she have been scared at all? Would she have worried about her plan failing – about dying for nothing – or would she have trusted that Jayne, Lizzie and I would succeed even after she was gone? She must have had a *lot* of faith in us, confidence that we wouldn't just walk away – and for some reason that hardens my resolve to see this through. Emily believed in us.

Lottie crouches down by the fireplace, and picks up a poker. "Sit," she squeaks, shaking the poker like she's trying to threaten us with a whack if we don't listen. It slips slightly in her hand – her palms must be sweaty. I've never been less scared of someone in my life, but I've got no clue what's going on so I do as I'm told and sit.

Lottie remains standing, holding onto the poker. "So, please tell me," she says. "Why are the three of you trying to frame my father for my mother's murder?"

The Present
Devi

My first thought is, *Crap*. My second thought is, *How did she figure it out?*

Jayne and Lizzie are sitting either side of me, and haven't said anything. I realize they're waiting for me to speak.

"I don't know what you're talking about," I say. My voice is smooth, but inside I'm scrambling to try and work out what we should do. What game is she playing?

"I've been doing some investigating," Lottie says, and my heart sinks. "Specifically, into you, Jayne and Lizzie. It was a coincidence, you three being there the night my mother died – of course, I knew you couldn't have killed her, but all the same..." The poker slips from her hand, falling to the floorboards with a dull thud. She makes no move to pick it up. "I thought it was odd. I searched her office, for her burner laptop – yes, I did think it was odd she had a burner laptop, with a burner email account logged in, but that was my mother. The police didn't

329

find it, of course, because she hid it well. Her password for the laptop was Bramble Estate, can you believe it? She'd deleted most of her emails, and was careful, of course, but in one draft email I saw your names mentioned *before* she ever met you. You're all connected to my dad – although, Devi, that's just a guess for you since I didn't find anything obviously linking you to him."

I don't say anything, trying to keep my expression blank, although inside I'm screaming. Why the hell was Emily putting our names into an email? *Who* was she emailing? She'd screwed us over. How would we explain why Emily knew about us before we were ever supposed to have met her? Unless we can spin this to make it seem like Emily *lured* us to the house or something? If all Lottie has is an email with our names, she's got no proof of our plan.

"So, I assumed all three of you had a grudge against my dad," Lottie carries on. "But *he* wasn't murdered. I considered whether it was a mistake, whether you meant to kill him instead. But obviously you couldn't have done, because there was no way you could have been in the dining room… And then I found out about my mother's diagnosis and things clicked into place…" She pushes a strand of hair out of her eyes.

"I still don't know what you're talking about," I repeat.

"Where's the laptop?" whispers Lizzie, which is an excellent question – is there any way we could nick it? But to my surprise, Lottie crosses the room to a cabinet and pulls it out, placing it on the table. Immediately I want to reach over and grab it, but I force myself to be calm – now is not the time to act recklessly, even if it goes against every instinct.

"My dad wanted to have a dinner with everyone who was there the night Mum died, to see if he could find out anything else the police haven't," Lottie continues. I hold back a snort – of course Charles thinks he's better than the police. "But I was in charge of the invitations, and I put an earlier time for your arrival so I could speak to you alone first. I want answers – my mum hid *so* much from me, and now she's gone and I just... I always knew she didn't like me. I didn't think she *hated* me. But she must have done, right? Because she knew my dad is all I have, and she wanted to take him away from me."

I try not to roll my eyes. It's a bit self-centred to think Emily did all this because she wanted to get back at her daughter for having a favourite parent.

Lottie seems to sense my derision. Her eyes fix on me. "Please, tell me the truth."

Lizzie opens her mouth, but I shake my head at her. We're not gullible enough to fall for this – the plea for honesty. For all we know, Lottie is faking it – she could easily have been put up to this by Charles. "How do we know you're not secretly recording us, or wearing a wire or something? Or that your dad's not secretly listening in?"

Lottie's smile is sad. "Dad's in his study. Douglas and Tate are on the PlayStation upstairs. There's no passageways to this room – no one could be eavesdropping. I'm not going to do anything with the information you tell me – look, you can even take the laptop." She pushes it towards me. "I know you want it – and you've got my word, however much that's worth, that I haven't made copies of the emails. No one else knows about Mum's burner account. Just...*please*, I need the truth." She's now looking at Jayne as she pleads, and I have no idea why. But maybe Jayne has a softer side than I gave her credit for, because she nods as she reaches forward and grabs the laptop.

"We won't tell you everything though," says Jayne. "Just…" She pauses, and I hold my breath waiting to see what she says, curious against my better judgement because I still think the best thing for us to do is say nothing and leave. "We're all connected to Charles Vanforte through the people he's hurt – the people he's killed. And he's hurt a *lot* of people. Your mum knew that – she wanted to punish him. She tracked us down, asked us to help frame him for her murder to punish him for the murders he got away with."

Lottie has been so softly spoken, so timid, so much of a people pleaser, I expect her to nod along with Jayne. But instead she wipes her eyes and seems to steel herself, straightening her back. "I don't believe you. About my dad being…being a killer. That's *ridiculous*."

"Why would we lie?" I snap, familiar anger rising in me – it's always there, bubbling away; it won't go until I've got justice for Dylan.

"Because…because you've listened to my mum and she's a *liar*," says Lottie. "Do you think she cared about you at all? No, she died and she left you to deal with the consequences of her poorly thought-out scheme. Because that's all everyone else was to her, you see. Pawns in her game." She curls her hands into fists. "While my mother was off saving the world, my father was *here*, going to all my piano recitals because he knew how much they meant to me. He was here helping me with my homework, and talking to me like a person and not a project—"

"Charles Vanforte is a monster—" I start.

"No, he's not!" yells Lottie. "My *mother* was the monster. My mother hated me so much she brought me here on the night she carried out this horrible plan so I could be a suspect in her murder – so I could watch her *die*. I'm going to have that image seared into my mind for ever. What kind of mother *does* that? She was a liar, she spent her whole life manipulating other people. You know…*she* was the one who told people that my dad had an affair and a secret child? She acted like it was just a rumour, but it wasn't."

"Why would she do that?" I frown.

Lottie folds her arms. "She wanted to punish my father. They always hated each other. I knew my father *did* have another child out there – and I'd been trying to find them for ages. But my mother sat on that secret for years – she held onto it until she found the best moment to use it against him. Which turned out to be when he started campaigning to get into politics. My mother loved every second of watching that rumour spread." She pauses. "You think my father is a bad person? You didn't know anything about Emily Vanforte."

The Present
Lizzie

I decide to speak, even though it feels like my throat has closed up and I'm panicked down to my core that Lottie knows what we've done. I *knew* this moment would be coming, that something would go wrong. "Even if your mother wasn't a good person, Lottie – your father ruined our lives—"

"No, he didn't," says Lottie, getting to her feet. "He didn't, you're just looking for someone to blame and my mother picked up on that. She liked exploiting people, using people—"

My father's last breath flashes before my eyes, and the words tumble out of my mouth without a thought. "That doesn't change what he did," I say.

"So, you didn't mind the fact your dad had an affair, and you have a sibling somewhere in the world that you've never met? And you don't mind that your dad has killed people we love?" says Devi, tilting her head.

Lottie's nostrils flare. "You're...*lying*..." She repeats the word again, like it's a life raft and it's all she can cling onto. "My dad would never hurt anyone—"

"Good lord," mutters Devi, and I can tell she's frustrated with how blinkered Lottie is, because her tone is getting sharper – but she's not going to get anywhere by being snappy. When people get annoyed with me, it makes me retreat into my shell more and I suspect it might be the same for Lottie. I want to tell Devi to be nicer, but I know she might turn her annoyance on me instead and I don't want that either.

Lottie takes a few deep breaths, her eyes flicking from Devi to me to Jayne. She looks like she's on the verge of saying something else – but then she seems to change her mind, because she turns to leave the room.

But before she can, Devi is on her feet and racing across to the door, blocking it.

"You absolutely can't tell the police about us having connections with Charles Vanforte," Devi says. "Or your father. Because if you do... If you do... I'll say you tried to kill me. Or something less stupid." Her face flushes red. "Think about the *reasons* we're connected to your father, Lottie. Do you think that coming out will hurt him or help him in this investigation? It's a coincidence that we had a prior connection to Charles – that's all the police will think. And who knows, maybe our stories of what he did could be evidence of his ruthlessness – making it way more likely that he had it in him to kill his wife." She thrusts her arms out, like she's imagining invisible chains tying her to the door, making it clear that she's not going to budge.

"Lottie won't say anything," says Jayne, her voice calm as she looks at Lottie. She's sitting with her arms folded, her dark eyes unreadable as they flick between Lottie and Devi. I have no idea how she can be so sure, but then she glances at me and her eye twitches – she's bluffing.

"I won't," says Lottie. "And you can't just keep me in here for ever, Devi."

Devi seems to come to the same conclusion, that she can't trap Lottie inside her own home. She steps aside reluctantly, and Lottie leaves.

"Dinner's in half an hour," she says over her shoulder.

"Why the hell did you agree to speak with her?" Devi wheels around to face Jayne. "We should have just kept our mouths shut—"

"We didn't tell her anything she didn't already suspect," says Jayne calmly. "All she wanted to know was *why* we were doing this—"

"She *suspected*," said Devi. "But she didn't have any proof."

"She still doesn't have any proof," says Jayne, getting to her feet. "It was always possible that the police might look into our backgrounds. We can be better prepared if they ask about any connections to Charles now." Jayne is collected, not panicked at all – I feel myself relaxing. If she's not worried, then I don't need to be.

None of us speaks for a moment, but surprisingly it's Jayne who breaks the silence.

"I want to see Ms Bromley," she says, picking up the laptop and tucking it under her arm. "I want to see how she's doing... Especially since she's apparently been put in charge of this dinner all on her own."

I forget that Jayne actually *knows* Ms Bromley, that her part of the plan involved working at the estate. Neither Devi nor I say anything, so Jayne gets to her feet and leaves.

Devi and I remain in silence.

"Lottie was right, you know," says Devi at last. "We didn't know Emily Vanforte."

"But we did know Charles," I say. "Whatever we find out about Emily – that doesn't change what Charles did, who he is."

Devi nods, as voices float towards us – loud, angry voices. Immediately I'm flashing back to the last time I saw Emily, standing at the top of the stairs and looking down on the four people at the bottom. She'd told us she would start a fight in the hallway, of course, so we were ready and prepared to go and listen and then feed back to the police that she'd been threatening to drop a "secret", a nice little motive for her murder. But this time Devi and I are left looking at each other, not knowing what we should do.

It's Devi who gets up and leaves, to see what's going on. I hurriedly follow her to the entrance hall. Tate is standing in the middle of the hall, looking up to the balcony, his mouth hanging open.

Douglas and Charles are both on the balcony; Douglas is shouting. "You're a liar," he yells. "I would never—"

"Get out of my house and never come back," snaps Charles, his voice echoing down to us. "Stay away from my daughter."

"You think I haven't *wanted* to break up with her?" says Douglas, his voice bitter. "You don't think it's been torture for me, keeping this relationship up? She deserves better than a piece of crap like me, but she *loves* me, even after I've treated her awfully. She would never give up on me because she's a *good* person and the best thing I could do is leave her, but I *had* to stay with her, she's my ticket out of the mess my parents made. But *you* – you pretend to be a saint – and the worst part is, you believe it too—"

"They've been arguing for like five minutes," mutters Tate to us. He doesn't seem surprised to see us half an hour earlier than we were supposed to arrive. "I'm not clear why…" His lips are pressed together, and there's a slight look of concern on his face. I think he knows exactly why they're arguing, exactly why Lottie was Douglas's "ticket out" of his own family's drama.

The three of us stand and gape upwards, transfixed by the argument.

And then, louder than anything I've ever heard before, a *bang* rings out and Douglas starts screaming.

Tate immediately drops to the ground, dragging me and Devi down with him. "That's a gun!" he shrieks, and I look up as a second bang shatters around the room.

"Oh my God," Charles is screaming. "Douglas – Douglas!"

Devi is struggling to her feet – I have no idea what she's doing. But she's running up the stairs – not to where Charles and Douglas are, but towards the sound of the gun.

"Get back here!" yells Tate, as he gets to his feet. He's up and running too, and I am as well, not really sure what I'm doing, as I follow him up the stairs. I reach the landing, to find Charles on the ground, clutching Douglas – and I don't know where to look, but I am standing, staring, transfixed. Douglas's eyes are fluttering and he's breathing rapidly, and there's blood spreading across his shirt.

338

All of a sudden I am not in the room any more – I am thirteen years old, and I am holding my father and telling him, *Wake up, wake up, wake up*! But he won't wake up and I don't know why he's not listening to me, but I know it's the end of the world, the worst thing that will ever happen to me.

And I'm back in the entrance hall of the Vanforte mansion as Charles holds Douglas, then lies him down.

He's been shot.

I stand frozen, gaping as Charles tries to take his pulse, but I know there's no point getting my phone out to call an ambulance, because I have seen this before and I know what is happening. Douglas's skin is ashen, his breathing is laboured, blood is pooling around him. His eyes dart around before they fix on me.

"Tell Lottie I'm sorry," he whispers. "I…never got to be better." And his head lolls back, and I see the moment the life goes from his eyes.

Douglas Treefair is dead.

The Present
Devi

I don't know what takes over me. It's a fight or flight situation – and I want to fight.

The second gunshot rings out and I'm suddenly on my feet, running towards the noise. A part of my brain is screaming at me, telling me I'm being stupid, that I need to get *away* from the gun, but another part doesn't care.

There's yelling behind me as I run up the stairs and go right, to where the bang came from. I'm in a corridor – and it's empty.

Whoever pulled the trigger can't have gone far. I keep going, feet pounding, turning a corner – and there's no one there. I'm running again, down the next corridor, because surely the shooter is close by. I stop, panting in the middle of the corridor while I stare at the empty hallways leading away on either side of me.

"What are you *doing*?" Someone grabs my arm. My free hand is balled in a fist and I'm swinging a punch before I can even think about it.

Tate catches my hand, stopping me.

"What are you doing?" he repeats, breathing heavily. He's twitching, looking back in the direction of the main entrance hall where Charles and Lizzie and Douglas are—

I don't want to think about what I just witnessed. I want to think about the shooter.

"There's a killer in this house," I say. My entire body is trembling, and Tate is still holding onto my hand. I stare at it, then at him, because my mind has been hurtling so fast that I've forgotten something important. *Tate was the last person to have a gun.* I know he wasn't the shooter because he was with me. And though it might have been a toy one, it probably wasn't, because he'd had a gun and now—

And now Douglas is dead.

I can't not think about him. The way he crumpled to the ground is lodged in my mind, and even though there's a slim chance he could still be alive, I know deep down that he's gone.

He was a horrible person to me. He threatened to stab me, and he called me a liar – but there were flashes, moments when I thought he wasn't as bad as he seemed. But now he's dead.

He's *dead*.

"Someone shot Douglas," I whisper, staring at Tate. He's nodding, and his throat bobs as he swallows. He's in shock – just as much as I am. Maybe more. Because he knew Douglas, properly. He went to school with him, grew up with him there. Maybe there was more to Douglas than the awful boy I met, there had to be.

I'll never know though.

I look down the corridor again, but it's empty – of course, it's not like the shooter is going to come back.

Jayne, Lizzie and I thought we were the ones in charge of everything that was happening in this house, that we were in control – but what if there's someone else playing our game? Someone unknown killed Douglas…

A bolt of electricity shoots through me at the thought of the unknown, because I've run through loose threads after the night Emily died again and again, things I didn't understand. And one of them was the fact I saw *someone* dressed all in black leaving the West Wing, and later looking up at a portrait of Emily – giving me Charles's diary extracts. That might have been Tate – but it might not. The question bursts out before I can think further.

"You didn't leave extracts from Charles's diary for me to find the other night, did you?" I ask him quietly. He stares at me blankly, obviously with no idea of what I'm talking about. So, if it wasn't Tate who left me those extracts… It might have been the same person who just shot Douglas.

My mind is racing and I know it's partly because I don't want to think about what just happened, but I don't care, I feel like I'm about to figure out something important. The person who left the diary extracts was tall and bulky – a broad-shouldered man. Something about that niggles in my head – I *have* seen pictures of an older man before, linked to the family; the mysterious older sibling Lottie was searching for.

There are so many places in the Bramble Estate someone could hide. I made jokes about horror films when I was chatting to the police, about killers living in secret, waiting for the right moment. But what if I was on to something – what if Charles's secret son has been with us in the house the entire time, and he wants revenge on Charles for never acknowledging him? Maybe he's got a vendetta against the Vanfortes, and anyone associated with them, and wants to pick them off, one by one?

The theory is obviously ridiculous, of course it is.

But the seed is planted in my mind now – Charles's secret son might have killed Douglas. And he might not stop with him.

I don't want to go back to the entrance hall, but it's like there's something drawing me to it, a piece of the puzzle I might see. So, I turn on my heel and walk silently back, Tate staying on my heels like he's in some sort of daze and has latched onto the idea that I know what I'm doing.

Charles is still kneeling next to Douglas, staring at him, his face pale with shock. Jayne and Ms Bromley are coming from the kitchen corridor down below, and Lottie has appeared from the corridor behind the body, and Lizzie is leaning against the far wall, breathing slowly in and out like she's trying to stop herself from panicking.

"Someone call an ambulance," gasps Lottie. "Someone call an ambulance!" she screams this time, because we're all just standing and staring. I can hear her, but I don't move to get out my phone – because it's clear there's no rush now.

Douglas is dead. Nothing we do now will bring him back.

Lizzie is looking at me, shaking her head, and I look down at Jayne, whose hand is clapped over her mouth in horror.

And finally, it properly hits me – we helped Emily stage her own murder.

But now there's a real murderer at large.

The Present
Lizzie

It takes ages for the police to arrive – I guess the icy roads slow them down. We wait for them in the dining room. I sit with Devi on a bench in the corner of the room. Jayne has disappeared somewhere, so I cling onto Devi's hand, and she doesn't tell me to let go.

Then the door opens and Jayne quietly enters, sitting down next to me and hunching over.

"I put the laptop in my car," she mutters, staring into space. I'd completely forgotten about the laptop – all I can do is think about Douglas. We need to be alone, to discuss…

Tate sits on one side of the dining table, Lottie on the other. Tate is tapping a rhythm on the table, while Lottie stares into space, her eyes blank. Her face is pale and tear-stained. I wonder what she's thinking.

Charles isn't with us. He's probably burning everything he was wearing when Douglas died. That's what I would have wanted to do – when Dad died, I threw out everything that reminded me of that day, and scrubbed at my skin until it was red and raw, like that would be enough to wash away the memory of what had happened.

Ms Bromley is back in the kitchen. She looks so frail, clutching her chest as she stares at Douglas, I'm half worried she might drop dead from the stress.

My blood is pounding in my ears, because unlike last time, when Emily died, I know there is an actual murderer about. Maybe it would have been better if there was a ghost haunting the estate after all, something supernatural picking off its victims. We could say its motive was just that it was naturally evil. It's almost worse, somehow, that we know the killer is human. That somewhere in their minds they thought it was okay to kill a seventeen-year-old boy; that they thought there was a good reason to do that. Douglas was never my favourite person, but he didn't deserve *this*.

What is going on?

We thought we were in control, that we had a handle on things. We were the ones who knew the truth about what had really happened the night Emily died. I was terrified the entire time, but I was living with the fact my father's murderer had walked free and I knew I could finally do something to *make things right*. Charles swapped Dad's heart medication like it was nothing, the easiest thing in the world, because he didn't want to deal with the fact my father would tell the world the truth about how evil he really is.

I wish Dad was with me now. He always knew exactly what to say. There was one time when I was eleven and I came home

345

from school crying, because Natasha and Hannah had decided to go on a walk at break-time and hadn't bothered to include me. I was left sitting alone on a bench, pretending to read like I didn't care. I knew I was oversensitive – Natasha and Hannah had told me so enough times – and that in the grand scheme of things it was a stupid thing to be upset over. But I was sobbing to Dad, and I couldn't get out the words to explain why seeing them walk around the school fields without me cut so deeply. I couldn't explain that my whole world was school, and it felt like nothing else mattered but fitting in with everyone else, and being liked – having someone to sit with at break-time, having someone to partner up with in class. I had a constant hope that tomorrow would be better, that I would finally be included – and that hope was wearing me down, because when I got to tomorrow I found it was never better. I walked around wondering why people couldn't just *like* me? Why could Natasha and Hannah not just include me?

What was wrong with me?

I didn't say any of that to Dad – it was too embarrassing to admit that I didn't have any proper friends, but he seemed to understand all the same. He didn't tell me that one day none of it would matter, that I would look back on high school and wonder why I cared so much. But he *did* stroke my hair and tell me that there was nothing wrong with me, that I was a wonderful, special person, and I wouldn't always be *everyone's* cup of tea – but I would always be his. And then he went off and made me a cup of tea, and I remember clutching it in my hands, the heat scorching through the mug, and this warmth spreading through me as he sat next to me and let me cry.

Ever since Dad died – no, ever since he was *killed* – I have drunk a cup of tea whenever I am upset. I have a feeling if I ask for one now I might get some odd looks, even though that's all I really want.

A single tear trickles down Lottie's face and my heart gives a little twang. Lottie was following Douglas around that evening, trying to get his attention. She wasn't seeing that he didn't care about her – probably like how I'm only just starting to see Natasha and Hannah don't care about me.

I let go of Devi's hand, hardly thinking as I cross the room to sit next to Lottie. I catch Devi's eye and I can tell she wants to ask me what I'm doing. Jayne is still staring blankly into space.

Lottie looks at me, confused. "Can I help you?" she asks.

"I, er…just wanted to ask if you were okay," I say.

She blinks at me. "Am I…*okay?*"

Her repeating the question I've asked highlights how absurd it is. Of course she's not okay.

I notice, out of the corner of my eye that Tate is staring at us. "I just thought…" I trail off as Tate shifts uncomfortably.

"Leave her alone," he says wearily.

I slip back to my seat, my cheeks burning.

The police escort me and Devi back to the hotel, and say they will question us properly later. I try to hide the fear their words put in me – what if Lottie decides she's going to tell them what she suspects about us? What if they think it's more than a coincidence that we were strangers who were in the house *twice* when a murder took place?

347

The moment the police are gone and Mum finally leaves us alone – after asking me three times whether I am okay – Devi messages Jayne to come up to us. She followed us in her car, but the police don't know that.

"What the hell is going on?" says Devi at once, pacing back and forth across my hotel room. "What the *hell* is going on?"

She has summed up exactly what I'm thinking.

"Someone killed Douglas. *Douglas*," she says. "Why? Why the hell…?" She's breathing heavily as she collapses onto my bed. "I think…I think there's another person playing our game," she says. "Person X. The person Jayne and I saw walking through the West Wing before it was locked off, and who left Charles's diary entries for me to find. The person Lottie was searching for – her older brother. I think he's been hiding in the house and he's possibly out for revenge, wanting to pick the Vanfortes off one by one—"

"That's so far-fetched," I interrupt, frustration at having no idea what is going on overriding my usual need to be polite. "Why would he want to kill *Douglas*? I mean, he wasn't pleasant—"

"An understatement," mutters Devi.

"But killing him because of that?" I carry on. "I don't know…" Suddenly, I'm tired. The kind of tired where my eyes are heavy and my thoughts are woolly. But what's happened seems to be affecting Devi differently – it's like she's been injected with adrenaline. She's pacing back and forth across the room like she can't sit still.

"There's something weird about all of them in that house, you know?" says Devi. "Do you think they're *all* in on this?"

"What do you mean?" I ask, rubbing my head. It's beginning to hurt.

"Lottie knows what we're doing – Douglas is dead, so right now just Charles and Tate don't know about us and our plan," says Devi. "But maybe Charles *does* know, and all three of them are trying to get us back by killing Douglas to…er…scare us…" From the way she trails off I can tell she knows it's a rubbish suggestion. "Okay, maybe that doesn't make total sense, but if it's not Person X, the alternative is it's Lottie who killed Douglas, right? Because Tate was with us, and Charles was obviously standing next to Douglas… But that doesn't add up, because Lottie doesn't really seem the *type*, you know? Doesn't seem like she's got a violent bone in her – it *has* to be Person X."

Devi finally sits down at the writing desk, glancing over to Jayne, who is standing by the window, looking out into darkness – the back of the hotel faces open countryside. She turns, and she looks about as bad as I feel. Her black hair hangs limp around her face, and there are dark circles under her eyes. From what I can tell, she always wears black – it seems fitting, somehow, now that we're surrounded by so much murder.

"I deleted the emails on Emily's burner laptop," she says quietly, then lapses into silence again.

"Lottie might still tell the police about us," says Devi. "I know she said she wouldn't, but we had no reason to believe her before, and everything must have changed for her now that her boyfriend is dead. Even if we *do* have the laptop."

Jayne nibbles her bottom lip. "I think…I think we might be safe from Lottie for now. It seemed like she really just wanted to know what happened to her mum. And after Douglas… Her attention might not be on us at all. She obviously knows *we* didn't kill him." She folds her arms as she leans against the windowsill. "But I wonder... Maybe Emily's and Douglas's deaths *aren't* separate. Maybe...I don't know. Emily planned this as well. Maybe it's all part of a bigger show she wanted."

Devi looks lost as she gets to her feet and heads to my mini-fridge. She opens it and stares for a few seconds before closing it again, shaking her head. "I just... I don't know what we're supposed to do."

There's frustration in her voice, which is odd to hear, because Devi *always* seems sure, even when she isn't. Some people might call it unearned confidence – but I think she puts on an act, trying to seem tougher than she really is.

She flops onto the big hotel bed with its crisp white sheets and folds her arms.

Jayne doesn't look like she'll be making any further contribution any time soon, so I decide it's time for me to suggest the idea that has been niggling in the back of my mind. I lick my lips. "Maybe we should tell the police that Emily wasn't murdered," I say. "Not the whole truth," I add hastily, as Devi and Jayne both turn to stare at me. "But that we think Emily's death was a suicide – so they know Douglas's murder isn't related to Emily's death. Otherwise they might go down the wrong path trying to find the killer."

"But what about all that evidence we planted about Charles?" says Devi, getting to her feet. "What about everything we've worked for—"

"We haven't been working to turn *into* Charles," I say, getting to my feet as well. My voice is shaking horribly and I want nothing more than to be tucked up in bed at home. "If we keep quiet then we'll be helping a murderer walk free – we'll just be saving our own skins. We'll be doing exactly what we *didn't* want to do—"

"Charles doesn't get to get away with this just because Douglas is dead," yells Devi, the sudden anger in her voice making me jump.

I flinch back, but I will not let myself be cowed, not when I know we would be doing the wrong thing – all I can think about is Dad, and how *he* did the wrong thing and died guilty, before he could fix his mistake. "Douglas is *dead*. And we know something that might help the police – we need to do this!"

"No," says Jayne, her voice firm. "No, what we need to do is figure out who killed Douglas – and why. Maybe the most important thing at the moment is figuring out who this Person X is, and how they're involved. If we can do that, who knows – the police might even take all our evidence about Charles more seriously, because it'll show them we know what we're talking about."

"We can't figure out who killed him," I croak. "We're not *detectives*—"

"Why not?" says Devi. She folds her arms. "Why can't we be detectives? Why can't we solve this? We were running the show the night Emily was killed, and no one even knew it. No one suspected it because we were just three teenage girls stupid enough to be out in a snowstorm and get stranded somewhere. They didn't expect anything of us – so why don't we solve this murder now, and get back to convincing everyone else we've solved the *first* murder?" She looks from me to Jayne. "It's time for everyone to stop underestimating us."

71

The Present
Jayne

The three of us sit in a circle on Lizzie's hotel-room floor.

"First of all," says Devi. "After Emily's death, after he pulled the knife on me, Douglas *said* someone had threatened to kill him. He said that was the reason there were knives in the bedroom I was staying in. They were his secret note-giver's stash or something."

Lizzie nibbles her lip. "Right – so our suspects for that are… er…Lottie, Tate, Charles, or Person X. But we *know* Tate and Charles can't have killed Douglas. So case closed, either Lottie or Person X is the murderer?"

Devi shakes her head. "No, we don't want to be too simplistic. It's possible the person who threatened to kill him *wasn't* the person who actually killed him."

"Or he might have been lying about receiving a death threat," I mutter without thinking. Devi and Lizzie look at me, and I shrug. "It's possible – it might just be a coincidence that he said someone had threatened to kill him and then he actually died. We can't just take him at his word."

Devi nods vigorously. "That's right, we can't. But the knives are a good place to start – I saw them in that room, that's a solid clue. And if it wasn't *Douglas* who put them there, who else would have had access to that room? And why *that* room? They would have needed to know the house well enough to figure it wouldn't be used…"

"That doesn't rule *anyone* out," says Lizzie. "Although…" She hesitates. "We haven't considered Ms Bromley?"

Devi snorts. "Yeah that'd be class, wouldn't it? Sweet old lady turns killer. I do quite like the theory, though—"

"I was with Ms Bromley when Douglas was killed," I interrupt, before Devi can get going on what I guess will be a ridiculous, long-winded theory. Of course Ms Bromley didn't have anything to do with it. "Remember, I went to see her and that's when the gun went off."

"Okay, and what about this Person X, then?" says Lizzie.

"Mr Creepo," mutters Devi. "Possibly Charles's long-lost son… We know Lottie was looking for him – maybe she actually *found* him, and invited him to the house not realizing he was dangerous? Or maybe he's someone else with links to Douglas. Or any of the others, actually."

A mysterious fifth guest.

"Maybe," whispers Lizzie. "Maybe there *wasn't* anyone else in the house."

"Oh, not the bloody ghost again—" begins Devi, but Lizzie gives her such a fierce look that she shuts up.

"No, I *mean* that Emily didn't seem like the type of person to let things get past her. If there was someone else in the house, I bet she would have known," says Lizzie. Devi looks confused, just like I feel. "Emily was *tall*. She could have worn something bulky… And you said the person you saw in the West Wing was tall and bulky…"

Devi blinks at her. "But I *also* saw that same person looking up at a portrait of Emily… *After* she was dead."

A shudder goes through me, though I don't know why. Except, from what little I know of her…Emily was not a good person. And Emily liked to play games.

"Maybe Emily *didn't die*," says Lizzie.

"No," says Devi firmly. "She's dead. We might not have seen the body up close, but the police are investigating. That means *they* saw the body and have confirmed she's dead. Unless…the police aren't the police and this is part of some elaborate hoax…" She grins, to show she's joking. "I love a conspiracy theory as much as the next person, but it's not massively helpful right now. Let's get back on track – just before Douglas was killed, he was arguing with Charles on the stairs. He basically said he wanted to break up with Lottie and didn't love her at all. I know she doesn't seem the murdering type, but what if she heard that and…snapped or something? If a boyfriend of mine said that about me I'd be raging."

"You wouldn't *kill* him though, would you?" points out Lizzie. Devi shrugs.

"Not everyone is as level-headed as me," she says.

I snort. Then try to cover it up with a cough.

"Logistically, Lottie would have had time to get round to that side of the house to shoot Douglas – and then run back so she appeared to come from the opposite corridor later on." Devi speaks slowly as she thinks. "But surely I would have *seen* her… It's really a shame there's no way *Charles* could have killed Douglas. That would have been so nice and neat – him actually committing a murder after we've been trying to get him convicted of another one."

"You know what else is neat?" says Lizzie slowly. "Tate. He was with us when the shot went off. The one person who we *know* had a gun at one point…absolutely couldn't have been the person who fired it."

"He's a weird one," says Devi. "He's sort of kept himself to himself…*but why did he have a gun in the first place?* Even if it *was* a toy? That's weird anyway."

"This is ridiculous," says Lizzie, putting her head in her hands. "I can't believe we're in this position – and we're going to have to have *another* interview with the police—"

"We can just tell the truth this time, though," says Devi. "We were invited to dinner at the estate, we went because we're just super curious, we spoke to Lottie in the dining room – although they might ask what we spoke about. Crap – we'll just say we talked about boys or something, I bet they'd believe that. We need to make sure Lottie will go along with it – I guess the fact that she's the most likely suspect in Douglas's murder will make her want to be as inconspicuous as possible – and if we let her know we're willing to tell the police she dropped a bunch of hints about wanting to off Douglas or something she'll definitely keep her mouth shut—"

"That would be a *crime*," snaps Lizzie, her normal timidness vanishing at the thought of lying to the police.

"So's basically everything we've done so far," says Devi cheerfully. "What's a little more perjury? Anyway, we can tell the police that after we spoke to Lottie, we walked out, saw the argument – and Douglas was shot."

"Except the police will want to see our invitations to the estate," I say slowly. "And our invitations all say, *I know what you three are doing* on the back, thanks to Lottie."

"We'll just say we threw them away," says Devi confidently. She seems to have all the answers, even if there are probably loads of holes in them. "Lottie won't deny she invited us – she let us in and chatted to us!"

Lizzie looks at me. "What do you think we should do next, Jayne?" she asks.

"I think…" I hesitate, because I don't really know what our next move should be. I don't like this question, being put on the spot. Luckily Devi can't go too long without inserting herself into the conversation.

"There's a clear line of questioning for us," says Devi, nodding her head like that will show how confident she is. "We don't know why Tate had a gun – and the likelihood is, it's the same gun that was used to kill Douglas. So, let's go speak to him."

The Present
Lizzie

Devi and I tell her grandma and my mum the next morning that we're going for a walk. We were only supposed to be staying in this hotel until our interviews were done, but we've been asked to stick around for more interviews now... For obvious reasons. Lottie's apparently happy to keep paying, because we haven't yet been kicked out. Maybe with everything that's been going on she's forgotten she's still funding our stay.

I expect Mum to tell me I shouldn't be leaving the hotel, that she's got a migraine and I need to stay and look after her. Instead she's on the phone to journalists, telling them to leave me alone. Suddenly I have a rush of gratitude for her – every time I think about what happened to Dad, I think about how I watched him die and couldn't help. I always seem to forget Mum was there too – to pick up the pieces afterwards, even though I knew how much she was struggling as well. I know she's overprotective, but it means she loves me.

Devi messages Jayne to tell her we're going to find Tate, but Jayne replies to say her grandma isn't letting her leave the house.

"Sucks for her," mutters Devi, as we get into my car.

When we arrive at the Bramble Estate it's to find a policewoman standing outside and police tape across the gates, unsurprisingly. I stop the car and wind down the window.

"This is a crime scene," begins the policewoman, though she frowns at both of us. "Wait – aren't you Devi Mistry? And Lizzie Newton-Hill? Hey – Jeff!"

She calls to a man who was rooting around the bushes. He gets to his feet, and Devi grins.

"Hey, it's detective man!" she says with what I know is genuine enthusiasm. For all her big talk about how the police treated us like silly kids, I know she actually quite liked the detective who interviewed us originally. He might have been condescending at times, and apparently sometimes doubted Devi, but she has pointed out correctly that he *did* listen to us, and thinks Charles murdered Emily… Which, okay, means he probably isn't the *smartest* policeman in the world, but it's much better for us to have him on the investigation. Although…I think the real reason Devi likes him is because he gave her loads of snacks while they were talking.

"What are you two doing here?" says the detective. I scramble to come up with an excuse, but Devi is already speaking.

"We're looking for Tate, actually," she says, and I look at her in horror, my mouth open. Why is she telling the truth?

She ignores me, staring at the detective.

"Why?" he says.

Devi shrugs. "Want to see if he's okay," she says smoothly. "He seems like a nice guy – quite funny too…" She lowers her voice. "Lizzie has a bit of a crush on him and thinks this is the way in…"

"I do not—" I start. Devi elbows me, hard. I stop and glare at her, and she widens her eyes at me in return. "I do not want that information *shared*," I say, looking back to the detective and trying to smile like I'm embarrassed, which isn't hard because I am.

The detective and the policewoman look at each other and smirk, and I realize what Devi is doing. She's still playing up our act – stupid teenage girls, more worried about their love lives than the fact we witnessed a murder.

"The family are staying at some cottages they own further along this road, since their home is now a crime scene," says the detective. "Tate is in the one at the end…"

I nod, rolling up the window and we drive off.

"Look at that," says Devi in disgust. "We witnessed someone getting killed yesterday and they believe we're trying to get you a date."

We drive up the road. Sure enough, further down, are a group of cottages which are all in darkness.

"Park your car a bit further along," says Devi. "So if Charles or Lottie look out they won't see it."

We hike back to the cottages, and Devi peers into the far one. "There's someone inside – it's Tate… He's seen me." She waves, pointing to the door.

A second later the front door opens and Tate looks out, his

face scrunched up in confusion as he looks from Devi to me. He's in pyjama bottoms and a T-shirt, his hair rumpled like he's just woken up.

"Hello," says Devi, like us dropping by is the most normal thing in the world. "We're coming in now."

And before he can say anything she's pushed past him and gone inside.

He looks completely confused.

I shrug, in what I hope is an apologetic way, and follow Devi in.

The Present
Devi

The cottage looks like one of those holiday ones you rent online. The entire first floor of the cottage is one room: a tiny kitchen in the corner, while the rest of it serves as a living room with a coffee table in front of a fire. Even though it's freezing outside, the room is stuffy, dimly lit by a few lamps.

"How's it going, *Tate*," I say, letting his name click against my tongue. I can't help but observe that he looks *very* good, even though he's just woken up – all rumpled, with his hair standing up in little patches. "If that's even your real name." It doesn't really mean anything, but saying it makes me feel like a badass in a film and I also don't know what I *should* be saying. I know he's not Douglas's murderer, but out of the five people who were there the night Emily died, there are only three still standing – and he's one of them. And he had a gun. Which means he surely knows *something*… And could potentially be dangerous, so I don't want to piss him off.

"Er…" Tate looks confused. "You're right… Tate isn't my real name."

I stare at him, my heart thudding, because this isn't what I expected at all. Is detective work really this easy?

"Tate isn't my real name," he says. "It's a nickname – short for Nathanial." His mouth twitches – he's messing with me. I stop myself from rolling my eyes, even though I secretly find the joke quite amusing. It's the sort of thing I would do.

I can't be distracted though, and figure the best course of action is to just keep asking questions in the hope one of them sticks. "Why did you have a gun?" I ask, speaking as quickly as I can in the hope he'll get confused and let something slip. "And don't tell me it was a toy. That was obviously rubbish, wasn't it? Because you panicked and couldn't think of anything else. We want to figure out who killed Douglas, seeing as we had the misfortune to be there when one of you Vanforte lot shot him, and the police don't seem very good. We're not leaving until we've got answers."

Tate shakes his head. "That gun," he says. "That *bloody* gun – the bane of my existence, let me tell you that… I didn't think it would work, you know? I thought it was so old there was *no way* it could work. I just thought it was super valuable…"

The Present
Lizzie

Devi folds her arms as she stares at Tate with her mouth hanging slightly open. Something seems to be occurring to her.

"The knives in my bedroom – the *antique* knives," she says. "The Vanfortes have loads of valuables in their house…" She looks at me, her eyes wide like she's expecting me to read her mind. "Antiques are expensive, Lizzie. They would get a lot of *money*…" She emphasizes the last word, and I finally get it.

"You were stealing from the Vanfortes?" I ask Tate. "But… Douglas was the one who was interested in the knives…"

"Look, I told the police this after Douglas was…murdered." His throat bobs, but he carries on. "So I guess it doesn't really matter any more. It was the gun *I* stole that ended up being used to shoot him – but Douglas and I were *both* stealing from the Vanfortes."

I look at Devi, who is frowning, like this doesn't sound right to her either. Tate and Douglas seemed to strongly dislike each other – how could they have been working together? But I don't interrupt, because Tate is still talking like he's relieved to get it off his chest.

"Douglas thought the Blue Room that you were staying in, Devi, wouldn't be used – so that's where he stored the knives," continues Tate. "Apparently there was some other valuable stuff in there – a lamp, or something?"

"I hit Douglas with the lamp," mutters Devi.

I gape at Tate. Douglas was stealing from his girlfriend's family? It makes me glad I'm single.

Tate rubs his head. "I was in charge of stealing the guns. They were really valuable, apparently – they belonged to someone famous years ago or something… They were supposed to be a pair, but there was only one out on display and I was too worried about someone coming in and finding me to search for the other one. And that *stupid* gun…"

"Wait, just so I'm following – why are you so certain it was *your* gun that killed Douglas?" I ask. "Because if it *was* the gun you stole that killed him, we can narrow it down to people who knew the gun was in your possession… So, er…Douglas…" I trail off, scratching my head as I see the flaw in what I've just said.

"Of course it was Tate's stolen gun," says Devi with a snort. "In detective films, if you see a gun, then that gun is going to go off. Chopsky's gun."

"Chekhov's gun," says Tate, the corners of his mouth twitching as he looks at her. "And that rule isn't always *literally* about guns—"

"Whatever," waves Devi. "Point still stands. We know about

364

this gun. Someone stole it – that means they used it to shoot Douglas. It's the most obvious explanation."

"Yeah, and the police prefer the *obvious* explanation," says Tate, his tone turning bitter. "Even if there's holes in it. I *told* them the guns were a pair but they're stuck on the fact that they analysed the bullet that killed Douglas and it matches the type in the gun I stole."

Devi takes a deep breath. "And no one else knew you and Douglas were stealing stuff? Lottie didn't?"

He shakes his head. "It's not like I had the gun very long before someone stole it from me – they must have been watching me."

Person X – I can almost make out Devi mouthing the words as she looks at me. A shudder goes through me again, the idea of Lottie's long-lost half-brother secretly sneaking through the Bramble Estate. The fear that there's a bigger game at play.

"How did you and Douglas even start working together?" Devi says. "It's not like you had much in common."

To my surprise, Tate grins. "I've always hated my aunt and uncle – and my own parents, to be fair. They've never cared about me. My dad just wanted to dump me somewhere so he wouldn't have to see me around the house... Douglas and I are – were – at school together, he knew how much I hated my family. And I knew *his* dad's business wasn't doing well any more – not as well as Douglas would have liked, because he had quite expensive tastes. He approached me about the whole scheme, and I figured they're so rich anyway it's not like they'd miss most of the stuff. I was going to use my share to go travelling. Get away from my parents – they wouldn't have funded me, they would have thought it was pointless."

"Why didn't you just get a job?" asks Devi, pointing out something so obvious I can't believe I didn't question it as well.

"My parents wouldn't let me." Tate shrugs. "They were worried people might think they had no money or something stupid – not that they'd give me anything, they're so tight with their cash. But stealing from my aunt and uncle felt a bit like a victimless crime – Douglas knew some people through his dad, who'd take the stolen stuff off our hands, and then they'd sell it abroad."

Devi is nodding along – I guess she has similar sorts of morals. Her face is thoughtful. "So that means...Emily was right about Douglas wanting a taste of Lottie's money. And on the stairs before he died, he *said* that she was his ticket out of the mess his parents had made. He *was* only with her for her money."

"I've got no idea when Douglas decided he would steal from our family," says Tate. "I mean – he was with Lottie for a year. He must have liked her in the beginning, right? But I guess his family was having money issues and he knew Lottie was rich." He shrugs. "I've never really got on with Lottie, we're just too different – I tried to warn her about Douglas once, you know, but she told me to keep out of it. Douglas could be charming when he wanted to be. And I think deep down he did have a weird sort of conscience – he stayed with Lottie because her family had money, but I think a part of him wanted her to dump him. That's why he treated her so badly. Like...the day Aunt Emily was killed, Lottie wore this cream outfit. And Douglas told her he liked her in dark clothes, cream washed her out – so she went and changed." He shrugs. "I think what Douglas didn't get was that Lottie wouldn't *ever* dump him. Not because she's a saint of a person or anything, but because Aunt Emily always ignored her, so she's spent her whole life trying to earn approval from Uncle Charles – and so that's what she thinks love is. Something you need to earn."

Devi looks at me, and I can tell she feels sorry for Lottie. I do as well. I wonder who the real Lottie is, the one who isn't trying to get approval from the men in her life.

"But Douglas didn't leave her…because he wanted to rob her?" asks Devi.

Tate nods. "I think Charles found out what he was doing – just before he got shot."

"See, this is why you shouldn't keep loaded guns in your home," says Devi. "In case someone uses one to shoot your child's boyfriend."

There's a niggling feeling in my mind, from what she's just said.

Guns.

Plural.

There were two guns – they were supposed to be a pair. But one was already missing when Tate tried to steal it.

Where had that one gone?

"And you've got no theories on who might have shot Douglas?" says Devi. "Like…could there have been anyone else in the house?" Her mind is clearly on Person X, while I'm now fixated on the idea of there being two guns.

"Why would anyone else have been in the house?" Tate frowns.

"Well…there was that rumour about Charles having a secret son," says Devi. "And I have this feeling that someone else is involved…"

Tate shrugs. "I mean, I *think* I did once hear my dad talking about Charles's secret child – how it was better she was kept a secret because she might have competed with Lottie…"

Devi's eyes narrow, and she looks over at me. I can tell she's thinking something, but I'm not sure what.

Her mouth falls open.

"*She*," Devi repeats back.

"Yeah?" Tate glances at me, like I can shed any light on what Devi is getting at.

"And when you say competing with Lottie…" Devi is breathing heavily now, though I can't tell whether it's excitement or panic. "That suggests they're around the same age?"

"That was part of the whole scandal," says Tate. "Charles cheated while Aunt Emily was pregnant…"

Devi looks at me, and it's definitely panic in her eyes. "Oh my God," she says.

75

The Present
Devi

Lizzie is protesting that we can't break into a crime scene, but I don't listen. The cottages back onto the grounds of the Bramble Estate, and Tate has agreed to let us sneak onto the estate and out again the same way. He seems bemused, but like he wants to help – I half thought he might ask to come along with us.

Even as we're hurrying across the expanse of lawn, my mind is whirring. When I was going through the files in Emily's office, the night she died, I saw something odd... Well, I think I did. I wasn't really *looking* at the papers, obviously, just enough to quickly describe them to the police – and then really focus on the ones I added in, about Charles's bank account. But I've always trusted my gut, and it's telling me now that this is important. Because I just trusted what I was told, and Tate's revelation just now shows me that was the wrong thing to do.

I go straight to the window of the corridor we were staying in. It opens easily – no point locking it, of course. Not when you're in the middle of nowhere and there's apparently no bad people about – no thieves…no murderers.

We slip down the corridors, Lizzie following silently behind me. The police will be mainly focused on the front of the house, where Douglas's murder actually happened.

They won't be looking at Emily's office – surely not…

We manage to get to it quickly, the route familiar as I retrace the steps I took what seems like forever ago, when I was running around planting evidence and feeling invincible.

We enter the office and I go straight to Emily's files… The ones on Douglas are gone, of course – they'll be evidence now…

"What are you looking for?" says Lizzie.

Ms Bromley's file is still there – but there's another one missing, another one that shouldn't be, because there wasn't even anything in there…

Nothing in that file but an application from Jayne Faraway to work for the Vanfortes with a date on it…

With a date that I'm sure…I'm *sure*…is actually two weeks before Emily Vanforte got in contact with us.

Which means when we all arrived to speak to Emily Vanforte and she told us about her plan to frame Charles for her murder—

She already knew Jayne.

"Why did Jayne say she wanted to get involved in this?" I say to Lizzie, who is standing confused by the door, peering out in case anyone comes along.

"I don't know – but can we *go*?" Lizzie asks.

"She *didn't*," I say. "She just said her story was similar to yours – and we didn't press her, because it became clear pretty quickly she's not much of a talker."

Lizzie is looking at me now. I can see the same realization dawning on her face.

"And Tate said he heard his dad talking about how Charles had a secret daughter – around the same age as Lottie." I'm speaking quickly now. "What if there were a load of rumours going around and things got confused – and Charles *didn't* have a son, he had a daughter? Younger than people thought? Including Lottie?"

"Jayne?" whispers Lizzie.

"She's been lying to us," I say, staring at Lizzie. The three of us haven't known each other long, of course, but I thought we had a special bond, something that made us friends on a deeper level. Except that might not be true at all. My sense that we were all in this together could be false. We're all liars, we lied to the police. But I didn't ever consider we might lie to each other. "Where was she when Douglas was murdered?" I say, my heart beginning to pound with fear, because I don't want to ask the question – I don't want this answer. Jayne had said she was with Ms Bromley – but we never confirmed that with Ms Bromley, we just took Jayne at her word.

Lizzie and I had been together.

And Jayne was somewhere else.

The Present
Jayne

I am sitting in my bedroom, at my desk. Gran keeps asking if Devi and Lizzie will be coming by. She suggests I go out for a walk.

She pops her head round my door, her eyes wide with worry as she asks if I am okay. Am I *sure* I'm okay. I just stare blankly back at her until she finally leaves me alone.

Alone.

I have always been alone.

I am not like Devi and Lizzie. They are better people than me; they are doing this because they are noble people.

I am not noble. I am a bad person.

I swivel round on my chair, turning towards my desk, and I lift up the cloth covering the object in the centre.

I wish I could go back. But it is too late – too late to go back.

I stare at the gun.

INTERLUDE TWO

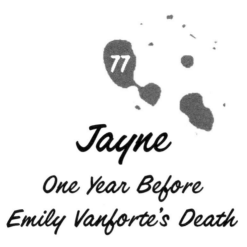

Jayne
One Year Before
Emily Vanforte's Death

Devi and Lizzie left the building, but Emily had quietly asked me to stay behind. She remained sitting, while I got up and stood by the door with my arms folded. Just in case I decided to leave.

"Have you considered my idea?" said Emily, leaning back as *she* considered *me*.

I stared at her, biting my bottom lip, careful to keep my face blank. Of course I had considered her idea. I had thought of nothing else from the moment she suggested it, turning it over and over in my mind. Examining all angles. Calculating all the risks.

"I just need to make sure this works," said Emily, her voice gentle. "That he's properly punished…"

"And your idea *does* do that," I muttered, because it was true. The idea she had presented would make sure that, no matter what, Charles would be punished.

"I am not the person the world expects me to be," said Emily. "They expect me to be a good woman, because of my charity work, because of how much money I give away. Pah, I say – it's easy to give money if you have millions more coming in. I wasn't lying when I told Devi and Lizzie earlier that I *wanted* to be a good person – don't we all wish to be seen as kind and caring? But the truth is, at my core, I am terrible. I collect secrets about people, collect knowledge, so I can use it against them. But Charles…"

"Have you also killed people?" I said, keeping my voice deadpan as I stole another glance towards the door. Emily was telling me what a terrible person she was… And I could believe it. From the cold way she was talking, the icy look in her eyes. Her voice didn't tremble as she spoke about plotting Charles's demise. She could have been discussing the weather.

"Well, Charles and I have the same…darkness, in us," says Emily. "I can admit… Having Lottie in the house the night of my death won't be pleasant for her. But if the scenario is a cosy family dinner you just happen to crash, it makes sense for her to be there. Collateral damage. The important thing is Charles goes down for this. He *must* go down for this…" Her throat bobbed. "I do care about Devi's friend and Lizzie's father – about the fact they prove what an awful man Charles is. But what I *really* care about…is me. Charles had an affair, resulting in a child, who he has been paying for in secret for sixteen years… That is the real betrayal. Being *tricked,* for *sixteen years.*" Emily's voice was laced with venom as she looked at me.

I'd only found out Charles was my dad about three weeks earlier. Mum had asked him for money to help get me through university. He'd said he would toss her – and me – out on the street if she didn't leave him alone.

He *owed* Mum money – help for my university costs would barely make a dent in all the years of child support he hadn't given. We had the house because Gran worked at the estate, not because Charles was being generous. He couldn't kick *Gran* out without Emily's permission and she would ask questions if he suggested it (and would never do what he wanted anyway). But Mum and I were *technically* not supposed to be living with her.

Mum pleaded with him to let us stay. He said he "wouldn't make a kid homeless" and as a nice compromise, only she should go.

It was a power play. He wanted her to *thank* him, like he had done *her* a favour. She found a bedsit a few miles away, but I didn't go with her. It was small and grotty and barely had any space for me. And Mum was never really a proper adult; Gran was the one who did all the sensible stuff. Like buy me clothes and make sure I ate vegetables and did my homework.

I'd always dreamed about who my dad might be. I thought he had no clue he had a daughter, that was why he wasn't in my life. But once he found out, he'd accept me for who I was. He wouldn't think I was strange, or odd. I didn't have much of an imagination, but I imagined that much.

Except the truth was, Charles had known about me my entire life. I was so *close* to him, and yet he didn't care. He didn't acknowledge me. He didn't speak to me. My whole existence was nothing but shame to him.

Something had stirred in me. Anger. I'd hated Mum for lying to me about the fact my father was a few hundred metres away my entire life – but I could see why she'd done it. While *she* just wanted to protect me, *he* really was a villain.

But despite that, despite what he had done, forcing Mum out, I had wanted to see him, just once, knowing he was my dad. I wanted to see if that would make any difference to how I felt about him. And maybe he would see me and change. Parents were supposed to be better people for their kids, right?

I hadn't been planning on confronting him, or yelling at him. But I had wanted to just…know.

I applied for a weekend job at the estate, just for an in so I could enter the house. After my interview with Emily's assistant, I strolled through the Bramble Estate casually, pushing open doors and trying to figure out if any of them led to Charles.

Instead, I found Emily.

Jayne

One Year Before
Emily Vanforte's Death

"Charles must pay," said Emily, tapping her fingers together. Devi and Lizzie were long gone now, and she was speaking to me like we were co-conspirators. "And what better way to do that than by destroying him? He ruined our lives, my dear. The extent of what he did… How he treated me like a *fool*." She spat the word out like it was the most disgusting curse in the world, like she couldn't think of anything worse. "I like the idea of sending him to prison for my murder – I like it very much. He'll never be able to stop thinking about me…" She smiled at the thought. "But of course he might *not* go to prison – as Devi and Lizzie have pointed out, he's powerful. He's got away with everything his whole life. And so…"

She reached under the table and pulled out a box.

"If it seems like he's going to get away with my…murder…" She opened the box, to reveal a gun. Her voice was calm as she said, "I want you to shoot him."

PART FOUR

THE REVENGE

The Present
Jayne

Devi and Lizzie haven't texted me to tell me how things are going, whether they've found out anything from Tate. I'm still in my bedroom, the gun in front of me. I know it probably would have been better to go with them and speak to Tate, because they'll be asking about his gun. And I have its twin. But I find it hard to lie to them, so I stayed away.

I can't keep sitting still and waiting – I need to move, clear my head. Gran is right – I need a walk. I grab the gun as I go. It feels wrong to leave it behind.

The air is cold but fresh, and the gun is heavy in my pocket. I crunch through fields, then finally, I can't be patient any longer.

Is everything okay? I type to Devi. She doesn't respond, which is weird because she normally replies instantly. I *know* it can't have anything to do with me. There's no way to link me to Charles. Beyond me living close to him.

I had heard the rumours about Charles's other child years ago. Everyone who lived locally dined out on the gossip for ages. I thought it was just talk. Until Mum told me otherwise.

When I showed up at the Bramble Estate and spoke to Emily, her first reaction was to scream at me. She'd heard rumours about Charles having an affair, maybe even started one rumour herself, but she'd never believed them – she thought the idea he'd cheat on her while she controlled the purse strings was ridiculous. She overestimated how fuelled by money he was.

But then I showed up and told her Charles was my father. She didn't take me at my word. Made me take a DNA test, with expediated results that would come back in a few days. It seemed a fairly sensible move.

The results confirmed Charles had been lying to her for years. I think that's what she really hated – that Charles had managed it for so long.

No one got the better of Emily Vanforte. That was what she said when she first told me of her plan to frame Charles. That she would be inviting Priya and Lizzie and having a conversation with us all about it. She didn't spring the gun on me until after they'd left – I think she'd been stewing about what would happen if something went wrong with her plan, because she couldn't stand the idea; it would mean Charles had won.

Emily had left my original application to the estate on file. I hadn't thought much of it, because it became part of my actual cover story. It had the date I originally applied – which wouldn't matter to the police. But Devi and Lizzie would know I had submitted it before Emily ever got us all together to discuss the plan.

Devi had looked through Emily's files – we planned that – but she wouldn't have noticed the date on it. Surely not.

What did you find out? I try again.

No response.

I check when she was last online – a minute ago.

She's ignoring me.

And I suddenly have a horrible feeling. I try once more.

What's Tate said?

I know it's out of character – me messaging so much. Devi and Lizzie will know this too. But I need to be *sure* – they can't know. They can't…

But there's a voice whispering in my head, insistent.

They know.

And suddenly I'm running back through the fields. I clutch the gun, glad to have it.

Just in case.

The Present
Lizzie

"Let's ask Ms Bromley," I say suddenly to Devi. She's looking around Emily's office now, just in case we've missed anything else. "Jayne said she was with her when the gun went off… And she did actually arrive with her after Douglas was shot. So that could mean she didn't… She didn't…" I don't want to believe Jayne killed Douglas, but for all our discussions about how we didn't really know Emily… Did we ever consider that we don't really know each other? I thought we were all in this together – we *were* all in this together. We *are*.

Devi looks uncertainly at me – maybe she's wondering about me as well. But we were together when Douglas was shot – I can trust her, surely. And she *must* know the same about me. We both got involved in this plan for the same reason…

"Yes, let's go ask Ms Bromley," she says at last, and I almost sigh in relief. At least we two are together, on the same team. She leads the way as we leave the room and sneak down the corridor, back out the way we came.

We slip through the grounds and down the path towards Ms Bromley's cottage. It stands alone, a ten-minute walk from the house. There's smoke coming from the chimney and Devi marches up and knocks.

We wait for a moment before Ms Bromley opens the door. She's stooped over and looks tired and worried.

"Hello," she says, surprised to see us. "I wasn't expecting a call… The police came to see me this morning, of course…" She shakes her head. "Would you like to come in? Have some tea with me?"

Devi and I nod. Devi looks around curiously at the little cottage. The front door leads directly into the living room, which is small, crammed with furniture – but it's spotless. Next to the little television is a bookcase stuffed with what looks like fat romances and a few notebooks. There's a fluffy red rug on the stone floor and the curtains are made of a thick, red material – the whole room is very cosy.

Ms Bromley leaves for a few minutes, and comes back with a tray laden with a pot of tea, some cups and a cake. Her hands shake as she sets the tray down, one of the cups falling over. I feel sorry for her, at once righting the chipped cup. Then I decide I should pour the tea for all of us, because she deserves to relax.

"This whole business with Douglas has just been terrible, hasn't it?" she says as she sits down. "I hope you both are okay…" She lets the last word hang; it's clear she's got no idea why we've come to visit her.

Devi swallows. "Er…last night… Did…?" I've never seen Devi struggling with words, but she is now.

"Did Jayne come and visit you?" I ask.

Ms Bromley looks from me to Devi, her mouth open in confusion. "What do you mean?" she says.

"Just before Douglas was killed, Jayne said she was going to pop over to the kitchen to see you," says Devi. "Did she?"

Slowly, Ms Bromley shakes her head.

The Present
Devi

I look at Lizzie; the question in her eyes reflects back in my own. *Why would Jayne kill Douglas?*

My phone buzzes with messages – *Jayne.*

I ignore them, feeling sick. Had she taken our revenge too far, because, as Charles's secret daughter, everything was a lot more personal for her? She *could* have been capable of murder – it was clear I didn't really know her at all, because she'd kept this secret about her parentage… Maybe she'd been aiming to shoot Charles – and missed and got Douglas instead. Wrong time, wrong place.

I had made a joke about killing Charles, but I never would have gone through and *done it*. Jayne had always played her cards close to her chest though, and she'd never actually told us why she wanted revenge on Charles.

Like father like daughter.

Ms Bromley is blinking at us.

"What's going on?" she says.

"I… Nothing," I say, feeling queasy. "Ms Bromley, can I use your bathroom?"

She nods. "It's just through there," she says, pointing at a far door. I go through it to find myself in a dark space, with stairs leading one way, a partially open door that leads to the kitchen and a second door that I guess is the bathroom. I hurry inside, shutting the door behind me. My heart is pounding as I splash water over my face, and my stomach continues to churn. What have Lizzie and I been involved in – *who* have we been involved with?

What have we done?

I did all this because I wanted justice for Dylan and Priya – except, Priya never asked me to do it for her – and I bet Dylan wouldn't have either. They wouldn't have wanted me to risk everything for them.

The truth is, I did this for *me*. I thought I would show the world they couldn't beat down the little guy, that we were people who matter too, that even if they think we have no power, it isn't true.

But what have I done to get here? I didn't want to let Charles exploit any more people – but have I been exploited instead?

I put the toilet seat down and sit on the lid, taking deep breaths. *In, out, in, out.*

I try to focus on the room around me – it's small and dark, with a roll-top bath and no shower. The walls are dark-panelled wood, like those in the main house.

I frown, noticing a slightly darker patch of wood on the wall and remembering what Jayne had told me about how to spot

390

the beginning of a secret passage. But it can't be – where would the passage be leading? The cottage is tiny.

All the same I lean over and press, and part of the wall silently slides back to reveal a passage…going down deep into the earth.

Ms Bromley and Mrs Vanforte know all the secret passageways on the estate.

Not in the house – on the *estate.*

Implying there are passages outside of the house.

A way to sneak in and out without anyone knowing, without footprints showing up in the snow… Get into all the rooms – take a valuable gun from a thief's bedroom…

But Ms Bromley is old. I'd seen her hobbling around – surely, she didn't have the strength—

Except she seems pretty strong. She looks after the kitchen, sometimes on her own. It doesn't take *that* much physical strength to pull a trigger on a small gun – and the shooter had missed. They'd had to fire twice, which meant their aim was poor… Or maybe it was their eyesight.

But how could she have got to the upstairs corridor in order to make the shot, and back down to the kitchen in time to walk out with Jayne without anyone seeing her? The timings were impossible – unless there was another secret passage linking the two.

I thought about Ms Bromley walking around all hunched over. But maybe if she walked with her back straight, she'd be tall. As tall as Emily, at least. She could wear a thick black coat which might make her look bulky…

Ms Bromley used a cane, so I assumed she had trouble

walking. But what if the cane was a prop? What if the weak old woman image was an act?

But why would Ms Bromley *want* to kill Douglas?

My earlier thought about why Jayne might have killed Douglas comes back to me: what if Ms Bromley was aiming for Charles and missed? Douglas and Charles were standing very close…

My next question follows naturally – why would Ms Bromley have wanted to kill *Charles*?

I look around the bathroom again, but of course there aren't any clues. There might be something elsewhere in Ms Bromley's cottage that explains things though. This could be my only chance to find out the truth – and I know I don't have much time.

I slip out of the bathroom and up the stairs, praying they won't creak. The stairs are narrow and steep, and there's just a rope acting as a handrail to pull myself up with. The first floor has three doors, one on the left, and two in the centre. At the far side of the little landing is another, narrower staircase.

Quickly, I open the left door, and peer inside. It's a double bedroom, with a bed neatly made and not much else.

I decide I'll just glance into the other rooms, before I do a proper search of Ms Bromley's bedroom. The second is a tiny room, with just a toilet and a sink. The third is another bedroom, but the bed has been stripped. I take a quick glance into the wardrobe, the only other piece of furniture in the room – it's empty. No one sleeps here.

I head quickly up the staircase leading to the next floor, which must be right in the eaves of the house, and wince as one of the steps creaks. I pause briefly, half expecting Ms Bromley to appear at the bottom of the stairs and ask what the hell I'm doing.

But she doesn't appear – hopefully Lizzie is keeping her distracted.

I reach the top of the stairs to find one tiny room... A small bedroom – much smaller than the unused one below. Dark. With a single bed placed under the only – minute – window.

A thought occurs to me, but it can't be right, surely not...

There's a picture on the desk, of Ms Bromley – and Jayne.

My heart trips over itself. Jayne said she lived with her grandmother. Jayne said she lived close to the Bramble Estate... Missing out the fact that she lived *on* the estate.

Jayne never properly explained how she was connected to Charles – or that her whole family was too.

My heart is thudding hard now, as I back out of the room and down the stairs. We need to get out of this cottage – it was a mistake to come here.

I go carefully down the two flights of stairs, and back into the living room. Ms Bromley and Lizzie are chatting, discussing the police officers that have arrived to figure out what's going on at the crime scene.

"Are you okay?" says Ms Bromley, looking up at me. "You were in the bathroom a while."

"Upset stomach," I grunt. I want to signal to Lizzie that we need to go, but I don't know how. She's happily sipping her tea, reaching for another slice of cake. "Er...Lizzie, I think we need to get back to the hotel. My nani's just messaged."

Lizzie looks up, her cup halfway to her mouth. Maybe she

senses there's something odd in my voice, because she doesn't question me. She frowns, then sets her cup down.

"We'll see you round," I say to Ms Bromley, as I head to the door. My heart is still pounding as my hand curves round the handle. But then I hear a click behind me.

I turn round to find Ms Bromley holding a gun to Lizzie's head.

The Present
Jayne

I take the long way through the fields to Tate's cottage, just in case there are any police about. It's a useless precaution, because I don't see a single officer. They must all be at the front of the house, where Douglas was killed.

I arrive at Tate's cottage to find the door slightly ajar, and push it open.

Inside, Tate is pacing. He wheels round to face me.

"What are you doing here?" he says.

"Where's Devi and Lizzie?" I ask.

He shrugs. "They said they were going to the house to check on something…except I saw them, about ten minutes ago, heading towards Ms Bromley's house…"

Why were they going to *my* house?

I frown at him. I must have *just* missed them.

"They were going to see Ms Bromley?" I ask sharply. I call Gran Ms Bromley at work because she thinks it's more professional. I hadn't really wanted to tell Devi and Lizzie or the police too much about me. The police obviously know she's my grandma, and that we live in the grounds. But it hadn't seemed relevant to the story we were telling.

Plus I had wanted to share minimal details. Just thinking about them makes me angry. The fact I've been *raised* on the estate, that Mum had *worked* for Charles... That he'd abused his power over her, even though she was so much younger than he was. That he'd acted like she was a problem he could fix by throwing money her way. That he'd known about me and watched me grow up and hadn't cared. Hadn't bothered to make contact. Never bothered to speak to me. Not once.

I pushed those feelings down, did my best to come across as detached as I could. Sometimes it felt like burying that anger meant I needed to bury every other emotion as well. Better to feel emotionless than open the floodgates.

"Yeah," says Tate, his face confused as he looks at me. "I mean I assume so. There's nothing else that way is there? Except a bunch of fields?"

But why would Devi and Lizzie be going to see Gran? Were they trying to figure out whether I'd been with her last night, when Douglas was shot? I used her as a bit of an alibi, because instead of going to see her straight away I had first slipped along to Emily's office, to get that stupid piece of paper with the date of my application on it: the only thing that might give me away. I didn't know whether Devi had already seen it when she was planting evidence in Emily's office, but either way it was my last loose end.

I had been walking from the office to the kitchen when the

gunshot went off somewhere else in the house – I didn't know where. Then a second one went off. And all I wanted was to get to the kitchen, to check on Gran. I ran into her on my way. She told me the gunshot had come from the main entrance…

There's something wrong with that explanation though, now that I think about it. The house is really big – but she was very precise about the location of the gunshot…

Emily had spoken to me about getting revenge on Charles. And killing him if the revenge plan failed.

But Gran also had a vested interest in wanting to see him suffer…

I know she blamed herself for what happened with Mum. It was because of her job with Emily that she and Mum lived at the estate in the first place. Which means, in a way, it was because of her that Mum met Charles. He was the reason Mum was always so…bitter about things. Why, Gran told me, she sort of gave up on herself and allowed herself to be treated so awfully by a man she convinced herself she loved – who told her he loved her too. It almost explained why she had been so absent in raising me even when she was around, why Gran was the one who was really in charge. Mum was *so young* when she had me. Barely out of her teens – basically a kid herself. Gran said it was almost like her life stalled after Charles, like she was waiting for him to change his mind and be with her.

He was the reason why, in the end, Mum had to leave us – we weren't always happy, but we got by – and then our family was torn apart.

I know Gran hates Charles. *Hates* him.

Much more than I do. Because Mum's life wasn't *completely*

ruined by Charles, was it? She got *me* out of it, that has to count for something.

But Gran sees someone who made her child suffer. And she'd do anything for Mum – and for me, too. Maybe to the point she'd be willing to do something extreme.

Tate is still giving me a confused look, like he's expecting me to say something.

When I have ordered my thoughts, though, I won't be telling him. What I'm thinking is stupid, it has to be. But I reach into my coat, for the gun. I wouldn't use it, of course. It will be good to have, though.

I push past Tate and go to the back door of the cottage, heading outside.

Towards Gran's cottage.

Towards home.

The Present
Devi

"You took a while in the bathroom," says Ms Bromley. She's looking down at my ankles. "You've got a bit of dust on you there, my dear," she says. "And my house is spotless. That passageway in the bathroom makes a small sound when it opens, did you know that?"

I nod along, my eyes fixed on the gun and Lizzie's face. Her eyes are wide, her lips pressed together to stop herself from crying. Her hands are up, to show she's not going to struggle, but Ms Bromley's eyes are locked on me.

I glance back at the door – the police are so near, just on the other side of the estate, and yet we could be the only people in the world.

"Why'd you kill Douglas?" I say at last. I need to keep her talking while I figure out how the hell I'm going to save me and Lizzie.

"I was aiming for Charles," she says. My theory was right,

then, but I don't find any satisfaction in that. "I thought he would go to prison for killing Emily – which is what he deserves for what he did to my daughter. For how he ruined my beautiful granddaughter's life by treating her like a *mistake*—"

"Jayne," I whisper.

"But the more I think about it, the more I think prison isn't enough." Ms Bromley keeps going like I didn't speak. "I think the only thing he truly deserves…is death."

The gun she's holding to Lizzie's head is shaking – not with anger or excitement, but simply with age. She hasn't been lying about that part – she is actually an old woman.

But that doesn't mean she isn't also deadly.

She's us, I realize. Us if we were older, had more time to let our anger fester. No one pays attention to teenage girls, and no one pays attention to old women.

We didn't.

"Emily told me about this plan she had, to destroy Charles," Ms Bromley says. "Emily thought she was a good friend of mine, you see… But she told me to call her Mrs Vanforte while I was working, to make sure I always knew my place, and I watched her act awfully to anyone she thought was below her, always knowing I was being paid to keep my mouth shut. So of *course* she wasn't really my friend. She was furious when she found out Charles had had an affair and then let his child be raised on her property. She raged against my daughter – not even *thinking* about the power imbalance between a man like Charles and someone like my daughter – which cemented my dislike of Emily. So I didn't particularly care that she was going to die. But her *plan* – her plan seemed good to me. I wanted to help…"

Things are clicking into place – we *did* have a mysterious person giving us extra evidence, after all.

"I left a little extract of Charles's diary for you to find and give to the police, one that showed what he really thought of Emily…" continues Ms Bromley, unaware that my mind is whirring away.

"You were the hooded person looking at Emily's portrait," I breathe. Ms Bromley straightens her back – she's tall, very tall. And her coat, hanging by the door, is bulky. There was never a Person X – only a person we didn't see. "You were trying to *help* us."

Ms Bromley nods. "I truly wanted Emily's plan to work. But I saw some flaws in it – the motive was the biggest issue for me." She smiles slightly as she looks at me. "You didn't see the issue with the motive that Emily planned as the reason Charles killed her, did you, my dear?" The way she's talking to me is so casual, like Lizzie's not standing terrified in front of her.

"No, what was the issue with the motive?" I ask, keeping my voice as casual as possible. I try not to look at Lizzie, because I don't want her to see how scared I am – if ever there was a time for me to put on a bold front, it's now.

"Well, the whole thing about Charles killing Emily because she left him money in her will…" said Ms Bromley. "It was… *stupid*. Emily made it clear how much she hated Charles – so why on earth would she give him ten million pounds upon her death? Charles never questioned it of course, he thought the money was owed to him. But anyone with a *brain*…" She shook her head. "He's kept diaries for years, you know. Hides them in a little chest he keeps locked in his study – Emily gave it to him as a gift, and didn't tell him the chest had *two* keys, one of which she kept. I borrowed that key just after Emily told me of her plan, stole a few of his diaries while I was cleaning... He always stayed with me in the room while I cleaned, but never *looked* at me, or what I doing. I was invisible to him. I knew he wouldn't notice a couple of missing diaries, he had so many. I took them away and read them at leisure – and though a lot of the entries showed a contempt for Emily, there was one which was *perfect* – paragraphs demonstrating a deep *hatred* of Emily, one so strong he might be driven to kill her. I wanted, just like you did, for Charles to face justice." It was almost as if she wasn't even speaking to me, like she'd been waiting so long to say these words aloud they were pouring out of her and it didn't matter who heard.

"Please," whispered Lizzie, squeezing her eyes shut. "Please just let me go."

"But I needed to be prepared in case Emily's plan went wrong," Ms Bromley continued. "There were too many variables in it... Like you three – your ability to lie *well* was a crucial factor and Emily just trusted you'd be up for the challenge without knowing a single thing about you. And it relied on Lottie providing evidence against her father, who she loved – something Emily never truly appreciated. She just assumed Lottie would unknowingly go along with what she wanted because Lottie has always been a bit of a pushover... Easily manipulated..." She rolls her eyes, contempt in her voice. But then her expression lightens as she continues. "You know, the night of Emily's death, I went home just like I said." It's almost like she's gossiping with us now. "But I came back via the secret passage in my bathroom to plant the diary extracts, and overheard Douglas and Tate talking about a gun Tate had stolen…so I used the passages in the house and I slipped into his room and took it. Just as a contingency plan."

"There's a passage to Tate's bedroom," I say slowly. "And there was a passage from the corridor where you shot Douglas leading down to the kitchen."

Ms Bromley nods. "Maybe you're cleverer than I thought," she says. "You know… No one ever suspects pensioners – harmless little old lady, that's all I am. But I got so angry when all the newspaper articles started coming out after Emily's death, suggesting Charles might get away with it, that he might be able to worm his way to freedom like he's done his whole life. So when I heard him and Douglas yelling last night about something so *stupid* – a few trinkets being stolen, like that even *matters* – I knew what needed to be done. Charles was distracted, and I had the gun. So, I went to the landing and I pulled the trigger…" She frowns, her mouth twisted in displeasure. "Of course, I've never shot a gun before – I didn't quite grasp how to aim the first time, which is why I missed – so I shot again. The second time I was *sure* I would get him… But somehow Douglas was there instead." Her voice wavers. "I regret that. I really do. I'm not a *bad* person. I just wanted my revenge – for my daughter and granddaughter. It has all been for *them*."

I ball my hands into fists. Lizzie's eyes are open now, and wide, terrified as she stares at me.

"Well, that's enough talking, I suppose," says Ms Bromley, and she raises her elbow a little. "It's a shame, a real shame…"

"Ms Bromley, you need to put the gun down," I say, trying to speak slowly. I don't want to do anything that might make her jump and fire accidentally.

"Yes," says a soft voice from behind me. "Put the gun down."

The Present
Jayne

I hold up the gun Emily gave me, the gun I know I never could have used. But Emily didn't know that, because I was a puppet to her. We were all puppets to her. Me, Devi, Lizzie... Even Gran. We thought we were stopping the manipulation, the lies, taking power... But we weren't.

We just swapped Charles for Emily.

"What are you doing, my dear?" says Gran. Her voice is calm, but there's a hint of steel in it. I've never seen her like this before. Surely, she wouldn't actually pull the trigger on Lizzie? She's not a monster – Lizzie is so...innocent.

I look to Devi, whose head twists between Gran and me.

She has to know – she has to know I'm not a murderer, that I could never do what Gran is doing. She has to know she needs to do *something* to stop this.

Gran doesn't move.

But slowly, she nods.

And I lift the gun and fire at the ceiling.

The Present
Devi

Jayne's shot goes off and my mind is clearer than it's ever been. I run towards Ms Bromley and fling myself at her.

As we're crashing to the ground everything seems to slow down – another gunshot blasts out, and I feel a woosh of air beneath my ribs, whistling past me. My mind is screaming that Ms Bromley was still holding the gun and she pulled the trigger as I crashed into her. The scream in my head carries on as I realize it's *not* in my mind – someone else is yelling.

I roll off Ms Bromley, wrenching the gun from her hands – sprawled on the floor and blinking confusedly up at the ceiling, she doesn't try to fight back. As I get to my feet I look around wildly for Lizzie and Jayne – they're both safe, though Lizzie is the one screaming, pointing at the door of the cottage. I turn, to see Lottie in the doorway, clutching her arm. Blood is slowing spreading across the sleeve of her white jumper and she's staring at it with shock on her face.

Tate is standing beside her, still in his T-shirt and pyjama bottoms and clutching a poker stick – but it falls to the ground with a clang as he stares at the blood blossoming out across Lottie's jumper. He looks up at me. "I thought Jayne was acting weird when she came to see me," he croaks. "I called Lottie over so we could investigate together."

"I've been shot," gasps Lottie. We're all frozen, but her words get me moving again.

"Sit down," I say, trying to sound like I know what I'm talking about. "Press down on the wound, try to stop the flow of blood. Lizzie – tie your jacket round the area where she got shot. I guess the landline still isn't working?" No one answers me, they all stare at me blankly. "Someone *talk*! Does anyone have enough signal to call an ambulance?"

"No," says Tate. "But the police are over at the house—"

"Go get them. *Now*," I say. "Run as fast as you can!"

He nods and turns on his heel and starts sprinting towards the main house. Lottie is whimpering as she collapses into an armchair in front of the bookcase. Lizzie wraps the sleeve of her jacket round the top of Lottie's arm and ties it tightly, and I stare hopelessly, not knowing what else to do but wait. I'm still clutching the gun – I don't know what to do with it, but I don't want to let it go just in case something else horrible happens.

There's a noise behind me, and I whip around to find Ms Bromley has pulled herself up and is limping to the door that leads out of the room.

"I do apologize for the accident, Lottie," she says calmly as she pauses at the door. "I'm just going to wait for the police in the kitchen."

A part of me screams that I shouldn't let her go anywhere, that we should keep her with us to watch what she's doing, but a bigger part is numb with shock – and simply doesn't care. It's the police's job to arrest her, not mine – thirty seconds of being a hero is enough for me, and I'm only just processing the fact I leaped at a person holding a gun... *And now I'm still holding that exact gun.*

Jayne stares as the door swings shut. "I didn't know what Gran did... What she was capable of..." Her voice cracks, and a single tear drips down her face, which she hurriedly wipes away. "I would never... You've got to understand – I'd never do what she did..." She's breathing heavily, pressing her hands to her cheeks. "Emily gave me a gun and told me to kill Charles. But I wouldn't have. I'm not an *executioner*. I thought her plan to frame Charles would get me the justice I wanted..."

"Let's go outside," I say cautiously. She's looking really pale – the fresh air might do her some good. Lizzie looks up, confused, but Lottie doesn't even seem to hear us.

"I've been *shot*," she says again.

"Tate will be back soon," says Lizzie slightly desperately.

I step outside with Jayne, partially feeling relieved to get away from Lottie. I know she's been shot and she's bleeding and in a lot of pain, and I don't know how bad the injury is, but I also know I can't do anything to help her. Lizzie seems like the right sort of person to be holding her hand – she's naturally caring and sweet and just the sort of person you'd want to be beside you if you were bleeding out.

Except Lottie is *not* bleeding out, she's talking fine... Though that might just be the shock. But either way, Lizzie is right –

Tate will be back soon with the police. And when they arrive I can give them the gun, which is still in my hand.

Outside, the air is freezing. Jayne stands a little away from me, staring in the direction of the house like she's expecting the police to appear from behind the trees at any second. "I'm Charles's daughter," she says without looking at me. "I guess that makes Lottie my half-sister. I had no idea until my mum told me a year ago. I went to Emily and I told her who I was, and that's when she started on this plan to get revenge on Charles. She didn't care about any of us – all she wanted was to punish Charles for betraying her. She even told me to kill him if we didn't manage to send him to prison. I didn't want to. But obviously…Gran *did* want to. I didn't realize how far she would go, that she would threaten you and… I didn't know, I…"

I could have been mad at Jayne, for lying. I'm not though – she showed up when we needed her, she was absolutely on our side. "It's not your fault," I say. I don't add that I could understand how Ms Bromley ended up like she did, fuelled by a single-minded focus on revenge, even at the expense of other people getting hurt – that could easily have been me. Because ever since Dylan's death I'd had a low level of rage simmering within me – time didn't heal my bloody wounds, it only made me feel them more. And that rage might have sparked into something bigger one day, had Emily not sent that letter to Priya.

But maybe Jayne knows how I feel, because she smiles slightly at me.

"No – calm down!" someone yells from inside the cottage. I run through the door, to see Lottie is standing up, waving a red book above her head. Lizzie is the one who yelled.

"Why does Ms Bromley have my dad's diary?" demands Lottie. Her face is pale, and tears are dripping down her face – I wonder if she's getting a surge of adrenaline or something, from the gunshot. Like she's past feeling the pain.

Ms Bromley had kept the diaries she took on her *bookshelf*? She was absolutely *not* a master criminal.

"I don't understand what's been going *on*," heaves Lottie, and it's like something has burst inside her, because she's now sobbing as she drops the diary. "What happened to my mum and Douglas and why did Ms Bromley shoot me…? She worked for us my whole life and I…" Her face crumples as she holds onto the place she was shot. "I'm *so sick* of the secrets…"

Lizzie picks the diary up, and opens her mouth, but whatever she's about to say is interrupted as the police burst into the room, followed by Tate, and everything is chaos as two policemen help Lottie to her feet. The last thing I see is her tear-ravaged face as she looks back at me, then Lizzie and Jayne, a silent plea in her eyes as the police discuss getting her to a hospital.

"Where's Bromley?" one of the police asks.

"Kitchen," I say, nodding towards it. He goes inside, but a second later he's back.

"It's empty," he says. "Right, clear out of this cottage."

"What do you mean? Where's my gran?" asks Jayne, as we're all pushed towards the door.

The policeman looks at her. "She's gone."

The Present
Devi

I head to the main house with Lizzie, Jayne and Tate, with the police bringing up the rear. Jayne and Lizzie walk behind, while Tate falls into step beside me. He's shivering, running his hands up and down his bare skin.

"We were facing a gun," I say to him. "The gun *you* stole. And you thought you'd be able to fight it off with a poker?"

He looks like he's a few minutes away from turning blue and dying, so I shrug off my coat and hand it to him silently, rolling my eyes as I do so. It's too small for him to put on, but he wraps it around his shoulders like a blanket.

"B-better than nothing," he says, his teeth chattering. "I mean... You took on that gun...empty handed. What's with you and jumping *at* guns?"

"Okay, we're *both* stupid," I concede.

"You are, without a doubt, the most unpredictable person I've ever met," he says. For a second I can't tell whether I should be offended, but then he smiles at me, his entire face lighting up, and it's like the sulky persona is a mask that's now gone, and he's showing me who he really is. And I'm smiling back, and there's a warm feeling in my chest, because I get the sense that, even though he doesn't know me that well, he understands me.

We head into the house, which is nice and toasty, and he gives me back my coat as we head to the entrance hall. Our fingers brush a second longer than they need to, his eyes lingering on me as Jayne and Lizzie and the other police catch up.

The detective who interviewed me is standing with his hands in his pockets as he speaks in hushed tones to a colleague. They both look around as we arrive.

"How's it going?" I say cheerfully. "I solved the murders for you, in case that's of interest."

My favourite detective looks confused.

"I told you," I say to him. "I should have your job."

PART FIVE

THE TRIAL

The Present
Devi

Ms Bromley has been missing for the past month, and it's unlikely she's ever going to be found. Which means she may never face trial for killing Douglas, or reckless endangerment or whatever regarding Lottie.

We'd forgotten about the secret passageway in the bathroom, and Ms Bromley must have vanished down it – a stupid oversight on our part, because she shouldn't get to evade justice. Luckily, Lottie's gunshot wound turned out not to be that serious after all.

Of course, it's not *just* us who let Ms Bromley go – the police weren't fast enough to catch her; she ended up being quite speedy for an old lady, as well as ridiculously ruthless. The police *were* quick to pin Douglas's murder on her after that though. It was well known Douglas had been rude to her the few times he stayed over – Jayne helped nudge that reasoning along – and I guess they felt that was sufficient explanation as to why she killed him. A stupid, petty reason that thankfully didn't give away the fact she'd been attempting to kill Charles – because if *that* had come out, Emily's whole plan might have followed, and our role along with it.

I don't think Jayne knows how she feels about her grandmother, beyond the fact that it's painful – she doesn't seem to want to talk about it; her whole world has been shattered. The three of us have gone our separate ways, back to our different corners of the country, and though Jayne seems okay over text it's hard to be sure.

It seems that one good outcome to come from the mess of everything that happened is Jayne being reunited with her mum – Charles has obviously got bigger things to worry about than the two of them living together once more on the estate. But from what I glean in messages, things initially aren't rosy; Jayne's mum was never much of a parent – she always struggled as a mum, which meant Ms Bromley was the one who *really* raised Jayne. That issue hasn't gone away. So they turn to Jayne's grandpa for help – Michael Faraway, who Ms Bromley divorced years ago. Bromley was Jayne's gran's maiden name, which explains why their last names are different. Jayne and her mother decide they're going to live with Michael. Away from the Bramble Estate, closer actually to me in London. They will both be getting a fresh start, and Jayne seems hopeful that this is also the beginning of a proper relationship between her and her mother.

Lizzie was slightly weird about Jayne for a few days – she said she didn't know if she could trust her. But she realized she was being unfair pretty quickly, because you can't go through what the three of us did together and come out the other side *without* trusting each other. Our group texts flow constantly.

In more excellent news, Charles has finally been arrested for Emily's murder. I guess even with the question mark around whether he had the opportunity to kill Emily at dinner, the police think they have enough evidence to bring charges. He's got a strong motive with his money issues and his proven hatred of his wife: he had the means to be able to get the poison, especially with his history of purchasing sleeping pills under the Edward Smith alias, and Tate had seen him talking to Emily alone at dinner.

I half want things to be neater – for Emily to have conveniently planted one last piece of evidence that shows up and shocks us all and really nails him. I hoped there might be something in Charles's diaries that were in Ms Bromley's cottage – Lizzie kept them, and sent us photos. I carefully read through all the pages, determined to find something juicy.

But there was nothing – they were mostly about how brilliant Charles thinks he is.

I even found the part of the diary where Ms Bromley ripped out pages to give to me. I could see why she stopped where she did, because the diary carried on to mention Jayne. The original extract I read said *I gave my daughter £1000 for her university fund. I don't have the money, of course, but what can I do? She deserves—.* And the next page reads "*nothing. But her ridiculous mother won't stop asking about the money. You owe it to Jayne, she keeps repeating. Doesn't believe me when I say I really don't have the funds. At least my* other *daughter might be more profitable. I was dreading Lottie's stupid piano concert – if mediocrity was a person, it'd be Lottie – but thank goodness I went. There were so many networking opportunities there. I can get back on top, I know I can.*

The next thing that happens is that Charles is released on bail and his trial date set. I expected it to be months away, but thanks to the media frenzy around him, it's due to start in a few weeks.

Lizzie, Jayne and I are back at school, but we're all being prepped by lawyers for the prosecution, coaching us on how to be witnesses.

Sometimes I wonder if we are doing the right thing, because this whole plan was Emily's idea and she was not a good person. But that, I realize, is how Charles usually wins. He does something terrible, then points to all the other bad things in the world and suddenly *he's* not so bad any more.

Well, he's not getting away with it this time.

I've been speaking to Tate as well. It turns out he lives near me, in London. Him in the fancy part, me not. But I don't envy him at all – not after what I've learned about his parents. It must suck, to have a mum and dad who don't seem to care about you beyond how you help their image.

We've met up a few times, for coffee, and we discuss everything other than the Vanfortes and the upcoming trial, which will be taking place in London. I ask him about Lottie, and he says that she's healed up nicely from the gunshot wound, but that she's constantly with her lawyers.

I wonder what it is she's planning on saying at the trial. She was the one part of Emily's plan that didn't work out, after all – since she didn't tell the police Emily's final words, that her drink tasted funny after Charles had had access to it, the *opportunity* part of the equation still hangs in the air. Plus, she'd be a good character witness for Charles – his sweet daughter, who would be left motherless... And fatherless, too, if he went to prison for life.

Lizzie thinks we should try getting her on our side. She messaged to say she had posted Charles's diary back to Lottie, to make sure she knew who her father really was. I could see the benefit of having Lottie on board, but didn't think the diary would make much difference. We had already *told* Lottie what Charles had done to our families, so she was well aware of the way he treated her. But she hadn't spoken up, or turned against him.

On the flipside though, she was keeping her word to us, since she hadn't told the police about our plan to frame Charles.

Either way she's a very big loose thread – and I don't like it at all.

The Present
Devi

The trial begins and Charles sits quietly in his fancy suit next to his fancy lawyers. There is a crowd outside the courtroom and loads of media coverage because Charles is a big-name politician, well liked – he's never lost a single election – and up till now people have been arguing any negative press is wrong because he's just a grieving husband. His approval ratings had never been higher than directly after Emily's death – that image is now shattered since he's been accused of her murder, and it's delightful.

Lottie Vanforte is due to be called as the last witness; she sits at the back of the courtroom, quietly listening to everything going on.

When I am called as a witness, I am able to tell the story exactly as I told the detective, because everything I saw at the Bramble Estate that night *did* happen. Emily was right – staying in character then makes it easier now. My lawyer has told me not to be "too moody". I do my best, staring straight ahead and giving my facts. I am not the best witness, but not the worst either.

The cross-examination is tough, but it feels like Charles's lawyers are slightly desperate, because they don't poke holes in my story, which might have actually helped things. Instead, they poke holes in *me*, trying to trip me up, show that I can't possibly give reliable evidence.

Lizzie and Jayne are also called as witnesses, and it's worse watching them because I'm so on edge that they're going to slip up. But they're both calm, sticking exactly to the story. Lizzie comes across best, her red cheeks flushed and her eyes blue, making it look like she is close to tears. I think this makes the jury want to protect her.

For the most part, though, I can barely focus on the trial – my mind keeps drifting back to Dylan. There's a particular memory of him lodged in my brain, from when he was fifteen or so, and it replays over and over. He's sitting at the kitchen table at his house, and he's laughing – the sun is shining through the window, across his face, and there's glee in his warm eyes as he tells a joke. I don't remember what he said, but I wish I did – and worse still, I can't fully recall how his laugh sounded, or his voice. I attempt to fill it in, but it's wrong – and the frustration at the memory not being entirely accurate turns into an ache in my chest. I wish I'd known how special that moment would be, because I would have paid more attention.

Without me even realizing, there's only one more day left of the trial, and just one more witness to give evidence before closing arguments. We'll finally hear what Lottie has to say.

I am sitting at home having dinner with Mum and Dad when there is a knock on the door. At once I am alert, tense, ready for armed men to come charging in, sent by Charles.

Then I remember that he is currently on trial for murder, and probably doesn't have time to be worrying about three teenagers who have just given evidence against him – nor does he have the means to enact revenge.

I open the door, and to my shock Lottie Vanforte pushes past me. She is dressed head to toe in white – in a cream top and trousers combo, with cream boots.

Mum and Dad get to their feet, both wearing identical looks of confusion – but I don't have any answers for them, because I've got no idea what's going on. Mum raises her eyebrows at me, then follows Dad into the kitchen.

"What are you doing here?" I say to Lottie the moment the kitchen door closes. "You're not supposed to talk to me about what I said in court—"

"Ms Bromley killed Douglas," she says to me. Her voice is the most self-assured I've ever heard it. "But she was aiming for my father, wasn't she?"

I don't know why she's come to see me about this – surely Jayne would be the right person to answer questions, seeing as though she happily told Lottie all about our plan to get revenge on Charles before. Plus, there's the whole sibling thing – it's so weird that they're half-sisters, I don't really see any resemblance… Although Jayne *does* cover her face with her hair and dresses like she's allergic to colour.

Before I answer, I take a moment to try and figure out if

there's some way she could use this to trip me up. As far as I know, she's got no hard evidence of our plan. And Lizzie sent Charles's diary to her because she thought she deserved the truth. I think about how much *I* would hate it if I was kept in the dark about things. Slowly, I nod.

Lottie looks me up and down, and I can't read her expression. "I'll see you in court tomorrow."

89

The Present
Devi

Lottie is dressed in a plain white suit as she takes the stand. She answers some basic questions, and then the lawyer asks what she saw that evening.

Of course, no one saw anything, because Emily poisoned herself.

But Lottie doesn't say that.

She takes a deep breath, then she says she saw her father, Charles Vanforte, put a few drops of something in her mother's drink. Her mother told her that her drink tasted funny – and then she died.

The courtroom explodes into whispers, and I'm expecting someone to stand up and yell "objection", for the judge to bang his gavel and ask for silence.

Instead, Charles's lawyer keeps asking questions, but he is obviously wrong-footed.

I wish I could see Charles's face, but I'm in one of the last rows and all I can see is the back of his head.

Lottie sticks to her story – the part about what Emily said is true, she *did* say her drink tasted funny. But the part about seeing Charles poisoning her – that's a *lie*. I've got no clue what she's doing, what game she's playing. At the end of the questioning her eyes briefly meet mine, and I try to figure out what she's thinking, but I can't. Then she looks away.

I barely listen to the closing arguments; I've got no idea whether we've done enough. Dylan is in my head, sitting at the kitchen table, mouthing something but no words come out – his voice is gone. From my memories, from the world, for ever.

Tate has asked me to meet him for dinner, but when I arrive at the restaurant it is to find Lottie sitting alone at a table, sipping a glass of water.

I sit down opposite her as she puts the water down.

"Why did you do it?" I ask. There's no point beating around the bush.

"I heard Dad yelling, the night Douglas was killed," says Lottie. "I saw the first shot go wide. And the second shot might have gone wide too – had my father not used Douglas as a human shield. Protecting his own skin, of course." She swallows. "You were right. He's a murderer." She takes a deep breath, gulps more water. I bite my tongue, even though I want to make lots of comments, because I can tell she's still not finished. "There was still a part of me that didn't want to believe what I'd seen. And yeah, he wasn't always *nice* to me, but he was an important man, sometimes he could be snappy or forgetful, that was just how he was. I always had an excuse for him. But…then I got one of his diaries in the post… I'm guessing one of you sent it?"

She barrels on before I can reply, but all I can think is *Lizzie was right. Well done her.*

"I read a bit of his diary where he called me mediocre. I've always thought that about myself, but aren't your *parents* supposed to think differently? There was a piano concert I was doing, and it was a huge deal for me because it was the biggest one I'd ever played – and Dad just said he was there for *networking* opportunities." Lottie looks at me sadly. "Mum didn't bother showing up to that concert, so I thought Dad actually cared because he came. But he wasn't there for *me*. He'd never been there for me – and sometimes I could convince myself I'd misinterpreted things, that my memories weren't right and he hadn't been as nasty to me as he was. Or maybe I deserved being belittled. But that diary…there was no way for me to lie to myself when I saw it written down. And I realized I don't deserve that – no one does."

"You've been really lonely, haven't you?" I say quietly, because I feel like I understand her a lot better now that I don't have Emily's idea of who she is in the back of my mind, clouding what I think of her. After all, Emily always assumed she would be able to manipulate Lottie into going along with her plan – she didn't consider, even for a second, telling Lottie the truth. The very idea had made her laugh. But Lottie wasn't the person her mother thought she was – and that was Emily's biggest mistake. "You were lonely, and that's why you were searching for your secret sibling."

"I found out about Jayne a few months ago – I'd been looking in the wrong places for this other child my dad was supposed to have." She smiles slightly. "I should have been searching a lot closer to home – and none of my investigations even mattered, in the end. I just accidentally overheard my mum talking to Ms Bromley about her. I wanted to be friends with her, you know, I wanted… I guess I wanted someone to talk to, to confide in, because I knew Mum didn't care about me. And deep, deep down I knew Dad didn't either."

"You've spent your whole life trying to find validation from other people," I say. "But *you* helped yourself, Lottie. You got your dad the justice he deserved, and you freed yourself from someone who never cared about you." That feels a bit too cheesy for me, so I add, "Plus, you'll be inheriting the Bramble Estate, won't you? Even if Emily didn't leave you everything, you'll still be mega rich soon."

I expect the jury to take *weeks* to reach a verdict, but we're back in the courtroom only two days later. I sit in a row with Jayne, Lizzie, Tate and Lottie, but I barely even register they're beside me. My heart is hammering as I wait, my stomach swirling in circles. Dylan is laughing in the kitchen, he's kicking a football at me, he's dying alone on the construction site. His mouth is moving, but there's still no voice coming out.

The judge starts speaking, and there's only one word I hear, ringing around the courtroom.

"Guilty."

90

The Present
Devi

If anyone else talks to me, I don't hear it. The moment we're allowed to leave the courtroom I am running through the corridors, out into the fresh air and through the streets. My feet slap against the ground and I am running, running, running.

I find a small patch of green in between some tall buildings and sit down on a bench and call Priya. She picks up on the first ring.

"Guilty," I say, and she breathes out once, quickly. "He's guilty. It's over."

There's silence for a second. Then, she says, "How are you feeling?"

Euphoric. Ecstatic. Empty.

I never told her how devastated I was after Dylan was killed, even though I know she probably figured it out. But I always thought that whatever I was feeling didn't matter, because she would have been twice as devastated as me. For once, though,

I decide to tell the truth. "I miss him."

"Me too," she says, and there's another silence down the phone. I know later I will go round to her house, and we will talk properly, and maybe we'll speak more about Dylan and things will seem lighter. But for now I'm aware the only person either one of us wants to talk to at this moment is Dylan, to let him know he finally got justice. Charles made him voiceless but I gave his memory peace.

I end the call, and stare into space. There's a few people in suits walking purposefully past, but the patch of green I'm in, which is too small to call a park, is empty.

Who am I without my need for revenge?

Someone sits beside me, and I look up to find Lizzie smiling sadly at me. Jayne is on my other side.

"What now?" I croak.

To my surprise it's Jayne who speaks up. "Now," she says, "we move on."

"For the past four years this has been my entire life," I say. I don't know how to explain it, but everything I've done has been with the knowledge that Charles killed Dylan. I figured out it was his fault, but it wasn't enough, because Charles got away with it. I've been screaming, trying to get the world to listen – and it finally did, and now I don't know what to do next.

Jayne suddenly reaches out, gripping my hand. "We did a good thing," she says. "Not just for us – Charles Vanforte won't hurt anyone again. We've helped a lot of people. And now we help ourselves – by leaving this all in the past."

"Dylan's still gone, though," I say. "He's *always* going to be gone and I'll never get to talk to him again. All I have are memories and they're…they're going to fade. I can't even remember what his voice sounded like, not exactly." I look at Lizzie, who is crying.

"You've done everything you could for him," says Lizzie. "We've *all* done everything we could." She grabs my other hand, and gives it a strong squeeze – and her saying that reminds me she's basically the reason Lottie finally turned on Charles.

"How did you know sending the diary to Lottie was the right thing to do?" I ask. "How did you figure out you could get her on our side?"

Lizzie wipes her tears away, and straightens her back. "Because I saw Lottie was like me – scared. I know now being scared doesn't make you a *bad* person. It doesn't make you weak. And I had you two to help me be brave, and Lottie deserved someone to believe in her too."

I'd been wrong, to get frustrated with Lizzie in the past and to overlook Lottie, because they didn't act like I did. Lizzie was braver than me, because she had a deep understanding of all the risks and did scary things anyway. And she was strong enough to help Lottie, too.

There is a knot in my throat as I speak again. "It's just…it doesn't really feel like anything's changed. I thought after this was over I'd feel…better. Or different. Or *something*."

"Well, I know one very big thing that has changed," Jayne says. "I have friends now. And… Well, I was never interested in forming a relationship with Lottie before. But she's not who I thought she was. She's someone I think I'm very lucky to know."

"It's great we've all got a murderer in common," I mutter, and Jayne starts laughing, and so do I and then so does Lizzie, and the laughter is slightly hysterically but all the same it feels good. It feels like water is flowing through me, dousing all my flames, washing away my anger.

And we grip onto each other, and for the first time in a long time, everything is okay.

SIX MONTHS LATER

Devi

Unsurprisingly, I am late. My room is a tip, and in the middle is a half-packed bag. It is the first week of the summer holidays, and I am at Nani's house. Next, I am going to visit Lizzie, along with Jayne. We talk regularly, message constantly, but this is the first time we are seeing each other since Charles's guilty sentence.

I sometimes think about the six other people who were at the Bramble Estate that night. Two are dead: Emily and Douglas. One is missing: Ms Bromley. One is in prison: Charles. One is abroad: Lottie went off for a fresh start to a school in America, though she keeps in touch with Jayne. They're developing quite the sisterly bond… She's also in constant contact with Lizzie, because they help each other through tough spots – and she frequently chats to me, too. My friendship with her is based on a mutual admiration, because we both agree that we are badass – and, surprisingly, we have an equally deep love of crappy reality TV.

And as for Tate…

He's sitting on my bed, watching with amused eyes and making absolutely no move to help me.

"Why did you only start packing *now*, right before our train is supposed to leave?" he says. He's not coming to Lizzie's with me – he's driving back down to London. Nani took a great liking to him, tells me I've met my match.

"Why did you start packing now?" I mimic in a high-pitched voice that sounds nothing like him. "You sound like my grandma."

Finally my bag is packed and we're heading out of the door, getting into his car to drive to the station.

I check my watch.

"Drive faster," I demand. "I'm not missing my train because you drive like Nani."

"Nani and I have a lot in common," he says. He's driving carefully, way under the speed limit. It was one of the most surprising things I learned about him – he's actually quite responsible. It's a pain in the arse sometimes – like now, as the light changes to amber and he slows down instead of speeding up.

"You could have made that," I say, folding my arms.

"How are you feeling about seeing Jayne and Lizzie again?" he asks me. He knows the truth about our plan – Lottie told him, after the trial was over, but if she hadn't I would have. He was annoyed we didn't tell him soon enough for him to help, but otherwise thinks what we did was brilliant and brave.

I shrug, because in truth I don't know how I feel about seeing them. We'd considered never meeting up, just in case it looked suspicious to the outside world. But after the trial and the verdict, the world quickly went back to ignoring us. I've stayed in touch with Tate, and it makes sense for Lizzie and Jayne and me to want to see each other again – we went through something terrible together.

He brings the car to a halt right in front of the station and squints at the board outside. "Oh, look," he says. "Your train's delayed by twenty minutes."

I swear. "No one knows how to be on time, do they?"

He grins at me as I unbuckle my seat belt, and leans forwards and kisses me.

I remember the first time I kissed him. We'd been hanging out for a few months and were in a park, sitting on a bench. He was complaining about people at school being stupid and looked all serious and broody, with his leather jacket and his tousled hair. And out of nowhere I asked him something which had been nagging at me.

"When I first met you, you said something dodgy," I said. "You said one of the people in the house might be a murderer – and that it might even be you. Did you…did you know what Emily was planning? Did you suspect anything?"

He grinned. "Er…no. I just wanted to troll you. You said you didn't scare easily – I wanted to…poke the bear a bit."

I kissed him.

I break away from the kiss now, running my fingers through his hair. "See you," I say, as I get out of the car and grab my bag.

* * *

437

Lizzie is over the moon to see me. She squeals and hugs me and I hug her back even though that doesn't really go with my cool reputation.

"Jayne's already here," she says.

I go inside Lizzie's house, looking around curiously. It's overstuffed with items. All the couches in the living room are frilly and pink and hidden under a mass of pillows. Jayne looks out of place, perched on the edge of a couch with her arms folded.

Her scowl lifts when she sees me.

"How's it going?" I say with a grin, and she grins back.

"Is your mum's car fixed yet?" she says.

"Broke down again," I reply. "And I scratched my dad's car so I'm banned from driving."

"Do you know what day it is?" says Lizzie, as she looks at us both. She plops to the ground. "It's exactly six months since Emily's death."

What an anniversary.

My phone bleeps with a notification and as I glance down I nearly faint.

I have an email – from Emily Vanforte.

"What's wrong?" says Lizzie. My heart is thudding as I open up the email, and start reading it aloud.

Dear Devi, Jayne and Lizzie,
It has been six months since my death. Do not fear – I am indeed dead. I scheduled this email to send.
I never had a doubt you three would manage to do what needed to be done—

"Except that's not true, is it?" I say with a snort. "Because she gave Jayne a gun and told her to shoot Charles if things were going to crap. Wait…Jayne, I thought you'd deleted all the emails in her burner email account?"

"I deleted everything in her inbox, sent mailbox and trash," says Jayne. "All the drafts too… But I never looked in her scheduled folder…"

"Keep reading," says Lizzie, her eyes wide and horrified. It's like she thinks Emily's actual ghost is speaking to us all.

—but if I'm honest, I never for one second thought you would get away with it. I assume you've managed to dispose of Charles – but got caught in the process. Never mind, it was to be expected. You're just three teenagers, after all. To that effect, though, I never want it to be said I didn't help those who have helped me. You will each receive – through a transfer that will never be traced back to me – £100,000 to pay for your legal fees.

Good luck, dear girls.

With all the love in the world,

Emily Vanforte

"What a *cow*," I say, clenching my phone so tightly it digs into my hand. "A *cow*. The whole time, she thought we'd end up getting caught – from the sound of it, she thought we'd get caught having *killed* Charles – then she thought she could just chuck some *money* at us…" I trail off as I reread the email, my initial anger giving way to a tingly feeling in my stomach. My insides begin to warm up. "She was wrong," I say with a small smile, looking up at Lizzie and Jayne. They're both still looking a mixture of angry and horrified. I start to chuckle.

"What's so funny?" asks Lizzie, her eyebrows bunching together. Jayne's expression has switched to one of confusion – she's catching up to where I am.

"She thought we'd be using our £100,000 each for legal fees because she underestimated us," I say with a snort. "But she's just gone ahead and given us each six figures to do whatever the hell we want with."

And Jayne laughs, and Lizzie laughs, and it's not because we're suddenly all going to be a *lot* wealthier than we were a few minutes ago – but because we're together. And that feels much more valuable than anything the Vanfortes ever had. As we're laughing, I feel lighter than I ever have before.

Because it hits me properly that we did it.

We did it when everyone else underestimated us, thought that we weren't smart enough, that we could be manipulated. We proved them all wrong.

We're the ones with the power. And we always have been.

THE END

ACKNOWLEDGEMENTS

Thank you to my brilliant editors, Sarah Stewart and Becky Walker. Sarah, thank you for all your time pondering over the plot with me. Becky, thank you for your endless enthusiasm for this story. Thanks as well to Anne Finnis and Beth Wetherfield, who were second readers on early drafts – I'm sure I would have lost sight of all the clues and red herrings in this book without your comments. Thank you as well to Helen Greathead for your insightful copyedit, Gareth Collinson for proofreading, Kath Millichope who designed the absolutely stunning cover, and Violet Tobacco, the cover illustrator, and Sarah Cronin for the interior design. A huge thank you to Hannah Reardon Steward, Fritha Lindqvist and Jessica Feichtlbauer in PR and marketing, for helping *This Book Kills* and *Catch Your Death* find their readers.

Thank you to my agent, Alice Sutherland-Hawes, for your professional guidance and immense support, and Saffron Dodd for your behind-the-scenes efforts. And thank you to all the co-agents who have worked so hard to find homes for my books across the world.

A huge thank you to all my writing friends – I'm so lucky to have found such a great community. Thanks to Tess James-Mackey for reading a *much* earlier version of this book and puzzling everything out with me, and to Megan Painter, for always being ready to chat plot.

Thank you to my friends. Matt, Alice, Rachel, I wouldn't tell you a single thing about this book until it was finished, but I always made sure you knew exactly how much progress I had made – whether you wanted it or not.

Finally, thank you to my family. My aunts, uncles and cousins, for enthusiastically picking up all my books and reading them and telling everyone else to read them too! My brother, for waiting patiently for each new book. And my mum, who continues to be my biggest cheerleader.

MORE MURDER, MORE SUSPECTS AND MORE TWISTS...

Discover another bestselling thriller from
Ravena Guron

OUT NOW

I'll make it clear from the start: I did not kill Hugh Henry Van Boren. I didn't even help. Well, not intentionally.

When Hugh Henry Van Boren, one of the most popular and richest kids in Jess Choudhary's school, is found dead, the student body is left reeling and wondering who the murderer could be... Jess, a student under strict instructions to keep her record clean or risk losing her scholarship, finds herself at the centre of the investigation when it's revealed that Hugh died in the exact same way as a character in a short story she wrote.

And then Jess receives an anonymous text thanking her for the inspiration.

With time running out, Jess knows if she doesn't solve this mystery she'll finally have something in common with Hugh Henry.

She'll be dead too.

"An awesome book, full of mystery, friendship and sass."
The Sun

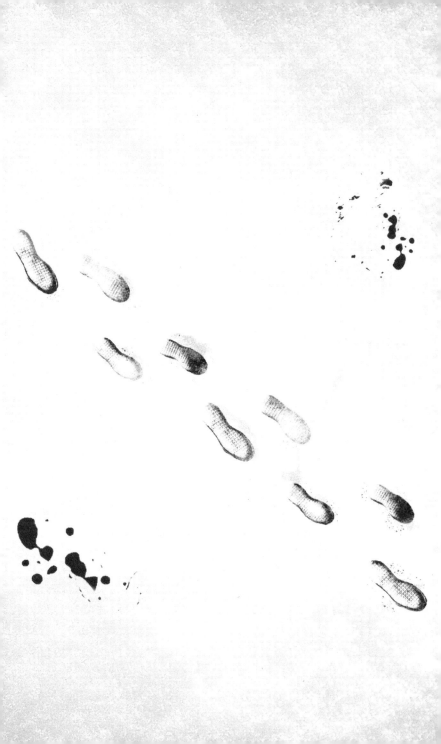

LOOK OUT FOR MORE NAIL-BITING
MURDER MYSTERIES FROM
RAVENA GURON...

COMING SOON.